MIGRATION

Species Imperative #2

JULIE E. CZERNEDA

DAW BOOKS, INC.

DONALD A. WOLLHEIM, FOUNDER
375 Hudson Street, New York, NY 10014
ELIZABETH R. WOLLHEIM
SHEILA E. GILBERT
PUBLISHERS

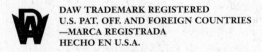

For Roger . . .
Once more, because.

Acknowledgments

Hardcover part deux! If I'd known the rush I'd get from signing these beauties, I'd have been too excited to finish writing the first one. My sincere thanks to all who took home copies of *Survival,* including the way you've brightened my days since with calls for "more Mac!" Here you go.

The gorgeous look and hopefully sensible contents of this book owe themselves to my always insightful editor, Sheila Gilbert, and the talented folks at DAW Books. A special thanks to Colleen Clarke, of Penguin Canada, for her enthusiastic support. I'd also like to thank these intrepid souls who read first draft: Jihane Billacois, Jana Paniccia, Ruth Stuart, Kristen Britain, and Janny Wurts. Your comments were more than helpful. As I wrote, I was reassured by the wonderful comments of C.J. Cherryh (fan-girl moment), James Alan Gardner, Robert J. Sawyer, Catherine Asaro, Doranna Durgin, and Jack McDevitt on *Survival.* Thank you all. And I'd be remiss not to mention the superb launch hosted by Bakka Books, where salmon was indeed served.

My first-ever visit to the west coast took place while writing this book. I'd like to thank my gracious hosts: in Seattle, Leslie Howle, Greg and Astrid Bear, and the SF Museum, Nathan Azinger, and Duane of University Bookstore; in Prince George, Rob Budde (UNBC), Lynda Williams, David Lott, Derryl Murphy, and Mosquito Books; while in Vancouver, Dan Archambault and Donald Derrick (Green College, UBC), Walter and Jill of White Dwarf (wow), Margaret McKinnon-Cash, Hazel and Fred Peschl, and

Douglas Starink. Hugs to you all! Ahem. About this cover art. You know I wish only the best for Vancouver, but isn't it glorious how Luis Royo destroyed it for me?

As for *Migration,* I've done my best to reflect what is known now, from geoducks to landscapes. My thanks to these folks for lending me their expertise: Kim McLean (geology and earthquakes), Nathan Azinger (food), Erin Kenny (language), Kevin Maclean (New Zealand), Isaac Szpindel (yet more optics), and Dr. Sally Leys (glass sponges). I was privileged to meet with Dr. Scott Hinch at UBC (a man who knows his salmon). Any factual errors in this book are mine. (If I've neglected anyone whose brain I picked for this, please accept my heartfelt apology and/or smack me with a salmon.)

There are real people whose names appear in this story. Gentlemen John Ward and Lee Fyock are back. From charitable auctions come: Frank Wu, who designed and commands his own starship, with teacup; Cathy Palmer-Lister, who named and runs a store in the north woods, and Wendy Carlson, a fine character. A newsgroup contest enlisted Lara Herrera and her son Rob to create a name for me, as did Bobbie Barber and Carol Gaupp, while David Brokman was his noble self. As always, any resemblance to an actual person is unintentional, except for the good bits.

A special note of affection and respect to my dear friends, the Heiers: Linda, Arthur, Mary, and, for always, Eddie. You've been with me from the start and I've appreciated it more than I can say.

As for my family? Yes! A hardcover book with my photo in it! You believed, so I did, too.

- Table of Contents -

CONTENTS

By what measure

should we

condemn ourselves?

Survival is

a moral choice.

(Recent corridor inscription,
Progenitor's Hold, Ship.)

- Encounter -

THE GREAT JOURNEY has been renewed. That which is Dhryn has remembered. All that is Dhryn must move.

That which is Dhryn . . . *hungers*.

That which is Dhryn remembers this place, knows its *Taste*.

All that is Dhryn must move.

It is the way of the journey, that all follow the Taste.

It is survival.

The language of the Eelings didn't lend itself to emotion. There was no need; the bioluminescent beings were able to flash patterns of excitement, joy, or strife.

Or fear.

"We have incoming ships," the transect technician reported. His voice didn't change, but his lithe body was suddenly ablaze. "Sir."

There should have been no reason for such a display. There were always incoming ships. The Naralax Transect was like an artery to Ascendis, the Eeling home world, anchored between the orbits of her two moons, constantly pumping trade goods to and from the lush planet, bringing ships to her famed refit stations on the nether moon, sending them away again faster and more powerful. And in debt.

"Multiple collisions. Sir."

"On my station." Sometimes a freighter strayed from its assigned path; dealing with aliens and their differing perceptions made that inevitable. The supervisor, as suited One Responsible, covered his feelings beneath an opaque cloak. Despite that caution, as he took in what his own screen now showed, alarm ringed each wrist with light and spilled past his collar, catching fire on the spikes of chin and frill.

The screen showed mayhem. Over fifteen ships were reporting hull impacts, several careening into other ships in turn. But there was no time to think about those lives, lost or at risk. For the legal traffic had virtually disappeared among a cloud of new arrivals. This was no confused freighter captain. It wasn't a convoy of audacious *iily* poachers, orbiting Ascendis herself while their servo scoops netted blossoms, relying on surprise and speed to evade the rangers who protected the rich forests of the north.

This was . . .

The supervisor drew himself up. "Send a planet-wide alarm. Do it now."

The cloud wasn't assuming orbit; it was heading for the upper atmosphere. It expanded at the same time, sensors translating the splitting of each new arrival into multiple targets, those into more, then more, all on the same trajectory. To the surface.

So many ships were breaking through the atmosphere at once, they set off weather control alarms as they shattered programmed winds and burned through clouds. Thousands, perhaps millions.

"What should I say? What are they?" The technician glowed so frantically the supervisor wondered he could see his own screen past that light.

Not that any of them needed to. Not now.

Now was too late.

The supervisor pulled his cloak closed, dousing the flickering light of his despair.

"The Dhryn."

1

RECOVERY AND RESUMPTION

"**Y**OU ASK HER."

"You."

"Not me. Don't you know who she is?"

"Doc Connor."

"*The* Dr. Connor, Mackenzie Connor. The one who lost her arm in that terrible accident last fall. You know. When the moorings collapsed under the pods and dozens of students were killed—"

"Five, not dozens."

"Whatever. Well, I heard it wasn't completely an accident."

"What do you mean?"

"Sabotage. I'm not joking. And when Dr. Connor tried to stop it, the ones responsible took her best friend, a scientist on contract here. They've never found the body." A meaningful pause. "What kind of person could come back and run this place after something like that?"

"Oh."

"Yes. 'Oh!' "

"Weellll . . . Someone has to ask her. He can't stay out there all day. Go on. You do it."

"Not me . . ."

Mac, who could hear the whispered argument quite well through the half-open door to her office, ran her fingers through her hair and gave those short curls an impatient tug. *A reputation for solid science and fair, if tough, marking was one thing,* she thought. *But these ridiculous rumors spreading through Base were be-*

coming a royal pain—not that she had any hope of setting that record straight. The Ministry of Extra-Sol Human Affairs had been succinct, if highly unhelpful. Mac's role was over. The rest of humanity had been informed. Measures were being taken by the Interspecies Union. There was, with perverse predictability, no hysteria and barely any press.

After all, any threat was out there, to others.

If anything, humanity's reaction had been rather smug, as if reassured to learn that, like themselves, another species had its share of troublemakers. *Somehow,* Mac thought with a sour taste in her mouth, *her kind seemed to view the entire business as over, now that the "unpleasant neighbors" had been found out and—oh so conveniently—left "town."*

Meanwhile, there was the small, inconvenient issue of what had happened here, on Earth. Now that friend was foe, and foe possibly friend, the politics were, to put it mildly, mud.

So Mac was to say nothing, accept whatever lies they'd planted in her absence, and get on with her life as if nothing had happened.

Some days, she almost could.

Others?

"I'm not deaf!" she snapped.

The ensuing silence could only be described as terrified.

Eyeing the door to the hall, Mac poked her forefinger into the workscreen hovering over her desk, the gesture sending the files she'd been updating back into the Norcoast main system. Those waiting for them would doubtless notice she hadn't finished and complain vigorously over lunch. She stretched and gave a rueful smile. *At least some things never changed.* The salmon would migrate, come what may. And those at Norcoast Salmon Research Facility would be ready, watching, learning, and . . .

Two heads appeared in the door opening, one above the other. "Dr. Connor?" hazarded the topmost.

Mac crooked the same finger, blue-tinged through its pseudoskin glove.

The students sidled into her office, each doing his or her utmost to stay behind the other without trying to be obvious. *Ah.* Lee Fyock's newest arrivals, shortly to be sent up the coast to sample intertidal zones. *Interesting pair*. The young woman so worried about disturbing her, Uthami Dhaniram, was already published, having spent three years studying sea grass dynamics in the Gulf of Mannar for Bharathiyar University. She'd arrived eager for her first winter, an ambition that would have to wait a few months.

In every way a contrast, tall, fair, and freckled Cassidy T. Wilson would likely consider Norcoast's mild, damp winters a joke, given he came from a family-run North Sea trawler. No academic credentials on his application, but experience enough to have drawn fine creases around his washed blue eyes and leave permanent ruddy patches on his cheeks. A deep-water fisher. Mac looked forward to his insights.

If Lee could keep him. Case, as the young man preferred to be called, had originally applied to work with the Harvs, the research teams investigating the Human lines of the salmon equation. A logical choice.

Until Dr. Kammie Noyo, Mac's coadministrator of the facility, decided otherwise. As Mac had been an unfathomable number of light-years distant at the time—on a world without oceans, let alone salmon cruising their depths—she could hardly protest after the fact.

Not that she would. Kammie's instincts were often on target. This wouldn't be the first time she'd deliberately cross-fertilized a lagging area of research by dumping an unwitting and typically unwilling student into the mix. If the student lasted and had talent, the results could be spectacular.

Of course, since Lee's research moved young Mr. Wilson into the so-called "Wet" half of Norcoast's projects—an arbitrary division based on the likelihood of wet socks at any given time—and Kammie administrated only the "Dry" now that she was no longer in sole charge, making sure this student lasted became, naturally, another of Mac's responsibilities.

"Sorry to bother you, Dr. Connor," Case began, ducking behind the hint of an awkward bow. His voice, higher-pitched than one would expect from his frame, tended to squeak. There were beads of sweat, not rain, on his forehead.

Mac raised one eyebrow in challenge. " 'Mac,' " she corrected.

Uthami's dark eyes widened into shocked circles. Before she could argue, Mac continued, lifting a finger for each point: "We're doing the same work. We live in the same place. And I can guarantee you, we'll smell the same in a very short time."

A broad grin slowly spread over Case's face. "Mac, it is." He looked suddenly younger.

What was it like, to be so young, to know so little yet be so sure?

Mac shrugged off the feeling. "Now. Who can't stay out—and where's out—all day? And why?" The hammering of rain on the curved ceiling underscored every word, but the weather was hardly noteworthy. Castle Inlet, where the pods, walkways, and docks of Norcoast's Base nestled, was surrounded by coastal rain forest for good reason.

"There's a man who came with some Preds this morning, Dr.— Mac," Uthami explained, gamely stumbling past the name. "Security won't let him in because he doesn't have a pass, but he won't leave. He's been waiting outside the pod since before our last class, a couple of hours at least. Tie—Mr. McCauley—said just leave him there, but we—we thought—you should be told." Uthami stopped and looked to Case, patently out of her depth.

Mac felt a little that way herself. Security. Locked doors. Things hadn't all stayed the same; most of the new changes hadn't been for the better. *Even these youngsters could see it.*

"Did you talk to him? Get his name?" she asked, venturing over the abyss of a startling hope. *Could it be?* Then common sense took over. Nikolai Piotr Trojanowski would hardly be stopped by the very security he'd put in place before leaving.

To go where?

Someplace she couldn't.

"No. We just saw him, standing in the rain."

From the fresh worry on both faces, she was scowling again. Mac forced a smile. "Then I'd better go see for myself. Thank you, both."

Norcoast Salmon Research Facility, or Base, as those with even the slightest acquaintance with it learned to call the place, was made up of six large pods pretending to be islands, connected by a maze of mem-wood walkways from spring through fall, with equally temporary docks and landing pads for its fleet of mostly operational skims and levs. Base was staffed, again from spring through fall, by a varying number of research teams who followed their equally varied interests along the coastline and into the waters of not only this inlet, but from Hecate Strait and the Pacific to the smallest glacier-fed lake that fed a stream that completed the circuit traveled by salmon. For that was Base's unifying purpose: to learn about these fish whose daily existence mattered to other life throughout this part of the world.

It was a part of the world Mac loved with a passion, from the rain-drenched forests to the wave-tossed ocean, from the wood-strewn beaches to the gravel beds high in the mountains that edged the coast. She loved Base as well, with its tidal flow of activity and eager minds. It didn't matter if they struggled for funds, like any research institute. They were experts when it came to getting the most done with the least. There was pride here, a feeling that creative solutions were the best kind, and self-sufficiency mattered. In a sense, they worked the way their subjects lived: finding a way around any barrier, fixed on goals beyond themselves.

Goals kept you sane. Mac listened to the echo of her own footsteps, no longer muted by carpeting. Pod Three had been lucky: no major structural damage above the first floor, only one anchor pylon ruined beyond repair. A mess inside, mind you, having been tipped on its side by the Ro, but most of that cleanup had been finished before Mac's return. The only lingering change was on the floor. It had been more economical to remove the seawater-soaked carpet than replace it. The cleaning staff were happy.

And these days, Mac preferred to hear footsteps.

Goals were better than waiting. Repairs to the rest of Base had taken all winter, and everything they'd had. Like an echo from the past, when Mac herself had been a student helping to repair storm damage to the original Base, winter staff and students had put aside their own projects to work alongside the construction crews. The months had sped by in a frenzied blur of activity, indoors when forced by wind and ice, outdoors whenever the elements cooperated, however slightly. The salmon would come again in spring—their goal was to be ready to greet them, intact.

And they were, Mac told herself proudly. Aside from minor cosmetic work that could be done over the summer, Base was back in business.

And if Mac had thrown herself into the reconstruction more than anyone else, if she'd lost more weight, gained more calluses, suffered more frostbite and cuts, no one had appeared to notice. It was just her being Mac.

And if she'd needed drugs to sleep without nightmares, if she'd dared not think beyond mem-wood rails and skim repairs, if she'd clung fast to what she could do, to escape what she couldn't—well, that wasn't anyone else's business but hers.

What was happening, all those light-years away? What had already happened? When would the other shoe drop?

Pushing such thoughts away, deep into that cold, distant place she'd learned to keep them, Mac trailed the fingers of her right hand along one wall, lifting them to avoid a fresh cluster of hand-drawn posters. The corner of her mouth twitched. A little early in the season for a challenge between Preds and Harvs, but then again, the rivalry served to get the new students' feet wet. Literally. Today's posters were inciting an improbable combination of sponges, bats, and beer.

Pod Three—being administration and thus blessed by "official guests," usually without notice—wasn't supposed to have posters, particularly this type. Someone more concerned with official appearances would take these down later. Later still, they'd go back up. Mac grinned.

A pound of feet from behind. She glanced over her shoulder for the source, ready to leap out of the way if it were Preds heading for their skims. Whale song of any type tended to get them moving, in a hurry. *Not Preds.* Mac raised an eyebrow in surprise at the lanky man hastening toward her, his hands grabbing at the air as if to hold her in place. "John?"

"Mac! Wait!" John Ward, her postdoc student for several years, wasn't a person to raise his voice indoors. Come to think of it, she'd never seen him run indoors either. *An alarming combination.*

"What's wrong?" Hearing the edge in her voice, Mac took a deep, calming breath as John panted to a stop in front of her. *They couldn't be under attack.* Things were back to normal. Earth had defenses and, as Mac had been told in no uncertain terms, there were People In Charge. What had happened here last year would never happen again.

She'd never let it.

Somehow, Mac pushed her dread aside, realizing there was a likelier scenario. "Did the new Harvs burn lunch?"

John's scowl turned puzzled, then he shook his head and scowled again. "Maybe. Probably. But that's not what's wrong, Mac. You have to do something. Dr. 'My Way or No Way' Noyo has gone too far this time. Too far!"

This, from someone who wouldn't criticize the weather, let alone a colleague? Mac leaned her shoulders against the wall to gaze up at the distraught man. The corridor was a bit public for a discussion of staff politics; on the other hand, it offered a choice of escape routes. *Bonus.* "What's Kammie done now?" she asked, resigned. In Base, getting from A to B typically involved the entire alphabet.

"Only hired my new statistician without so much as asking me first. Honestly, Mac, one minute I'm so qualified you two make me overwinter here to help run the place—the next, I'm not consulted on what impacts my own department."

"Your department?" Mac narrowed her eyes at him. Postdocs didn't, in her experience, morph into administrators without notice. "And what department would that be?"

John turned pink from collar to hairline. "Oh. It's not really a full department—not yet. You're right, I shouldn't call it that, but—"

"What are you talking about?" Mac interrupted.

"You know," he insisted, then looked perplexed at the slow shake of Mac's head. "You don't. Oh, dear."

"Enlighten me."

"But . . ."

"Now would be good."

John took a deep breath. "While you were—gone—and since I was stuck here over the winter anyway—I sent a proposal to Norcoast to offer a couple of new courses in stats, some higher level stuff, you know." He warmed to his topic. "Filled the classes through to next fall with the first mailout. It was amazing! Which led to this little extra team of us, an office in Pod One, the need for a new theoretical statistician . . . of course someone who can add to ongoing research . . ." John's voice trailed away as Mac continued to stare blankly at him. "It was in Kammie's report," he offered, then the pink drained from his cheeks so quickly he might have had chromatophores under the skin, like the octopi he loved. "I'm sorry, Mac. I didn't mean—I know—it hasn't been easy for you—"

Whatever showed on her face by this point stopped him in his tracks. "Sorry," he finished lamely.

Would it ever end? Mac made the effort and shrugged off the apology. It hadn't been possible to arrive back at Base and pretend she was the same person. There was the new hair, for one thing. The new hand and wrist, for another. *Not that her postdoc, her friend, was agonizing over those changes.* He meant the brain damage they'd been told Mac had suffered in the supposed skim accident that had taken her hand.

That the damage was nothing of the sort, but rather the consequence of a series of high-handed and ruthless reconstructions of the language center of her brain to suit the needs of others? That when she was tired, words on a screen or page turned to gibberish and she'd resort to audio?

That when she dreamed, it was in no language spoken on Earth?

Not things she cared to admit to herself, Mac decided, let alone explain. But it wasn't John's fault.

She shrugged again, conscious that her silence wasn't reassuring. "No need to apologize, John. You know what Kammie's reports are like."

He nodded his understanding. Kammie Noyo might be one of the foremost soil chemists on this or any planet, but her administrative reports were the driest possible combination of numbers and lists imaginable. *Not to mention the woman's compulsive use of footnotes.* Even before Mac's 'accident,' she'd read Kammie's reports under bright light, with loud music and a cold ocean wind blowing through the room. *And still nodded off.*

After receiving Kammie's mammoth accounting of what had happened at Base during her absence—and after one too many frustrating nights trying to puzzle through it—Mac had cut to the "Work Needed" list and filed the rest for later. Much later. If ever.

It seemed she'd been a bit hasty.

"Tell me now," Mac scowled. "Starting with where you two found funds to expand teaching programs when a third of this place needed repairs." The insurers had, with uncommon, if unknowing, accuracy, declared the destruction due to an act of war and refused to pay. Base might have been left crippled in the water, if it hadn't been for Denise Pillsworthy, who, it turned out, had bequeathed everything she'd owned in life to Norcoast, including her patents.

They shouldn't have been surprised, Mac reminded herself. Denise had only been happy when locked into her claustrophobic lab in Pod Six for days at a time, wearing thirty-year-old clothes, wrapping wire and her considerable brilliance around inventions she'd blithely toss at the world so it would leave her in peace. She'd had no family, only colleagues she alternately ignored or badgered. A couple of closer ties, perhaps, but none she'd let interfere with her work. "Don't tell me you tapped Denise's legacy—"

"Mac! No. I'd never use the repair funds. Kammie helped me apply for a grant. I thought—" He achieved a striking likeness to a puppy caught with a well-slobbered slipper. "I thought you'd be pleased."

Mac remembered seeing the budget, albeit vaguely. Those hadn't been numbers to her. They'd been faces. She'd blinked fiercely and skipped to the next section, having shed her tears for those lost in the attack last summer, when Pod Six had been sent to the bottom of the inlet by the Ro. Drowning the acoustics lab. Drowning friends and colleagues. *Denise . . . Seung . . .*

She stopped herself before the roll call kept going. Some nights, it ran an endless loop . . . a list of loss.

Which mustn't tarnish the future. "Of course I'm pleased," Mac said, her firm nod for both man and concept. "More stats up front? Just what we need around here. I've been hoping to find a way to boost students' analytical skills—get them to the level we expect. My apologies for any misunderstanding, John. My fault."

John still wore that anxious look, as if she hadn't finished grading his latest paper. "I never meant to surprise you with this, Mac."

Mac rolled her eyes theatrically. "I'm getting used to it. Just don't assume I know everything, okay?" She tapped him lightly on the chest with two fingers. "So, what's the problem with your new staff member? Not qualified?"

One of John's virtues, both as a scientist and a person, was his transparent honesty. Mac watched the war between offended dignity and the truth play out on his face, and carefully didn't smile. "She's more qualified than I'd hoped," he admitted glumly. "It's just . . ."

". . . you expected to be involved in such an important decision," Mac finished for him. "Nothing wrong with that, John. Look at it this way. If the new prof doesn't work out, you can fire her." His look of dismay was almost comical. "Hadn't thought of that?" she asked innocently.

"Mac—!" he sputtered.

Mac chuckled deep in her throat. "I suppose congratulations are in order. It isn't every day I lose a postdoc and gain a department head."

"You're worse than Kammie."

Her smile broadened.

"Fine," John surrendered, hands in the air, relief brightening his expression. "You on the way to lunch or Box Hunting?" *Valid question.* This time of year, preparing gear for shipment to the varied field stations assumed the proportions of an emergency evacuation. Tie was already in his protective huddle over Base's stockpile of tape, rope, bags, and crates. No matter. Students and staff were resourceful scroungers, not to mention creative. The only rule, unspoken but upheld—mostly—was packed boxes were off limits. If taped and labeled. And someone was sitting on them.

"I'll have you know I finished my packing last week," Mac informed her new department head serenely. The move to the field was something felt in her bones; she grew as impatient for it as her salmon for their natal streams. *This year,* she told herself, *more than ever.* To get away from everything and everyone. To lose herself in work. To escape the temptation to obsessively scan every available news release, looking for any signs of . . . "Lunch," Mac blurted. "I'll meet you there." Turning to leave, she paused and smiled at him. "Don't worry, John. The day will come when you get to trample over other people."

"Thanks. I think."

With a chuckle, Mac headed for the lift. She squeezed in with a group of damp, noisy Misses, short for "miscellaneous," the catchall phrase for those researchers looking at areas other than predator/prey interactions or harvesting issues. On the way down two floors, to the surface level and walkway, she listened with half an ear to their discussions, a jargon-rich blend of technical chatter and shameless gossip. Not to mention an impassioned debate on the aerodynamics of flying monkeys.

At moments like these, if she hadn't seen the Ro come close to destroying this pod for herself, she could forget it had ever happened. She could forget the sinking of Pod Six, the rooms ransacked by one or more of the invisible beings, Emily being abducted—or rather recruited—by them. She could believe the story planted by the Ministry of Extra-Sol Human Affairs: that a fringe group of xenophobic Humans had used violence to protest the first visit of a Dhryn to Earth.

Above all, she could forget the Dhryn.

"You coming, Mac?"

A student was holding the lift door open for her. The rest had already walked out. Mac managed a smile and nod. "Thanks."

The main floor was jammed shoulder to shoulder with people bustling to or from lunch in the large common gallery. This early in spring, with teams waiting to head to field stations or out to sea, Base bulged with its maximum population. Late fall saw the return influx, but most went back to their respective universities or institutes for the winter, to write papers and take other courses. Mac and Kammie stayed year 'round, with those few whose work continued despite the ice, or because of it.

In normal years.

Mac made her way against the flow of foot traffic, nipping between those intent on their companions, their stomachs, or both, and managing, for once, not to sacrifice her toes. Mac wasn't short, but it seemed each new crop of students arrived larger and more oblivious than the last. She could use warning lights and stilts at this rate.

The noisy, moving crowd thinned, then was gone by the time Mac reached the main entrance. She nodded a greeting to the two in body armor standing to either side, receiving an unusually wary look from both in return. Today's pair was Sing-li Jones and Ballantine Selkirk. Quiet, reserved men who, being lousy poker players, had already "donated" most of their free time to Tie's pod repairs. *Knew why she was here, did they?*

They were part of the team of four security personnel assigned by the Ministry to Norcoast, initially ordered to remain discreetly anonymous. This silly notion had immediately inspired the curious denizens of Base to a series of escapades aimed at filching underwear as well as identification.

Moreover, the notion had annoyed Mac. She expected names and personalities from everyone around her, even those whose job was to overdress, stand in one place, and loom. She got them.

Not that she'd needed them, she reminded herself. Selkirk was the tallest, Norlen shortest, Zimmerman had virtually no neck, and Jones tapped his left forefinger against his holster when thinking. *Anonymous? Hardly.*

Nothing against the men themselves, but on any given day, Mac's feelings about guards of the looming variety ranged from still-annoyed to resigned. The suits of black gleaming armor made them easy to spot, if about as useful as coded door controls. At times less useful, given last week they'd let in three tigger-splattered tourists and a census taker for the upcoming local election who'd insisted on interviewing everyone despite Mac's repeated assurance only five people on Base qualified as residents, of whom only two ever voted.

If anything, the blinding obviousness of the guards at their post made Mac suspect other, more subtle precautions in place, not that any of the four had yet to admit it. All to protect this one pod against the return of a nonexistent group of fanatics.

Mac wouldn't mind being guarded against the return of the real culprits, the Ro. After all, according to all experts and the Ro themselves, their previous attack had been aimed at her alone.

Not the flavor of the day, she reminded herself.

No mistake, anywhere the Ro had been, anyone they'd touched, was being watched. But the Ro—the powerful and mysterious My-rokynay—were now sought-after allies, popular with everyone. *Everyone else,* Mac corrected to herself. Apparently they'd been aware of the dangers of the Dhryn all along; supposedly they'd tried to communicate that peril without success; the assumption was, they'd been on guard.

There was no doubt the Ro *knew* about the Dhryn and the Chasm worlds. And that knowledge was now the most important commodity in the Interspecies Union.

For regardless of anyone's guesses as to their actions or motivations, one thing seemed clear: the Ro had been about to destroy the Dhryn Progenitors once and for all. But in a classic case of mis-understanding, the IU, with abundant and clever help from humanity, had managed to grant the Dhryn the means to expose their ancient enemy by defeating the Ro's stealth technology.

The Dhryn? They'd vanished into the unimaginable depths of space encompassed by the transects and the planetary systems those pathways connected.

The Ro? They hadn't been heard from since, despite what Mac was sure were frantic efforts by any culture with communications technology to reach them.

Aliens should come with labels, she grumbled to herself. "Friend / Useless / Planning to Eat You" would cover the current possi-bilities nicely.

Were the Ro friends? Not by any standard Mac accepted. The enemy of my enemy? She knew the logic. She didn't believe it for an instant.

Actions mattered.

As now. Mac didn't bother asking questions. The entrance was transparent—from inside, anyway—and she could see the reason for Jones' and Selkirk's "she's not going to like this" looks for herself. *Though why they'd chosen* this *poor soul to lock outside was anyone's guess.*

The rain was striking so hard that each drop bounced back up from the mem-wood walkway, as if simply falling from the sky wasn't insult enough to the solitary figure standing in its midst.

Miniature waterfalls poured from every crease of his yellow coat and hood, giving him something of the look of a statue abandoned in a fountain. A hunched, thoroughly miserable statue, staring at the shelter so near and yet so unattainable.

"For the— Let him in," Mac snapped. Instead of waiting for her order to be obeyed—or debated—she headed for the entrance control herself.

Jones and Selkirk scowled in unison. "He's not authorized—" the latter began.

"And you started caring about this when?" Mac asked in disbelief. "Need I remind you about certain tourists? Or Ms. Ringles, the Census Queen?"

The two managed to look abashed and determined at the same time. "We have our orders, Dr. Connor."

"Here's your new one. Authorize him once he's out of the rain." Knowing full well neither would stop her, although both shifted automatically to loom in the appropriate direction, hands closer to weapons, Mac keyed open the door.

Without hesitation, the figure stomped inside, ignoring the looming guards and instantly creating his own small pond as water from rainsuit and hood puddled around his boots. Then he yanked back that hood to glare at her.

"About bloody time, Norcoast."

Should have listened to Selkirk, Mac sighed to herself. Aloud, and before either guard could do more than look interested, she said quickly: "It's all right. I know this man." Then Mac frowned. "Since when do you make house calls, Oversight?"

Charles Mudge III, the man who was the Oversight Committee for the Castle Inlet Wilderness Trust, which made him her—and Norcoast's—personal demon, stood shivering with cold and damp. His eyes were no less fierce than his voice. "When I revoke a license to enter the Trust. Your license."

Fresh-caught and grilled salmon, geoduck chowder, fiddleheads, new potatoes bursting their skins, wild rhubarb pies—a promising menu, though tasting would be the proof. Spring meals tended to alternate between triumph and disaster. This year they'd added a brand new kitchen to the equally new cooks. Mac was fond of the irony that by the time any given set of student cooks gained enough experience to be reliable in the kitchen, everyone, including those cooks, would be too busy to make or eat anything but cold pizza and oatmeal.

Despite today's tantalizing aromas, Mac found herself with no more appetite than her "guest," who'd brusquely refused her offer of lunch. Nevertheless, she'd brought Mudge to the gallery, hoping the sheer volume of voices and clattering utensils would keep him from shouting at her immediately. At least until she knew what was going on and could justifiably shout back.

She hoped his threat was simply to get her attention. Surely revoking their license would require hearings, presentations, proof. *Not that proof would be hard to obtain,* Mac thought glumly, staring uneasily at her visitor. It might not have been her fault, or Norcoast's, that the Wilderness Trust lands had been disturbed so profoundly on the ridge overlooking Base. That didn't matter. They'd joined in the lie that nothing had happened, agreed to a silence that sat on Mac's stomach as an uneasy weight, on her conscience as a stain.

She'd hoped not to face Mudge. Not this soon. Kammie had handled the applications for the spring/summer research before Mac's return, saying the approvals had been given. Everything was routine.

Nothing in the haggard face watching her warily from the other side of the table agreed with that assessment.

"What's this about, Oversight?" Mac asked, bringing her imp on top of the table, ready to call up the active research proposals. The imp, or Interactive Mobile Platform, could use its own data or access that held within Norcoast's main system. In use, it projected a workscreen almost as powerful as her desk's. Given the number of people currently eating lunch through hovering workscreens of their own, imps were likely the most common portable technology in the gallery after forks.

"Can we talk here?" he whispered. "Talk freely, I mean."

Was everyone around her going to act like a damn spy? Mac glowered at him. "We don't have vidbots hovering everywhere, if that's what you mean. No budget and no point." Not to mention it was illegal to put surveillance on private individuals inside their homes, which Mac considered Base to be. She'd threatened her new security force on that issue until their eyes glazed.

"If that's so . . ." Mudge paused and leaned forward, eyes intent. "Where have you been, Norcoast?" Quiet and quick, like a knife in the dark.

"Didn't Dr. Noyo tell you? In New Zealand—at the IU's consulate."

Quieter still. "Why are you lying?"

Mac tapped her imp against the table, then put it away in its pocket. She knew what she was supposed to say; she'd said it often enough. To her father and brothers. Her friends. Total strangers. Somehow, this time, the words stuck in her throat. Maybe it was the innocent din from all sides, people in her care as much as the land nearest them was in this man's care. *Their care.* When neither she nor Mudge had any real power to protect them.

"You didn't come here and stand in the rain to ask about my trip," she said instead. "What did you mean, revoke our license?"

Mudge hadn't removed his rainsuit. Not camouflage, since the only other person at Base who knew him on sight would be Kammie. The students and staff likely thought he was another insurance adjuster. No, Mac decided, he stayed rain-ready in case she had him tossed back outside. *Tempting, that.*

As he laid his arms on the table, the fabric made a wet rubber protest. His face, usually flushed, was mottled and pale. *Gave up the beard,* she noticed, with that distressingly familiar jolt of missed time. "Please." Again, a whisper. "No one will tell me what's been going on. No one. I waited for you, Norcoast, but they wouldn't let me talk to you. I still can't believe I made it this far."

"What are you talking about?" Mac resisted the urge to look over her shoulder, but couldn't help lowering her voice to match. "I've been right here. You haven't called me. You've been dealing with Kammie—Dr. Noyo—"

"Pshaw! I've dealt with no one. And yes, Norcoast, I called *you.*

They'd connect me with some nameless fool who'd prattle on about how busy you were. So I came in person. Twice." He stabbed at the tabletop with a thick finger. "The first time, I made the mistake of using the trans-lev from Vancouver like a normal visitor. They stopped me at the dock and sent me back. This time, I didn't tell anyone where I was going. I bribed some of your students to bring me here with them. I wouldn't give a name or ident until you showed up at the door. Wouldn't let them have a chance to send me away again." He stopped to catch his breath, managing to look outraged and smug at the same time.

They. Them. Mac didn't doubt who'd been keeping Mudge away from her. The Ministry. The arm of Human government that dealt with offworld issues of interest to humanity, now patently interfering on Earth.

Answering the question of how much they relied on her willing silence, Mac told herself, feeling cold. If they could impede the movement of a government official, however annoying, who knew what other powers they'd been granted since declaring the Dhryn a threat to the Human species? *Obviously no paralysis of jurisdictions in the way.* Given the circumstances, Mac supposed such streamlining was reasonable, probably even commendable.

She just preferred her bureaucracy a little more on the cumbersome side, with things like forms, delays, and names attached.

Mudge was distracted by students with trays crowding past him, forced to lean sideways to avoid a close encounter with chowder; distracted by her own thoughts, Mac was grateful for the reprieve.

She'd drawn too much comfort in the lack of news, believed it impossible to keep something as noteworthy as attacks on entire worlds a secret, assured herself she'd be among those to know. *Had she been naïve?*

What might be happening?

Enough, Mac scolded herself, reining in her imagination. It wasn't as if knowing would make any difference in her life. She was packed for the field; she had experiments to run. So what if the Ministry had reserved to itself, and presumably key leaders of Earthgov, the right to decide how much truth to release about the Dhryn? That was their job. The press releases had been masterworks of reassurance. "The Dhryn posed an unspecified hazard" Late-night comics joked about explosive alien flatulence. "The Dhryn had gone missing." Enterprising, if unscrupulous, individuals advertised colonization rights on their abandoned worlds. "System approach controls were to report any sightings." Shipping schedules and security hadn't changed.

Avoiding panic, keeping order in space-bound traffic, concealing needful preparations for defense or attack. Those were valid reasons.

Weren't they?

The truth might come out in years, never, or this afternoon. Mac feared the timing would depend more on how soon the crisis grew out of control than on anything more sensible. But she wasn't a politician.

She was someone who understood the need to protect others. Maybe secrecy was the best way. It wasn't hers, mind you. *But they hadn't asked her opinion.*

"Pardon? What did you say?" Mudge demanded. His rainsuit squeaked as he turned to face her.

"Nothing." Mac pressed her fingertips, real and artificial, against the tabletop. It resisted without effort, being as hard as the truth. *Truth.* She licked her lips, trying to think of the best approach. "It was a mistake to come here, Oversight," she told him at last. "You have to leave. Now."

He settled deeper into his chair.

Oh, she knew that look. Growing roots and planning to be as stubborn as one of his damned trees.

As easily cut down.

Mac closed her eyes briefly, then gave in. "Let's continue this in my office."

She'd picked one of the smaller tables, off to the side. It didn't share the ocean view afforded by the rest of the room, though it made a decent spot for watching hockey or vids when those were playing. It was, however, close to an exit. Mac had grown convinced of the value of such things. Now, spotting the intent pair approaching them as Mudge stood up, she was even more grateful. "Don't talk to anyone," she hissed. "Out this door, left to the end of the hall. Take the lift to the third floor, last office on the right. Wait for me there. And don't touch anything," she added hastily, suddenly beset by the image of Mudge rampaging through her drawers. "Go!"

He walked away as John Ward came up to introduce his companion, a companion who not only gave the departing Mudge a curious look, but was also someone Mac hadn't expected to meet again—and certainly not here.

"Mac. This is Dr. Persephone Stewart, my—our new theoretical statistician. She arrived ahead of schedule." To say John was beaming was an understatement. He practically radiated joy. His companion smiled at him, then at Mac.

Emily would say this Dr. Stewart had done her homework, Mac decided. An older, but athletic figure, their new statistician was dressed to blend in a casual, not-too-trendy shirt and skirt. An interesting personality was hinted at by intricate rows of red, bronze, and turquoise beads braided scalp-tight over the top of her head like a tapestry cap, dense black hair below framing her ears and neck like ebony mist. Slung casually over one shoulder was a well-used portable keyboard. No wonder the students in the gallery were tracking Dr. Stewart's every move. John, hovering at her side, was patently smitten.

So much for his complaint about Kammie's high-handed decision-making.

"Call me 'Sephe," invited the tall dark woman, her smile as magic and mischievous as Mac remembered. "Everyone does."

Oh, she remembered the smile. And the name. And more. Mac remembered the weapons, ready in each hand, as this woman guarded her against the Ro. 'Sephe might well be a statistician.

She also worked for the Ministry, not Norcoast. *Why was she here? Why now?*

Mac's mouth dried. *Something had changed.*

"Everyone calls me Mac. Nice to meet you," she said calmly, offering her hand.

But Mac wasn't sure if it was in welcome or self-defense.

2

SECRETS AND STEALTH

THE OUTER RIDGE of Castle Inlet curled its arm against the Pacific, hoarding an expanse of coastline virtually untouched by Human intervention for over three hundred years. It was a steep, tree-encrusted coast, where eagles perched at the bottom of clouds and rivers gnawed the growing bones of mountains.

The land might trap the eye, but water defined it. Waves alternately slapped aside cliffs or gently lipped fallen logs to shore; mist, rain, or snow filled the air more often than sunlight. Water, locked in glaciers and snowcap, even set the distant peaks agleam by moon or star.

Today's downpour had eased to the point where Mac, looking out her window, could see the toss of waves and the mauve-gray of cliffs, if not the trees above and beyond. She didn't need to—those trees were the heritage of the man standing beside her. In a sense, Charles Mudge III was the Wilderness Trust.

In all the years they'd tussled, spat, and outright battled over scientific access to this Anthropogenic Perturbation Free Zone, she'd always respected that. *Now?* "They've promised me privacy here," Mac said finally, turning to look at Mudge. "If that's a lie, I've no way to know. I can only warn you."

"The same 'they' who wouldn't let me talk to you."

Mac nodded.

The Ministry of Extra-Sol Human Affairs. An office on each Human settlement, station or colony, two or three local staff.

Census-takers. Bureaucrats who arranged travel visas and sent inoffensive messages of congratulations or condolences as necessary, keeping somewhat neglectful track of humanity's widespread offspring. Mediators, when Human expectation collided with alien reality. There was a central office on Mars, ostensibly to be close to the transects anchored outside Venus orbit, but also because matters within Sol's system, or on Earth herself, hadn't been part of the Ministry's jurisdiction.

Until aliens came to live and work here as well, and that jurisdiction began to blur. For who better to forestall any interspecies' confusion, than the component of Human government accustomed to dealing with it daily?

Mac had been brought home on a Ministry ship. On the journey, as her arm had healed, as she'd grieved, as she'd answered their interminable questions and received few answers to her own, she'd made a pact with herself. She'd think the best of those who'd taken control of things, do her utmost to believe they meant her well and could do their jobs—at least until there was clear evidence to the contrary.

On those terms, Mac tolerated guards on her door and accepted 'Sephe as staff—assuming the woman's work as a scientist measured up to Norcoast standards—even though that acceptance meant ignoring the other aspect of their new statistician.

Mudge's complaint, however, was another matter.

He appeared uneasy. Perhaps he hadn't believed her assurance of privacy. Mac wasn't sure she believed it either. She watched Mudge pace around her office, pausing beside her rebuilt garden—presently receiving an overdose of chill mist which made the floor nearby somewhat treacherous. Its weather mirrored that of Field Station One: last to feel summer, first to freeze again. Of course, since the floor near the garden consisted of fist-sized hunks of gravel embedded as if the bottom of a river, walking with care was a given. Her staff had worked hard to restore what the Ro—and, to be honest, the Ministry's investigators—had torn apart. The reconstruction had been a pleasant but unsettling surprise upon her return, Mac remembered. Unsettling, because she could look over there and believe nothing had changed.

Almost. Mudge didn't glance up at her collection of wooden salmon, swaying on their threads below the rain-opaqued curved ceiling. If he had, he would have seen that not all were carvings. Between the stylized Haida renderings, the realistic humps of pinks and the dramatic hooked jaws of coho and chum, hung slimmer, more nondescript fish, fish with hollow bodies filled with motion sensors and alarms.

It was likely Mudge also missed the significance of the reed curtains beside both doors into Mac's office. At night, she pulled them across. Not for privacy: the walls themselves could be opaqued at will. No, like the false carvings, the reeds were hollow and contained metal chimes. When touched they made, as Tie bluntly put it, "enough noise to wake the dead." Low-tech security, perhaps, but comforting nonetheless.

Everyone else might want a visit from the Ro. *Never again,* vowed Mac, with a restrained shudder.

Did her staff and friends consider her obsessed by her midnight visitor? Maybe. For Mac's part, she was appalled by how completely everyone else had accepted the Ministry's version of events: that she and Emily had surprised vandals planning to sabotage the pods; that Emily had seen too much, and been taken to keep her silent, that Otto Rkeia, career thief and presumed ringleader, had met his death by misadventure during that sabotage.

As if "death by misadventure" could somehow encompass being glued to an anchor of Pod Six, thirty meters below the surface of the Pacific.

Not only had everyone at Base let Emily Mamani slip from their lives, they actually believed they themselves were safe. That anything was safe.

What was she thinking, Mac chastised herself, *bringing Mudge here, hinting she'd reveal secrets others had died, were likely dying, to protect?* "A threat to the species . . . where on that scale . . ." She refused to remember the rest of that voice.

Heedless of her inner turmoil, her unwelcome visitor stopped to point at a shoulder-high folding screen of black lacquered wood, presently perch to three gray socks, a large lumpy brown sweater, and a pair of faded blue coveralls twin to those Mac wore. "Don't they give you living quarters?"

Mac waved at the lab end of her office. "I like to stay with my work." He gave the worktables loaded ceiling-high with boxes and storage bags a doubtful look. "Incoming postdocs," she lied, unwilling to admit she'd had no students apply to work with her this season. Why would they? She'd abandoned Base last year, produced no results, attended no conferences, ignored messages, missed interviews. *Unreliable. Unproductive. Unworthy.* Mac was counting on the coming season and its results to set things right.

The boxes and bags were Emily's. Her belongings kept being sent here, without warning, from wherever they were found. Thoroughly searched and documented before Mac saw them, with no explanation or advice on what to do with them; she let them pile up. Archaeologist's tools and flamboyant jewelry from the dead home world of the Dhryn. Slashed silk and broken furniture from guest quarters on Base. Sleeping bag and tent from Field Station Six. A collection of erotic novels and exotic kitchen gear from the Sargasso Sea. Mail-order llama statues.

Flotsam from a woman's life. *How far could you drift before being lost?* Mac wondered.

The Ro had taken part of Emily's flesh and somehow traded it for no-space, so she could travel with them, talk to them. *How long could a body endure that connection? How long could a mind?*

Well aware of that connection, the IU and the Ministry desperately wanted to find Emily Mamani and any like her, to reestablish communication with the Ro. The real reason for their attention to Base. To Mac. *Emily's things?*

More bait.

Forgive me, Emily had asked, the night she'd left.

She was a hero now, of sorts. To those who knew. A Human who'd given up everything to try and stop the Dhryn. She'd known the truth; tried in vain to tell Mac.

Forgive me, Mac thought, then tensed as Mudge laid his hand on a nearby crate, one of several forming a lopsided pyramid in the center of the large room. The stack, Emily's equipment from Field Station Six, looked regrettably like a shrine. No guarantees any of it still worked. The Ministry had left it in pieces. Mac had reassembled the console as best she could, but Emily would have to rebuild the tracers, test everything first.

It had been Mac's decision to keep Emily's field equipment at hand and ready, a decision those who'd been here last year acknowledged with silent, dismayed looks whenever entering her office. Especially Lee, once hopelessly smitten with Emily's lush looks and boldness, who'd found the love of his life in quiet, shy Lara Robertson-Herrera from biochem a mere month after Emily's disappearance. When he saw the crates, he'd actually flinch.

Did they think she didn't notice? She was stubborn, not blind.

The waterproofed gear she'd use this field season was stacked outside on the terrace, ready for pickup by t-lev. Mac was simply ready for Emily's return.

Whenever that might be.

Mudge tapped one crate with a stubby forefinger, as if he'd guessed its contents from her reaction. "Haven't you found a replacement for Dr. Mamani yet? Surely she had collaborators."

Oh, yes. Invisible aliens, able to sidestep space, utterly ruthless and bent on genocide. Mac shook her head. "No. No one available, that is," she qualified. His skeptical look made her fumble for an explanation. "The tracer technology we were using was imported." The present euphemism for anything alien, although eager innovation rapidly blurred whatever was in Human hands for more than a week. Patent law was a booming business. "Em— Dr. Mamani was working with it on her own."

As far as Mac knew. From scuttlebutt through academic channels, she'd heard how "officials" had swept through the Sargasso Sea Research Outpost, Emily's other home, with such fierce thoroughness that lawsuits had been filed and lost, five doctoral students had attempted to transfer elsewhere, an effort that resulted only in attracting further scrutiny (Mac had heard the phrase "scoured to their toenails" used and didn't doubt it), and the reputation of the scientists left rocked by Emily Mamani's wake best described as "tenuous."

The "officials" had claimed to be hunting clues to Emily's disappearance. Mac wondered how long anyone would continue to buy either the excuse—or its truth. Emily's younger sister, Maria, wouldn't take Mac's calls anymore. *Not that she had news to give her.*

Mac's troubled thoughts must have shown on her face. Mudge came back and sat in one of the two chairs in front of her desk, eyes fixed on her. "This place is what I expected, Norcoast. Not you." His eyebrows drew together. "You've changed."

Somehow, Mac knew he didn't mean her new haistyle or lack of The Suit. "People do," she said noncommittally.

"It's more than that." His frown deepened, acquiring puckers beside his eyes. "But I didn't come here to pity you."

Ouch. Mac almost smiled. "You came to revoke my license," she reminded him.

His eyes gleamed. "I would if I could, believe me."

"What do you mean?"

"They've taken the Trust away. Surely you knew?"

Mac was grateful her desk was close enough she could put her hip to it for support. "There was," she ventured, "some talk of emergency measures during the—incident—last year."

"Some talk?" Mudge slammed his palm against the arm of the chair. "The government—don't ask me what branch, because I get a different set of names every week—took control then and kept it. I get no reports. Your Dr. Noyo's applications went over my head . . . approved without my so much as seeing them. I spent months waiting for the one person I could expect to tell me the truth about the Trust, only to find I wasn't permitted to talk to her. In all but name, Norcoast, there is no more Trust."

Her heart fluttered in her chest, as if looking for a way out. *If this was some favor from Nik, it was no favor at all.* "I didn't know," Mac said. "I—I'd assumed Kammie was a better negotiator than I'd been. Or that, under the circumstances, you'd been unusually—" she changed *kind* to "—amenable to this year's projects."

"Convenient, your being away."

Provoked, Mac lunged to her feet. "I was looking for my friend—"

Mudge waved his hand placatingly. "Sit down, Norcoast. You might be pigheaded and narrow-minded, but I never believed you were a willing part of this."

Sorting a compliment from that could cause a headache. Mac settled for a testy: "Thanks. Given you can't revoke my license, for which I won't deny I'm grateful, why did you come?"

"I want to see for myself."

"See what?" Mac asked, dreading the answer. Sure enough, Mudge thrust a thick finger in the direction of shore. "No. Absolutely not. I can't possibly—"

"Why? If there's nothing wrong, what will it hurt?"

"With you," Mac pointed out, "there's always something wrong."

He leaned back in the chair and didn't quite smile, although Mac sensed Mudge felt close to victory. "I'm willing to overlook your people's usual transgressions," he said generously. "The footprints, the broken limbs, the misplaced sample vials. Picnics."

How about the massive scar from a Ro landing site—the tracks from teams of investigators—the doubtless intact passage left by a panic-stricken Dhryn carrying her up the slope? Aliens where they didn't belong. Not part of Mudge's worldview.

Or, until recently, her own.

Mac swore under her breath.

"Pardon?"

"I said it's not possible." As his face clouded, she temporized, "Yet. The webbing lines to the shore haven't been set up. No way to get there. You'll have to come back in—" Mac gauged the limit of Mudge's patience and doubled it for negotiating room, "—say, two weeks."

He pursed his lips, then shook his head. "Too long. The undergrowth will be up, obscuring details. You have skims, levs. I'd settle for a kayak."

Feigning shock, Mac widened her eyes. "I can't believe you said that, Oversight. After all the precautions, the truly extraordinary care Norcoast insists on using to protect the Trust lands—"

"Where *were* you?" With a quickness as surprising as his change in tactic, Mudge lunged forward to try and capture her left hand. *Her new hand.* "How did that happen?"

Mac stepped back, putting her fingers out of reach. "A skim accident."

"You don't lie well, Norcoast. Not to me."

"I've never lied to you," Mac protested.

"Until today."

Was this some bizarre test of her obedience? Had Oversight been part of what happened last year? Was his arrival within the same hour as one of the few of the Ministry's agents she knew on sight, 'Sephe, a coincidence or by plan?

Her head hurt. *Spies and lies.* If it weren't for the stakes involved, she'd gladly forget both. "You've missed the last transport, Oversight," Mac informed him. "I'll have someone set you up with quarters for the night."

Mudge stood, looking as dignified as possible considering he was still dripping wet despite his rainsuit and patently frustrated. And angry. Possibly even betrayed. *Oh, she knew that mix.* "We'll find you dry clothes," Mac offered. With an inward shudder at the thought of Mudge in conversation with anyone else at Base, she continued: "But I'll have to ask you to stay in your room. Supper will be sent up. There'll be a t-lev at dawn to take you back to Vancouver."

"Don't bother. I'm not leaving."

Mac blinked at him. *This was her tactic, not his.* Salmon tipped and touched overhead, music on the damp sea breeze coming through the partially open door. "There's a time to be stubborn, Oversight," she began, "and a time—"

"Would you?"

She didn't dare hesitate. "Yes. In your place, I'd go home."

"Lying. I told you that you aren't good at it, Norcoast."

They glared at one another. Mudge's usually florid face was pale and set. His thick fingers fussed at the fasteners of the raincoat he'd kept on, as if confident they'd be leaving at any minute now to head out in the rain. That she'd give in.

The worst of it? Mudge only asked for what was right and due. Mac thought of the interminable arguments they'd had through the years. Those she'd lost had been exactly like this one, where the moral high ground hadn't been under her feet, but his.

She steeled herself. The landscape had changed. The stakes

weren't research proposals or summer funding. She owed loyalty to more than a single stretch of glorious wilderness.

"Go home, Oversight," Mac said very gently.

These days, Mac's office boasted a couch that could reassemble itself into a bed. A handy place to dump her coat in the daytime; convenient at night, for the long hours she'd been keeping in order to catch up with her work. Comfortable enough, given sleep had become a duty she'd rather avoid. It went without saying that the security team applauded her decision to stay in one location, instead of reopening her separate living quarters upstairs. Equally obviously, her friends and colleagues trusted this wasn't a lifestyle choice she planned to foist on them, too. As far as Mac could tell, they'd at last abandoned hope she'd return to normal herself.

Tonight, as usual, Mac didn't bother changing the couch to a bed. She shrugged off her coveralls and left them on the floor. Turning off the interior lighting, she padded barefoot to the door to the terrace. She pushed it wide open with one hand, stepping around the half-drawn curtains, and stood gazing out.

No stars in sight, but the rain had taken a rest, leaving drops to line the undersides of every surface. The drops sparkled, refracting light from the dimmed glows marking step and rail, catching on spiderwebs. The ocean was dimmed as well, its ceaseless movement damped to a complex murmur rather than a roar. That would change with the tides and the wind.

Mac absorbed the calm of the world, breathed in its peace.

It was only the chill dampness that raised gooseflesh on her arms, belly, and legs. It was only her supper, sitting uneasily on a day that put Charles Mudge III in guest quarters and a Ministry spy on her staff, that made her flinch at a splash in the distance.

Mac refused to admit otherwise, for the same reason she came outside every night, to stand in the dark until it was clearly her choice to go inside and turn on lights.

She would not be changed by *them*.

The near shore of Castle Inlet was out of sight from here, even in daylight. "I should talk to Kammie," she whispered aloud. *And say what?* That this year, approval for Norcoast's research would have been granted for anything? That this year, they wouldn't have to confess their missteps to Charles Mudge III? "And I'm sorry about it?" Mac asked the empty sky.

Maybe that was why she was still awake, well past midnight.

Patter patter patter. Thud.

Heart pounding, Mac rushed to the railing and peered downward, trying to find the source of the sounds. *There!* A hunched silhouette passed in front of the lights on the walkway below, then ducked under the railing.

A *splash*—followed by the rhythmic sound of someone beginning to swim, badly.

"I don't believe it," Mac muttered, wheeling to run into her office. *Give the security team some real work?* After all, Mudge was hardly an athlete; he could drown. "Solving a few problems," she spat, but ignored her imp, instead grabbing her coveralls from the floor. She didn't bother trying to find shoes.

A moment later, Mac was in the lift tapping the clearance code for the lowermost level of Pod Three. She paced back and forth during the seconds it took to reach her destination, then squeezed shoulder first through the opening doors.

The smell of the ocean was intensified here, seasoned with the tang of protective oils and machinery. Like the others, this pod was open to the ocean underneath. Unlike the others, a third of that access was at wave height, through a gate wide enough to accommodate their largest t-lev, though with some admitted risk to paint and toes. Pod One held the fabrication and maintenance shops for the equipment and submersibles. This area was reserved for the repair and storage of Base's well-used surface fleet—Tie McCauley's domain, his meticulous nature clear in the gleaming order of tools and parts lining the curved wall. Woe betide the student—or staff—who disturbed a single item without permission. It was astonishing how unlikely timely repairs could become.

Tie had been elsewhere during the partial sinking of the pod. *How guilt had stained that joy, to have an old friend safe when so many others . . .*

An assortment of craft bobbed at anchor or hung from cabling. Mac headed for the gate itself, running along the dock that floated down the center of the expanse. Without a wasted move, she keyed open the inset access port within the gate, then dropped into the antique but always-ready skim Tie kept berthed next to it. The combination of grad students, fickle ocean, and Saturday parties made a quick retrieval craft an essential resource.

Mac ducked as she sent the skim beneath the half raised port, swinging it in a tight turn toward shore the instant she cleared the pod wall. Her hair somehow found its way into her eyes, despite its shorter length, and she shook her head impatiently. The skim, true to its name, paralleled the water's surface once in motion. She kept it low, needing to slip under the walkways between the pods to find Mudge. It meant a teeth-jarring ride as the repellers—at this intimate distance—faithfully copied every tiny rise, shudder, and fall of the waves beneath.

He would pick the middle of the damned night, Mac growled to herself. There was barely enough glow from the walkways to pick out the pods on either side. That wasn't a problem; Mac could have piloted through any part of Base with her eyes closed. But she wouldn't find Mudge that way. Fortunately, Tie had rigged this skim with searchlights. Mac aimed two over the bow as she slowed, sparing an instant to hope everyone else was in bed sleeping.

The fool should be right there.

And he was. Mac let out the breath she'd unconsciously held as the light passed over the sweep of an arm against the black water. She brought the skim down in front of the swimming figure and leaned over the side, steadying herself as the craft rocked from end to end with each swell. "What the hell do you think you're doing?" she demanded as quietly as she could given her mood and the water.

Goggled eyes aimed up at her. Mudge had come prepared; she gave him that, noting the wet suit and hand flippers. One of those flippers waved at her. "Get—out of my—way." Gasping, but not out of breath. Mac was impressed. Not always behind a desk, then.

It didn't change anything. She glanced over her shoulder, checking for any sign they'd been noticed. All quiet, but Mac knew it couldn't last. "Get in the skim, Oversight."

His answer was to put his head down and start swimming around her.

Mac muttered a few choice words and restarted her engine.

It was worse than arguing with him face-to-face. They played a game in the dark, under the dips of walkways and around the massive curves of pods. Mac would circle ahead; Mudge would have to stop. Then he'd duck beneath the night-black water, swimming under or past the skim, and Mac would have to circle again to get ahead of him.

After her third try, sorely tempted to use the boat hook to knock some sense into the man, Mac admitted defeat, along with a grudging respect. "Get in," she told him, "and I'll take you to shore tomorrow."

Mudge bobbed in the water like a dubious cod from some myth. "Your—word—Nor—coast."

The boat hook had such potential. Mac sighed. "Yes, yes. I promise. Just get in. Please?"

With an effort that had them out of breath by its end, Mac managed to get Mudge onto the skim's bench. For all of his bravado and wet suit, he was shaking and alarmingly cold to the touch. She wrapped a self-warming blanket from the skim's emergency chest around his shoulders, laying another over his lap. "Damn you, Oversight, you could have drowned," she accused, rubbing his back as hard as she could.

"Ther–rre—ther–re's worse—things," he sputtered.

Mac's hands stilled for an instant on the blanket.

"Yes," she agreed numbly. "There are."

Either Mudge had believed her, or he'd swallowed enough ocean for one night. Mac didn't particularly care which, so long as he stayed in his room. She yawned her way down the night-dimmed corridor to her office. With luck, she'd get a few hours' sleep before having to deal with what she'd promised.

It wasn't going to be easy. They'd somehow avoided being noticed tonight, but tomorrow, with all of Base awake and moving, it would be a different story. Not to mention the tiggers, the automated pseudo-gulls which reacted to any unauthorized intruder with an arsenal ranging from ear-piercing alarms to adhesive droppings containing any of a variety of unpleasant and increasingly debilitating substances. Mac didn't put faith in Mudge's assurance the tiggers should still be programmed to let him pass into the Trust lands. She'd have to find some way to circumvent them.

But how?

"I study salmon," Mac protested out loud as she let herself into her office. She didn't bother with lights, aiming straight for her couch after closing and locking the door behind her. The night was going to be short enough.

The lights came on anyway.

Somehow beyond surprise, Mac squinted at the figure seated all too comfortably behind her desk, chin resting on her hands, brown eyes fixed on her: 'Sephe.

Was no one going to let her sleep?

"It is the middle of the night," Mac observed.

"So it is. Where have you been, Dr. Connor?"

Mac straightened from her tired slouch, enjoying a welcome surge of adrenaline-rich anger. "Is that why you're here?" she snapped. "To check on where and when I sleep? There's no—"

"Answer the question, please."

"I took a walk." Mac marched to the couch, where she thumped her pillow into submission and threw it to one end. "Now about that sleep."

Rapier-sharp. "This isn't a game, Dr. Connor."

Mac yanked her oversized sweater from the screen and laid it on the couch, adequate blanket for a warm spring evening. "If you say so."

"You can't take Mudge ashore tomorrow."

Her back to 'Sephe, Mac squeezed her eyes shut, her heart giving a heavy, hopeless thud, anger draining away. *They'd promised her privacy, at least here, where she lived.* Like a fool, she'd believed.

Had they made charts of her sleepless nights? Recorded her cries when she did sleep and the nightmares woke her? Counted the times she'd called out their names? Emily. Nik.

Brymn.

Mac unfolded the fists she'd unconsciously made and turned. "If you heard that much, you know I gave him my word."

Dark fingers flicked the air. *Dismissal.* "Tell him you lied again."

At the somber look in the other woman's eyes, Mac choked down what she wanted to say, settling for the blunt truth: "That won't stop him. He's determined to check on the Trust lands. He'll do it by himself if he has to."

"Unfortunate."

A pronouncement of doom? With the bizarre feeling of having switched places with one of her students called to task, Mac went and stood before her own desk. "Oversight isn't part of this, 'Sephe," she insisted. "Leave him alone."

The Ministry agent stood as well, her full lips thinned with disapproval. "That's not your—"

"Leave him alone," Mac repeated, forced to look up. *Had she shrunk since this morning?* "We'll go onshore tomorrow. I'll show him the bare minimum, trust me. Oversight will go home and write a scathing report about our mistreatment of his hillside that your people can bury however deep they want."

"Inadequate." 'Sephe's expression didn't change. "Stick to your fish, Dr. Connor. On-site risk assessment and management are my responsibility, not yours."

"At least use what I know!" Mac retorted. She shook her head, then leveled her tone to something if not completely civil, then hopefully persuasive. "I've handled Oversight for fourteen years. Believe me—the best way to deal with him, the only way, is to let him see what's there with his own eyes and file his own report. Anything else will simply raise more and louder questions than your Ministry is willing to answer." She hesitated, worrying she'd gone too far—*or not far enough?* "Don't underestimate him," Mac continued. "He has connections at every level of Earthgov." She spared a moment to be grateful Mudge wasn't one of those eavesdropping. *Pleading his case was something she'd never live down.*

A long, more considering look. Mac kept quiet under it. Whatever orders 'Sephe had to follow, surely she had some discretion in how.

"Fine," 'Sephe said abruptly. "Take him. Give him the tour. But not first thing in the morning. I'll need time to manage the ramifications."

Mac guessed those "ramifications" would include briefing those who watched over Base. *Sensible.* "That works," she replied, relieved and willing to show it. "It'll probably take me till noon to find a way to get Mudge past the tiggers anyway."

The magic smile, the one that pretended they were old, dear friends. "Leave that to me." The smile disappeared. "But keep your friend away from the Ro landing site."

Mac's nod was heartfelt. She'd no desire to return there herself. "Thanks," she said.

Another dismissive gesture. "Next time, don't make promises you shouldn't." Her face softened. "It's good to see you again, Mac. Even if you have tamed your hair."

"Easier to keep bugs out," Mac said, giving the curls a deprecating yank.

'Sephe chuckled. "I'll take your word for it. Good night, Mac." The Ministry agent walked to the door.

She knew better. Mac couldn't stop herself. "Wait. Please."

'Sephe paused, eyes never blinking. She had a way of becoming still that went deeper than not moving, as if she disengaged everything but her attention. *Her students,* Mac decided, *were going to find that ability disconcerting.*

"Have you—is there—" *She sounded like a blithering idiot.* Mac took a steadying breath. "It's been over four months. I'm not asking you to breach protocols or orders," she hastened before the other could say a word. "I—it hasn't been easy, not knowing what's happened, who might be . . ." her voice failed and Mac coughed to cover it. "If there's anything you can tell me, anything at all, I'd be grateful."

Maybe 'Sephe had listened to her nightmares. For the briefest of instants, Mac saw sympathy in the other's eyes and felt a rush of hope. Then 'Sephe shook her head. "Mac, I can't. News is locked up tight, these days. Even if I had any myself, it would be classified by the Interspecies Union. It's not just the Ministry, or Earth, in this. You, of all people, know that. We aren't alone—or even the ones most at risk right now. We can't think in terms of one species, let alone one person."

Aliens. Had there really been a time, Mac wondered, when they didn't matter to her? When she'd truly believed that what took place outside this one world's thin coat of atmosphere was insignificant, without meaning to her life? She wouldn't go back to that ignorance, would never again accept so small and inaccurate a view of reality. No matter the cost.

As well think salmon didn't need trees.

"I understand." She lifted and dropped one shoulder. "I'm sorry I—"

"Don't apologize," 'Sephe told her, shaking her head in emphasis. "You didn't ask to be involved. Hell, none of us did."

Mac surprised herself by smiling at this.

'Sephe took a step closer and lowered her voice. "I can tell you one thing, for what good it does. He checks on you, Mac. As often as he can. There's a breach of protocol for you." A flicker of a grin. "Drives the deputy minister bats."

He? Nikolai Trojanowski. *If it were true . . .* Mac locked her reaction away so quickly even she wasn't sure how she felt. It didn't matter. 'Sephe was trying to distract her, deflect her curiosity in a safer direction.

You need lessons from Emily.

Mac had learned the hard way to ignore outrageous claims about men. She'd have never lasted one Saturday night out with Em otherwise. "I appreciate everyone's efforts, whether security or on staff," she said blandly, refusing to ask anything else. *It revealed too much, at no gain.* "Speaking of staff, 'Sephe, I hope you enjoy being busy. At Norcoast, we keep our people on the run."

Chuckling at the in-joke, poor as it was, 'Sephe's eyes brightened. "I'm looking forward to it. In case you had doubts, I am an excellent statistician."

She hadn't, actually. No matter what references or threats backed an applicant's claim, to get past Kammie in an interview, 'Sephe would have to be exceptional and prove it. "A skill useful at the Ministry, no doubt."

"Extra-Sol Human Affairs. That wretched hive of bookkeepers

and actuaries." Mac must have looked skeptical, for 'Sephe gave a short laugh. "I'm not joking. When the alert came from the IU, the Ministry had to scour the ranks to find anyone with the right clearances who qualified for fieldwork."

Like a certain someone who'd looked more at home skulking around in camouflage and armor than in suit and cravat. "Nik," Mac suggested. "And you, of course."

"Me, qualified?" 'Sephe's eyes turned bleak. "You could say that. Lasted three years in an orbital colony where revolution was the polite name for anarchy. Made me the logical choice to accompany you to the way station." Her full lips twisted. "Make that the only choice, given the other three in the Earthside office at the time couldn't find the arming mechanism of a hair dryer on a good day."

Which implied too much about 'Sephe's current assignment, Mac realized, her mouth suddenly dry. "Is there going to be trouble here?" she demanded. "Is that why you've been sent?"

"Gods, I hope not."

Mac blinked at the vehemence in the other woman's voice. 'Sephe hesitated then lifted her hands in the air as if in surrender. "They didn't exactly send me."

"Pardon?"

"They didn't send me. I asked to apply for the job."

There had to be something wrong with her hearing. "Job? What job?"

"I found out you, I mean Dr. Ward, was looking for a new staff member. I took a peek at the listing, just out of curiosity, and—" *Was that a blush warming 'Sephe's ebony skin?* "—it was perfect. I did my doctoral thesis on topographical analysis of multidimensional systems. Assessing failures in glassy metal moldings. My work has obvious application to the analysis of dissolved substance variances in tidal currents."

"Obvious . . ." Mac's eyebrows rose as she stared at 'Sephe, becoming convinced despite herself. "You're really here to work with John and his crew." Her lips twitched, then curved up. "Don't tell me. Let me guess. You had no trouble getting approval from your superiors at the Ministry, who have a vested interest in this place and in me. All so you can do topographical analysis." She couldn't help laughing. "Some spy you are. Anyone else know?"

'Sephe looked offended. "I keep secrets for a living."

Mac could picture Emily rolling her eyes at this.

"It's not that I don't take my work for the Ministry seriously—"

"But if you can serve and do what you love at the same time, why not?" Mac offered as the other woman appeared to hunt for words.

Another smile. "Exactly. I knew you'd understand."

So now she had a reluctant spy—or was it an enthusiastic statisti- cian—on staff? Mac sighed to herself. Still, it had to be an im- provement to work with a spy who valued their research. She cheered. Maybe, with luck, 'Sephe would become so engrossed in her own work she'd ignore minor details such as who was swim- ming among the pods in the middle of the night. *Or was it morn- ing?* Mac stifled a yawn.

'Sephe noticed. "I'll let you get some sleep, Mac." She paused, having almost made it to the door again. Mac, almost to the couch again, waited politely, if impatiently. "I'm glad you know," the erst- while agent confessed. "I'll do my best for Dr. Ward and his team. But I'll have to follow orders from—you know who—over his or yours."

"Just hope Kammie never finds out," Mac said. At the other's puzzled look, she smiled: "You'll learn. Good night, 'Sephe. And thanks for your help with Oversight."

"It's Nik I hope never finds out," the other echoed back to her.

"Mr. Career Spy," Mac quipped before she could stop herself, then waited, curious how 'Sephe would react. *It was late enough for them both to have lost a little mutual caution.*

Sure enough, 'Sephe actually winked at her. "I'd take that bet. Scuttlebutt says Nik's posting Earthside was an early retirement, but no one knows from what. He must have traveled outsystem a fair amount, though."

Mac fluffed her pillow. "What makes you say that?"

"From the day Nik arrived, he was the one the consulate would call to nursemaid the, well, call them "less familiar" aliens visiting

Earth. The weirder the better. Some of the stories he'd tell? Let's leave it that if they weren't in filed reports, I'd say he made them up."

Mac had no wish for 'Sephe to give an example of "weirder." Her own studies into alien life-forms and their cultures had progressed sufficiently to realize her wildest imaginings probably brewed beer or its equivalent, gambled on a preplanned vacation at least once in a lifetime, and contemplated their existence in terms of joy, tedium, or despair, depending on the moment and substance involved. It didn't help her feel capable of understanding an alien mind. It did help explain why the IU had picked Nikolai Trojanowski as Brymn's guide while on Earth.

Nik's motivation? *Nothing so simple.* The Ministry had had its own agenda, which included maneuvering Mac herself offworld to learn more about the Dhryn.

She'd learned too much.

And not nearly enough.

'Sephe mistook her thoughtful silence. "Mac. He wants you safe. We all do. Don't resent the precautions we're taking, our presence here. But—"

"What we want can't always come first," Mac finished calmly. "You don't need to tell me, 'Sephe. Nik and I have had this conversation."

"Watch yourself. Okay? He can be a ruthless bastard."

Mac blinked. She considered taking the bait for no more than a heartbeat. *Trust was earned,* she told herself. And she'd prefer to learn about Nikolai Trojanowski on her own terms. "Isn't that part of the job description?" she replied.

"It's recently been added."

Lines drawn and acknowledged. The two women shared a moment of perfect understanding, then Mac yawned so widely her jaw cracked. "We've all summer," she concluded. "You are planning to work the full season." It wasn't a question.

"Unless the world ends."

"Not funny."

"No."

"Where on that scale . . ." Odd, how the reminder was a comfort.

Exhaustion from chasing Mudge through the dark, Mac decided. Or maybe it was finally having someone else who *knew,* so she could believe she wasn't the only one facing the truth.

"Good night, Dr. Stewart. Welcome to Base."

"Good night, Dr. Connor. And thanks."

Later, as Mac lay sleepless in the clarity of the dark, she clutched the sweater covering her upper body with hands real and synthetic, and considered the truth.

Had Nik, who doubtless knew 'Sephe very well indeed, made sure she heard about the opening in John Ward's fledgling department, so suited to her true interests?

Mac nodded to herself. *Likely,* she decided. Why? How better to get 'Sephe here, close to Mac, than to have the woman think it was her own idea? More importantly, how better to convince Mac herself that in 'Sephe she had a potential new friend, someone to let close?

It would have worked, Em, before you.

Mac shook her head. Too much left to chance. *Nik* made *opportunities. He didn't wait for them.*

So. Easy enough to orchestrate that opening on staff. Mac could have done it herself. Simply arrange a flood of applications for John's proposed new courses. Applications weren't students nodding in their seats Monday morning.

Still too much chance.

What if the request for a new staffer had been tailored to match 'Sephe's own passions?

An image of John Ward in Trojanowski's trademark suit and cravat floated up behind Mac's eyelids.

Where had that come from? If there was one thing Mac could be sure of, it was that her transparent postdoc was incapable of anything more clandestine than his biweekly beer run for the Misses, a trip John somehow continued to believe was his deep, dark secret. No one had the heart to tell him his routine was so well known that Mac herself put in orders on occasion.

Perception was everything, Mac mused.

Or was it nothing? However Persephone Stewart had been brought to Base, Mac could only be sure of one thing: it wasn't to follow the dream of applying her training and knowledge to the statistical analysis of dissolved substances in tidal currents. Or any other research.

"Poor 'Sephe," Mac whispered into her sweater.

Which brought her inevitably back to one question: why was the Ministry's only other "field-ready" Earth agent in Pod Three?

She nodded to herself. *Because something terrible had happened. Or was happening, even now.*

Mac got up to find a real blanket.

- Encounter -

THERE were tales told of ships that appeared in the right place at just the right time. Heroes were made of such tales. Legends were born.

It was yet to be determined if the anticipated arrival of the dreadnaught *Guan Yu* into the definitely unanticipated chaos that was the Eeling System qualified.

"Report!"

On that command, displays winked into life in the air in front of Captain Frank Wu: feeds from navigation, sensors, ship status. The first two pulsed with warnings in red, vivid yellow, and mauve—matched to the circulatory fluids of the *Guan Yu's* trispecies' crew. Threat should be personal.

"What in the—" Wu leaned forward and stabbed a finger into the sensor display to send its image of the planet they were approaching to the center of the bridge, enlarged to its maximum size. "The Dhryn!"

"Mesu crawlik *sa!*"

No need to understand gutter-Norwelliian to grasp the essence of that outburst from the mouth cavity of his first officer, Naseet Melosh. Wu shifted back in his chair, instinctively farther from the image, fingers seeking the elegant goatee on his chin out of habit. *Nice if swearing would help.*

The bridge of the *Guan Yu* grew unnervingly silent as everyone, Human, Norwellii, and Scassian alike, stared at the sight now hovering in front of them all.

None of them had seen a planet being *digested* before.

Two of Ascendis' land masses were visible from their approach lane. Both had been verdant green, dappled with the blue of waterways and the golden bronze of the Eelings' compact, tidy cities. Now, huge swathes of pale dirty brown cut along perfect lines, as though the world was being skinned by invisible knives.

The lines grew even as they watched in horror, crisscrossing one another, growing in width as well as length, taking everything.

The cities? They were obscured by dark clouds, as if set ablaze.

Perversely, the sky itself sparkled, as if its day was filled with stars. *The number of attacking ships that implied . . .* Wu swallowed. "Tea, please," he ordered quietly, then "Amsu, are there any more in the system?"

His scan-tech started at her name and bent over her console. "No. No, sir. No other Dhryn. There's scattered Eeling traffic heading—there's no consistent direction, sir."

"Yes, there is consistency," Melosh disagreed. "They go away." His voice, a soft, well-modulated soprano, was always something of a shock, coming as it did from deep within that gaping triangular pit lined with writhing orange fibroids. "They flee in any direction left to them. These are not transect-capable vessels; the Eelings have no refuge within this system. I must postulate hysteria."

"Understandable. Communications, I want every scrap of sensor data transmitted to Earthgov. Start sending relay drones back through the transect. Two-minute intervals. Keep sending until I tell you to stop or you run out." Wu didn't wait for the curt affirmative. "Anyone come through the transect after us?" He accepted the fine china cup from the ensign. Out of habit, he sniffed the steam rising from the dark liquid. Odd. He couldn't smell anything. Still, the small habit comforted.

"No, sir. Not yet. But I can't raise the Eeling's transect station to confirm and—" the scan tech waved her display to replace the planet, "—it's a mess out here. Damaged ships is the least of it. There's no organized defense."

"There's us," Wu corrected.

"Us? We came here for an engine refit," Melosh reminded his commander. "We off-loaded our live armaments. We cannot close the transect from only one end. We cannot save whatever remains of this world. We can run, but the Dhryn could follow."

Wu turned and met his own reflections in each of the Norwelliian's immense emerald pupils. Not surprisingly, he looked grim in all three.

Timing, Wu knew full well, didn't make heroes. Resolve did.

"You're right, Melosh. There's only one way we can hope to stop the Dhryn and that's to catch them on the planet surface. Get the crew to the escape pods." Putting his tea aside, Wu stood, straightening his uniform jacket with a brisk tug. "But first, find me the weakest spot on this planet's crust."

The mighty *Guan Yu* spat out her children, all nestled in their tiny ships, then sprang in silence toward the twitching corpse of a world. Her captain sat quietly at the pilot's console, tea back in hand, ready to do what had to be done.

No hero. Not he.

A chance, nothing more.

He'd take it.

Then, the scope of the nightmare made itself known as the Dhryn's Progenitor Ship came into view from around the far side of the planet, catching the sunlight like a rising crescent moon. Glitter rained down from her to the surface, still more returned, until it seemed to any watching that the mammoth Dhryn vessel didn't orbit on her own but instead floated atop a silver fountain of inconceivable size.

Then specks from that fountain swerved, heading straight toward the *Guan Yu*. Hundreds. Thousands.

He had no means to destroy her.

Wu's lips pulled back from his teeth and he punched a control. The *Guan Yu* hurtled downward even faster than before, seeking the heart of what had been the home of the Eelings.

He could only make the Dhryn pay.

The escape pods went first, each disappearing within a cloud of smaller, faster ships. Swarmed. Consumed.

Clang. Clang. Clang.

Wu tossed aside his teacup and secured the neck fastenings of his helmet. Lights flashed and dimmed, flashed and dimmed. The *Guan Yu* lost atmospheric integrity. One or more seals had failed.

Dissolved.

"Don't worry. I'll take you with me," Wu promised his unwanted guests.

As the first feeder, clothed in silver, drifted down her corridors, the *Guan Yu* screamed her way through the atmosphere and stabbed into the weakest part of Ascendis' crust. Shock waves rippled across the continent, setting off quakes and volcanoes.

The air itself burned.

The Great Journey must continue until home is attained. That which is Dhryn has remembered. All that is Dhryn shares that goal.

There will be danger.

There will be hardship.

It is the way of the Journey, that most will not reach its end.

So long as that which is Dhryn achieves safe haven, all sacrifice is joy.

3

TOUR AND TROUBLE

"I TOLD YOU to go, *Lamisah*. Why didn't you listen?" A soft, reasonable voice. The voice of friendship, of trust.

The words. It hadn't been those words. Those—were wrong.

She'd go, but she couldn't see.

Mac shoved her hands outward, pushing at the darkness.

The darkness *burned*.

She screamed as her fingers dissolved, as the backs of her hands caught fire, as the bones within her palms curled like putty and dripped away. *Drip. Drip.*

She screamed as the drips were sucked into mouths—into mouths that insisted, in their soft, reasonable voices, voices of friendship, of trust:

"We told you to go, *Lamisah*. We warned you. Didn't we?"

Her arms went next . . .

Mac rubbed her hands up and down her arms, shudders coursing through her body until it was all she could do to sit still, to stay on the couch, to fight for calm.

"That was—" she began, then pressed her lips together. *A familiar nightmare, although it usually started at an earlier moment.* If she had to dream it, Mac preferred this version. She'd rather face a floating bag of organic acids than look into those familiar yellowirised eyes and see their warm glow dim, see them sink, watch him become . . .

"No!"

She leaped to her feet and went to her desk, gripping it with both hands. *One hand and one substitute,* Mac corrected herself, always aware of the difference, though she couldn't feel one. *Illogical.* Both delivered the same sensory information. One simply used nonbiological circuitry.

One wasn't hers.

No chance of more sleep, not with her body wringing wet with sweat and her heart jumping in sickening thuds within her chest. Mac unopaqued the wall and ceiling, hoping for dawn.

Close. No stars, but the distant peaks snarled against a paling sky. *Time to be up and moving,* she assured herself. Not that she felt like either.

A shower, short and cold, a fresh set of coveralls, and a barefoot prowl after coffee made the coming day seem slightly less impossible. Merely onerous. Before it had to really start, Mac took her steaming mug outside, finding a perch on the stairs leading up and around the wall of Pod Three where she could watch the rest of Base wake up.

The muted, directionless light of predawn made mysteries of pods and walkways, turned them into pale-rimmed shadows curved one into the other. The walkways were still damp from yesterday's rain, evaporative drying rarely a factor around here. *Something a few new students hadn't learned yet,* Mac decided with amusement, eyeing a series of towels hanging heavy and soaked from the terrace of Pod Two. *Probably wetter now than last night.*

The moisture played tricks with hearing, too. The lapping of ocean against pod and rocky shore was as intimate as breathing; footsteps and yawns loud and clear well before Mac spotted the first group of students making their way to Pod Three for breakfast.

The sun leered over the mountains at her, a reminder time wasn't patient. She cradled her mug between her hands, lifted it to savor the rich aroma of coffee on sea air, impatient for it to cool. Habit. Mac tended to ignore minor details such as how long her cup had sat on desk or workbench, so she'd grown used to what she gulped being cold, eventually liking it that way. Unfortunately, grad students were prone to random helpful acts, and she'd scalded her mouth more than once since coming to Base when someone reheated her coffee without warning.

What first: Mudge or breakfast? She was not combining the two. "Mind if I join you?"

Mac turned her head with a smile. " 'Morning, Case." She gestured to the stair beside her and the student sat down. He was dressed for diving, though his wet suit was open at the neck and sleeves, the hood hanging down his back. His bare feet were porcelain pale and his toes, like his fingers, boasted reddish hairs at their joints. Like Mac, he carried a steaming mug in one hand. In the other was a promisingly plump bag.

Case grinned at her interest. "Muffin?"

"Thanks." Mac pulled one from the proffered bag. Warm, yes. Also lopsided and unexpectedly green. *New cooks.* She took a generous bite, chewed, and swallowed. "Mint," she said, raising her eyebrows. "Now that's original."

"But is it edible?" Case examined his own muffin dubiously.

"You'll have worse," Mac assured him. She was pleased he'd sought her out; it took some students a tedious amount of time to realize research staff were people, too. They ate in companionable silence for a moment, watching a raft of bufflehead ducks bobbing on the swells. "Where are you diving today?" she asked.

"We *were* heading for the reefs—down to the glass sponge observation station." He didn't try to hide his disappointment. "I've seen remote images of the deep corals off the coast of Norway, but nothing as up close as you have here."

"Were?" Mac had learned long ago how to instill a wealth of interested neutrality into both voice and expression. Lee's plans weren't hers to question—in front of his still-shiny student, anyway. "What changed?"

Case looked taken aback by her question. "That's what I was going to ask you. A memo came through everyone's imp, just when we were suiting up. No diving. No skim traffic. Nothing onwater today. Even the t-lev from Vancouver's been delayed until tonight." A sideways, very wise look from those sea-faded eyes. "That's not usual stuff here, is it, Mac?"

"No, Case. No, it's not." Mug in one hand, Mac dusted crumbs from her thighs with the other as she rose to her feet. "Then again," she smiled, "what is? Someone's probably forgotten to post they're running a sensitive assay in the inlet this morning. I'll look into it. Thanks for breakfast."

His "You're welcome," hardly registered. Mac's thoughts were racing ahead even as she climbed the stairs to her office at her normal pace.

Seeing the tactic for what it was, knowing she had no reason to feel any special bond to 'Sephe, any friendship, didn't help. Mac still felt betrayed. *What was 'Sephe up to?* Whatever it was, if she'd interfered with Base operations . . .

She'd be leaving on the next t-lev.

"We're leaving. Now."

As if accustomed to having his breakfast interrupted by an infuriated woman in hiking gear, Mudge put down his coffee, calmly wiped his mouth with a napkin, and left the table to find his rainsuit. He pulled on the garment, still without a word.

Just as well. Mac doubted she could engage in reasonable conversation at the moment.

She hadn't found 'Sephe. She had found, however, the source of the stay-put, stay-dry order.

Dr. Mackenzie Connor.

Not by name, but 'Sephe—or someone—had used Mac's codes to essentially shut down operations for the day, on a day when a good third of Base should be heading out to the field. The day before Mac herself planned to go, meaning she'd be delayed at least that long herself. She wasn't the only one upset. Her incoming mail this morning ranged from polite protest to profanity, although Mac had taken a certain satisfaction from replying "wasn't me" each time.

If the Ministry agent thought this would keep her from taking

Mudge to the ridge, Mac fumed to herself, *'Sephe hadn't read the right files.*

Meanwhile, Mudge had fastened his last boot and now looked at her interrogatively, his small eyes bright with anticipation. Mac jerked her head at the door, then led the way.

A shame security didn't try to stop them. Mac had prepared several versions of a scathing protest at such misuse of her codes, her people, and her facility. But no one appeared to notice another two figures in rainsuits wandering the corridors, so she filed her protest for later.

Mac waited for an empty lift to take them to the pod roof. Stepping out first, she reached back and punched in the command for the lowermost level, sending the lift where it would wait until someone from administration could be found to input the retrieval sequence. This early in the season, when students were having trouble finding their own boots, let alone responsible staff? Her lip curled with satisfaction. *Why make 'Sephe's life easier?*

"This way," she told Mudge, walking through puddles. The rain hadn't started again, but yesterday's deluge had filled every depression and dimple on the roof. Not that the roof was large. In point of fact, it wasn't supposed to exist at all, being another of those "handy, that" modifications. The original pod design had called for an irregular upper surface, transparent from within and appearing as mauve-and-gray stone from without. No one and nothing else was to be on it. Ideal camouflage, sure to appease those who wanted no sign of Human presence in Castle Inlet.

Which had lasted as long as it had taken the first grad student to find a hammer. Tell imaginative and curious scientists they couldn't use the top of their own building? *Who'd thought that would work?* All but Pod Six eventually grew a small roof consisting of a labyrinth of narrow bands and bulges made of mem-wood, often, but not always, flat. Each new bout of construction had been justified with a scientific purpose: to secure an antenna or collector, to house a weather assembly, and so forth. Over the years, as the roofs became more useful and used, those purposes had expanded somewhat.

Mac led Mudge past planters filled with mud—the planters had withstood the Ro attack but last year's vegetable gardens hadn't fared well, around the jumbled heap of newly replaced lawn chairs belonging to the Norcoast Astronomy Club—though the frequent cloud cover made precious little difference to attendance at "meetings" and almost none of the members could tell a star from a planet—and, finally, to a small, sturdy shed that had, alone among all the structures perched on Pod Three, been constructed to look as much like a natural rock formation as mem-wood, plaster, and imagination could allow.

It had been a nice gesture. It might even have worked, had it not been for the giant parrot adorning one side of the shed. *Appeared five summers ago,* Mac recalled, patting the bird's technicolor wing fondly. Preposterous thing, but with a cheerful, jaunty look. There was a pirate flag firmly in its beak; the traditional skull and crossbones replaced by a salmon skeleton. Barnacle Bill, they called it, and students learned to sing the parrot's exploits in bawdy detail. *Emily knew every verse.* Mac had once accused her friend of making up the worst of them to shock her new students.

Emily had only smiled.

The memory might have been a floodgate. Mac tried to concentrate on stepping over real puddles, even as her mind swam with questions. *Had Emily left with the Ro? Had the aliens truly left? And what did "leaving" mean to beings who could make their own transects through space at will?*

Or had Emily been taken? But by whom? The grim, black-garbed defenders of Earth? Their counterparts from any other threatened world?

Or was Emily on Earth, sipping margaritas in a bar decorated with parrots, teaching bawdy verse to handsome tourists . . .

Swearing under her breath, hiding the trembling of her hands, Mac yanked aside the weather screen covering the end of the shed.

Was Emily dead? Had it happened months ago?

Or had she waited for rescue, for friends, only to die alone?

"It's nothing fancy," she warned Mudge, her voice less steady than would have been reassuring under the circumstances, "but it'll get us to shore."

"In one piece?" he asked, eyes dropping from the parrot to stare in dismay at the personal lev cowering inside the shed. It was, as Tie referred to it, at that delicate age between junk and vintage. To survive long enough to be vintage, it shouldn't have belonged to Mac.

She wiped cobwebs from the yellowed canopy. "It's this or nothing. Help me push it out."

Together they wrestled the old lev out of its shelter. The gentle light of early morning wasn't kind. There were more patches than paint on its sides, the upholstery had endured too many buckets of overripe salmon, and a regrettable, although essentially harmless encounter with a barge had permanently resculptured its prow. Remarkably, last year's tip and righting of the pod didn't seem to have added any more dents. *As far as she could tell.*

Mac gave the lev a surreptitious kick for luck. She'd bought the thing well and truly used her first year of tenure at Norcoast. Granted, it had been shiny, clean, and intact back then. Even better, dirt cheap. It was only later that Mac learned why few people bothered with levs for anything smaller than freight transport. Compact antigrav units were, to be generous, finicky beasts prone to suicide.

Levs, boots. Same thing. Mac was satisfied when either got her where she wanted to go with dry feet, although she had noticed footwear was more reliable. Little wonder everyone at Base conspired with Tie to arrange to ferry their coadministrator from place to place, keeping her lev in this shed and out of his workshop.

Which kept it out of inventory, too. *More problems for 'Sephe and crew,* Mac rejoiced.

Much to Mac's surprise, the engine started on the first try. No death rattle or strange clanking marred the steady hum. That slightly strangled wheezing? *Hardly noticeable.*

"You get in first," Mudge said after a moment's thoughtful consideration.

"Brave man," Mac quipped, not entirely sure herself. Then she looked out at their destination, the outstretched arm of Castle Inlet, where mist hung like dust-gray garlands around the deep green trees. "Let's go."

Besides, she told herself optimistically, *it wasn't far.*

Mac shut down the lev's engine, which continued to wheeze and gasp noisily as if to prove its rise into the air, plunge to a hand-breadth above the ocean, and subsequent erratic hobble over the boulders and logs of the shore to land here had been a fluke.

"WE COULD—" the last wheeze died and Mudge stopped shouting to be heard over the racket, "—swim back," he finished.

Mac patted the lev. "It just needs a rest." *Not a bad landing,* she congratulated herself, hands sore from holding the controls perhaps a little tighter than useful. The tendency of levs to simply drop if their antigrav failed had crossed her mind on the way here. Several times. Over a combination of height, wave, and rock that didn't make such a drop appealing in the least, given the high probability of deer mice in the safety chutes. *This was much better.*

Much. Mindful of the Trust, and her companion, Mac had brought them down on a bare outcropping on the ocean side of the ridge, close to one of the pathways leading up the ridge. The minimal damage caused by landing here would be easy to record. Mudge couldn't fault her on this. *Could he?*

Rather than ask, Mac looked out over Hecate Strait, the cool, salt-fresh wind playing with her hair and teasing the hood on her shoulders. Clouds were getting organized for the day, small puffs scudding above the waves as if on parade, longer wisps holding court above, a tumultuous line forming in the distance. There would be salmon beneath it all, driving through the depths. The young smolts preoccupied with filling their own stomachs while avoiding being food themselves; the mature, powerful adults who would never eat again, guided by the tastes and scents of home, answering that one final call, to spawn—

"Ahhh."

The soft exclamation drew her around. Mudge had his back to the ocean. His arms were outstretched, his head tilted, his body dwarfed before the rising ranks of trees that began mere footsteps away. *To someone else,* Mac thought, *he might look foolish.* A man past middle age, wearing a faded yellow rainsuit that had doubtless fit better several kilos earlier, what hair he had tossed by the wind like stray grass. Standing in what could only be called worship.

Mac felt a tightness in her throat. She didn't interrupt. Instead,

she looked where he did, tracing the underlying ridge in the arro-
gant skyward thrust of pine, cedar, and redwood with her eyes, understanding one thing at least.

She'd been right to bring Mudge here.

"I should never have brought you here," Mac snapped, catching
the branch whipping toward her face in the nick of time.

They were walking three meters above the forest floor, using the
suspended walkway set up by last year's researchers. That forest
floor was visible beneath their feet, the walkway of a transparent
material which allowed the passage of not only light, but rain and
small objects. *Minimal presence.* It conveniently glowed a faint
green with each footfall, so they knew where to step next. Repellers
kept the surface clear of spiderwebs and other nests.

Repellers didn't stop branches from growing or leaning across
their path. Mac fended another from her face. Mudge either didn't
realize that what he pushed out of his way would spring into hers,
or didn't care.

His voice floated back to her. "Why? Do you have something to
hide, Norcoast?"

*Should she count on her fingers or pull out her imp to do the calcu-
lation?* Mac snorted. Aloud, she said: "No. I don't have anything
to hide. But you're—OW!" The tip of a branch snapped against her
cheek despite a last second duck. "Will you stop!" she shouted.

Mudge, for a wonder, did just that. Mac fingered her cheek and
glared at him, breathing heavily. Ever since she'd showed him the
path, he'd hurried along it as if possessed by demons. *If she didn't
know better,* Mac thought darkly, *she'd believe he had a destination
in mind.*

As this particular path swung all too close to the Ro landing site
at the top of the ridge, she sincerely hoped not. *There were some
things she needed to believe,* Mac admitted to herself as she studied
his sweating face. Among them, that Oversight was here for his
trees, nothing more.

He was fumbling in a pocket. Before Mac could do more than

tense—*when had she developed that appalling reflex?*—he pulled out a wad of white and pressed it into her hand. "Here. You're bleeding."

Mac lifted the tissue to her cheek. "What's the rush, Oversight?" she asked, holding his gaze with hers. His face was flushed with effort. *No surprise.* They were both too warm in their rainsuits and had their hoods down, even with the light drizzle falling. Drops collected in the creases beside his eyes and erased what hair he had.

"Was I rushing?" All innocence.

Mac waited.

"Oh," Mudge gave an embarrassed-sounding harrumph. "I—Sorry about that, Norcoast. It's all a bit—much, you know. Being here." He looked up and around, eyes wide, then back to her, his expression somehow desperate. "I must make as complete an inspection in the time we have—" he raised the hand holding the recorder, "—but there's no way to see it all. No time."

"Beautiful, isn't it?" Mac commented.

"Beautiful?" Mudge blinked raindrops from his eyes. "Of course it is." She merely gazed at him, letting silence speak. Finally, he heaved a sigh and lowered the recorder. "Of course, it is," he repeated, more slowly and with emphasis. "Thank you, Norcoast." He looked past her again. "It's worth everything we do, isn't it," he said softly.

Mac nodded, drinking in the sights, sounds, and smells for herself.

Spring. Regrowth, renewal, reproduction. They stood encompassed by living things answering those imperatives, urgently, impatiently. Birdsong, from hoarse to heartbreakingly rich, filled the air. Pollen powdered highlights of yellow on the bark of trees. Green shoots burst through the dark soil below like fireworks exploding in a night sky, their color so vivid, so intense, it seemed to leave a taste. Anywhere sheltered from the tiny raindrops, the air was filled with motes, some in flight, some adrift, all intent.

Mac drew a deep breath through her nose, savoring the rush of molds and damp wood, of distant flowers and brand-new leaves. *Regeneration.* She could feel it, just being here. She would know it, when she was at the field station, waiting for the first migrating salmon of the season. Her life would regain its purpose, its balance—

"It's stopped working."

"What's stopped working?" she echoed.

"This thing." Mudge banged his recorder against the palm of his other hand. "It's gone dead on me."

Mac couldn't pull air into her lungs. Her eyes searched the surrounding maze of crisscrossing branches and shadow. Not that those she feared would trouble to hide. *The Ro.* Masters of stealth, when they wished.

And their favorite tactic? To interfere with power supplies, broadcast or stored.

Their strange allies. Who could be close enough to touch, and neither she nor Mudge would know.

The Dhryn?

Mac didn't dare look up. If there were any above them, it was already too late.

Mudge's annoyed: "Well, Norcoast? Where's your imp?" made her jump.

"My—" Her voice caught.

"What's the matter with you?" he demanded, but went on without waiting for an answer, hoarse with frustration. "You did bring it? Oh, I know it's not ideal. This—" a wave of the recorder, "—would be better, much better, more complete and reliable." He shoved it into a pocket, the rubber protesting. "Piece of junk. I assume your imp has at least basic data recording capabilities, ambient conditions, that sort of thing? I have to collect as much as I can . . . make notes."

Nodding, Mac took out the small device and laid it on her palm, unable to help stealing glances in every direction. She tapped in her code with a finger, lower lip between her teeth.

The workscreen formed before her face, its display so bland and normal she gasped with relief.

"Good," Mudge said, either oblivious or assuming Mac's emotions reflected his own. "Let me use it."

Without warning, the current display, a checklist of her field supplies, disappeared. In its place, a string of incomprehensible symbols tumbled among the raindrops in the air, flaring yellow, then red. *A message?* Mac jabbed a finger through the 'screen to save it.

As she did, the symbols were replaced by a flicker of light that, so briefly it could have been her imagination, formed a face.

Then the display winked back to its list of equipment, tents, and rations.

Mac closed her fingers over her imp. Rain washed her cheeks, conveniently hiding the tears she couldn't control. *Of joy or terror? Interesting question,* she told herself. But whatever she was feeling, Mac knew she hadn't imagined what she'd seen. Or rather who.

Emily.

"Well? Are you going to let me use it or not, Norcoast?"

"What? Oh. Not. Sorry." Mac opened her rainsuit and secured the now-precious gadget in the upper zipped pocket of her coveralls. "Old model," she said smoothly. "Forgot it doesn't have direct data recording. Try yours again."

His expression was the familiar "are you nuts?" one she'd grown accustomed to ignoring over the years. Presumably hers was the equally familiar "willing to wait forever" one, because Mudge didn't bother arguing. Instead, he grabbed out his recorder and activated it one more time, grumbling under his breath all the while. Then his eyes widened. He gave her a shocked look. "It's working!"

Why wasn't *that reassuring?* As Mac suspected the answer involved the Ro, or at least their technology, neither far enough away, she was proud of her calm: "Oh, good. Shall we proceed?"

"I expect you to show me what's been happening here, Norcoast," Mudge scowled fiercely. "No tricks." He started moving without waiting for an answer, the walkway edges flashing green with each impatient step.

So much for sharing the beauty of the place, Mac sighed to herself. "I don't know what you think you'll find, Oversight," she informed his back as she followed behind. "There's been no one here since the last field season and you've seen those reports."

The walkway climbed with the mountain, each step etched in light. Mac forced herself to stop looking for Emily at every turn. She'd been given a message, that's all. 'Sephe and company would help her find out what it meant. At least now, there was hope.

If only Emily's face hadn't looked so . . . strange.

Mac and Mudge soon reached the section where the walkway spiraled both up and around a series of mammoth tree trunks, each wider than a transport lev, rising vertically as if they were columns supporting the unseen sky. *An otherworldly place,* Mac thought, trying to shake free of the aftermath of Emily's message. There had been a time when being here gave her a sense of permanence, of safety, of life that needed nothing but itself to continue.

Having walked on one of the lifeless worlds of the Chasm, she knew better. *The trees were something else at risk. Something else to lose.*

The rain collected in the dense canopy of leaves, branches, and moss far above their heads, so drops continued to fall long after cloudbursts ended for the day, an absentminded deluge that skewed time the way the scale of the trees skewed perceptions of self and importance. Mac could see it affecting Mudge. His pace gradually slowed from impatient to reverent, the recorder in his hand lifting until he held it like a torch.

They were still some distance from the Ro landing site, and well away from the trampling done by, well, several individuals including herself last year, which was why Mac didn't pay attention when Mudge disappeared from view around the next trunk. He was only footsteps ahead. Besides, the bark on that tree trunk was festooned with a string of amorous slugs, so Mac paused to do a quick count, admiring their glistening yellow and brown. *Quite dapper beasts.* Five . . . six . . .

Snap. It was such an ordinary sound, Mac didn't bother glancing up. Branches cracked all the time. Eight . . . nine . . . There was a red velvet mite, vivid and soft, climbing up the back of the tenth slug. Mac peered closer, curious as to how it was managing to find traction in the slime.

Crash, snap, CLANG!

"What the . . . ?" Abandoning her slugs and muttering under her breath, Mac hurried around the tree trunk, light flashing underfoot with each step. A bell-like metal-to-metal clang wasn't ordinary. *What was Mudge doing?*

She stopped in her tracks.

Mudge was standing in the middle of the next rise of the walkway. His arms were being held by two large figures encased in the Ministry's black armor from head to toe. Even their faces were hidden behind gleaming visors. A scuff mark on one of those visors, and the sad condition of the recorder lying at Mudge's feet explained the *clang*.

The rip through the forest ahead explained everything else.

Another new Ro landing site. This time, they'd knocked over giants, flattened centuries' old growth, scraped soil to expose the mountain's very bones. Not a large area, as if they'd lost control and crashed, but of a certain size, a certain shape, as if they'd come down and shoved aside whatever was in their way.

Levs, the silent, expensive, probably-always-work type, hovered between the standing trees. More figures, twin to those confining Mudge, moved through the debris on the forest floor. Mac sniffed. There was a faint charred smell to the air. *Gone,* she reasoned.

After Emily sent her message.

Had the Ro ship been waiting for her? *Had they spied and known she was coming? Or had they been here all along and only now been chased away, the message a last minute attempt—at what?*

Mac shook her head free of questions. They only served to make her more anxious, not less. "Let him go," she told the guards holding Mudge. "I'll take him to Base."

"You know about this, Norcoast?" Mudge struggled, futilely, against his captors. "I demand an explanation! Do you see what's— what's—" words appeared to fail him as he looked out at the destruction. Then, eyes brimming with tears, he turned to her. "What have you done?"

Mac winced. She wasn't sure what was worse: the horror on his face, the ravaging of the forest, the return of the Ro . . .

Or the way every visored head in view was now aimed right at her, as if waiting for something.

"Tomorrow," Mac said loudly and clearly, so there could be no possible misunderstanding by anyone or anything in earshot, "I am leaving for Field Station Six. To study my salmon."

How many times and in how many ways had the Ministry told her they didn't want her involved any longer?

Fine. She'd give them Emily's message. As a bonus, she'd also let them explain a major Anthropogenic Perturbation of a Class Three Wilderness Trust to its Oversight Committee.

Who would never talk to her again, anyway.

"Your Mudge is not a happy man."

Something she had no authority or ability to change, Mac thought sadly. She tilted her office chair back so she could rest her bare feet on her desk. Her toes complained about their time in wet socks and she wiggled them slowly. "What will happen to him?"

'Sephe shrugged, her loose-fitting yellow shirt bright enough to use as a signal flare. If she'd been one of the black, visored entities on the ridge, there was no sign of it. *Unless,* Mac told herself dourly, *you counted snug black jeans.* She'd come quickly enough when Mac sent for her.

Which had been after Mac had had the dubious thrill of hiking all the way down the ridge walkways to her lev, finally getting it started during the worsening rain, and somehow keeping it running until it squatted safely on the roof of Pod Three. Where the machine had given every indication of coughing out its last breath. *One day,* Mac vowed, *she'd get a ride home.*

Oh, they'd have taken her in one of their levs had she mentioned the message in her imp, Mac knew, spinning the device in circles with pokes of her big toe. *But likely not back to Base.* She'd learned a few things about the spy mind-set by now.

"I can't speak for my superiors, Mac, but Mudge was in the wrong place at the wrong time—and so far he's refusing to keep quiet about it. He's been taken home, but with a security blackout on his communications."

"That can't last."

"Maybe he'll give in—see how important it is to cooperate with us."

Mac snorted.

"It's to everyone's advantage," 'Sephe insisted. "The consulate's satisfied with our reports, but if news of a Ro landing here gets out to the public, we'll have to allow who knows how many IU representatives to come and inspect the site. Then there's the media. Think they'll respect the Trust? You know the stakes—"

"Oversight won't care." *You are such clever little toes,* Mac congratulated her feet as they managed to roll her imp back and forth.

"You do."

Mac couldn't stop the look she gave 'Sephe.

"Sorry," the other woman said quietly. "If I'd known about the new site, Mac, I'd never have let you go with him."

"You tried hard enough to stop us as it was."

"The travel ban?" 'Sephe raised her hands. "Don't blame me. That came straight from the head office when the sensors detected Ro activity. We didn't want to spook them."

"To not 'spook' them, you disrupted normal routine here and sent in storm troopers?" Mac shook her head. "Excuse me for missing the logic."

"Our people only moved in after the Ro launched, to preserve the site and look for clues or messages." 'Sephe made an exasperated noise. "Which they had to do, because you and your friend chased the Ro away! Thanks for nothing."

"Ah." Mac stretched forward to snag her imp with one hand, then brought her feet flat on the floor with a triumphant thump. "Thanks for everything, you mean."

'Sephe's eyes narrowed. "What haven't you told me, Mac?"

Ignoring the slot on her desk, where she'd normally insert her imp in order to use the desk, Mac activated her imp's workscreen. With a flick of her fingers through the display, she brought up the Ro's message.

The glyphs scrolled to the end.

Emily's face flickered in and out of view.

"Dr. Mamani's alive," 'Sephe whispered.

"It's only an image," Mac said, resisting the temptation to replay the message, stare at that face, hope . . . *Hope was reckless.* "The message—that should tell us more. You can decipher it, can't you?"

"We've resources," the other said noncommittally. "I've certainly never seen anything like it before." 'Sephe drew out her own imp, identical to Mac's but doubtless more sophisticated.

Probably comes with a stunner, bomb, and ropes as well as self-destruct, Mac told herself, only half kidding.

'Sephe set her display beside Mac's. Without needing to be told, Mac stroked through the control portion of her display and pointed to its neighbor, sending the message to 'Sephe's device.

"Thanks. Did you copy it?" 'Sephe asked.

Mac gave another snort. "I'm not about to dump Ro coding into Norcoast's vital systems."

"Good." 'Sephe touched one end of her imp to Mac's where it lay on the desk. Mac's workscreen winked out of existence.

With a wordless cry, Mac picked up her imp and tried to reactivate it. Nothing. "You've wiped it," she accused, leaping to her feet.

"Just the message." 'Sephe put away her imp. "What did you expect?"

She'd hoped otherwise. Mac didn't bother to scowl. "I expect to be told what that says."

"I'll relay your request. That's all I can do."

Not enough. "Promise you'll tell me if it's really from Emily. If she's asking for help."

'Sephe frowned. "Why would she need help?" she demanded, her tone sharp. "The Ro aren't the enemy."

"Easy for you to say. You didn't see her," Mac countered. "You didn't see what they'd done—how it was affecting her—"

She might have struck a nerve. "Your Emily isn't the only one making sacrifices for the good of all," 'Sephe interrupted passionately. "At least she might be alive. At least she hasn't been sucked into one of their—" The full lips pressed into a thin line, but it was too late.

"So," Mac dropped the word into the ringing silence their shouts had left. She felt numb, having the truth arrive like this. "What happened in the Chasm—it's begun again. The Dhryn have attacked a world, haven't they? Which one?"

'Sephe sat on the couch as if she'd lost the strength to stand, her hands cupping her imp and Emily's message. "Ascendis." Just the name.

It was enough. "They went back for more," Mac said tonelessly.

"I don't know what you mean."

"Yes, you do. The letter I received from the Secretary General of the Ministry—" *The one that had started it all,* Mac thought, remembering her name in mauve crawling over the envelope's blue and green. The colors of a threat to the Human species itself. "It listed a series of mysterious disappearances. One of them concerned an eco-patrol that went missing on Ascendis." She glared at 'Sephe. "Why isn't this on the news? People need to know the threat is real—and that there's evidence the Dhryn have been—" Mac paused to think of a word and rejected *tasting* "—scouting."

"We're aware. So is the IU. So are the worlds who may have suffered previous Dhryn attacks. What would a more public news release say, Mac? That the Dhryn were able to enter a populated system without warning, pass any defense, consume what they wanted, and leave? No one wants panic." 'Sephe hesitated, then went on: "The IU wouldn't have informed us about Ascendis—not yet—but a Human ship was there. Her captain sent home every bit of information he could before—"

"Before what?"

'Sephe's dark eyes were haunted. "Before his crew was consumed—and he crashed his ship into the planet in a futile attempt to stop the Dhryn. Would you like to know his name, Dr. Connor? It was Captain Frank Wu." Her voice rose, became husky with emotion. "Would you like the crew list? Would you like population stats for the Eelings? Biomass data? A complete list of the devastation?"

"Yes." Mac held up her imp, her voice sounding cold and set to her own ears. "I want all of it."

'Sephe blinked. "What did you say?"

"I said yes. If we are going to understand the Dhryn, we need to know what they do, the impact they have, every scrap of data. Thanks to this Captain Wu's quick thinking, there's finally something other than rumor and legend. Can you get it for me?"

"To do what? You study salmon—isn't that what you're always saying? What good could you do?"

The words were like a slap. Mac gritted her teeth. "Can you get me the data from Ascendis or do I have to ask someone else?"

'Sephe's laugh wasn't amused. "You want to be locked up with Mudge?"

"No," Mac snapped back. "No. And I don't want him locked up either." She held her breath, then said more calmly: "I want to help."

"Then listen to me, Mac. Keep doing what you've been doing. Run this place. Study your fish. Forget last year and let us do our job. The message from Dr. Mamani? That's crucial. Thank you. But even that—" a dark look, "—you shouldn't have waited to give it to me, Mac. You can't make decisions like that."

Em, she's definitely not read the right files. Mac sat down in her chair and propped her bare feet on her desk, wiggling her toes thoughtfully. "I understand. But what about Oversight?"

"The Ministry is putting together an explanation for him, something to cover what he's seen. It may not satisfy him, but it should keep him from convincing anyone else."

"You're good at that."

"I—" whatever 'Sephe started to say, she decided against it. She got to her feet, the movement awkward. "I have to go—get the message to those who can make sense out of it. Mac, I promise to ask if you can know what it says. That's all I can do."

"Help Oversight. He can be too stubborn for his own good."

'Sephe's dry: "So can you," made Mac smile.

Almost.

"We're on the same side," she reminded 'Sephe. "You, me, even Mudge."

The Ministry agent's lips twisted. "It's never that simple, Mac."

After she left, and the door closed, Mac leaned as far back as she could, pressing the heels of her hands against her eyelids. "It is for me," she said, not caring who overheard.

- 4 -

CALAMITY AND CONSEQUENCE

T HE MINISTRY'S NEED to explain anything to Charles Mudge III expired at 6:01:34, Pacific Time. The earthquake lasted one minute and twenty-three seconds, with a recorded epicenter 2.34 kilometers below sea level, directly under Castle Inlet's protecting arm.

The coast knew earthquakes. After all, something had to give—and often did—when three immense tectonic plates met to argue about who'd reshape the ocean floor and resculpt the edge of the continent on any given day. Seismic warnings from the network of waiting sensors set off alarms. Signals sped up and down the coastline, out to sea and inland, sent via every means of transmission available. The birds, of course, hadn't required one. They'd launched themselves from trees and rocky shoreline as the first tremors began deep underground. But people needed time, time to shut down systems at risk, time to seek shelter, time—

They had barely moments. As the tremors intensified, the sharp shifts of the ocean floor moved up Pod Three's anchoring pylons to jiggle its infrastructure. Mac's hanging salmon clashed against one another, setting off the independent motion sensors. Adding to the cacophony, the curtain reeds on the door clanged in warning.

Base's internal alarm system, a varying shriek of light and sound penetrating every nook and cranny, was something of an anticlimax.

Mac couldn't tell what woke her, too torn by the dual assault of sensation and memory to think straight. Haven, the Dhryn home world, had shaken like this under attack by the Ro. It had split in every direction as the great buried ships of the Progenitors tore themselves free of the planet, seeking the safety of space. *Brymn had held her in his arms to keep her safe—*

Brymn? Mind suddenly, terribly clear, Mac pressed her hands over her ears as she ran outside. "Damn you, Emily!" she cursed, unable to hear herself past the din. "Don't do this again!"

The outside terraces on each pod were filling with staff and students. Mac sagged with relief at shouts of "earthquake!" among steadier voices, hearing those taking charge, giving orders. *When had a natural disaster become less threatening?* she wondered inanely, gripping the rail with numb hands even as the world stopped trying to shrug them loose.

Then she roused herself to follow the procedures she'd practiced with the rest. The gates would have opened to release anything captive in Pod Six. What remained was to make sure everyone was safe and inside, ready for what would follow.

For the mere heave of earth and stone wasn't what threatened Base.

It was water.

Imagine lying in a bathtub, legs out before you. Imagine lifting and dropping your legs, not too high but very quickly, to make your own small quake. Watch the water as it hurries to fill the void, then is pushed aside again as your legs settle. The quake is over.

Now watch how the water surges to crash over your knees and threatens to spill over the sides of the tub.

The bathtubs used by the designers of Norcoast Salmon Research Facility were larger, and featured immense paddles instead of legs, but the principle was the same. They knew there would be earthquakes. And when there were earthquakes near water, that water would move. *Tsunami.* The giant waves that raced away from the disturbance faster than a skim, traveling entire oceans as a line of shadow, a mere ruffling of the surface, until cresting to a hideous destructive height against any shoreline, a threat to all who lived in sight of the sea.

Enclosed areas, like bathtubs, like Castle Inlet, faced their own maelstrom. Here, confined by cliffs, the water shoved aside would surge back, racing from side to side, tumbling up slopes and down again, over and over until it built into huge tortured piles that would slam against anything in their way with inescapable force.

The designers knew this and planned for it, as much as technology could plan for nature. If an earthquake of sufficient force was detected by the pod anchors, they would loosen their grip and become tethers. Walkways would disconnect. Shielding meant for ice and storm would wrap around the walls of the pods and doors to the ocean would close. The pods would rise and fall with the water. A bumpy ride at best, but survivable. Hopefully.

While inside . . .

"I'm just saying—I hate this part."

Mac leaned shoulder to shoulder with Kammie Noyo, and couldn't disagree.

Leaned wasn't exactly the word. Like everyone else in this pod and all the others, she was pinned where she'd last stood in the corridor by the protective foam hardening around them. It had erupted from orifices throughout the interior of the structure the moment the pod's sensors had detected the terraces were clear of people and the storm shields were in place, filling labs and rooms, holding objects in place as well as people.

"And I don't see why it has to be the color of bile."

Mac had remembered to keep her arms up as the foam rose up their legs and bodies, stopping chest high on her. During a test of the system, years ago, she'd left them down and spent three hours unable to deal with a maddening itch on the side of her nose. The foam was harmless, if you didn't mind the paralysis aspect. You could lie down on the floor and be completely covered. *Not her first choice.* The foam arched overhead as well, following the wall and ceiling material to effectively seal anything that might otherwise shake loose and fall on their heads. Its join was, presumably, also waterproof. Even if the pods were flipped right over, they should be safe.

The Ro had known. They'd known to disable the pods' protections before sabotaging their anchors. They'd been told how by Emily Mamani, their spy. Emily, who had come to Base to find out why Mackenzie Connor and her obscure work so interested a Dhryn. Emily, who had come to use that interest to hunt the Dhryn's weakness, their Progenitors. Emily, who with the Ro had used Mac to befriend a Dhryn and betray his kind, for the good of all others.

"Forgive me."

"Mac? How can you sleep through this?"

"Thinking, not sleeping." Mac looked down at Kammie. The other woman's pupils were dilated. Otherwise, she looked calm enough. Mac glanced along the corridor. Everyone in sight looked reasonably comfortable, if a bit nervous. Understandable—the floor was tilting beneath them and, from the feel of her stomach, the pod was dropping at the same time. Mac raised her voice. "Hope you like roller coasters, folks. At least none of us has had breakfast yet."

A few laughs at that.

"There'll be a few more tremors—aftershocks. And probably a few wave events—" The pod gave a sharp roll back and left, its pinned occupants gasping in reaction. Mac waited until everything settled, then continued. "Like that. The foam will be dispersed once the sensors—" This time the swing of the pod was to the right and up, putting Mac and those with her temporarily where the ceiling should be. Several students now below her hooted and waved as the pod rocked back to level, trying their best to intercept someone's hat as it tumbled along the foam's surface. Beside Mac, Kammie shook her head in disgust.

"—once the sensors say everything's settling down," Mac finished. "Meanwhile," she grinned at Kammie. "You might as well enjoy the ride."

"Three skims are still missing, but I 'spect those will turn up on shore someplace. You can see for yourself the condition of the walkways. They're a total loss. Otherwise— Mac, are you listening?"

Skims. Walkways. *As if those mattered.* Mac rested her chin on her fists, elbows on the cowling of the lev, and tried to pay attention to Tie's briefing. They were circling the pods, assessing damage, and it was all she could do not to cry.

Base had survived. The pods had bobbed like so many corks, and several people had to be treated for nausea, but the foam had vanished under the mist of dispersal agent and very little had been shifted, let alone broken.

She couldn't say the same about the landscape.

The ridge that stretched between Castle Inlet and the strait beyond had been scraped clean, as if the coating of forest and soil had been a frosting licked away. Close enough. The quake had momentarily liquefied the sandy substrate beneath, creating a downward sag and flow rather than a landslide's bump and tumble. Now only rock showed in a swatch stretching from the highest point to the shoreline, the fresh dark line of a fault plain to see. The shore? It was a confusion of mud and debris, leaves and branches sticking out at random as though a child had decorated a mud pie. Scale was impossible. What appeared twigs from this distance were giant tree trunks, snapped and torn. What appeared lines of gravel and sand were boulders. Mac spotted an eagles' nest, half covered by the remnants of a mem-wood dock. Streams and river mouths would be choked, some completely dammed.

The air stank of ruined trees and rotting kelp.

The sea hadn't been spared. It was brown and clouded as far as she could see, dotted with drowning bits of land-adapted life, sediment quietly smothering what aquatic life couldn't swim away.

At least it had been a minor earthquake, 4.3 on the revised Barr-Richter scale, barely rattling cups in Prince Rupert, unnoticed in Vancouver or Anchorage. A local event. Hadn't brought down anything more than this slope. Hadn't seriously affected rivers beyond this side of the inlet.

Hah, thought Mac.

One of her first priorities would be to assemble a team of researchers to record the state of land and water, to monitor the successional stages as the ecosystems rebuilt. Some of the scientists were, very quietly, overjoyed by the opportunity. It was rare to have such access to the destruction of a well-studied area, to be the first to see life restore itself. Their work would have immense value.

Mac watched as a gull settled on a root now aimed skyward, perhaps attracted by the line of silent, unmoving tiggers perched on a nearby scar of rock. The servos were still on guard, protecting what was to come.

"Mac. Stuff happens."

She looked at Tie. His weary face was streaked with drying mud and a line of grease. A bit of pink foam was stuck in his hair above his left ear. "That it does," she agreed. "Let's head back. I've seen enough."

And if she believed this earthquake "happened," Mac told herself, so far beyond mere fury she felt nothing but cold, *she should invest in that fabled bridge across the Bering Strait.*

A few meetings were actually fun—those rare events involved pizza, a tub of ice-cold beer, and the joyous task of celebrating a colleague's latest success, whether publication or offspring.

Most, like this one, were thinly disguised battles, usually with the outcome predetermined and of no joy to anyone.

Mac planned to make it quick. Speed didn't help when pulling off bandages, but she hoped in this case it would limit the fallout. With any luck, everyone would leave mad at her instead of each other.

She hated meetings.

"Let's get started," she ordered quietly, surveying the gallery from the centermost seat at the head table. That table was raised on a small dais, allowing the entire roomful of people a clear view of Mac, Kammie, and the other five senior scientists. Or guest speakers, hired bands, talent shows, and the like.

No one expected entertainment today, not with Pod Three reverberating each time a floating, dying tree bumped and scraped against its supports, not with the view out the transparent walls showing an ocean stained with the blood of a mountain.

"We've conferred with—" *everyone possible,* Mac almost said, then changed it to "—experts. The bottom beneath the pods is stable, but seriously disturbed. You've seen for yourselves the state of the shoreline. Rather than reinstall the permanent anchors and resume our work here—" The shock traveled across the room, mirrored in all of their faces. *Did they think nothing would change?* Mac raged—but kept it to herself. They didn't need her pain as well as their own. "—Pods One, Three, Four, Five, and Six will be towed to a new site."

From any other group, there might have been pandemonium or some protest. Not here, not now. Three hundred and fifteen faces looked back at her, many of them familiar, some new, very few she didn't know on sight yet. Her eyes couldn't find Persephone, but she took that as a positive. *Someone better be investigating what had happened.* Just as likely, 'Sephe hadn't dared face her. Mac spotted Case, sitting with Uthami and John Ward. Everyone was silent, waiting.

They knew there was more to come.

"The process, barring storms or more rumblings from beneath, will take three weeks. Norcoast is sending haulers to tow the pods. We'll have to secure all gear—move out what's going to be needed during that time. Check your imps for details. The sooner we're ready, the sooner we can get moving."

"Where?" came a voice from the back.

Mac glanced at Kammie. That worthy stood, having learned long ago her soft, high-pitched voice needed all the help it could get to project past the first line of tables. She smoothed the front of her immaculate lab coat with both hands. A nervous habit. *Who wasn't on edge?* Mac thought with sympathy. "We're returning Base to its original home, beside the mouth of the Tannu River itself," Kammie informed them. "It's an ideal location. And was ideal, until the natural disaster before this one. I assume that when history repeats itself, Base will be towed back here again." Her comment drew a laugh and Kammie smiled faintly as she sat down.

Mac resumed her part of the briefing. "Pod Two is being refitted as a self-contained research unit, to accommodate what will be an ongoing, multiyear, and very well-funded exploration of the successional recovery of the life in this area. Congratulations to those who will be staying. We look forward to your findings." Martin Svehla, freshly minted head of the new unit, beamed beatifically at the world at large. Mac was reasonably sure he wasn't hearing much else.

A hand rose.

"Yes, Case."

He stood, glancing once around the room before looking up at her. "Dr. Connor. What does this mean for those of us packed and ready to head to the field?"

"It means—" Mac began answering.

Kammie stood so quickly her glass of water rocked on the table. "It means a temporary postponement," she interrupted, steadying the tumbler. "You'll have the choice of going home for three weeks, travel costs covered by Norcoast, or joining some of us on the University of British Columbia's campus for course credit. I believe there will be four topics offered."

So this was how it felt to be ambushed by a puma, Mac told herself. Only the cat had good reason for pouncing on you from behind and driving its fangs into your skull.

"Dr. Noyo is talking about some individual circumstances," Mac said harshly. *If you didn't want to be lunch, you fought with whatever you had.* "Each case will be decided on its own needs and merits—"

Unfortunately, tiny Kammie Noyo was more dangerous than a hungry puma. "Now, Dr. Connor," she interrupted again. "We mustn't confuse the issue. Norcoast will not be broadcasting power during the tow. The main system will not be operating. There will be no backup of data, no supplies, no—"

Mac leaped to her feet. "So bloody what? I don't need all this—" she waved her hand around furiously, "—to do my work. I'll use a pencil if I have to!"

But the others at the head table didn't meet her eyes when she looked to them for support.

"Norcoast has been very clear, Dr. Connor," Kammie said into the painful pause. "They won't send anyone into the field until Base is up and running to support those efforts. It's only three weeks—a month at most."

"A month—" The first runs would be over. The first salmon would be dead, their legacy mere specks of eyeball and yolk left in the redds, the nests their mothers dug in the gravel upstream.

Mac closed her mouth, afraid of what might come out next, afraid she was wrong, that she was overreacting for reasons incomprehensible to both mystified students and troubled colleagues.

Most of all, she was afraid of staying here one more instant. *What else would she lose if she did?*

She sat, slowly. With an effort that left her dizzy, she nodded at Kammie, gesturing graciously that the other was to continue.

Mac didn't hear another word that was said.

The foam wasn't supposed to leave a residue. Maybe it was her imagination that everything she touched in her office was faintly sticky. Mac ignored the sensation as she ignored everything but the task at hand. She was packing. Quietly, quickly. One small bag. They'd been told to take only personal valuables, to leave everything else behind. For three weeks.

It wasn't Kammie's fault.

Kammie had anticipated Mac's reaction to the "take a hike" order from Norcoast perfectly. She'd known better than to bring it up in private, giving Mac a chance to launch herself at those responsible, fly to the head office, make a pointless nuisance of herself and possibly lose her post here altogether. It wasn't only potential students who were wondering about the qualifications and commitment of a particular salmon researcher.

It wasn't Kammie's fault.

If she'd anger to spare, Mac thought as she zipped up her bag, she'd save it for those lackwits who'd forgotten how real scientists worked. Hands-on, with nets and serum syringes, scales and insta-freeze pouches. A zapper to discourage bears who preferred her fishing techniques to theirs. She'd done it before.

Not that they'd listened.

There was temporary power throughout the pods, enough for lights and to run whatever systems needed to go through an off cycle before storage. *Enough for coms to work,* Mac noticed morosely, as hers gave a fainter-than-usual chime.

Listen to them? She grabbed her sweater instead.

A second chime. A third.

Fine. "Mac," she said, thumping the control with the side of her fist. About as satisfying as slamming a door when no one else was there to appreciate the gesture.

"Hi, Princess. Going that well, is it?"

Oops. Mac sank down on the corner of her desk, shaking her head at herself. "Sorry, Dad. I should have called you back." They'd all contacted family and friends after the earthquake, taking the time to give reassurances if no details. *She'd really meant to call again.* "Did an inspection. Held a meeting. Packed. It's been hectic."

There wasn't power to waste on the vid 'screen—not that Dr. Norman Connor had ever needed to see her face to know. *Sure enough.* "What's wrong?"

"Norcoast is shutting us down for three weeks." *Shutting* me *down,* Mac told herself, penning in her now-familiar frustration. *It wasn't his fault.* "They're moving the pods back to the Tannu."

"While you're away in the field. Sounds like good timing."

"You'd think so." Mac sighed and stared out the window at the fittingly sullen sky. "But they won't authorize any work until Base is up and running again."

"That's bloody ridiculous," he exploded. She could picture him pacing angrily around his apartment, dodging the table he insisted belonged in the middle of the floor. "Since when do you need all that? This ridiculous nonsense of interactive data-feed. Voyeur-scientists, that's what they are! Never get their feet wet or dirty, but oh, they want their input, oh, yes."

Dr. Connor Sr. had spent most of a century doing fieldwork on owls, from an era when that meant disappearing for weeks at a time. His indignation, right on target, eased some of Mac's own. "Trust me, Dad, I argued the point. But it's a done deal. I—" A plan crystallized Mac hadn't been aware of forming until now. "Is that guest room of yours ready? I haven't been to your place since, well, since I came back." When he didn't answer immediately, she went on, feeling suddenly desperate: "We could take a trip, maybe even visit William. You could play granddad while I play aunt."

"I'd love to have you here, Mac, you know that, but—" her father's voice trailed away, then returned. "Now might not be a good time."

"Why?" she asked, surprised into worry. "Is something wrong there?"

His "No. Nothing's wrong," came out too fast, too definite. Mac stared down at the com control, as if it could transform into his face.

"What is it, Dad?"

A pause, then, slowly: "There are vidbots hanging outside my building, Mac. Outside your brothers' homes as well. All authorized and legal—we checked. Our guess is some nosy reporter hopes to catch you away from Base. I really don't think you feel like giving interviews."

Attract media attention? Oh, the Ministry would love that. Mac shuddered at the thought of black-armored Ministry agents trying to loom discreetly among her father's geraniums. *Bad enough she'd had to lie to her family already. How to explain that?* She rubbed her hands over her face, as if to scrub away the image. "You're right, Dad," she agreed. "It was just a thought. I need a break from all this." Mac realized how wistful that sounded and went on more firmly: "Don't worry. I'm sure Kammie could use help with her courses."

"That's hardly taking a break," he protested.

Mac shrugged, even though he couldn't see. "Best I can do."

"The ice is off the lake, Mac."

The family cabin? She snorted. "I haven't been there in—in a very long time. And neither have you."

"Blake went up last month. He said the place was in great shape."

"Have you seen Blake's house lately?" Mac retorted. "His idea of great shape is knowing where the leaks are so he can avoid the puddles."

Her father laughed, but went on, a warm, coaxing note to his voice. "Think about it, Mac. May at the lake. Peace and quiet."

"I don't need to think about it. I remember. Black flies. With occasional flurries. No thanks."

"The birds will be coming back."

Mac closed her eyes, tilting her head back, her hands tight around one knee for balance. "You know why I don't like it there anymore, Dad."

"Maybe it's time. Things change. People."

"I don't."

Mac imagined her dad shaking his head ruefully, that half proud, half exasperated look on his face she usually managed to elicit at least once a visit. "Fine. But it's yours if you want it."

"Kammie will need me—" Mac began.

"No, I won't," an unexpected voice interrupted, startling Mac's eyes open. Kammie Noyo met her scowl with a wink. "Hi, Dr. Connor," she added, approaching the desk. "It's Kammie. How're you?"

"Frustrated," her father answered. "You ever try explaining the concept of a vacation to my daughter?"

"You're a brave man."

Was she invisible? "I don't need a vacation," Mac growled at them both. "I don't want a vacation. I want to get to work."

"Well, if you change your mind, Mac, the door's open. Let me know what you decide."

"I will. Bye, Dad."

"Bye. Nice talking to you, Kammie."

"You, too, Dr. Connor." Mac turned off the com.

"Go."

She glared at Kammie. "Pardon?" she said at last.

The chemist put her hands on her hips, a posture which combined with her oversize white lab coat to make her resemble a small bird ready to take flight. *A whirlwind temporarily touching down was more accurate,* Mac thought warily. "You heard me," Kammie stated. "I want twenty-one days without you. Go."

"That's harsh."

"The truth."

Mac swung her leg back and forth, then gave the other scientist a thoughtful look. "I've been that bad?"

"You got a few hours?" Kammie's stern expression faded into something worried, a little frightened. She touched Mac's shoulder, let her hand drop. "Mac. You're the strongest person I know. But even you can break. You've—it's been hardest on you, these last months. We've all seen it. Listen to your father. Listen to me. You need some time. To look after yourself first for once."

Mac stood and took a step away, stopping to study her garden, with its sprouts of growth through the melting snow. *Plants had such optimism.* She felt stiff and cold inside. "What I need is my work," she said. *It wasn't Kammie's fault.*

"That's not what Em—" The other's voice broke.

Mac turned, catching the pain in Kammie's eyes, meeting it with her own. *Not forgotten after all.*

"I know exactly what she'd say." Mac shook her head, her lips twitching involuntarily. "But loud music and sex aren't the answer to everything."

"She'd argue it," Kammie chuckled, her dark eyes sparkling with mischief now, instead of tears. *Something had eased,* Mac decided, *but she wasn't sure what.* "So. You going to take that vacation?"

Mac grimaced. "Let me fight the concept a while longer."

"And then you'll go," the tiny chemist nodded with satisfaction. "See you in three weeks, Mac." With that, she sailed out of the room, lab coat snapping as if finding the perfect wind.

"If not sooner," Mac muttered under her breath. She bent to pick up her bag, wondering who'd won that little encounter.

"Mac . . . Dr. Connor? Do you have a minute?"

She straightened to find Case standing in the doorway to the terrace. *Bother.* Her own fault. She'd left the door ajar, open invitation to the sea breeze as well as anyone passing by.

Mac smiled a welcome. "Always. Come in, Case. I thought you were off to the family trawler."

"I'm on my way. Getting a ride to Kitimat with some of the Preds," he told her, stepping into the room, carefully avoiding the gravel section of the floor and giving her garden a bemused look as wet snowflakes began plopping down from its weather grid. May was a chancy month at Field Station One. "I wanted to say good-bye."

"Good-bye? That sounds rather final. It's only three weeks—so everyone keeps telling me," Mac added darkly.

"I—well, that's what I need to talk to you about, Mac. Unless you're in a hurry." He looked pointedly at her hand.

"Oh, this?" Mac dropped the bag, nudging it aside with her foot. "No rush. The haulers won't connect until the wee hours of tomorrow morning. Besides, I haven't made up my mind yet where I'm going. Have a seat." While Case folded himself into one of her chairs, she took the other. The unhappy set of his mouth, the shadows under his eyes? Something was up. *Though students,* Mac reminded herself, *could escalate a minor problem to a full-fledged life crisis if they worried hard enough.* Which didn't make the problem less real or painful.

She deliberately settled deeper, stretching out her legs. "So. Looking forward to some time at home?"

"Looking forward to it? Not really." Case gave a strangled laugh. "But I need the open sea. I can't hear myself think in a place like this." This last, hurried and thoroughly miserable. His shoulders hunched.

"You don't like it here," she suggested, disappointed but not showing it. *Hadn't picked him as one of the terminally homesick.*

His glance up at her was shocked, followed by a quick blush Mac didn't try to interpret. "Of course I like it here. I love it. Base is great. Everyone's—everyone's great. That's not it. I need time alone. I've a decision to make. I don't want to make the wrong one."

So that was it. Mac nodded triumphantly. "A decision about coming back. You're not sure about working with Lee."

"How did you know?" He gave her such a soulful look, Mac had to stop herself from smiling.

"Educated guess. Why?"

"I'm a deep-sea fisher." Case held out his hands. They were crisscrossed with a maze of white scars. Filleting knives, hooks. Even with gloves and the latest tech, harvesting wasn't for the thin of skin. "Tidal ecosystems are interesting, I grant you, but not what I came here for."

Mac pursed her lips. Then asked: "Are you good at it? Harvesting, that is."

His pale eyes gleamed. "Wilsons have been heading out to the North Sea for thirteen generations. I've more family drowned than buried." A hard shrug. "Why won't Dr. Noyo just let me work with the Harvs? That's where I belong, Mac. Isn't it?"

Ah. Not homesick. Intimidated. Mac put her hands behind her head and considered Lee's troubled student. *Just as well this had come to a head now,* she decided. She had a feeling about this one; she didn't want Base to lose him. "In your opinion, Case," she said carefully, "from what you've seen so far, nothing else, does Lee's line of research have any relevance whatsoever to harvesting?"

Another shocked look. "Of course it does. He's examining nutrient cycling within estuaries. Those are key feeding grounds for fish in transit, not to mention habitat and spawning nurseries. The list of species affected? Everything we'd want to haul aboard, as well as their primary food source and predators. You should see the prelims he's done on the impact of mitigation upstream on the yield of . . ." Case's passionate voice trailed away as he took in Mac's rather smug smile. "You know all of this."

"I should," she agreed calmly. "And you find his work interesting?"

Case actually squirmed. "Yes, but that's not the point, Mac. Lee, Uthami, the rest in the team—they're experts at this stuff. Me? I don't know anything."

"Yet."

"Sure, I could learn it. But in the meantime, I'm dead weight," he protested. "What can I contribute? With the Harvs, at least I'd understand the terms—know what I was doing. I'm useless as a Misses."

Mac brought her arms down and leaned forward on her elbows, holding his eyes with hers. "Listen to me, Case. You know what a catalyst is, right?" At his nod, she continued: "Kammie and I share a fondness for them. Mind you, to her, being a chemist, catalysts are what make a reaction more likely to occur—in many instances, make it possible in the first place—without being consumed themselves. But here? In a place like this? Catalysts are those individuals who can connect different lines of research. They bring together ideas which wouldn't meet otherwise. That's crucial to what we do here."

He rolled his eyes. "And I felt inadequate before? You aren't helping, Mac."

She sat up. "Yes, I am. Think about it, Case. You bring the perspective of a Harv, the knowledge of your deepwater fishing heritage, to the work in tidal systems. Every question you ask will have the unique value of coming from that knowledge. Bottom line? Lee and his team don't know what you know, and they'll benefit from your insights." Mac grinned. "I admit there's the chance you'll drive Lee nuts—but I think his new lady love is already doing that."

There was something immensely satisfying about the stupefied look on the young man's face. "You're saying Kammie assigned me to Lee's research team because I don't have a clue about his work and he doesn't have a clue about mine."

Mac nodded cheerfully. "Couldn't have said it better myself."

"That's not—I'm really—Mac?" He gave her a desperate look. "What do I do now?"

"You go home," she advised. "Spend some time on that open sea. Think to your heart's content. Just be back here in three weeks, 'cause we have work to do this season, despite earthquakes and Norcoast."

Case stood when she did, then offered his hand. Mac took it, enjoying the feel of warm calluses, noticing the strength. "You believe I can do this," he told her. Almost a question, as though he had to be sure.

"I believe neither of us will know that until you try," she said honestly. "I hope you will, Case."

His grip tightened before letting go, his freckles prominent on his very serious face. "I promise. Thank you."

The ensuing pause had the potential to become awkward, but Case relaxed and smiled before it did. An unexpected mischievous smile. "So if I'm to try what Kammie says, will you do the same? Take a vacation?"

Mac raised one eyebrow. "Eavesdropping?"

"The door was open," he said, appearing completely unrepentant.

Grad students, she sighed to herself. "I'm considering it."

"You're welcome to come home with me." The young man

blushed and added hastily: "Don't worry. My parents and sister will be on the trawler, too."

One of the few times to be grateful Emily wasn't *around.*

Mac coughed. "I appreciate the offer, Case, but I'll probably help Kammie with the courses she's running. Or there's a taxonomy conference in Brussels—"

"When was the last time you took a vacation?"

Mac found herself at a loss.

"Aha!" Case crowed. "I bet you've never taken one. I bet you don't even know how!"

"Of course I do," Mac huffed. "I haven't bothered."

He gestured at her cluttered office. "So it's true!"

"What's true?" she asked cautiously.

"What they say. You really do live here all the time. Year in, year out. You don't even bother with sleeping quarters."

"There's nothing wrong with a passion for one's work," she said primly, then winced. *No doubt about Emily's response to that line.* "Don't you have a ride to catch, Mr. Wilson?"

Unfortunately, grad students loved nothing more than a mission. Case, Mac realized glumly, happily relieved of his own conundrum, had his teeth firmly in this one.

Which would have been fine, if it wasn't her.

"I promise to think about it, Case. Oh, no," Mac forestalled his next outburst. "This is where I get to pull rank. End of argument."

He chewed on his lower lip, then nodded. "You promise, though."

"Go chop fish heads," Mac suggested with a grin, making a shooing motion with her hands.

She closed and, as an afterthought, locked the door to the terrace, before making one last walk-through of her office and lab. She opened cupboards. Counted Emily's boxes of belongings. Found a hose clamp in the wrong drawer and put it with the rest.

Strange, how final it felt.

Mac shook off the foreboding. She was tired. Tired and thoroughly offended by the current state of things. Neither led to peace of mind.

Of course, it didn't help her mood to return to her office to find two black-garbed monoliths guarding her desk.

They'd left their visors down for some unfathomable reason. *It had to be hot in there,* Mac thought, not for the first time. She scowled until, one after the other, they flipped them up on their helmets. The revealed faces shared a sheepish look. "Jones. Zimmerman," she acknowledged, feeling uneasy. *Nice guys; but they never came to her office like this.* "What can I do for you?"

"Hi, Mac," Jones said. "We're here to help you pack."

Mac reached down and grabbed her bag, holding it up for inspection. "Done."

Zimmerman, dark-skinned, dark-haired, and perpetually dark of mood, so far as Mac could tell, heaved a sigh, rattling something loose among the weapons clipped to various parts of his armor. "Told you we didn't have time for supper, Sing-li."

"I thought you'd left by now," Mac commented.

"We're waiting to take you to join the others at the university," Jones informed her.

Were they, now.

Mac tightened her grip on the bag handle. "Why?"

The two exchanged looks, likely reflecting on other situations involving that question in that tone from Mac. "It's a nice campus. Great facilities—"

She lifted an eyebrow. "I do know the place. The point, gentlemen?"

Jones managed to shrug his encased shoulders. "It's a secure option, Mac," he told her. " 'Sephe's already there, doing the prep work. After what's happened—well, we all felt some extra precautions might be necessary. I know you won't be happy about this, but—"

"Why wouldn't I be? Sounds perfectly reasonable," Mac said blandly. "Just give me half an hour to locate the samples I'm taking from storage. One of the courses we're teaching has an anatomy component. Where shall I meet you? Front entrance? Back here?"

They probably should leave their visors down more often, Mac decided, amused by the war between suspicion and relief on their faces.

Suspicion won. "We'll come with you," Zimmerman said. "Help you pack."

Mac smiled. "Perfect." She slipped her arms into the shoulder straps of her bag, and waved her "helpers" onward.

Mac had no idea what Kammie and the University of British Columbia would make of five preserved orca heads, two bottles of giant squid eyes, and fifty-three huge, "too good to discard but on the way to rancid" clumps of mutually cemented rock barnacles. If they got there.

As expected, however, her "samples" made admirably awkward burdens for two overly helpful Ministry guards.

By the second load, they'd begun working together, leaving her to pull out the next load from the stas-unit in Pod Four.

By the third, Mac was no longer at the stas-unit, but on her way to Kitimat, having squeezed herself and her bag in with a bunch of homebound and very happy Preds students, much to the delight of Case Wilson.

"Vacation, here I come," she told him, dropping into the tiny space they'd cleared her for a seat.

She hoped the universe would behave itself while she was away.

- Encounter -

*O*EISHT WALKED restlessly up the hillside, each step bringing front legs forward, brace, then drawing the hind set through. The rhythm was soothing and efficient. *Oeisht* covered ground rapidly, each step a surge of muscle and bone.

Behind *oeisht,* on the lower third of the slope, *aisht* huddled in the homes of the settlement, *isht* of every life stage safe in their pouches.

Safe. Was there meaning to the word? This far from kin, *oeisht* panted with despair. *Oeisht* had seen for *oeishtself* the desecration of the farmland in the next valley to this. A single *isht* had survived, jammed inside a hollow roof pipe, the only living thing between the hills of scoured rock. Too young to grieve; too young to have concepts for what had happened.

But Others knew. Others had sent urgent messages. Travelers, the infertile *aisht,* restless, always seeking, ever curious, had interpreted their meaning for those who dwelt within the Pouch of their kind.

Oeisht let the latest swing forward of his hinds stop, easing to his haunches. By the new thinking, the Pouch was far larger than this one place. *Oeisht, aisht,* and *isht* lived on a world within its star system, that star within a cluster of stars, that cluster, within others. *Oeisht* wasn't a theologian, but this new concept, that the dark sky of night was itself the inner folds encompassing the universe, had a good feel, a comfort to it.

Oeisht had come to the hilltop for comfort. Now, *oeisht* gazed upward, elongating and thinning *oeisht's* eyestalks to sharpen the focus of the stars winking above. Each, if *aisht* were to be believed, might have worlds, worlds with those who had eyes looking toward *oeisht. Oeisht,* out of sight of *aisht,* who might think *oeisht* foolish, flared ears in greeting. Then, *oeisht* crouched, retracting ears and eyestalks.

The stars were wrong.

The stars were coming closer.

Oeisht leaped to all fours, surging downslope in prodigious leaps, moaning *oeisht's* despair.

The stars were faster.

And they brought the Dhryn.

It is the way of the Great Journey that what can be gathered cannot satisfy. That which is Dhryn cannot be filled.

That which is Dhryn . . . *hungers.*

Only at Haven, will there be enough.

All that is Dhryn must move.

Or all that is Dhryn will end.

5

REST AND RECRIMINATION

MAC COULD SEE them all now. Case, triumphant. Kammie, openly smug. The Ministry's finest probably still explaining the presence of orca heads and the absence of hers on campus. Her father, who'd let her pretend this trip had been her idea all along.

"Vacation, hah!" Mac grumbled to herself, staring out the window of the public lev. "Bet I last two days before I'm bored sick or resorting to chocolate."

Since she'd been one of the last to leave, there hadn't been an onerous round of good-byes. Suited her mood. *They wanted her gone for three weeks? Fine. She'd go.*

From Kitimat, Mac had caught a public lev to Whitehorse, another to Ottawa—in which having two seats to herself meant room to nap—and this last to North Bay, where she'd stood for the final leg to let a family with young twins and even younger kitten sit, or rather squirm.

Par for the course. *Weren't vacations supposed to be relaxing?* So far, Mac hadn't seen any evidence of it. Other things, yes. Vidbots hovered everywhere, in the doorways and passages of transit lounges and hotels, even hung from the ceilings of stores and restaurants. Governments swore those in public areas were reactive and nonrecording, keyed to switch on only if a disturbance was detected or during special events to provide news feeds. Rights groups kept testing that claim; the average person hardly noticed the things anymore.

Mac did. They weren't allowed in Castle Inlet. Away from that refuge, she resented their little shadows, felt their presence like weights on her shoulders, knew a steady anger that they kept watch on her family.

She liked the devices even less, having been tracked by one on the Dhryn world. *Emily's trick.*

Then there was the pace. Mac was used to taking transit off-hours and to odd locations. Now, she was forced to join the brunt of the Human stampede. *Worse than students heading to supper on Pizza Tuesdays.* Her initial curiosity over why all of these people had somehow picked her route to follow soon changed to a frantic hope they'd all go somewhere else entirely.

Fortunately for her sanity—and peace aboard public transit—by the time she reached North Bay everything eased to a civil crawl. The station received only one lev an hour, so she disembarked to welcome, open space. *No more elbows and backpacks threatening her nose.* Even better, the ever present vidbots became scarce, then nonexistent. Not much to watch in the northern woods, and fewer places where being watched was permitted. *Part of the charm.*

From the station, Mac shared a ride with a group of cottagers just in from Toronto to the Misty River Cottage Association docks. The courtesy ferry was, as always, nowhere to be seen, so the cottagers shared their picnic with Mac while they waited, along with their eagerness to check on their respective properties after the long winter. Ice breakup north of Algonquin had been two weeks later than predicted; relying on such predictions, Mac agreed with the cottagers, was about as smart as feeding bears from your porch.

They were pleasant, cheerful people, intent on leaving their mundane lives behind while "up at the lake." Much as she hated to admit it, Mac began to warm to the concept. Maybe this enforced vacation wasn't such a bad idea. Each stage of her journey had seemed to lift a layer of dread from Mac's shoulders. Each took her farther from what might be, back to a time when her biggest concern had been getting Sam to notice she was a girl. That, and making it into the school of her choice.

She had a new definition of life crisis now.

The ferry arrived midafternoon, an actual float-on-water boat with an equally quaint waterjet engine that purred quietly to itself as its operator brought it to dock. Wide and low to allow room for cottagers and whatever paraphernalia was going up with them this year, the ferry's only protection from the elements was an awning over its stern half. The awning and seat cushions had once boasted vivid red, purple, and yellow stripes, now mellowed to pastel by sun and time.

The sun, as suited mid-May, was set to brilliant, as if it had forgotten all about spring and gone straight to summer. Mac drank in the intense blue of the sky, marked only by a few puffy white clouds stuck behind the low rolling hills to every side. The ferry headed upriver, loaded with carryalls of food and other supplies, bits of cottage-ready furniture, and a stack of mem-wood for a tree house that would be a surprise for a trio of lucky great-grandchildren.

They chugged peacefully alongside tilting cedars, reflections mingled with the lichen-stained boulders of the shoreline. The forest had a manicured look, branches starting a tidy two meters or so up every leaning trunk. Not the work of a gardener, just the heavy snow pack pressing lower branches down until they snapped. There were still patches of dirty white snow here and there in the shadows, the remnants of deeper drifts that grudgingly melted away.

Mac sat on the bow, bare feet dangling to either side despite the occasional splash of still-cold water, elbows on the gunnel so she could lean forward with her chin in her hands. The sun was warm on her back; the ferry slow enough she could see the river bottom clearly. Mac watched for turtle scrapes and schools of darting minnows, counted mussel beds and spied the tail of a pike, lurking beneath a sunken log. A beaver nosed by, bubbles streaming from its fur, staring up at Mac before ducking below the surface.

She smiled.

The river took a wide bend, then they were at the lock to Little Misty Lake. Rapids tumbled white and busy beside the structure which lifted water and shipping more peacefully between levels. Like much in this part of the world, the lock was revered as an antique worth saving and considered a hopeless and expensive bottleneck to progress. Usually at the same time, by the same people.

Once inside the lock, Mac helped slip the rope from the ferry's prow around the cable running from the top of the lock wall to below the water. She ran her real fingers along the corded steel. It was cold and wet, slimed with algae, utterly practical and simple. She experimented with her new fingers, trying to detect any differences in sensation. None. The cable and its predecessors had been here, doing their job, since before humanity achieved orbit. *Her new hand would probably outlast her, too,* Mac decided, amused.

The gates closed behind them and the lock began to fill. Mac and one of the cottagers at the stern guided their respective ropes up the cables as the ferry rose. The operator, meanwhile, was lying back in his seat, hat over his eyes. After a few moments, a gentle snore began to compete with the gurgling of water around the hull. *A little early in the season for the novelty to have worn off,* Mac thought, then yawned herself.

Little Misty, despite its name, wasn't small. It was one of those long and convoluted northern lakes, deep and cold, filled with rocky, tree-bearded islands. Its shoreline was a sequence of points and hidden tiny coves, making it possible to surprise a moose or otter every few minutes.

The ferry operator paid attention here. May meant deadheads in plenty—floating logs, often marked by little more than a twig dimpling the water's surface. There were rocks below as well. Mac could see them from her perch on the bow. Great jigsaw pieces of basalt loomed from the depths like the broken pavement of a giant's road or the ruins of a vast city. Fish cruised every edge, hovering over drops so deep the bright rays of sunlight faded to black. Other times, the ferry slid past uplifted stone whose eroded surfaces kept a painted score of past collisions at low water.

They put the cottagers ashore first. All were on Heron Island, the second largest on the lake. Someone's son had come a week earlier to set out the floating docks. Mac helped carry belongings and construction materials from the ferry to land, amid numerous, earnest pleas to visit sometime. Having seen the amount and quality of food these particular cottagers were laying in, she didn't say no.

Mac's destination was at the far end of the lake. She was as eager to reach it as the ferry operator, who reminded her, several times, that he'd have to be back through the lock by twilight or sleep over.

Around a final string of islands, ranging from bare rocks with the requisite possessive gull on each, to a stunning tower crowned by gnarled white pine. An osprey watched them from the skeletal tip of the tallest tree. Then, another cove, so much like the others the operator gave Mac a doubtful look.

"That's it," she assured him, tying her boots to her bag and making sure that was secure on her back.

No dock here. The operator brought his boat in until the keel kissed the sandy bottom. "Thanks," Mac told him. She hopped over the side, sucking air through her teeth at the bite of chill water on her warm feet and ankles, and waded to shore. She waved good-bye as the ferry headed home, not that the operator turned to look.

Mac dropped her bag on a flat stretch of rock and let out a sigh.

"Been a while," she whispered.

Behind her, forested hills, deep lakes, and flat marshes marched north until the tundra began, an expanse of wilderness punctuated only by small quiet towns and isolated camps. To live here year-round was to accept seasons, value solitude, leave doors open for strangers and, above all, depend on oneself. Preparation and habits mattered here, helping you survive when civilization wasn't around to help.

Cottagers—those summer migrants—who wanted only to play, party, and unwind didn't come this far, and certainly not to lakes like Little Misty where you couldn't zoom around on skims or have every modern convenience delivered to your door. *To come here . . . to stay here,* Mac thought, perching comfortably on that piece of driftwood the size and shape of a dragon's head, the one which had waited for her here as long as she could remember, *you had to let yourself assume another shape.*

She lay back along the wood, soaking in sun and silence, and let her tears flow.

Before the shadows lengthened too much more, Mac put on her boots, grabbed her bag, and headed up the hill. It was a steep slope, slippery with last autumn's leaves, but there was a stair of a sort. Where the winding path didn't take advantage of natural rises in the rock—themselves treacherous when wet, short pieces of wood had been set sideways in the slope to provide a foothold. Surprisingly, most were still intact, though Mac stepped carefully and, near the top, had to avoid eroded sections where the path had become steeper than the hillside.

She climbed past the cedars, through arrow-straight white pines, until a glint of reflection ahead marked her goal. A red squirrel, tail flailing back and forth, scolded her from a branch overhead. "Is that any way to welcome someone?" Mac told it. Unimpressed, the squirrel cussed louder.

The cabin sat within a circle of pines whose tops met far above. For a wonder, nothing seemed to have fallen on the roof besides pine needles and cones. It was a rambling structure built to take the weather, nothing fancy or pretty about it except the aging logs of its construction, and more bunkhouse than home. The senior Dr. Connor had routinely brought up students and visiting peers as well as family. Family, particularly Mac's brothers, had used it for the occasional party, inviting numerous friends. As far as Mac could recall, they'd found room for everyone. Somewhere.

The long building was T-shaped due to an addition tucked on the back, and had a second floor that was mostly slope and tiny, web-coated windows. It did boast that essential northern convenience, a covered porch which circled the front and sides. Visitors were usually taken aback to learn there was a separate outhouse farther into the forest. Not that there wasn't indoor plumbing, but it saved having to power up the cabin in winter.

Otherwise, the landscape was as it had been, a hush of moss and pine.

Mac climbed the five steps to the porch and unlatched the outer screen door, ready to jump to the side if any recent occupants made a run for the woods.

Nothing large, anyway. She opened the door to the cabin proper and could hear a rustle or two that likely meant squirrels in the rafters or mice under the floor. Stepping inside, she gazed around, admiring the abundance of right angles. Pod Three was home, but she'd developed a positive hunger for the perpendicular.

The first floor was divided in thirds, with sleeping quarters to the left and right. In the center was the common room, an expanse of dark wood and scattered couches, shelves and tables, with braided rugs tossed here and there on the floor. The massive fireplace on the back wall had been cobbled together from loose stone from the lake itself, glints from embedded crystals of pink, white, and amethyst now catching the low rays of sun entering through the porch and windows. Two narrow doors stood open on either side of the fireplace, one to the kitchen and the other to stairs leading up.

Other than the scurrying of four-footed houseguests, the cobwebs curtaining the windows and hanging from rafters, and the truly remarkable paper wasp nest hanging from the eaves outside, the place did look in "great shape," as Blake had stated. Not bad, considering Mac's father hadn't been up for at least ten years and Mac herself—

She hadn't set foot on the shores of Little Misty Lake or in this cabin since Sam had left for space and died there.

"On the bright side, Em," Mac said aloud, "I finally cut my hair."

While finding someone new to obsess over. Mac put her bag on one of the tables. She'd come for peace and quiet. It wasn't going to happen if her heart gave a peculiar lurch at the mere thought of Nikolai Trojanowski being here with her. Of being alone, just the two of them. Of what it would be like, to discover each other. To . . .

"He probably prefers cities, Em. And blondes. Curvy blondes who giggle and wear sequined nail polish." Mac giggled herself at this. *Though the idea of being here had merit.* Physical attraction, however intense, was one thing—cheerfully sharing an outhouse quite another.

Though, maybe, being a spy, Nikolai liked his women dangerous and full of secrets. Maybe . . .

Mac snorted. "And maybe I should get to know the man better before letting him in my head, let alone through the door. There's the difference between us when it comes to relationships, Emily Mamani," she said as she went to the kitchen. "I don't want any surprises in mine."

Not that getting to know Mr. Spy better was likely to happen.

There were, as Mac had expected, a few nests scattered through the cabin, the most palatial where a chipmunk had hollowed out a down pillow in the upstairs bedroom. All were abandoned, their occupants awake from hibernation and scattered to greener—and mate-filled—pastures. The pantry cupboards had kept out any non-Human guests, though many of the supplies were newer than the rest, implying others had used the cabin and courteously replaced what they used. Others who weren't Blake, Mac chuckled to herself.

Mac made a quick supper of self-heating stew and then took a cup of cocoa out to the covered porch, making room for herself among the cobwebs on the swing. She sat down with care; the old chains and wood held.

A loon called urgently in the distance, a spring arrival eager for company.

"Better you than me," Mac told him peacefully.

Compared to the vastness of mountains, ocean, and rain forest offered by Castle Inlet, or the glaciers, canyons, and powerful rivers of the inner ranges, the view from the porch wasn't much. A small sweep of dark blue lake, a couple of rocky islands, the approach to the cove below, all framed by pine branches, several bare of needles. If Mac went upstairs and bothered to clean a window, she could see a bit farther. Catch the osprey on its perch during the day, spot the Milky Way at night.

Yes, there were more dramatic vistas, but this one offered an intimacy she'd experienced nowhere else. With the exception of the stars, she could be part of everything she saw. She could climb the trees and smell sap on her fingers; lie on the rocks and be warmed by the sun; swim to the islands and hear her heart in the waves. She could cup lake water in her hands and drink, feel it trace the inside of her throat to become part of her.

And having been to the stars, Mac decided, *she'd take this anytime.*

Her father had picked this spot for his owls, several species calling this forest home year-round, the rest visitors in season. Tiny, opinionated screech owls, hopping through the bush at night. Curious great horned owls, who'd stare down from their perches, heads pivoting almost full circle to follow what Humans were doing. Busy barred owls. Arctic owls, alien and elusive. More. Mac planned to hike to some of the old nest sites while she was here. There had been three within a few hours' walk, ten more if they camped out at night. Some would likely still be occupied and Mac would record what she could. Her father'd be pleased to catch up with his "old friends."

Recording. Mac frowned. She'd left her imp on her desk at Base. Partly by accident during the rush to elude her keepers, partly consciously. She'd seen no reason to stay connected to the world or to her work while she was away on this forced rest. *Okay, maybe some petulance in there,* she admitted to herself. The Ministry hadn't wanted her input when she was accessible. *Why make it easy for them to contact her now?*

It wasn't as if she was hiding. Or could hide if she wanted to. Thanks to the nans injected into her bloodstream by Nikolai Trojanowski, her DNA signature had been replicated and concentrated in her liver and bone marrow. As a result, finding Mackenzie Connor—or her remains—anywhere on Earth took only the right equipment and motivation.

Mac shrugged. *Old news.*

Of course, right before the injection, which had hurt like hell, there had been that kiss. She traced her lower lip with a finger, imagined a tiny scar. There had been anger. Blood. Perhaps passion. Certainly, regret.

More old news.

She focused. *Owls.* There might be a recorder stored somewhere in the cabin. Or she could buy one when she went for supplies. Fresh-baked bread would be nice.

Mac pushed the swing into motion with one foot, having made enough plans for one night.

May in the great boreal forest shared one thing with the same month in Castle Inlet. *Life, getting on with life.* Mac shut the screen door on a horde of disappointed black flies and shook the remaining hitchhikers from her hair. It never failed to amaze her how the insects all seemed to emerge, ready to feed, on the same day. At least it meant hummingbirds and swallows wouldn't be far behind.

"Mackenzie? Mac? It can't be! *Bienvenue, ma petite!!!!* I can't believe it."

Mac was swept into a tight hug every bit as warm as the voice. "*Bonjour,* Cat." For an instant, she let herself indulge in feeling safe, of being known and loved without question, then pushed gently to free herself. There was no safety, even here.

But there was Cat Palmer.

The proprietor of Little Misty Lake General Store stepped back to study her with those bright blue eyes. Joke was that Cat could not only see in the dark, she could see a kid "thinking" how easy it would be to tuck that chocolate bar or fishing lure into a pocket. Kind eyes, with the puckered corners that sun, snow, and frequent smiles left behind.

Kind eyes that began to frown at what they saw.

"Place hasn't changed a bit," Mac said, looking away.

Cat shook her head, its tight curls barely up to Mac's shoulder, and grinned. "Who wants it to?"

The General Store sat where a point divided two coves. Sand and pine needles competed to cover the real wood of its porch and steps, while a gentle shoulder of granite sat companionably close to the east end of the one-story building, so those inclined could clamber up and eat fresh-baked pie while watching for loons. From the doorstep, a zigzag of uneven boards led to the water's edge in either direction. Going west brought explorers to where a small river entered the lake, sandbars and isolated clumps of reed grass framing its mouth. Moose wandered out at dusk, leaving plate-sized footprints in the sand below the water. Going east, a rickety dock floating on barrels stretched out in welcome to where the water was dark and deep enough for diving. It was presently owned by a pelican and several mergansers.

In deference to the waterfowl, dozing in the morning sun, Mac hadn't used the dock. Instead, she'd run her canoe on shore, then lifted it out to lean against the logs set along the beach for that purpose. Accommodating birdlife was tradition here. Any day now, swallows would start colonizing the roof overhang. Cat would fuss and pretend to chase them away, all the while keeping track of how many returned and how well they built their nests.

Inside, the store was a maze of too-close shelves, some filled until they appeared ready to fall, others half empty, as if they'd forgotten what they were to hold. Tourists dropping in to buy bug repellers, ice cream, or tent mem-tape invariably stayed longer. Their children found treasures. Maps to the best fishing holes, eyeballs painted on stones, balls and archery sets in brilliant colors, those card games no one bothered to play at home that kept everyone up at night here, gadgets that must be useful, if only you knew what they were. Cat would offer homemade cider and conversation while the children— and, truth be told, most adults—explored in fascination.

There were local crafts as well, fruits of those who spent the long, short-dayed winters here. Russell Lister, Cat's husband, couldn't say no to any budding artist. Some of those mercifully one-of-a-kind items had been on the shelves as long as Mac could remember.

She picked up a dusty ceramic pig, the eye that wasn't winking aimed at the ceiling, and grinned. "Still here?"

"I don't think Russ could bear to sell her after so long," Cat chuckled. "Now come. Millie sent over a batch of her Chelsea buns. They're still warm."

"Extra walnuts and cranberries?"

"*Mais oui!*"

Mac followed Cat to the end of the store where three hand-made tables competed for window space with a stuffed black bear. The bear was so old its fur had started falling out; years ago some-one had taken pity on the beast and applied a sticker to a bald spot. The whimsy became tradition and now the bear's glass eyes peered wistfully from a coating of funny slogans, comic book char-acters, beer ads, and sparkly place names from all over the world.

And beyond. As Cat grabbed mugs of cider to add to her tray, Mac squinted at the bear's left ear, now covered in a pale yellow sticker inscribed with lettering that looked faintly hieroglyphic.

"Imported," Cat confirmed proudly, taking a seat. "We've started to get a fair amount of traffic from 'out there.' Good spenders. Some of them, anyway."

Aliens. How small they'd made the world. Mac traced the sticker with a finger. "Ferry brings them?" she asked curiously, trying to wrap her head around the non-Human making the trip through the locks in that little boat. Once the ice broke up, Little Misty Lake, and the other rivers and lakes associated with this watershed in the heart of Ontario could only be accessed by canoe or on foot. An essential part of its allure.

"No. We take them tripping from here." Cat pushed over a plate barely wide enough to contain the bun, let alone the syrup and melting icing that oozed down its sides. The confection smelled even better than it looked.

Mac's mouth watered, but her fork paused in mid-assault. There had been only one kind of trip leaving the General Store when she'd last been on the lake. "As in canoeing and camping?"

A brisk nod. Cat was already into her first bite. Around it, she continued: "Russ worked out a deal a few years back with the IU, letting us advertise. He and Wendy—that would be Wendy Carlson, you haven't met her yet. Wonderful girl. Comes up each season. We let the consulate make sure whoever's coming can physically sit in a canoe, walk up paths, be out in full spectrum sunlight, breathe the air—the basics. Russ and Wendy pack whatever odd things have to be in the diet, but that's all the fussing we do. Portage with their own packs, paddle with the rest, sleep on the ground."

Mac blew nutmeg-scented steam from her mug and narrowed her eyes. "So how do the aliens get here in the first place?"

Cat winked. "At night, using one of those pricey stealth levs—the kind that no one notices." A sip of cider. "No complaints yet." She laughed at Mac's expression. "Don't look so scandalized, Mac. As if it's never been done before!"

Only in a bloody emergency! Mac thought, then her own lips twitched. "Sam used his skim more often than not," she relented. "He couldn't stand how long the ferry took." She'd tease him about being impatient; he'd counter about wasting time. The memory was like pulling on old slippers found in a closet, comforting and warm. Startled, Mac took too big a bite of her bun, syrup running down her chin, eyes smarting. Her only worry coming here had been facing the pain of such memories.

Not that the pain would be gone.

"He had plans," Cat said matter-of-factly. "Places to go." Her fingers touched Mac's, once, with understanding. "And he got there. That's more than many can say."

Swallowing, Mac wiped her mouth with a cloth napkin embroidered with mosquitoes, another craft success, then blinked hard to clear her eyes. "You take aliens canoe-tripping," she pointed out. "I doubt anyone else can say that."

If her voice showed any strain, Cat kindly pretended not to notice. "Probably not," she smiled. "You should come on the next trip. Be fun. We could use you."

"Thanks anyway," Mac said firmly. "But I'm up for some peace and quiet, not looking to shepherd novices through the bush—any kind of novice."

"C'mon," coaxed Cat. "You get along with aliens."

"I do?"

"Didn't you get pretty close to that—what was he called—Dhryn? We heard how he helped you during that attack, the one at that place you work. Everyone was so worried."

Mac's blood turned to ice. *Here,* she thought desperately. *Even here. Like a contamination spreading through her life.*

Cat misunderstood Mac's silence. *"Ma pauvre petite,"* she breathed, eyes wide. "What was I thinking, to mention that terrible time, to upset you? I'm so sorry. Here, have more cider. Let us talk of other things, happier things. The bears are awake. I saw a sow with three fat cubs just yesterday. Mac? Mac, don't go."

Mac had stood. "I'll be back for my supplies," she managed to say. "Thank you for—for the cider and dessert."

Cat stood also. She nodded, lips together in an unhappy line, but didn't speak. Another of her gifts, to know when silence was the only answer.

Mac went out the door, pulling it closed behind her. She ignored the clouds of hungry black flies competing to land on her face and ears.

She went straight to her canoe, launched it.

And paddled as if the Ro were behind her.

Three days passed. Mac aired the bedding on lines strung between the pines, keeping an eye on the squirrels to be sure none decided to snatch pillowcases for themselves. She flipped the mattresses in all nine bedrooms, twelve in total, and found only one more nest, this of mice and most certainly occupied, thank you. After relocating the litter and aggrieved mom to a new home in a box of rags, Mac swept the floors.

She tackled the shelves and rafters next, tying together some fishing rods and more rags to reach as high as possible. The windows had to be washed three times on both sides before recovering any sparkle. Cleaning the eaves troughs required a shovel and snips, since they'd acquired not only debris but healthy clumps of goldenrod and several optimistic tree seedlings. She caulked the gap under the doorsill leading into the kitchen, likely the entry for most of her current roommates.

The kitchen and indoor washrooms were in the best shape, likely because both had been used more recently than the rest. Still, Mac spent a morning scrubbing until every surface gleamed.

By the afternoon of the third day, she'd run out of chores. The powered systems had functioned normally from the moment she'd arrived, receiving a feed from North Bay Generation as well as solar backups contained in a pine that wasn't anything of the sort, the device so well camouflaged it hosted a raven's nest every year. Not that much in the cabin required power: a few lights, a boxed furnace which could sit in the fireplace and heat the main room if necessary, water pumps for the washrooms and kitchen, a huge walk-in chiller—presently empty—and a stove, though old, that would have been the envy of the cooks at Base. Dr. Connor Sr. liked to cook.

Not something she'd inherited, Mac grinned as she sat on the swing, now made cozy with clean cushions, and popped the top of a self-heating chili.

There was also a receiver. With an effort of will, Mac had left it wrapped and in its cupboard. The weather station on the outhouse roof would give ample warning of natural and programmed storms. Out here, anything else she'd need to know would be announced by shout from a passing canoe—eventually. She'd spent too many hours trying to eavesdrop on the universe. *It could function without her attention for three weeks.*

Besides, how could she trust the news? Ascendis had been attacked without a ripple of attention. *Better,* she decided, *not to try and sort lie from truth.*

As Mac ate, she admired the porch, brightened by rugs, its screens now free of years of pollen and dust so the breeze from the lake moved lightly through. Black flies and their ilk beat helplessly against those screens, attracted by her warmth and breath but unable to enter. No matter. They could afford to wait. She'd be going out again.

Mac curled her spine deeper into the cushions, feeling the pleasant burn of well-used muscles along with the occasional twinge. *A swim before bed would be just the thing,* she decided.

Tomorrow? Back to the store to apologize and get her supplies. She'd overreacted. "Hard to find peace in a place if you don't bring some with you," Mac informed the black flies.

She'd found a measure of it, tidying the place. Dirt and grime put things into perspective. They didn't belong; effort removed them. The final result was comfort for herself and pride of accomplishment. *Not to mention sheets free of eight-legged friends.*

The sun, about to dip below the southwest shore of the lake, touched fire to water and turned tree trunks to gold.

"Nice one," Mac approved.

Then, while the light lasted, as she'd done every quiet moment alone, Mac pulled a folded sheet of mem-paper from her pocket. Technically, she wasn't supposed to have a copy of Emily's message, if it was from Emily at all and not the Ro using her friend's face as some sort of signature. Or extortion.

Technically, the message had been erased the moment 'Sephe had wiped Mac's imp. Who hadn't been able to promise she could tell Mac its meaning, or if it could be understood by anyone at the Ministry.

Mac opened the sheet, holding it to the remaining light. The red symbols, aligned in columns, each intricate and no two obviously alike, meant nothing to her. From the onset, it had dashed that faintest of hopes, that the damage to the language center of her brain might actually be useful. She had no other resources or knowledge to even try to decipher whatever it said.

But making a clandestine copy for herself the moment she'd returned to Base? *Nothing easier.* "The Ministry should have enlisted students, Em," Mac said aloud.

No to mention have more respect for print.

Mac refolded the sheet and tucked it away. *Silly, to feel better having it.* "Probably a grocery list gone astray."

Or, finally, word from the lost.

The lake breeze was starting to carry a chill. Mac picked up her empty container of chili and went inside.

The moon was below the horizon when Mac walked down the hill to the cove. She didn't need its light anyway. The stars were enough to pick out the familiar path and her bare feet quite adequately informed her of the difference between moss, wood, and stone.

And they found sand.

Dropping her towel, Mac brushed away the solitary mosquito singing in her ear. Early for them. She'd waited until the black flies settled for the night, the chill air of May more than they'd tolerate, but there was always something hungry out here.

She walked into the water, blood-warm at the very edge from the day's sun. Her first few steps were through fine floating debris, the black sawdust and old leaves that drifted up against the narrow beach. Her next steps, the water cooling as it rose to her calves, were over small, sharp pebbles and the occasional larger, smooth stone that she avoided, knowing how slippery each would be.

Thigh-high and out of the shadow of the trees. Bitter here. Her skin tightened in reflex, hairs rising, and Mac's feet began to numb, though the upper water remained warm to the touch. She stretched out her arms, dappling the still water with her fingertips, real and otherwise, watching the ripples stir the stars laying in the lake.

For the water was more than calm. Except for where she touched it, the lake might have vanished, replaced by perfect reflection. Mac stood in the center of a sphere of stardust, divided only by the utter black silhouette of forested hills.

There'd be mist in the morning. She could taste it starting to curl into the air.

In a single swift motion, Mac drew her hands over her head and dove.

She kept it shallow, wary of rocks below. And no more than an arm's length below the surface, the lake was winter-cold. The lightless chill of it drove the air from her lungs and set her heart hammering. It was like some potent liquor, heat following the shock of taste. The water became satin to her skin, slipping between her fingers, catching on her palms, sliding along her sides and legs.

Mac rose with a sputtering gasp. *Awake now,* she grinned and rolled over to catch her breath, leaning her head back in the water so more of its heat escaped, taking tension with it. It was just possible to float with most of her in the relatively warmer layer. She relaxed and looked up at the stars . . .

. . . only to see them blotted out by the hull of a rapidly descending and very silent lev.

6

CANOES AND CONVICTIONS

"**S**HE'S OOZING red liquid. Is that normal?"

"Idiot. It's internal fluid. Blood."

"What about the oozing? Is that normal?"

Mac lifted her head to glare at her new guests. "Yes. No thanks to you." She went back to picking gravel from her right knee, thoroughly scraped when she'd swum frantically toward shore to evade the landing lev and managed to beach herself like a deafened whale. *There was,* she shifted uncomfortably, *gravel elsewhere,* but she wasn't removing her towel to find it.

Not in front of the three sitting in the common room, staring at her.

Well, Russell Lister wasn't staring. He was doing his utmost to demonstrate that not only wasn't he staring at Mac now, he most certainly hadn't been staring at Mac when the lev's floodlights had pinned her as she climbed out of the water.

At least the lights had helped her find her towel.

The lev, a monstrous self-important beast too large to land anywhere on the sloping land around the cabin, presently floated in the cove, its driver staying with it. Mac, wrapped in towel and dignity, had tried to ignore it as she limped up the path. But the others had followed her up here anyway, without invitation. Or warning about the eroded section. There'd been a fall or two.

Shame the porch door didn't lock.

"A light was on, Mac," Russell began. "I didn't think you'd

be—" He blushed crimson, something that appeared to fascinate his companions.

So much for not *looking.*

North woods protocol: a light meant an open door and willing host. Mac couldn't very well argue the point, having left a small lamp aglow in a window in case she'd needed a guide on her return through the trees. "I'm here now," she said, taking pity on the man's obvious distress.

Like his wife, Cat, Russell was a fixture on Little Misty. The couple had operated their store and guided canoe trips into the various connected waterways for over seventy years. A little weathered by time, like cedar grayed by the sun, but Mac had no doubt both could still outpaddle, outhike, and outlast any incoming camper, including herself.

Gracious, gentle people. Friendly, with a quiet reserve.

Mac finished cleaning her knee and glanced at Russell suspiciously. *Not to mention insatiable gossips with a wicked sense of humor.* It wouldn't be long before the man's embarrassment faded and the night's little exposé was thoroughly embellished—and shared all over the lake.

"It's okay, Russ," Mac gave in. "What can I do for you?" Her eyes slid to the two sitting together on the biggest couch and she automatically switched from English to Instella, the common language of the IU. "What can I do for all of you? My name is—" she hesitated, well aware cultural norms varied. *Then again, this was her family's cabin.* "—Mac."

The alien to the right gave a deep bow, its trisegmented torso letting it fold a disturbing amount while seated. It wore a beautifully embroidered caftanlike garment in shades of browns and golds, large and billowy enough to reupholster the couch. *It did a great job of concealing anatomy,* Mac thought curiously. Shorter of the two, the fabric-covered alien possessed a broad face, wider than it was high—Mac supposed she could call it a face, though there were no features showing through the mass of shaggy gray hair that covered head, neck, and shoulders. A pair of jointed eyestalks protruded from the hair on either side of the head, a purple beadlike eye at each tip. The upper eyes on both sides were looking at Mac. The lower "eyes" were lidded and to all appearances taking a nap.

Its voice was a smooth, immaculate tenor. "We are pleased to make your acquaintance. We are Mr. Kay and Mr. Arslithissiangee Yip, respectively. And how are you today, Mr. Mac?"

Before Mac could do more than blink, the other alien belched and announced loudly: "Fourteenth. You never introduce me properly. It's Arslithissiangee Yip the Fourteenth." This alien was close enough to humanoid norm to be wearing a Little Misty Lake General Store cap and sweatshirt, extra large, complete with leering moose on the chest. Close, but not that close. The alien's eyes were side by side, but too small, almost embedded in folds of sallow skin. The nose stuck out a little too far, and had a hard shiny surface. The mouth, however, had full lips, shaped like a Human ideal of sensual beauty. *Well,* thought Mac, *they would have been the Human ideal except for their color.* They were either naturally beige or the alien had made an unfortunate choice in cosmetics, given they parted over four yellowed teeth and a forked, white tongue.

Mr. Kay produced a pair of gloved hands from within the voluminous caftan outfit he wore and proceed to groom the hair down the front of his "face" in an agitated manner. "Having a number as part of your name is ridiculous. Mr. Mac does not. I do not. Mr. Lister does not. Mr. Carlson does not. Mr.—"

"Irrelevant. Irrelevant! IRRELEVANT!"

Mac and Russell exchanged looks as the aliens bickered. He shook his head and shrugged. She sniffed as a pungent odor that had nothing to do with pine trees, chili, or cleaning fluids began filling the room, then glared at the aliens. One of them, Mac decided, had released something.

Hopefully, it wouldn't stain the couch.

"Excuse me."

The two ignored her. "Fourteen!" "Do you require I give out your ident number too?" "Idiot!" "You're the idiot!"

Mac tightened the towel across her chest and stood up. "QUIET!"

The one who'd called itself Kay managed to look smug despite the hair.

"My name is Mac, with no 'mister,' " Mac told them. "I've got your names, including the number," she added quickly when Ar-slithissiangee Yip the Fourteenth opened its mouth. "Now, I'd like to know why you're here." Her look of inquiry included Russell Lister, whose fault this most likely was.

Sure enough, he was the one who answered. "These gentlemen booked a trip with us."

"Gentlemen" either answered the gender question, Mac thought, or Russell was guessing.

"So?"

"Five days and four nights. We're portaging into Crow Lake then taking the Sagani River over to that fabulous stand of—" Russell stopped as Mac frowned at him. "It was a last minute booking. They've arrived too early. We can't head in until Friday morning, so—"

"Oh, no," Mac interrupted, aghast. "Don't you even—"

"It's only two nights, Mac. We don't have room at the store and you have all these beds. Cat sent you supplies . . ." This last was delivered with a pleading look.

Two purple eyeballs on stalks and two beady ones did their best to copy it.

Mac gripped her towel and eased her weight off the leg with the throbbing and skinned kneecap.

"The place looks great," Russell added. "You've really cleaned it up."

A hairy head and a becapped one nodded.

If only there wasn't a standing tradition on Little Misty of sending overflow guests to the bunkhouse-style cabin of the Connor family. If only locals like Russell, lonesome after the winter, comprehended that not everyone wanted company.

If only she didn't owe Cat a few dozen favors, including an apology for her abrupt departure . . .

She was going to regret this.

"Fine," Mac growled. "Two days."

"Our thanks, Mac." Mr. Kay reached into his caftan and pulled out a small box, holding it up triumphantly. "And look! I obtained a game of cards from the store in anticipation of our time together."

The second alien gave a hum that sounded downright blissful. "There are numbers."

Okay, Mac thought, scowling at Russell, who was trying—and failing—to keep a straight face.

Already regretting it.

Mac threw her pillow into the air. She'd tried putting it over her head. Hadn't helped. Was it some kind of rule that aliens had to snore? Loudly, arrhythmically, and with alarming pauses as if one or the other had suddenly died? She should have known better than to put them at opposite ends of the cabin. The two front corners might be the largest, best rooms. It didn't matter an iota when she was the one inflicted with stereo snoring.

Mac lay on her back and studied the beams meeting overhead. The moon was up and full, bright enough to pull color from the old quilts on the walls. The racket had probably cleared the nearby woods of anything that could run, including moose and bear. The idea had its appeal.

Then a particularly piercing whistle, followed by a moist sputter and rising moan, made her giggle.

Mac covered her mouth with her hands, hoping their hearing wasn't as good as hers. But it was no use. She gave in, laughing so hard at each new improbable snore that tears poured from her eyes and her heels drummed the mattress.

Finally able to stop, though she still snickered helplessly every so often, Mac got up and sat on the bench under the small window.

What were they? She'd done her best to learn more nonterrestrial biology, but the number of intelligent species, let alone their spread beyond their original planets, made it impossible to know them all. If only she'd brought her imp, she could have accessed the considerable library she'd amassed.

And if wishes were horses, Mac nodded to herself. "I'll ask," she said aloud, wiping a last tear from one eye. "If it offends them, Em, they can leave. If not . . ." *Oh, she knew that itch—her curiosity was fully engaged.* Mac could no more ignore it than stop aliens snoring.

Then another thought widened her eyes. Mac hugged her knees to her chest and considered it.

She kept her promises. But was it her fault that no one, Ministry agent or otherwise, had ever asked her to not question a couple of alien campers about what was happening beyond this system? Casual questions, of course.

Seen any Dhryn lately?

There was no humor left in Mac's smile.

For some reason, falling asleep took no more than a return to bed and snuggling under the covers.

When Mac next awoke, it was to the drumming of rain on the roof. A reprieve, of sorts. She knew perfectly well Russell hoped she'd show Kay and Fourteen, as she'd come to think of the other alien, how to paddle a canoe. It wouldn't be this morning, unless the sky cleared.

She listened as she dressed. No snores, but a promising clatter from the kitchen. Mac pulled an old sweater over her head and fluffed her hair into a semblance of order—as much as the short, curly stuff ever had these days. Times like these she missed her obedient braid, sacrificed in *grathnu* to a Dhryn Progenitor. She'd been so proud of herself that day. Mackenzie Winifred Elizabeth Wright Connor *Sol.*

She'd believed she was close to understanding the Dhryn.

Fool.

And now, when she least expected it—and hadn't asked for it— she had a new batch of aliens to attempt to understand. *When was the universe going to remember her field was* salmon?

"They'd better not want any hair," Mac grumbled as she went downstairs in search of her guests.

The aliens were, as she'd surmised, busy producing breakfast. The long table, with its top of scarred maple, was set for three at the near end. Fourteen was pouring coffee while Kay stood in front of the stove, stirring something. Mac sniffed cautiously. Despite the condition of the path to the cabin, they'd brought up a considerable amount of baggage, including a crate of 'their' food packed in unidentifiable round packages, most of which had gone in the chiller. She'd learned to be wary of extraterrestrial diets.

Another, bolder sniff. *Bacon?*

An upper eyestalk bent backward, aiming its purple eye her way. "Good morning, Mac!" Kay greeted without leaving his task. "How are you?" He might not have a visible face, but his voice conveyed friendliness. *Always assuming,* Mac thought as she entered the kitchen, *a concept like friendliness meant the same to them both.*

"Fine, thanks. I hope you both slept well?" If there was a certain irony in the question, Mac felt it was deserved.

Fourteen looked up, his small eyes bright. "I hate sleep." Without his Little Misty River cap, she could see he possessed a fine down of reddish hair in a ring on the top of his head. It made him look more Human, one of those who chose to go bald with maturity. Yesterday, Mac had assumed these were young beings, perhaps adventurous students or wealthy offspring after an Earthly thrill. Now, she wasn't sure. "Sleep wastes time," Fourteen informed her. "Coffee?" As Mac nodded, bemused, he snapped at the other alien. "This cooking of yours wastes time, too. I told you to use something ready-to-eat if there wasn't any *poodle* to be had."

Mac blinked, then realized it must be a word without an equivalent in Instella. Still, good thing her Great Aunt Roxy, whose house swarmed with dog-type poodles, wasn't in earshot.

Kay seemed unperturbed by Fourteen's complaints. He turned with a large skillet in one hand, a spatula in the other. "It's ready."

Mac was about to protest she'd make her own, thank you, "poodle" or otherwise, when she saw what was in the pan. Scrambled eggs, fried tomatoes, golden-brown potato slices, strips of bacon. They'd all been in the supplies Cat had sent for her, the store owner foolishly optimistic in thinking Mac had finally learned to cook for herself. "Wonderful," she said weakly, sinking into a chair.

Fourteen finished pouring her coffee, then grabbed a basket of toast from the counter and placed it on the table between them. "Eating wastes time," he announced firmly, but sat as well.

Mac's mouth watered as Kay filled her plate. If it wasn't for the elongated, many-knuckled fingers gripping the spatula, light pink out of their gloves, and the faint, not-unpleasant dried hay smell of the being leaning to serve her, she might have been sitting down to one of her father's meals. That and the hair, which at this range proved to have fine strands like very tightly wound springs, more metallic than gray in color. It moved more stiffly than Human hair, too, and Mac wondered how it felt.

Without thinking, she lifted her hand to find out, then realized that might not be particularly tactful and reached for toast instead. "Looks great," she said truthfully.

Dividing the rest between himself and Fourteen, Kay joined them at the table, sitting to Mac's right. "Please, Mac. Enjoy your breakfast. We don't wait on ceremony," he assured her.

"I'd guessed that," she replied, glancing across the table at Fourteen, who was using a fork in each hand to deliver huge mouthfuls one after the other. Despite having front teeth, he wasn't, Mac concluded, chewing. Just shoveling and swallowing.

Kay's lower two eyes remained closed. Now the lids wrapping his upper ones did the same for a brief second, as if in exasperation. "You must forgive my companion, Mac," he said. "He does know table manners, I assure you." This last forceful and directed at Fourteen.

"Waste of time," came the reply, between rapid forkfuls of potato and egg. "Irrelevant."

Kay, on the other hand, waited courteously for her to start, so Mac took a bite of the egg. It was hot, fluffy, and flavorful. Perfect, in fact. She smiled and nodded at him. "Great," she repeated, having no problem being emphatic.

"Just wait until you taste supper," he assured her, seeming pleased by her reaction.

Trying not to be obvious, Mac kept glancing at him. *How would Kay deal with the hair in front of his face?*

He didn't have to, she discovered. The alien drew open the front of the caftan he wore, the same or identical to last night's garment. The fabric draped as though heavy and stiff but moved as easily as silk. His chest, below the hair hanging down from his head, was hairless and smooth, cream-colored except for a blue-tinged tattoo of what appeared to be a pair of eyestalks staring longingly at one another with lettering between, and a horizontal crease of skin marking a second waist, halfway up his torso from the first.

The crease opened by itself, like the mouth of a recycle bin. Mac's fork, with its delectable morsel of fried tomato, paused in the air a few centimeters from her mouth.

Kay picked up his plate and, using his knife, scraped its contents into the cavity in one tidy swoop. Next, he poured in his mug of coffee. Almost like an afterthought, he took a spoonful of honey from the jar on the table, and carefully dripped the sweet after the coffee.

The crease closed, Kay retied his caftan, then sat back. "Tasty. I do enjoy Human food."

"Just don't forget your supplements," Fourteen reminded the other. His own plate was empty, exhausted forks lying across the middle. "Ready? Let's not waste time."

Both aliens looked at Mac.

She finished putting her fork into her mouth, drew the now-cold piece of tomato from it with her lips, and chewed very deliberately, enjoying the flexibility of her tongue. She swallowed.

"You might want to play some cards," Mac suggested.

"Go fish."

"You 'go fish' yourself."

"You are withholding information."

"Never said I had the—" pause, "—purple spotted fat one with a hat. Go fish."

"I will not. I have counted the numbers! You have the card I need!"

"Do not!"

"CHEAT!!"

Mac shook her head and dried her hands. The argument in the next room was growing louder by the minute. She was sorry she'd even suggested they play. *Aliens.* Hadn't even helped with dishes.

"Is there a problem?" she asked, standing in the door of the kitchen. "Oh."

There were cards everywhere, including two stuck in Kay's hair. *And that smell again.* Mac wrinkled her nose.

"Trisulians always cheat," Fourteen informed her in a tone of vastly offended dignity. "It is their nature." Since he was the one balancing on a table, hands paused in midair, Mac didn't have to guess who'd flung the deck.

"We pride ourselves on flexible strategy," Kay rebutted, feeling for the cards stuck to his face. "That is not cheating. You, on the other hand, are a fine example of Myg predictability. I could tell your every move from the beginning. Boring. Boring."

"CHEAT!"

"BORE!"

"The rain's stopped," Mac announced, walking between the two glowering beings to open the door to the porch. "We could—" she winced inwardly, "—canoe."

The ensuing silence could only be described as shocked.

Mac turned back around. "You did come here to go tripping," she commented. "A little practice now will help."

Fourteen scrambled from the table. His center of gravity appeared more to the rear than a Human's, Mac observed. "But there was a storm!"

She glanced outside again. Beams of sunlight were beginning to slice downhill through the trees. The trees were dripping, but beyond that, she could see the water of the lake. Sparkling and peaceful. "Weather's fine now."

"We're not ready." This from Kay, who moved to stand beside Fourteen almost protectively. Almost, since the top of Kay's upstretched eyestalks barely reached the height of Fourteen's humanish ears. "And there must be preparations to make first. Many preparations."

"All taken care of," Mac assured him, starting to enjoy herself. "You two can easily fit into a regular canoe and we've several under the porch. Russell left personal repellers, on the off chance you end up in the lake. Just be in clothing you don't mind getting wet—"

They spoke in unison. "Have none." "Left mine in the lev."

Mac's eyebrow rose. Any of her former students would have recognized the look, the one that meant they'd better formulate a new approach now, or she'd do it for them.

"Then strip," she said firmly.

Stripping hadn't been necessary after all. In the face of Mac's determination, Kay had admitted his garment could withstand immersion if necessary. Fourteen had rummaged through the spare clothes Mac's father kept in a trunk until he found some that fit. They were a little musty, but the alien didn't seem to mind—or perhaps couldn't tell.

Oh, for a recorder, Mac wished. Between Kay's mane of overgrown hair and brown-bronze flowing caftan, and Fourteen's proud donning of a faded orange Ti-cats' football jersey and paisley shorts—which revealed rather too much of his lumpy calves— her eyes hurt.

But finally the two stood, albeit with obvious reluctance, beside their canoe. Mac's was nearby. She planned to go out with them, neither having been very reassuring about their ability to swim.

If she didn't know better, Mac wondered, having shown each how to hold and use a paddle, *she'd think canoeing was the last thing they wanted to do.* But they'd paid to go wilderness tripping with Russell. He wasn't going to give them time to adjust to life on the water. It would be heigh-ho, a full day of paddling to go. The least she could do was provide a few pointers.

"Fourteen, you get in the stern—that end," Mac told him after floating the canoe into the cove. She stood in water over her knees and held the craft in the middle, bow just touching the beach. The rain had eliminated the warm surface layer, so the sunshine was very welcome. "Climb down, keep yourself low, hold the sides. That's it. Easy. One step at a time."

Once the alien was turned and seated, he gripped the gunnels of the canoe as if it would tip any second. "Did you call me 'Fourteen'?"

Oops. "Sorry—" Mac tried to remember all the syllables of his name.

"Efficient. I shall be 'Fourteen,' on your world."

"Glad you like it," she said, relieved, and handed him a paddle. "Hold this across the canoe. Don't move till I say so. Kay, your turn."

The second alien, the Trisulian, took a quick step back. "The boat appears unsteady. It is dangerous."

"Idiot." Fourteen gave a loud belch and brandished his paddle in the air. Mac grabbed the canoe just in time. "I—the boring one—am already in position. What danger is there? Are you not 'flexible'?"

"Kay, you have to eventually," Mac coaxed, trying not to shiver as her blood lost heat to the water's chill. *Think hot, humid July,* she told herself sternly. "It's the only way to travel these lakes. You came a long way to do this. C'mon. I'm here. Take it slow. You'll enjoy it. Trust me."

Kay kept shaking his head. Hard to say if that meant no, or if he was trying to dislodge the black flies that clung to his every hair. Knowing the morning would involve passing through clouds of the wee things, Mac had hung a camouflage disk around her neck, and clipped one on the repeller belts each alien wore. The small devices emitted a compound that confused the sense organs of the insects so they couldn't decide where to land. The disks worked almost as well as Cat Palmer's legendary ability to sit outside all day without a bite.

Well, except on poor Kay. He'd continued to attract black flies as if exuding sex pheromones. The insects were particularly enamored of his eyestalks. All four were coated in tiny black specks, as if dipped in mobile pepper. *No sign they impaired his vision, but that had to be annoying.*

"No black flies out on the lake," she offered. "They prefer land."

Ah, Mac thought triumphantly. *That did it.* Kay went toward the canoe. He moved like a timid deer, arms up and back as if to keep as far as possible from the craft until the last possible moment, each footstep a painfully slow edge forward.

Fourteen began bouncing up and down with impatience, almost dumping himself and splashing Mac up to her chin.

"Stop that!" she snapped, teeth chattering in earnest now. Calming her voice, she continued: "Hold the sides and step into the middle, Kay."

For a wonder, both aliens did as they were told. Mac made sure Kay was turned and securely seated, with a paddle in his hands, before she pulled the canoe around to point out into the cove. She gave it a gentle push into deeper water. "Remember what I showed you about paddling. Try it now. Gently. At the same time, if you can."

Their first strokes weren't bad for amateurs, Mac decided. No flailing about or splashing. Not too much power. Reasonably straight. "Very good," she complimented, then added: "Just don't argue."

Mac hurried to shore to launch her own, smaller canoe. She didn't bother to dry off before jumping in to follow. The sun would do that.

As they left the cove, a curious loon took one look at the canoeful of nonterrestrials and submerged.

They may have hesitated and fussed, but the two of them worked together well. Their canoe left a zigzag wake, but was heading in a more-or-less consistent direction. Mac studied the movement of their arms and shoulders, comparing them with her own. Similar body parts, able to perform similar functions. Perhaps there was more muscle layering Fourteen's shoulders, but Kay, though shorter in height, had reach on him, and what appeared to be a more flexible elbow.

Mac called out some instructions; they listened and began moving in a straighter line. *Quick learners.* She had to dig into her paddling to keep up.

She was sure Kay and Fourteen had never canoed before, Mac mused as she eased into the soothing rhythm of reach, pull, twist, and hold, but judging by their ability and the way they carried themselves in general? She might not know the norm for their respective species, but she'd bet both were active individuals among their kind, able to use their bodies well—perhaps exceptionally so. Hardly unexpected in anyone who would travel light-years to camp in an alien wilderness.

Why make such a trip? she wondered. *Didn't their worlds have wilderness?*

Mac had only experienced two alien planets, both Dhryn. The first had been Haven itself, the world where the Dhryn Progenitors, mothers of their species, lay deep underground. Haven's surface had been totally urbanized, every square centimeter containing only the Dhryn and their buildings. The second? She had no name for it. The planet had been the Dhryn home world, before a cataclysm stripped it of all life, leaving wind to carve its haunted, dust-coated ruins. A cataclysm repeated throughout the hundreds of worlds of the Chasm.

The Ro claimed the Chasm had been caused by the Dhryn. That they'd destroyed their own world. That unless found and destroyed first, the Dhryn would wreak the same havoc throughout known space.

Green drops dissolving flesh. Mouths that drank . . .

Mac shuddered. She had sufficient nightmares—she didn't need them in broad daylight, too. "Keep to the shoreline," she told her pupils. No need to shout; sound carried admirably over the calm water. Fourteen lifted his paddle in acknowledgment and almost tipped their canoe. Mac winced, but they righted again. "And watch for logs and rocks," she advised.

She'd given them the novice craft, glad to have found it under the porch instead of borrowed yet again. It looked like hers, though a bit larger and heavier, being cream-colored with memwood seats and gunnels. Novice craft, however, had certain additional features. There was a keel that expanded downward if a strong broadside wind was detected, giving more control. If they struck anything, the canoe's bow would absorb the impact and, if they tipped too far to one side suddenly, the canoe would release a stabilizer bar to recover itself. *Not that she'd told them.* Russell's canoes were like hers, the classic dance-with-me-or-swim type. Kay and Fourteen might as well start thinking that way.

So far, the two were doing fine. As they entered the next and wider cove, Mac let her mind drift again. *Alien wilderness.* Until now, she'd focused on learning about various aliens and their cultures. There had to be so much more. There had to be worlds different from the Dhryn's, worlds like this one, with life everywhere you looked. She rested her paddle on her lap and gazed over the side of her canoe. Streams of tiny light-touched bubbles rose from the silt as bacteria digested debris. A twisted thumb-wide furrow led to a mollusk where it sat, pretending to be a rock. Fish fry—barely more than eyeballs and tail—skittered through the bubbles; their shadows flying over the shell.

What would she find in a lake on another world, under another sun? Mac shivered, not because she was still cold, but with the sheer delight of it.

Mac dipped her paddle again, shattering the view. The Dhryn. They were the puzzle. *How could such beings even exist?* She could comprehend, if not envy, those who lived apart from other living things. The Dhryn she'd met had fed themselves with cultivated fungi, simple organisms refined into an industrial process. There were Human colonies on inhospitable worlds who lived much the same way.

For that matter, she knew a few individuals on Earth who managed to live as though they were the only life on the planet.

"But we didn't start that way, Em," Mac whispered. "We can't survive that way. Not without technology to replace all this—" She gazed over the lake, up at the sky with its fading wisps of gray clouds, down again to the tree-fringed shore.

The IU had sent archaeologists to the Dhryn home world. Good as far as it went, but Mac had urged them to send those who would look much farther back, to when the first Dhryn had floated toward its prey. "There's an answer, Em." She nodded to herself, once, firmly. "There's a way being a Dhryn, how they live, all of it, makes sense."

Not that she had the faintest notion what that could be.

"Yet," Mac promised herself.

While distracted, she'd temporarily lost sight of her charges. Like all beginners, they'd learned to pick up speed before developing skill at maneuvering. Unworried, Mac sent her canoe around the next point, only to frown. No luck. She was about to activate the finder beacon—another handy aspect of a novice-level canoe—when she spotted a familiar brown and orange well past the next island, bobbing in the now-choppy water of the middle of the lake.

More speed, but less sense of direction.

Mac shook her head and paddled after them.

"Kay complains the world continues to move up and down, side to side. Along with his *douscent*."

"His what?"

Fourteen pursed his generous lips in thought, then gave a nod. "His pouch-storage-assimilation organ."

Mac didn't know how well Fourteen could read Human expressions. To be on the safe side, she arranged her face into something sympathetic. "Sounds as though he's seasick—a sensory conflict due to the motion of the canoe over the waves. If that's it, Kay should be better shortly." *A Human would be, anyway.*

Her compassion was wasted. "Irrelevant. He's a coward," Fourteen declared, "even for a Trisulian. Afraid of being hungry. Afraid of high places. Afraid of moving water."

Why the little . . . "You took him out there on purpose," Mac accused.

A sly tilt of his head. *Not quite a yes. Not quite a no.*

"Flat water is boring. Waves are fun." Fourteen settled deeper into the couch, stretching his arms along the back. His expression could only be called smug. "Kay ate too much Human food this morning and refused to take medication before our paddling. He has only himself to blame. Idiot."

Mac hoped this meant the Trisulian would be able to manage rough water during their trip with Russell. Otherwise, it was going to be a very long and unpleasant five days for all concerned. Except perhaps for Fourteen, apparently vastly entertained by his companion's discomfort.

At least she had her chance to talk to one of the aliens alone. She would have preferred Kay, simply because he had better manners. *And there was that smell.* Mac was reasonably certain it came from

Fourteen when he was agitated. *So don't get him upset,* she warned herself, resigned to whatever happened.

Mac draped a leg over one of the fat arms of her chair and made herself comfortable. It wasn't easy, when she felt anything but relaxed. "While we wait for Kay's *douscent* to recover its equilibrium, Fourteen," she said casually, trailing her fingers along a line of mending in the fabric of the other chair arm, "mind if I ask you a few questions?"

"You may ask, but there will be none of this—" Fourteen thrust his pelvis up from the couch with great vigor. Three times. It was quite a display, given the oversized paisley shorts. "Impossible. I don't have external genitalia," he explained.

Emily, Mac knew, *would be convulsing with laughter.* She, on the other hand, could feel her face flame with embarrassment. "I didn't—"

"I'm well aware of the Human preoccupation with copulation with aliens, Mac. Do not seek to deceive me. There was a brochure."

"A brochure," she echoed.

"At the consulate. It strongly recommended informing any Human making advances that I state an appreciation of the implied compliment but explain I am physically unable to participate and would prefer to be left alone." Fourteen paused. "I didn't waste time with the appreciation part. I don't feel complimented by your lust."

Mac blinked. "My lust."

Fourteen threw up his arms in what appeared to be exasperation, then clambered to his feet. "If you are so desperate for the act, I believe Trisulians have some capability. We will go to Kay and obtain his service for you."

"That won't be necessary," Mac assured him. "I—" Then, her eyes narrowed in suspicion. "I've taken a drug to subdue my carnal urges," she said matter-of-factly. "Being here alone?" Mac gave a theatrical shudder. "It would be so very—difficult—otherwise. I'm sure you understand. It must have been in the brochure."

It was his turn to blink at her.

Fourteen's mouth suddenly stretched in a huge grin, revealing that his teeth consisted solely of four squared incisors on top and a chitinous ridge along the bottom, with that disturbing white tongue lashing between. His inset eyes opened as much as they could as he gave a harsh barking sound Mac had no trouble translating at all.

When Fourteen finally stopped laughing, he claimed: "I had you! I had you!"

As if she'd admit that. Mac raised one eyebrow. "Not for a millisecond."

The alien pointed to the door to the west bedrooms. "We can try it on Kay. C'mon. C'mon." He was bouncing on the couch, his splay-toed bare feet slapping the wood flooring.

"No." Mac threw her other leg over the chair arm and slouched deeper. "And no. Just how immature are you?"

"As immature as I want to be," Fourteen asserted, sounding slightly offended. "I'm on vacation."

Mac grinned. "I can't argue with that. Though I confess I'm wondering why you've come all the way here. To Earth, I mean."

Fourteen dropped back down on the couch, looking pleased by her question. *His knees,* Mac noticed, *were another almost Human feature.* If you ignored those extra lumps on the insides. They sunburned like Human knees, too. He'd come prepared, she'd give him that, slathering an ointment over his reddened skin when they'd arrived back at the cabin. A bright green ointment with what appeared to be flecks of sand in it. *Positively alluring,* Mac chuckled to herself, *with the paisley shorts.*

Fourteen held up his five-fingered hand, folding a digit with each item. "Earth has exotic landscapes . . . varied cultures, hardly touched by those of other species . . . the legendary politeness of Humans . . . a most favorable exchange rate within the IU. And—" Fourteen paused, one finger still straight, and looked at her as if trying to read her face.

"And?" Mac prompted, fascinated by this view of her world. *Exotic? Polite?*

Another voice answered—Kay, from where he leaned one shoulder against the doorframe.

"And Earth has you, Dr. Mackenzie Connor."

Without realizing she'd moved, Mac found herself behind her chair, her hands gripping its back for support. Common sense had her eyes flicker to the door to the porch, estimate her chances of getting there first.

Curiosity held her still.

"Not on vacation," she stated.

"Unfortunately, no." Fourteen sat up, his posture subtly different. *The hand-me-down Human clothes,* Mac thought, *no longer looked quite so silly.* He reached into a pocket of his shorts and brought out an envelope that looked remarkably familiar, except that its blue and green was barred with gold. "The Interspecies Union is hosting a gathering of experts on our common problem, the Dhryn. We wish you to attend, Dr. Connor."

"Mac," she corrected automatically, while such fierce joy burned through every part of her, she had to struggle to keep it contained, to hold her expression to something resembling curious interest.

At last, a chance for answers.

"Mac," the Myg smiled. "Efficient as always. Please excuse our small deception. Mr. Lister will be paid in full, but we never intended to take his trip. We had to come in person. Our invitation was not reaching you through, shall we say, regular channels."

Why was she not surprised? The taste was bitter, as was the certainty others would have known about this—and how desperately she'd want to be part of it. "Then how did you find me?" Mac answered her own question: "You're spies."

Kay, weaving slightly, made his way to the opposite chair, sitting with a groan. "We are not spies," he denied stiffly. He reached for a cushion and pressed it to his abdomen. "*Usish.* The room keeps moving."

"Irrelevant," Fourteen snapped. "Do not withhold meaningful information. Mac should know how we found her."

Did she really want to know? A faint mental alarm went off. Ignoring it, Mac eased around her chair and rested a hip on the arm nearest the door. "It would be a nice gesture of mutual trust," she suggested. "Something I could use about now."

The two looked at one another. Kay's eyestalks dipped and rose. As if this signaled permission, Fourteen began. "Since your government would not let us contact you directly, nor pass along our invitation, we arranged for an individual in your facility to notify us when you left for your research in the mountains, somewhere we could contact you discretely, privately. We thought we'd lost that opportunity when the 'quake struck, then you came here. Everything was perfect!"

"*Perfect?*" Mac could argue the word choice, considering it encompassed an IU spy among her colleagues and students at Base. *Not to mention if these two had walked in on her at the field station, she'd have sent them packing so fast eyestalks would have spun.*

Fourteen offered the envelope. Sure enough, her name crawled across the surface in mauve. *Just like last time.* Then, it had contained a letter from the Ministry, proclaiming a threat to the species and requesting her help—the sort of request no Human would refuse, or could, without the most severe penalty.

Mac eyed the latest incarnation, but made no move to touch the thing. Yet. *Learned my lesson, Em.* No matter how badly she wanted to be part of what was happening, *to know*, she wasn't going to jump blind again. "Where is this gathering taking place?" she asked.

"Irrelevant," came the reply. "Even if we knew, it would be kept from you until reaching our destination. For security reasons."

"Do you object to travel offworld?" This from Kay.

Mac's fingers dug into the upholstery, the fabric a little worn and dusty. Worn by Human use. Dusty from the processes of life on this planet. Familiar. *Home.*

"No," she said calmly. "I'll go wherever I must." She didn't bother asking for a guarantee they'd bring her back again. In Fourteen's terms, it was irrelevant.

Instead, Mac took the envelope in her hands, feeling its familiar metallic texture between her fingers. She drew a breath, then prepared to rip it in half.

"What are you doing?" With that cry, Fourteen tried to snatch it back.

Mac hung on, startled. "I'm opening it."

"Violence is not necessary. Apply any body fluid." Kay then pressed the cushion tighter to his abdomen as if the idea offended his *douscent*.

"Ah." With a doubtful look at each alien, and doing her best to forget the envelope had come out of those paisley shorts, Mac touched the moistened tip of her tongue to one edge.

It unfolded in her hands like a flower, the envelope itself becoming a flat sheet of multisided mem-paper. Its now-white surface was coated in black text beneath the seal of the IU. But as she adjusted her grip to angle it toward the light from the nearest window, the words winked in and out of meaning, sentences fragmented. The more she tried to make sense of it, the less she could understand. It was Instella, the interspecies' language. Mac was sure of it. She should be able to read this with a little work.

Should and could were different things.

Rather than shout her frustration—*and reveal her ongoing issue with print* —Mac casually folded the sheet, which reformed into a sealed envelope in her palm. "Fine," she said. "When do we leave?"

"As soon as I inform the IU you are ready and willing—"

"Not so fast," Kay groaned from his seat, eyestalks tilting in different directions. "Some of us aren't up to moving vehicles."

Fourteen pursed his lips and made a ruder noise than usual. "Idiot. I told you to take your medication. Your discomfort is irrelevant. As soon as I inform the IU, arrangements will be made—including notifying your government, Mac, and the helpful Mr. Lister. Tomorrow would be the earliest for all to be in place. More likely the day after that." He made an expansive gesture at their surroundings, then bounced where he sat. "But is this not an excellent place to wait? We have Mac. And we have *poodle*!"

Kay muttered *"Usish"* again and turned his eyestalks from the exuberant Myg.

Mac tucked the envelope from the IU into a pocket, fastening it closed with a press of the mem-fabric. *One thing to be swept up in the moment, Em. Another to have time to think things through.* She hoped her courage would last two more days.

She slipped her leg over the arm of the chair and sat down. "What else can you tell me about this gathering?"

"It is unprecedented—if you are familiar with the politics of the IU . . . ?" Kay let those words trail into a question. Mac shook her head. "Ah."

"Idiot," Fourteen said promptly. Mac wasn't sure if he meant his companion or her. "All you need to know is that everything about the IU, everything it does, has a shape." His hands described a series of circles, each larger than its predecessor. "At its center are the oldest species, the ones first to the group. The Sinzi, of course, are at the core. Together, these are the decision-makers. Outside of this lie those species who are well trusted by the oldest and are wealthy, or wield some other power. These are asked to carry out those decisions and to communicate them to others. Beyond are all those species come recently to the transects, who haven't proved either economic worth or stability. Informed, but rarely consulted."

"This is the political position our two species share with yours, Mac," Kay broke in. "It would normally remain so, but our systems lie along the Naralax Transect. The IU realizes we must be all included—perhaps even in the innermost councils. This is what is unprecedented." He sounded more exasperated than grateful. Mac could understand that reaction.

Fourteen laced his fingers together, as if in prayer. "You see, the Dhryn are not some nebulous threat to us. They wait on our doorsteps, ready to strike either of our worlds next. Indeed, our closest trading partner, the Eelings, recently succumbed."

"I'd heard Ascendis was attacked. A Human ship was there—it sent a report." *Before it crashed and everyone died or was consumed by Dhryn,* Mac reminded herself, breath catching in her throat. "I don't have the details. What happened?"

"The Eeling light has been extinguished forever," Fourteen's lips trembled and he put his hands over his eyes.

"By the Dhryn?" Mac demanded sharply.

"The Human ship finished the job of destroying Ascendis," said Kay, his voice growing cold and harsh. "To their credit, many of the—feeders—were caught on the surface. But the planet can no longer support the life it knew."

Feeders on the surface . . . Mac shook off the horrific image, focusing on the puzzle. "I was told the Dhryn left the system."

"There was no one to stop them."

Mac leaned back and stared at the ceiling rafters, seeing something completely different, a world made of flesh. "Dhryn wouldn't leave without their Progenitor," she mused out loud. "So she wasn't on the planet when Captain Wu sent his ship into it. But why?"

"Isn't it obvious? They wanted to be able to leave quickly. As they did."

Mac looked at Kay. "Nothing," she warned him, "is obvious about the Dhryn."

"Except the destruction they leave behind," he countered, upper eyestalks rigid. "The only Eelings to escape had crowded into sublight ships and scattered through their system to hide. They are delicate beings, Mac, too delicate for such stress. Most died before they could be found and rescued. Those we did save were taken to our systems, Trisulian and Myg, but a pitiful few are of breeding age, even if they have the will. The Eelings didn't colonize other worlds."

Fourteen dropped his hands, his eyelids glistening with moisture. "It is the end of a vibrant species."

How could the mind comprehend a loss on that scale? Mac didn't even try.

"Worse than that," added Kay. His fingers were busy combing the hair down the front of his head. *A nervous habit*, Mac decided. "We fear—" he made a sharp quelling gesture when Fourteen opened his mouth as if to protest, "—we fear our systems will be next. We'll either feed the Dhryn, or become the chosen battleground where they are fought by the IU. That we will lose, no matter the outcome."

Bureaucracy. Hierarchies. When survival was at stake, Mac thought sadly, *how soon they could become a threat instead of protection. How little the parts could seem to matter, when the whole was in peril.*

She studied the two of them. Whatever else, she had no problem reading the anxiety in their body language—no matter how alien, they shared that peculiar tension of limbs needing to move but forced to wait. "Then we'll have to trust this gathering will think of safer alternatives." Mac tapped her head with a knuckle. "It might just be a case of digging out the right idea."

Fourteen lunged from the couch to grab Kay's arm. "Hurry!" he urged. "There are knives and a spatula in the kitchen!" He peered at Mac. "Perhaps a spoon."

Kay's left eyestalk twisted to glare at him and he shook his arm free. "Mygs have the most inappropriate sense of humor," he said to Mac.

Mac didn't quite smile. "It helps, sometimes."

"Exactly." Fourteen rubbed his palms together, then slapped them on his knees. He cried out and lifted his hands again. From the shocked look on his face, he'd forgotten both sunburn and ointment.

"Now that's funny," Kay announced, eyestalks waving.

Mac sniffed. *Sure enough.*

"Why don't we continue this on the porch?" she suggested. *Where there was fresh air.* "You go ahead. I'll make some coffee and bring it out."

Without waiting for an answer, Mac stood and went to the kitchen. Her hands were trembling as she lifted them to push open the door. She frowned at them. *This was no time to be thinking about a devastated world and its survivors.*

Yet she couldn't help remembering . . . Brymn had come to Earth, sought her out for one reason. Mac's work with salmon considered populations in terms of genetic diversity; she calculated evolutionary units, the minimum amount of diversity required for a group to respond to evolutionary stress without going extinct. The Dhryn . . . he'd asked her about determining the evolutionary unit for an entire species. For a world.

Without knowing what was to come, what he'd become, Brymn had desperately wanted to know it was possible, that she could produce a number, reveal some formula to show how many must survive, in order for some to continue.

Mac pressed her forehead to the door and closed her eyes.

They'd both been so dangerously ignorant. He'd asked for the sake of his kind, fearing their persecution by the Ro, sensing an approaching doom. She'd become his friend, begun to work on the problem, only to learn, too late, it wasn't the Dhryn who were threatened.

But what if Brymn had asked the right question, after all? Mac thought. Not about any one species. About the Interspecies Union. That population. That diversity.

How few species could it contain, and survive? At what minimum would the transects between systems fail, if they weren't first destroyed to keep out the Dhryn?

What if Earth was alone, again?

Mac shoved the door open with all her strength.

The resulting bang didn't startle the man sitting at the kitchen table, who merely leaned back in his chair.

"You do keep interesting company, Dr. Connor," Nikolai Trojanowski remarked.

- Encounter -

THE IMRYA fleet waited with the patience of their kind, settled into position where the Naralax Transect was locked into their system's space, orbiting Mother Sun with the other transects' mouths like one pearl among many. A perilous black-hearted pearl.

Such disturbing analogies were produced each day and posted throughout the fleet, from engine rooms deep in the bowels of every ship, to the suites of the battle cruisers where officers maintained households, from navigation arrays to the galleys. For the Imrya were a lyrical folk, renowned for their poetry as well as the interminable amount of time it took for them to get to any point in conversation.

Trade negotiations with non-Imrya were best accomplished by remote.

Months ago, an Imrya outpost had been decimated by Dhryn. Not that they'd had a name for the attackers back then. Imrya newscasters had spent weeks composing anguished rhapsodies about an unseen terror, an unimaginable power able to eat through safety seals and make entire crews simply vanish as if they'd never existed.

But now the IU had named this fear, that name and warning sent to all. The Imrya, as befitted a species who had contributed to the IU for generations, one of the strong arms upon which all depended, had received even more. Details of ship structure. Potential weaknesses. Unconfirmed rumors of attack strategy.

Warning that where the Dhryn had been, they would come again.

If the Dhryn dared return, the Imrya fleet would be ready.

Watching the poisoned fruit in their orchard.

That which is Dhryn feels fear, knows dread, but not of others.

There is only that which is Dhryn.

All else . . . *sustains*.

That which is Dhryn fears time, dreads distance.

Being too slow? Losing the Taste?

Either ends the Great Journey.

7

PRODIGAL AND PROBLEMS

MAC QUIETLY CLOSED the kitchen door behind her and latched it. *What did it say about her that her first thought on seeing Nik again, here and now, no matter what else was on her mind, was "yummy"?*

Emily would agree, of course. The Ministry's favorite spy was dressed camper-casual: a faded brown shirt with long sleeves rolled to his elbows and open at the neck, shorts, and sandals. The clothes revealed a pleasing expanse of tanned skin and the working of lean muscle. His brown hair had grown out its office trim, reaching his collar at the back, and was now more waves than curl. No glasses hid his hazel eyes, but a charmingly scruffy beard framed what was almost a smile.

Yummy.

Mac coughed. Her second thought: *keep it safe.* "Is this an official visit?" Cool, a little formal.

She thought he'd been about to rise and come to her, only to check the impulse as she spoke. *She was probably mistaken.*

For her part, Mac concentrated on the spot of floor beneath her bare feet, a spot she had no intention of leaving without answers. "Well?"

"No," Nik said, putting his arm on the table and rubbing the tabletop with his fingers. *If it made any sense,* Mac thought, *she'd swear he looked shy.* "I had some personal time coming."

As if she believed that . . . Mac focused. "Which doesn't explain why you're here."

"No?" The word invited fantasy. Mac felt herself blush. *Wood floor. Toes. Wood floor. Toes.*

"No," she echoed.

"I got a report about the quake. I wanted to see for myself if you were okay. Are you?" This last with concern.

How odd, Em, Mac said to herself, *to be almost more afraid of an answer than of asking the question.* She steeled herself. "Did you cause it, Nik? Did you destroy the ridge?"

"Oh." A wealth of comprehension in one syllable. "No, Mac," Nik said finally. "It wasn't me."

She hadn't been sure. It might have been a wild guess, a slip toward the paranoia she feared as much or more than anything else. To counter the tendency of the floor to betray her and tilt, Mac laid her hand on the side of the nearest cupboard. "So it wasn't natural. Those—" She launched into a lengthy description involving several unlikely acts and more than a few unprintable adverbs.

"Feel better?" Nik asked when she paused for breath.

"I knew it! An earthquake? How bloody convenient—for everyone but us."

"And our people on the mountain."

"What? Oh, no." Remembering those visored heads looking up at her on the mountainside, Mac stumbled to the chair next to Nik's. *There had been over a dozen.* "How—how many were trapped?"

"Luckily, only two. Robillard and Masu were guarding the Ro site. When the quake hit and the slide followed . . . they didn't have a chance."

"No, they wouldn't." Without thinking, Mac reached for his hand where it rested on the table and laid hers on top. "I'm sorry, Nik."

His hand turned, fingers wrapping around hers. Mac met his eyes as they searched her face, felt herself drowning.

Time stopped.

"Mac!" from the other side of the door. "Are you coming? Where's the coffee?" A rattle. "Why won't this idiot door open?"

"A spill. I'm washing the floor behind it," Mac explained, pitching her voice to make it through the hefty door. "I'll be right out,

Fourteen." She stood. "Have to go," she told Nik, starting to pull her hand free.

His resisted.

That and his smile did disturbing things to her sense of priorities. "Careful or I'll introduce you," Mac said.

"Later." Nik rose, still holding her hand, then brought it to his lips, pressing them to the inside of her palm.

"Will you—" His beard tickled her wrist, the sensation rushing up her arm. Mac blamed it for the quite remarkable difficulty she was experiencing putting words together. "Aren't you staying—" she heard herself say and flushed crimson. "I didn't mean—"

"Kay needs something for his *douscent,* Mac," the alien bellowed. "He says any bovine secretion will do, but he prefers ice cream. Idiot should have taken his medication when I said so." The voice faded, as if Fourteen muttered to himself as he walked away. "What's a vanilla, anyway?"

"Trisulian, I take it," Nik said.

"And a Myg," Mac sighed. "If I leave them alone too long, they'll get into an argument, there'll be shouting, the place will start to reek—you probably know who'll do that—and then stuff will be thrown around . . . it'll be worse than the last day of class, trust me."

"Always." Nik's eyes laughed down at her. Her lips twitched in response.

"It's good to see you," she confessed. *And it was. No matter why he'd come.* Emily would doubtless have something to say about that.

Nik traced her jaw with a light finger. "I promise I'll be back tonight. Probably late."

"Good thing we don't lock doors up here."

His teeth gleamed. "Think that would stop me?"

Mac put her hands on his chest and pushed gently. "What I think is that any minute now two aliens are going to break down that door in search of vanilla ice cream and coffee. Go. From the sound of it, we're here until tomorrow at least."

As easily push a cliff. "You're leaving with them?" Nik glanced at the closed door then down at her with a darkening frown. "What the hell's going on here? What do they want? Who are they?" He started to walk past her and she grabbed his arm. It was like iron.

"I don't have to tell you," Mac said quietly, "what you already know." Without letting go, since he seemed as tightly wound as a spring—*posturing or real?*—she used her free hand to open her pocket and pull out the envelope. "You came to stop me from accepting their invitation. You're too late. I'm going." She offered it to him.

He took it, all the while staring at her in obvious dismay. "Oh, Mac."

She swallowed her pride. "When you come back tonight—if—I need you to read that to me. Please. I can't."

"And you still agreed to go." Harsh.

"You knew I would. You—" She bit off the accusation that wanted to tumble after; there was no gain to it now. "Even if I'd wanted to say no—how could I? You know what's at stake, Nik. We all do."

"All I know is that you have a limitless capacity to worry me, Mackenzie Connor."

"That's never been my intention." Her hand, her real one, lingered on his arm, trapped by the heat of his skin, the texture of fine hairs, the corded strength beneath her fingertips. "I'd rather—" Mac stopped herself just in time, snatching her hand away. *Emily was the bold one; she wasn't.* "—I'd rather make coffee," she finished breathlessly, heading for the pot. "And you, Mr. Spy, should get going before you're seen."

Looking over her shoulder, Mac found herself alone in the kitchen, the back door sighing as it closed. She put both hands on the counter and leaned forward, shaking her head ruefully. "And how brilliantly smooth was that, Em?" she asked.

Did he guess what she'd almost said? What she'd wanted to say? Did she even know?

"Seasick alien on the porch," Mac reminded herself. "Serious questions to answer and ask. Saving the universe tomorrow."

She hadn't believed in the coincidence of Nikolai's arrival—less than a day after her new guests—any more than she'd believed in the earthquake. *Right on both counts, Em.*

But if she occasionally thought "yummy," Mac decided, *that was nobody's business but her own.*

The first interspecies' problem of the afternoon was, predictably, Emily.

The second, less predictably, involved poodles.

Mac took a long swallow of her beer and kicked the swing in motion. While she'd been inside, making conversation and coffee, the aliens had rearranged her porch. Kay, understandably not fond of swings at the moment, had brought out one of the overstuffed comfy chairs from inside. Fourteen, who probably did like swings, was not to be outdone, and had somehow maneuvered one of the couches through the door.

As befitted a proper porch gathering, they'd all switched to beer when the sun was low enough to hit the back wall, and were now too warm and comfortable to budge.

The two had listened eagerly to her synopsis of her experience with the Dhryn, asking few questions, seeming impressed—and occasionally dismayed. Now, however, both were firmly stuck trying to comprehend one aspect: Emily—or rather, Mac's continued loyalty.

"Dr. Mamani remains my friend," Mac insisted, trying to find the right phrasing. "Emily—" *lied and betrayed,* "—acted on behalf of the Ro in order to try and stop the Dhryn. I—we—hope she's still safe and with them. It's perfectly normal Human behavior."

Fourteen chugged his third bottle in one long swallow, then belched for an impressive five seconds. "Perhaps 'friend' in Instella does not convey the Human meaning of the word, Mac."

Back to that again. "Perhaps," Mac said, doing her best not to sound testy, "you could convey to me why finding a word to define my relationship to Emily matters, Fourteen. I keep telling you, we have shared experiences, we feel affection. We look out for one another. We get angry; we forgive mistakes. Call that combination whatever word you like and let's move on."

"The clarification is important, Mac." Kay, who'd been alternating scoops of melted ice cream with dollops of beer into his *dous-cent—which must be about to explode by now*, Mac judged—paused to wave ineffectually at the halo of black flies that had somehow passed the screens to find him. "We need any clue to help identify those of our respective species who might be, like your Emily, affiliated with the Myrokynay—the Ro."

"You believe they've recruited individuals from other species in the IU?" Mac considered this, then shrugged. "Maybe. But there's the issue of the Ro technology—I explained how Emily required an implant in order to communicate with them, to help her tolerate how they travel." *Her fine olive skin, rent along one arm to reveal the depths of space and wheeling stars where flesh belonged.* Mac blinked away the memory. "That's your best way to identify their representatives. But it's likely something not every species could integrate into their bodies."

"We neither believe, nor disbelieve, such recruits exist," Kay replied. "We can't discount the possibility. Such individuals could help us talk to the Ro, convince them to protect us. If the Ro prefer to find those who already claim loyalty and trust like yours, it is somewhere to start."

Mac stared into the forest for a moment. She had to squint to see past the tree trunks to the glitter marking the lake. "That won't help you," she said heavily, turning back to her companions. "Emily was working with the Ro long before we became friends. I didn't tell you—I didn't think it was important." *And still hurt.*

She kept it simple. How Emily had cultivated a rapport with Brymn, how she'd learned of his interest in Mac's work, how she'd managed to be hired at Norcoast, how she'd cultivated Mac as a colleague and as a friend—

Her voice faltered.

"That's enough, Mac," Kay said quietly. "We've no wish to cause you pain. At least, now we know you were right. The word 'friend' in Instella will not bring us any closer to those who work with the Ro."

Fourteen had pressed his hands over his eyes as Mac told her story. Now he dropped them down to gaze at her. "Your Emily did not have to become your 'friend,' Mac," he said. "She could have arranged what she did and still kept her distance from you, safe from exposure or compromise. Perhaps you were what she couldn't resist."

This, from a being who set speed records eating or drinking, and belched or released noxious fumes without warning? "Thank you, Fourteen. You are very kind."

The alien looked embarrassed. At least, that was how Mac interpreted the irregular pink blotches along his cheekbones. *One never knew,* she reminded herself. "Irrelevant," he barked. "It's time to take a break. Have supper. You ready to make some *poodle*, Kay?" To Mac, "This will be such a treat."

Kay's upper eyestalks had developed a droop. *The beers or time of night,* Mac judged. Now they shot erect. "Is this the right time? I thought we were going to save it."

"Idiot! Save it for what? What better time than now? With what our new friend, Mac, will share at the Gathering about our enemy—not to mention your success with the canoe? Tomorrow will be soon enough for more words, words, words, words!" Fourteen bounced on the couch with each repetition. Mac, listening to the creaks of protest, hoped the old furniture survived the alien's gusto. "Tonight, we party! We must have *poodle!*"

Kay patted his middle, having tucked away his *douscent*. "I am a little hungry," he admitted. "And I promised Mac a memorable supper."

So much for Human/alien relations, Mac decided, stopping her swing. "You really don't have to go to any trouble for me," she said cautiously. "Save your supplies."

"Idiot!" Mac supposed it was a positive sign that Fourteen now freely applied the term to her. "It is our duty to share with you the best of what we have brought." His beady eyes narrowed to tiny slits. "Or are you not familiar with *poodle?*"

Kay stood, smoothing his caftan and straightening the mass of hair tumbling over his face. "You insult our host, Fourteen. Mac is an intelligent, cultured being. Of course she's had *poodle* before— no doubt prepared by the finest Human chefs. I will have to make an extraordinary effort to compare. Extraordinary." With that, he strode into the cabin and Mac could hear his determined footsteps heading for the kitchen, presumably to be "extraordinary."

Mac glanced at Fourteen, who was looking insufferably pleased with himself.

They ate her food. How bad could theirs be?

Given her past experience with non-Human sustenance?

Good thing there was a med kit in the cabin.

"Humans didn't invent outdoor cooking, you know."

Plomp. Mac's stone hit a ripple and sank. "We were searing our meat on grills long before the first transect," she countered.

Fourteen took aim and launched his own pebble into the cove. *Tic . . . tic . . . tic . . . plop.* "Five!"

"You can't count the initial toss as a skip. Four."

They were sitting on the small stretch of sand that Mac's father proudly called a beach, having been banished from both the kitchen and the brick barbeque in the clearing behind the cabin.

It seemed "extraordinary cooking" required privacy and concentration.

"Irrelevant."

Mac found a nice flat stone and tried again. "What's irrelevant?" *Tic . . . tic . . . plop.* "Three."

"That your species has a long record of outdoor cooking. You originally obtained that technology from us, the Myg. Your own history tells of our visits." *Plomp.* "Doesn't count. That was a defective rock."

Mac snorted. "Let me guess. There was a brochure at the consulate."

Another of those sly looks. "Don't you believe your own mythos? That aliens have been here before?"

"Oh, those guys. They were looking for virgins in cornfields." *Tic . . . tic . . . tic . . . tic . . .* Mac lost count and whooped triumphantly. "Beat that, Fourteen!"

The alien made a show of shading his eyes and looking outward. "Beat what? I was watching this small creature dig in the sand. What do you call it?"

Mac gently bumped her shoulder into the alien's. "A beetle, and I win."

"Are there virgins in your fields?"

"All the time. We call them heifers."

Laughing, Fourteen wiggled his bare toes. They were wider at base than tip, so they looked more like miniature fingers than the Human version. Mac noticed he used them quite readily to sift the sand for skipping stones. "You are joking with me again, Mac."

"Maybe so," she said peacefully, resting back on her hands. "Tell me, Fourteen. What do you think of Earth? Of this place?"

He joined her in gazing out at the lake. The sun was about to set, its last rays seeming to calm every ripple. Near the shore, the dark water was already glass-smooth, except where water striders—and skipping stones—briefly disturbed it. A series of expanding rings marked the rising of a fish. Black flies skimmed the beach; midges danced in self-obsessed clouds.

As if on cue, the loon gave its throbbing cry. It echoed from the trees on the opposite shore, then faded to a waiting hush.

"You don't want to know what I think of it," Fourteen said in a strange, low voice.

Mac turned to look at him. There was moisture along his thick eyelids. Noticing her attention, he brought up his hands, as if to hide it.

Not so alien, after all.

"There's an answer to the Dhryn," she promised him. "I believe we will find it. I believe we'll save our worlds—yours, mine, all of them." Hesitantly, unsure if the gesture would be welcomed by a Myg, Mac put her arm around his broad shoulders.

Fourteen's hands didn't budge, but she heard a muffled: "No external genitalia."

"No one's perfect," she laughed, then squeezed his shoulders lightly before letting go. "Shall we go and see if the *poodle* is ready?"

The hands came down as Fourteen shook his head. "Waste of time. Wait until Kay calls us. If we go too soon, he'll have us skinning the creature." A sniff. "Trisulians don't mind that sort of thing, but I certainly do." He seemed to perk up. "At least he bought it already dead. If you don't, they make so much noise—well, puts me off the meal, Mac, let me tell you. Then there's all the jumping around you get with live *poodles*. It's a mystery to me why Humans didn't properly domesticate this food beast."

Aha! Mac hid her smile by reaching forward to collect a handful of stones. *A game was afoot.* She had to admit, these two had come prepared to do their part enhancing Human/alien relations.

"First to seven wins," she challenged.

"So. This is *poodle*." Mac swallowed. "Sorry to refute your lovely compliments, Kay, but I can't say I've ever had it."

Two purple eyeballs, atop their stalks, and two beady eyes, within their fleshy lids, were locked on Mac.

The table was beautifully spread. Kay must have gone through every cupboard to find serving platters, fluted glasses, and a wide, if inexplicable, array of cutlery. There had even been a candle, although tying twenty birthday-cake candles in a bundle had produced more momentary conflagration than light for dining. Once the fire was put out, leaving only a minor and hardly unique scorch mark on the tabletop, they'd settled to enjoy their repast.

Repast was the word, Mac decided, admiring Kay's ingenuity. Her mammalian anatomy might be a tad rusty, but even she conceded a resemblance between the mass of meat and bone in the center of the table and a small dog. *If you pressed the animal flat and took other severe liberties with its skeletal structure.* Four legs, similar in size but not quite, jutted proudly into the air at forty-five degree angles. Where there logically would be paws, Kay had affixed ones of foil. *A nice decorative touch,* Mac thought.

There was no head. Perhaps that had been too tricky to reproduce. But there was a distinct tail, with a white pompom of what looked suspiciously like cushion stuffing at its tip. Complete with pink ribbon.

Other dishes held an array of vegetables and fruits. Some, Mac recognized, some she didn't—marking the latter down as to-be-avoided, tactfully, of course.

It was a work of, if not art, then artistic determination. Mac did her best to look dismayed instead of about to laugh. Personally, she had no problem eating anything if hungry enough—being a biologist studying a carnivore who ate the same way tended to instill a certain "fits in my mouth" mentality.

Her great-aunt, though, would have needed her new heart immediately, not next year.

"Let me carve you the first piece."

"That's not really necessary, Kay," Mac said, her voice sounding appropriately strained even to her. *If she didn't laugh soon, she'd choke.* "You go ahead."

Fourteen leaned over the table. "No, no, Mac. This is our thanks to you. Our treat. You must go first."

"Oh."

Kay took the sound as a "yes" and began sawing away at the carcass with the largest knife the kitchen boasted. He was careful to keep his facial hair away from the food.

The "poodle" had a crispy skin that parted with a puff of steam and clear fluid. Mac sniffed surreptitiously but couldn't smell anything over the nearby plate of yellow-spotted pickle-things.

Kay carefully freed a large piece of meat, laying it on a plate with great ceremony. He passed it to Fourteen, who placed it in front of her.

They waited, staring at her again.

Mac gazed at the offering and pressed her lips tightly together. *It was that or grin.* "I didn't realize poodle meat was white," she managed to say.

"It is 'the other white meat,' " Fourteen quoted proudly. "As proclaimed by one of your famous twentieth century authors."

Before she lost all self-control, Mac took her knife and fork in hand. Moving very slowly, conscious of her rapt audience, she pushed the tines of the fork into the meat at one end and even more slowly cut a morsel free with her knife.

Mac lifted the morsel to her lips and paused, looking at her guests.

Kay's eyestalks were bent forward as if that helped him see her better.

Fourteen was quivering, as if he wanted to bounce but knew that might be hard to explain at supper.

Mac smiled to herself and plopped the meat into her mouth, chewing vigorously. As she cut a second piece, she commented: "Tastes like chicken."

Absolute silence.

"Mind?" Mac reached over and violently yanked one of the legs free. She tore off a bite with her teeth, chewed and swallowed, then glanced up at the others. "That would be because it is chicken," she told them. "Or rather several. Nicely done, Kay."

"What do you mean, Mac?" that worthy blustered. "I bought this before we came. From a certified poodle dealer recommended by the consular staff!"

Mac gestured a denial with her drumstick. "Chicken."

"Idiot!" shouted Fourteen. "You should have checked before telling me you had obtained this rare delicacy. Mac, I am mortified."

"Because it didn't work?" she grinned.

Both managed to look crestfallen, Kay by drooping eyestalks, Fourteen by sagging in his chair.

"Don't worry," Mac assured them. "You would have fooled quite a few Humans with this—and any non-Human you wished. I have some expertise, you know."

Fourteen's sigh was heart-wrenching. " 'Aliens Eat Poodles' was number three on the Human-Alien Mythos list. I knew we should have picked something else."

"There's a list?" she asked dubiously. "You aren't still trying to trick me, are you?"

"There's a list, Mac." Kay began carving meat for himself and Fourteen. "The consulate maintains an impressive collection of anecdotal and verified instances of Human presumptions about the non-Human. The funnier and more preposterous of those is put into a list. Any visitor to your system gets a copy. It's partly for humor's sake—"

"And partly to improve understanding," Fourteen finished, taking his plate. "How better to learn to tolerate an unfamiliar culture than by knowing its intolerance about yours?"

Mac did her best to wrap her mind around the logic or its lack, then shook her head. "That list can't flatter humanity," she said.

"Trust me, you aren't alone. There are lists like this on most worlds," Kay told her. "But I will admit an obsession with alien sex ranks uniquely higher on yours. Care to explain why that is?" His eyestalks gave a suggestive waggle.

Fourteen belched. "She didn't fall for that one either. Don't waste your effort, Kay. Or your poultry-poodle."

The serious, albeit momentary, business of eating "poodle" began. As Mac expected, Kay was finished in the time it took him to fill and scrape his plate into his waiting *douscent,* with Fourteen a close second. As they stood, she pointed her fork at each in turn. "No cards. Dishes."

"But you aren't finished yet, Mac," Fourteen protested, his tone implying this was some adorable silliness on her part.

"Don't worry about me. I'll keep eating while you tidy up." As they looked to one another, then back at her, Mac firmed her voice. "Cabin rule. No one leaves this kitchen until it's clean."

Efficient when they want to be, Mac thought moments later, helping herself to more mushrooms after checking them carefully for otherworldly origin. Kay and Fourteen were making quick work of their task, despite the quantity of dishes and implements Kay had used. The subject of almost constant complaint from Fourteen, of course. Whatever Mac hadn't wanted to eat had gone in the chiller. The grill outside had been sprayed with enzymes to digest any attractive poodle bits before a bear came to explore.

Mac yawned and realized she was not only full, but tired. Standing, she collected her things and added them to the pile beside Kay. "This is the last of it. Thanks," she said, grabbing another towel from the drawer to help Fourteen dry.

The three of them doing dishes might almost be Mac, her father, and Sam. She smiled at the memory. Sam would be talking about space; her father, his owls; and she—she'd listen to both and dream her own dreams.

"This is a waste. You should install a recycler," Fourteen commented.

Kay nodded, shaking both head and hair. "Not that this isn't charmingly archaic, Mac."

"A recycler requires power," Mac explained serenely, taking the next dish. "We enjoy sharing a task. Sometimes, anyway." She nudged Fourteen. "On vacation—a different pace and way of doing routine things." *Although this wasn't what Kammie et al had had in mind,* she thought happily.

"Idiot. Better things than dishes."

Mac smiled and took a stack of dried plates to the cupboard. "We'll need them tomorrow morning at least." Fourteen had sent his signal; the answer about the lev's arrival to pick them up had been the predicted "as soon as we know, you'll know." "Probably for lunch."

"You are more than kind, Mac, to keep us in your home," Kay replied, his voice warm.

"Least I can do," she said. "If it's going to be another day, are you sure you have everything you need? If not, we can canoe over to the store."

Kay shuddered, his mass of hair adding to the effect. Fourteen laughed. "A most excellent notion, Mac," the Myg proclaimed. "We shall obtain more card games! Numbers! Numbers!"

Mac didn't ask her guests how much sleep they needed, sure that if they roamed around the cabin in the wee hours, it could hardly be any noisier than their snoring. They seemed content to bid her good night when she was ready for bed, both going to their respective rooms. Perhaps fresh forest air made aliens groggy, too.

After checking that lights were off and window screens were secure, Mac walked through the darkened main room to the stairs, knowing the way. She put her foot on the lowermost step and stopped cold.

"I'll be back tonight."

She'd done so well, managing not to think of Nik until now.

Of course, now was the worst possible time, when there was no one and nothing else to distract her.

Mac considered knocking on one of her guest's doors, then could almost hear Emily's voice in her ear: *Coward.*

Be that as it may, she wasn't doing much good standing paralyzed at the base of the stairs, her heart pounding in her ears so loudly she'd never hear a door opening anyway.

With a sigh, Mac brought her foot down. With this much adrenaline in her system, she'd never fall asleep. She tiptoed across the common room floor and out to the porch. There, she snatched her towel from the line by the swing and headed for the lake. *A cold swim should solve this.*

The walk didn't. A *rustle rustle* seemed to follow her all the way down. Mac knew it was most likely a raccoon hoping she'd brought a midnight snack, but it made the hairs on her neck stand on end.

When she reached the cove, she breathed a sigh of relief. The lake seemed waiting for her, its water calm, dark, and inviting. Mac checked the stars, although she was reasonably sure there wasn't another stealth t-lev full of aliens about to land. And for a wonder, the mosquitoes were cooperating, showing a distinct lack of interest in her skin—which would likely change by tomorrow, given the way the evening air was growing warmer.

She stripped and headed for the water, then froze. *Rustle. Rustle.* Without a second's hesitation, she grabbed her towel and wrapped it around her middle, tight as a corset, then sat on the cold sand.

What was she thinking!

Mac picked up and threw a stone. *Plop.* The water even sounded welcoming.

Not tonight, she told it. *Not with Sir Nikolai possibly wandering the woods.*

"Never liked those movies, Em," she muttered aloud. The ones where the heroine, regardless of anything else happening around her, would plunge naked into the first pond she could find and stay put until her prince arrived. Usually to plunge as well, given the seemingly irresistible allure of soaking wet heroine. Pushy, presumptuous, desperate heroines. Wet, pushy, presumptuous, desperate . . .

Not that Mac didn't fully appreciate the underlying rationale. *Gods, her breath caught at the mere thought . . .*

"Official business." She threw another rock and managed to

miss the entire lake with it, hearing it thud against a log. "Stopping me from finding answers, from doing what I can. Keeping me locked away at Base while the universe moves on. He's here to do his job. That's it."

All of which was true, Mac thought. *So why not take advantage . . . why not enjoy the night?*

"Because I don't want just one," she whispered to the rising moon. "I don't know how to want that. I always want tomorrow. Nights without end. Endless tomorrows." Emily had understood. She'd given up trying to talk Mac out of her grief for Sam. The dates she'd arranged, when Mac couldn't avoid them, had been with men who were fun and forgettable. Her type, not Mac's.

Emily had teased her about having a heart with two settings: don't care and forever.

Which would be more helpful, Mac sighed, *if hearts came with a switch.*

Without another look at the cove, she climbed to her feet and trudged back uphill to the cabin.

"Mac. Mac. Wake up!"

She'd slept through the alien snore-a-thon? Mac rubbed her eyes and fought to pay attention. *Who?*

"C'mon. Wake up!"

That voice—it was like a plunge in the cold lake. Mac found herself on her knees, staring at the figure sitting at the end of her bed. "Emily! What? How?"

"I can't stay, Mac. They're calling me back already." Was it the moonlight that made Emily's face thinner, sharper, turned her eyes into black gulfs?

Choking on a sob, Mac scrambled to reach her friend, but Emily stood and moved away. "I can't stay, Mac. Not until you read my message. Why haven't you read it yet?"

The mem-sheet under her mattress. Mac froze. "I've tried, Em. We've all tried. Just tell me what it says! Let me help you!"

Emily pointed to the window. "See what you've done?"

Mac swiveled to put her bare feet on the floor. "What is it?" she whispered.

"See?" Emily pointed again.

Humor her, something in Mac said. The woman's been living with the Ro for most of a year now, or however time passed for them. Another part of her whimpered in protest even as Mac pulled a sheet around herself and walked to the window.

And looked outside.

Whisper: "You should have read it, Mac."

She should have seen the forest, the moon. Instead, Mac found herself standing on a rocky path, under a morning sky. The wind was sharp and she clutched the sheet to her body. *Where—?*

The air splintered.

At first, Mac couldn't make sense of it. Overhead, on both sides, silver objects were flashing by. They were part of the wind, or its cause, a mass moving together until, in the distance, so many met they obscured what should have been skyline. Lines of smoke curled up, there were explosions . . .

Mac squinted then gasped. She knew that shape. Those buildings. That curve of shoreline. This wasn't some alien landscape. This was Vancouver. The university was right there—Kammie and the students—

Then the rain began to fall. Green and hungry rain. It fell in great sheets and torrents that would have hidden what was happening from her . . .

Except that it fell here, too.

The flower buds on the scrubs beside her dissolved and washed away, leaves following, branches bending then gone.

Something slowed above her; it cast a shadow. Mac lifted her head and saw the arms dangling, coated in silver except for their mouths.

Whisper: "Why have you failed me, Mac?"

Then green rain struck her face and washed away her screams . . .

"Mac! Mac, wake up!"

"No," Mac begged, "not again! I'm sorry, so sorry. Emily, please not again—"

"Mac!"

That *voice?*

Mac opened her eyes, finding herself soaked with sweat and supported half sitting by a grip on each of her arms. "Nik," she greeted the latest apparition on her bed. "I've dreamed you before, too. It never ends well."

She couldn't remember a dream where he stroked the side of her face, or pushed her hair back from one ear with a shaking hand. "I can't understand what you're saying, Mac," Nik said. "It's Dhryn, isn't it?" He swore under his breath as he released her arms, only to wrap his around her and hold her tight. *That was new, too.*

Emily paying her a visit wasn't.

The Dhryn consuming her city wasn't.

The burning of her flesh wasn't . . .

Shuddering, Mac burrowed against a chest she hoped was real and not illusion, listened to a heartbeat she hoped could drown out the screaming. As both stayed strong and steady, her shudders stopped and she began to cry. No mere tears, but deep, heaving sobs that burst from her lungs and tore her throat.

The arms stayed around her, held her close. "They told me you still had nightmares," a low, uneven murmur into her hair. "Shhh. It's okay, Mac. You're awake. I'm here. Really here." He rocked her back and forth, very gently. "Shhh." She felt a blanket adding its warmth to his. "I won't leave, Mac. Rest. Shhh. Just rest, now."

The voice faded into darkness.

8

MEANINGS AND MISGIVINGS

MAC OPENED her eyes and winced. *It hadn't all been a dream, then.*

So much for worrying about Nik finding her skinny-dipping in the cove. *Let's try that other cliché, Em,* Mac told herself furiously as she tried to extricate herself from his arms. Woman screams herself hoarse in her sleep until Prince Charming visits her bed.

If this was a vid, she would have waked prettily to his call, hair and skin perfect. She wouldn't have sobbed herself into a stupor, said sobbing likely including both mucus and horrible noises. And now a pounding headache.

His arm lifted, letting her scramble out. "You okay?" Nik said sleepily.

Mac clutched something—a blanket—to her and scowled down at him. He was still in yesterday's shirt, with long pants instead of the shorts. Bare feet. The hint of morning light through the window stroked shadows along the planes of his cheekbones and neck.

Even rumpled—still yummy, she thought, and had to smile. He smiled back.

"I'm—fine. Thank you. It's not usually that bad." *No, usually it was worse,* she told herself honestly.

Nik raised himself on an elbow, resting the side of his head on two knuckles and a thumb to consider her. "Want to talk about it?"

Mac hesitated, then asked: "Would it help?"

"I can't see how."

She was surprised into a laugh.

Nik winked. "See? Now that helped," he boasted, sitting with a smooth, quick motion that brought his feet to the floor. For some reason, she clutched her blanket and tensed. As if it had been his intention all along, he eased back against the wall, arms folded. *Deliberately neutral,* Mac judged his positioning. Training or sensitivity to her mood?

They didn't, she realized suddenly, *preclude one another.* "I need to know why you're here."

"Officially here?" An eyebrow rose and dared her. "Or here—" he patted the bed.

Mac refused to blush or dwell on the intriguing dimple starting to show in the light beard beside his mouth. "I know why you're— there." *In her bed.* "You heard me having a—a nightmare. You heard me and came—" she stopped as Nik shook his head. "You didn't?"

"Here already, Mac," he confessed, that dimple growing deeper. "I was watching you sleep."

She blinked. "Why on Earth would you do that?"

"Spy. It's a lifestyle." Flippant and quick.

Trying to distract her. Mac frowned at him. "Then let me clarify my question for you, Mr. Spy. Fourteen and Kay said the Ministry wouldn't let the IU contact me. When they finally found a way, *poof,* you show up. It's no stretch to know you're here to try and stop me from going with them. Going there." Making sure one hand could hold the blanket securely, she lifted the other to point to the ceiling. "What I want to know is why."

Nik pushed himself off the bed in one lithe motion. Between the sloped ceiling and small room, Mac would have had to press against the window to let him pass and reach the door. She had no intention of budging.

But he wasn't trying to leave. Instead, he came close and gazed down at her. "I can't stop you," said Nik soberly. "You've accepted this from IU representatives, who will bear witness, believe me, if you try to deny it." A flick of the wrist, and the IU envelope was in his hand, held at his shoulder.

Mac's eyes locked on it. "What does it say?"

He folded it between his fingers. "I made a recording for you." His other hand tugged his imp from his pocket.

"I didn't bring mine," Mac confessed, feeling like a student caught without homework.

Nik didn't comment, simply tucked the device away again. "I'll get you one. Meanwhile, most of this is fairly harmless. Statements of common goals, common good, a mutual desire not to be consumed by the Dhryn. That sort of thing. There's a lengthy list of regulations and protocols regarding deportment at the Gathering, how to share information et cetera."

She could hear the *"But"* coming. "What is it?"

"You're expected to put the needs of member species of the IU ahead of your own. That goes both ways. This—" Nik passed Mac the envelope; it was warm from his hand. "—lets you demand help from any IU member. But not for yourself as a Human. Not from other Humans. Once you took and opened this, you were, to all intents and purposes, no longer a citizen of Sol System. Or of Earth."

"It's an invitation to a conference," Mac protested. *She'd been to dozens, probably more, ranging from fascinating to how-soon-could-they-hit-the-bar boring.*

"It's an invitation, Mac, to join an elite group drawn from all over the IU, whose sole function is to stop the Dhryn. However long that takes. Whatever it takes."

It was as if she heard trumpets, the call was so loud and sure. "If you think I regret this, Nikolai Trojanowski," Mac proclaimed, glaring up at him, "you're wrong. I want to find Emily. I want answers. If this piece of illegible text gives me access to the resources of the entire Interspecies Union, so be it."

His lip twitched. *A grin?* "And far be it from me to argue your flawless logic, Dr. Connor. Not when I'd do the same in your place."

Aha! "You disagreed with keeping me away from the IU, didn't you?" It was as though a weight had dropped from her shoulders. "You never intended to stop me accepting this. You—Nikolai Trojanowski—you disobeyed orders."

Nik made a show of looking offended. "Me? Never."

Mac snorted. "Just like you're never late."

"It took longer than I expected," he said serenely, "to find one old cabin in the woods." Then, his own expression serious: "I wanted this to be your choice, Mac, whatever you decided. If you'd said no, I would have taken the aliens with me last night and left you alone."

"Alone is overrated," Mac told him unsteadily.

He seemed closer without moving. "Yes, it is." Softly, searching her face: "Gods, do you have any idea—of course you don't—how dangerous your eyes are? A man could forget anything in them. Forget to breathe."

For some reason, Mac found herself intensely conscious of both breathing and wearing only a blanket. *What if she—*

A clatter from downstairs shattered the moment, restoring Mac's badly skewed equilibrium. "I've aliens in my kitchen," she explained. *Damn, he was too good at distracting her.*

And knew it.

"Worried they'll burn the place down?" That dimple again.

"No. Kay's a great cook. He— Stop changing the subject," she snapped.

Nik held up his hands in surrender. "Whatever you say."

Mac took a deep breath. She tapped the floor with a bare foot. "What I say is that the Dhryn, the Ro, Emily, even traffic reports on Little Misty Lake are higher on your list right now than—" *She hadn't meant to go quite that far.*

"You," Nik finished, his face now inscrutable.

"Yes." Mac stood perfectly straight and still, daring him to deny it, knowing that if he did, she'd never believe him again. "So why were you watching me sleep?"

Nik lifted his hands, then let them drop at his sides. "We don't—" he had the grace to look uncomfortable, "—have this place rigged. You took us by surprise, coming here."

"It's our family cabin," Mac said tightly. "Last time I checked, my movements weren't restricted, even if my privacy is."

He shook his head. "You dream Dhryn, Mac." As if that was sufficient excuse.

"You didn't need to climb into my bed to find that out."

The corner of his mouth twitched. "No, I didn't." That dimple.

"I'm here under orders, Mac. Allow that I can also be glad to be here. With you." This last in that low, quiet voice, the one Mac found disturbed things, things she didn't need disturbed while trying to think clearly.

She marshaled her thoughts. "If you're planning to stay until we leave, unless you want to introduce yourself as a Ministry agent . . . ?" He made a face. "Thought so. Then we'll need to explain your being here with me. In the cabin—not here," she added quickly, gesturing at her bed.

" 'Here' would keep it simple," Nik proposed, smiling down at her, eyes warm.

Mac couldn't smile back. Her hands tightened on the blanket until her knuckles turned white. *Coward,* she railed at herself. Fun was fun. She'd accepted offers before now, had a pleasant dalliance, forgotten names the next day.

It wouldn't be that way, Em. Not with him.

Nik lost his smile. "I see," he said, his voice grown thick. "It wouldn't."

Mac made an effort. "You could be my cousin, visiting for the week."

"Better if I could come and go without questions asked," he said, the sound reassuringly normal again. *Spy training,* Mac thought enviously. *Her voice still had a wobble to it.* "A neighbor?"

"You'd need a reason to hang around." Then Mac began to smile. "I have an idea."

Nik gave her a suspicious look. "Why does that make me nervous?"

"Depends. Are you any good with a shovel?"

"Good morning, Mac! I have made potcakes!"

"Idiot. Pancakes. It's not hard to remember," Fourteen grumbled. He busied himself pouring coffee, but gave Mac a quick wink.

Mac winked back. "Good morning. And thank you. It smells amazing." She took her seat in the kitchen, heart pounding. *Great spy she was.*

"We are serving you first, Mac," Kay announced, stepping to her side with a plate stacked five high with fluffy pancakes. Fourteen passed her the container of syrup. Both waited, watching her. "And will wait for you to eat."

"If this is so I can help with the dishes," she grinned, "it's a deal."

"Irrelevant," Fourteen claimed. "It is so I can tell if Kay has poisoned us with this concoction."

Kay's eyestalks, the two alert ones, bent to glare at Fourteen. "I refuse to serve cold poodle for breakfast. If you have to eat it, go outside."

Mac used her first mouthful of pancake to hide her smile. Their bickering, to her Human ears anyway, had an affectionate undertone, much like her brothers. It was odd how homey it was, sitting to a meal with them, despite the twisted gray locks that served Kay for a head, and Fourteen's dubious color sense. He must have raided the clothing trunk for that red plaid shirt. *If only he'd changed the paisley shorts.* It didn't help that his knees were again coated in bright green ointment.

Knock, knock. "Hey, Mac? You home?"

Kay and Fourteen froze at the sounds coming from the porch. Despite expecting Nik's imminent "arrival"—he'd slipped from her room and gone outside—Mac jumped in surprise. "Door's open," she called, recovering. The two aliens stared at her, then at the kitchen door, as if expecting the worst. "It's okay," Mac reassured them. "It's only—" *Oops. Nik went to the consulate regularly, his name would be on records.* "—Sam," she continued, taking a deliberately casual sip of her coffee. "Sam the landscaper." *Emily,* Mac sighed to herself, *would have quite a bit to say about that slip of the tongue.* "He's local," she finished lamely.

Nik/Sam popped his head around the frame of the kitchen door. "Sorry to intrude on your breakfast—"

"This is Sam Beckett," Mac said hastily, before Nik could introduce himself. He shot her a look she didn't dare read.

"How are you, Mr. Beckett?" Kay said, rising to the occasion like a born host. "Have you eaten yourself? We have plenty. Please join us."

"Call me Sam. And thanks. If that's okay with you, Mac?" a respectful salute of fingers to brow in her direction.

Nik must have taken the time to rummage through the workshop portion of the outhouse building. Her father's old leather tool belt hung around his lean middle, complete with ax-hammer and pliers. He'd put on a slouch as well, a subtle drop of shoulders and hips that stripped away his usual grace.

Mac narrowed her eyes. *He was enjoying this.* "Of course. Sam, this is Kay and Aslith—"

"Fourteen," that worthy interrupted. "Don't waste more time. Sit. Eat. Coffee? Potcakes?"

Kay, putting out another setting, stopped and pointed his eyestalks at Fourteen. "I thought you said they were pancakes."

"Idiot."

Mac giggled and everything seemed to settle, including her stomach. Nik took a mug of coffee as he sat, with every appearance of needing it. The aliens continued to chatter between themselves. *Checking out the new arrival,* she decided.

The new arrival was doing the same. Playing the role of "Sam the landscaper" with consummate skill, Nik somehow ate his breakfast while gawking at everything the two aliens did, up to and including a small gasp when Kay upended the last of the syrup into his *douscent.*

Being more familiar with her guests, or rather their skewed sense of humor, Mac had her doubts about this strategy. Sure enough, when Fourteen and Kay finished their meal—predictably before either Human—the Myg stood and scowled quite fiercely at Nik. "I have no external genitalia."

Fourteen's timing was impeccable. Nik sputtered and almost choked on the mouthful he'd been about to swallow.

"My companion has no tact," Kay said, his tone contrite. "What he means to say, with sincere regret and no disrespect to your species, is that neither of us are physically capable of satisfying your overwhelming urge to copulate. You'll have to use Mac."

Oh, she should have seen that coming. Mac shook her head with appreciation. Nik, meanwhile, had an alarming gleam in his eye. "Sam's too old," she informed them calmly, before he had a chance to say anything. *And make it worse.* "He doesn't have those urges anymore."

Fourteen blinked, then broke into his barking laugh. Kay drummed the palms of his hands on the table—presumably his version.

Nik?

The look he sent Mac wasn't official at all. In fact, it was the next best thing to ominous.

Mac grinned. "Hadn't you better get to work, Sam?"

After the dishes were done, and Kay had gone to his bedroom for, as Fourteen put it, time to commune with his overstuffed *douscent,* Mac left the Myg rearranging porch furniture for some obscure reason and went to check on Nik.

Black flies lifted from every leaf as she left the porch steps, hovering in confusion an arm's length away—aware she was close, but not knowing where. Mac waved at them cheerfully. *Technology wasn't cheating.* "Go chew a moose," she advised.

The top third of the path from the cabin was the most seriously eroded, convenient for Nik—since she assumed he'd want to overhear anything said on the porch. Mac edged her way alongside the deep crevices of exposed gravel and sand, keeping to root-tight soil. Unlike the coastal rain forest, here the dimly lit forest floor was a brown carpet of decaying needles, punctuated only by absurd balls of moss, vivid and vulnerable, and clumps of blushing mushrooms. If a tree fell, letting in the sun, the ground exploded with grasses, blueberry bushes, and eager saplings. If sun touched stone, the smallest cracks became lined with stubborn willow shrubs and packed with moss, its surface crusted with lichens.

The path bent sharply before the next drop; Mac heard the thud of his ax before she spotted him working just below.

Mac stopped, her real hand resting on the cool moist bark of the nearest tree. It wasn't hot yet, but Nik had already stripped off shirt and tool belt. More confused black flies circled his head, hunting a landing. He was chopping back a huge, upthrust root to make room for a wider stair. The new timbers were stacked behind him—they'd been stored under the porch for years, waiting for someone with time and inclination.

For once, Mac didn't wonder about Emily's reaction to the easy play of muscles over his shoulders and back with each confident rise of the ax, or the sweat plastering hair to his forehead and neck, glowing on his skin in the morning light.

She felt her own.

How complicated brains made the basics, she mused, putting her back against the tree, content to enjoy the moment before he noticed her. *Which biological drives remained untouched once you added intelligence and tossed in civilization? Breathing. Leaping away from flame.* Past that, even something so central to being Human as caring for a child evolved regulations and customs, habits and judgments.

Now, interaction with non-Human intelligence. What effect did it have, blending biology so three species could share breakfast, and thousands could share space?

What were they missing about the Dhryn? Mac frowned.

Nik chose that instant to look up and see her. "What's wrong?" he asked immediately, shifting his grip on the ax.

Mac found a smile. "Just thinking. You're doing a great job."

He used his forearm to wipe his brow. "It's a wonder you didn't break your necks climbing this," he commented, gesturing at the ground. This section did look worse in daylight, more dry gully than path.

"It keeps casual visitors down. Usually."

Nik glanced up the slope, then lowered his voice slightly. "There's nothing casual about those two. Fourteen's been at the Gathering for several weeks. I've asked for background information, his area of expertise, but nothing's come through yet. As for Kay—he's a more recent arrival, for all they seem pals. Does he only have four eyestalks?"

"That's all I've seen so far. Why? Do they come and go?" *Within that hair, it was possible.* Mac was quite taken with the notion. "How many should he have?"

"Four is normal," Nik said disappointedly. "But your Kay is no ordinary messenger, judging from the clout he had in arranging this little ambush in the woods. I'd have thought he'd have more by now."

"Care to explain that?"

"I—"

"Mac-ac-ac-ac!" They both looked downslope as the hail echoed across the lake and back. They could hear the rub of paddle against a canoe. "Mac-ac!!!"

"What? I don't believe it. That's Russell," Mac said, recognizing the bellow. "Fourteen told me he'd called to cancel their trip last night," she growled. "Should have done it myself. You'd better stay here," she said as she clambered past Nik and jumped the timbers, heading for the cove. He started to follow her anyway, and she paused to look back at him. "He'll know you aren't local," she warned.

"And not Sam Beckett."

He knew? Then she understood. *Damn Ministry dossiers.* "I had to pick a name," Mac defended, grabbing a handful of cedar for balance. "There wasn't time to consult."

"You don't let go of people, do you?"

"No." Mac's lips twisted. "Not first," she admitted, beyond caring what that revealed about her. "Just keep busy and out of the way. Trust me. Russell won't stay long."

Another of those offhand salutes, but his hazel eyes were troubled. She felt them watching her as she went down to meet the canoe.

"Wendy Carlson," Russell Lister introduced. The tall woman slogging through water to her ankles waved at Mac, then kept pushing her canoe up the beach. They'd brought the store's two largest, Russell fully aware how much gear Kay and Fourteen had brought.

"Nice to meet you," Mac said, taking the paddle Russell shoved at her. "But you've made the trip for nothing. They canceled their trip. I thought Fourteen—the Myg—called you last night about it."

"He did," Wendy said, then nodded at Russell. "Made us come anyway."

Mac turned to him. "Why?"

His face went bright red. "No reason. You're fine. I can see that. Plain as day. We'll just head back now. Sorry to trouble you, Mac." He reached for his paddle and Mac returned it with a puzzled frown.

Wendy, a friendly-faced young woman with a glorious mane of red hair blowing free in the wind, broke out laughing as she pulled the front of her canoe onto the sand. "Honestly, Russ, you're hopeless. Don't mind him, Mac. He expected to find you hanging from a tree in some alien bondage ritual. It was all Cat and I could do to stop him calling in the police last night to storm the place."

"Bondage . . . ?" Mac repeated incredulously. "You're kidding." *But from Russell's embarrassment, Wendy wasn't.*

Mac couldn't decide if she should laugh or tear out her hair. On second thought, maybe she should put Fourteen and Russell in the same room for a while. *Or maybe not.* "Russell? What on Earth put that in your head? You were the one who dumped them on me in the first place."

He rested the blade of his paddle on top of his boot, crossing his hands on the handle. "I know. Just made it worse, Mac. Worrying you'd come to harm because of me. Glad you're okay." He heaved a sigh, then shook his head. "I feel like such an idiot."

"You should," she agreed. "Alien bondage? You and Cat watch too many vids over the winter. I should send you some comparative anatomy texts." She put her hand on top of his, pushing gently. "Thanks for checking." Mac paused, then the light dawned. *Aliens,* she sighed to herself. "What exactly did Fourteen say to you?"

"That's the thing." Russell lowered his voice conspiratorially, although the three of them were the only beings in sight who'd conceivably hear. Wendy sent Mac a look of sympathy. "We weren't in, so he'd left a message."

Mac waited a long moment, swatting at an inquisitive—and precocious—deerfly. When Russell still didn't speak, she burst out: "Well? What did the message say?"

Russell gave her a hurt look. "Give me a minute, Mac. I'm making sure I get it right."

A spy on her path, aliens on her porch, and Russell taking his time. Mac pinched the bridge of her nose to make sure she was awake. "The gist," she suggested acidly, "will do."

"I heard it," Wendy volunteered. Ignoring Russell's *humphf,* she shifted into a credible imitation of the Myg's gruff voice. " 'The canoe trip is now irrelevant. The female Human meets our needs. Charge Kay triple and stay away. And send four more of your fine shirts to the address I left. Add them to Kay's bill.' "

Mac winced. *Damn Myg sense of humor.* "Okay, I can see how you might take that the wrong way. My apologies, Russell."

He rolled his eyes and didn't move, doing his own credible impression of Man Terribly Wronged. *The one that never worked,* Mac remembered, *but always made Cat laugh and give him a hug.*

She grinned. "Why don't you and Wendy come up to the cabin for a drink?" she invited. "We can get your bill settled there."

"Great!" Wendy smiled cheerfully and gave the older man a light push. "C'mon, Russ."

Nik had taken her suggestion and made himself scarce, Mac noticed as they negotiated the path to the cabin, although she suspected he was capable of hiding behind the thinnest tree. She led the way up the steps and opened the porch door.

The two aliens had arranged three armchairs around a trio of mismatched tables this time, and were busy playing another card game. So far, the cards were safely in their hands or on a table. *The IU's finest,* Mac grinned to herself.

"Mr. Russell! Mr. Wendy!" Kay greeted them warmly. "How are you this morning?"

"Fine, fine," Russell got the words out somehow, though Mac could tell he was still trying to regroup. Admittedly, aliens playing cards was a far cry from what Russell had imagined he'd find here. She was sorely tempted to knock his and Fourteen's heads together. Interspecies communication was difficult enough, without throwing in erotic and anatomically unsound vid dramas— *not to mention,* Mac fumed to herself, *brochures on human sexual behavior.*

"Are you sure you don't want to take the trip?" Russell had continued. Not being privy to Mac's thoughts, his voice was closer to normal. "It's an amazing opportunity—"

"Irrelevant," Fourteen interrupted. "You were told not to come. We have other plans. Be amazed without us."

Kay's upper two eyestalks—four in total, Mac confirmed involuntarily—bent to aim at Russell. "Ignore the rude creature," Kay told him. "Please, make yourselves comfortable. We will, of course, pay the full price for our trip regardless. Send my companion here the bill."

"But he said to send it to you," Russell protested, giving Mac an anxious look. Fourteen seemed oblivious, busy rearranging cards.

"You don't need to send anything, Russell," Mac said firmly, glowering at her guests. "They will each pay you double the cost of the original trips before you leave here. And you—" she pointed at Fourteen, who froze with a handful of cards in midair to stare up at her, "—will pay for your own shirts before they are shipped."

"Sounds fair to me, Mac," Russell said with a huge smile.

Since no one from another world seemed inclined to comment, Mac went on: "Coffee anyone?"

"Something cold, please, if you have it," Wendy answered. She'd been studying the card game. "What are you playing?" she asked Kay.

"Something he made up," the Trisulian answered morosely.

Fourteen grinned. "Involving more numbers and less cheating!"

Wendy looked entranced. "Would you show me? Please?"

"Be my guest," Kay stood, offering her his seat.

Russell dropped into the swing and put his head back on the cushions, closing his eyes. "Take your time, Wendy. We're in no rush. Oh, I take three sugars these days, Mac. Thanks."

Kay accompanied Mac to the kitchen, holding the doors for her courteously each time. "Should we prepare a beverage for Sam?" he asked.

"Got my own, thanks." Back in his shirt, sawdust frosting his hair, Nik leaned against the kitchen counter, sipping a glass of water. His eyes laughed at her.

She was going to put a tracer on him, Mac thought, exasperated.

She went to a cupboard and snooped through Cat's gifts until she found a bag of cookies. "So Fourteen invented his own card game—just like that?"

"He lives for numbers," Kay said, putting on the coffee. One eyestalk watched what his hands were doing, its partner swiveled between her and Nik, while the remaining two stayed asleep. Mac was fascinated.

"What does he do with them—when he isn't playing games?" Nik asked, stealing a cookie as Mac put them on a plate.

"Do? I've no idea." The aroma of coffee began filling the kitchen. "He is paid ridiculous sums for whatever it is and considers himself very clever. Numbers," Kay put out mugs, "bore me."

"What do you do?" Mac asked. "When not vacationing on Earth, that is," she added quickly. Remembering who was supposed to know what about whom was the worst of it. *Or was that who knew which who knew what?*

Mac's head threatened to throb. *Salmon,* she promised it, *were much simpler than spies.*

"I'm a—I believe the Human equivalent is civil servant. I obtain information, prepare meeting summaries, that sort of thing."

How—normal. Mac spooned sugar into Russell's mug, at a loss for what to ask next. *This,* she said to herself, *from the woman with a spy in her kitchen.*

Said spy was presently using his skills to sneak another cookie. Mac passed him the bag with the rest. "Help yourself."

"Thanks. By the way, I'll be gone a couple of hours. Need to get some setting posts from my shop."

Gone? She gave him a sharp look, but the Ministry agent seemed more interested in eating than clandestine signals.

"We have ample poodle. I will save you a sandwich," Kay promised.

Nik looked startled, then worried. *Was either expression real?* "It's okay, Sam," she said, playing along. "I had some last night. Delicious."

"If you say so, Mac. Till later, then." Nik gave her that half salute, then ducked out the back door.

"You're sure he's too old," Kay ventured. "Seems fit."

"Appearances can be deceiving." She hesitated. *How did one casually ask about eyestalks? Was there etiquette?*

"True for all species, Mac. Shall we serve our guests?"

Opportunity lost, for now, Mac followed Kay back to the porch.

Leftover "poodle" did make excellent sandwiches. Mac had Kay leave a plateful in the kitchen for "Sam," so he wouldn't mention the name during lunch on the porch. Wendy and Russell helped finish off the rest, both operating on what Mac's father had called "cottage time." In other words, lingering whenever politely possible until the next meal showed up.

Mac went down to the cove to help launch their canoes, just to be sure it didn't occur to Russell or Wendy to linger for supper.

Russell still had his doubts. "You're sure you want to stay alone with these guys, Mac?" he asked, standing beside his canoe. Wendy was pushing hers out. "They seem nice enough, but you never know."

"If I detect the slightest hint of evil intentions, you'll be the first one I call," Mac promised, then grinned. "I plan to wear them out anyway. A good long hike, probably a few days' worth into the bush," she improvised, "then I'll get a ride back with them to Base. Time for me to return to work by then. Tell Cat I appreciate the supplies and I'll visit more next trip." Then she beckoned Russell close to whisper: "We paddled a bit yesterday. Kay gets terribly seasick. Don't tell anyone—I think it's a pride thing with his species."

Russell drew back with a knowing look. "Ah. Thanks, Mac. Good to know."

And if their supposed itinerary wasn't all over the lake by midday tomorrow, Mac thought with satisfaction as she watched the twin canoes head out into the lake, *nothing would be.*

Just then, a v-shaped flock of seven huge birds appeared over the trees on the far shore, their powerful wings beating in synchrony, flying toward her and north. Swans. Mac smiled as she hooded her eyes to watch them pass overhead. The pelicans would arrive next, with their unwelcome nesting companions, the gulls. Cormorants were here already, competing for space with early arriving geese. Herons would push them both out soon, reclaiming their colonies.

It was like welcoming old friends home.

There was no sign of Nik as she walked through his construction site to the cabin. Mac didn't bother wondering where he'd gone—or how, since there'd been no sign of an additional canoe along the cove. The sun was blazing down now, bringing that heady scent out of the pines and adding a pulsing heat even in the shade. Late May.

Some years, that meant snow, Mac thought with a grin.

Kay and Fourteen were waiting for her, the latter curled into a ball on his chair, lumpy knees in front of his nose. Mac resolutely avoided looking at the expanse of strained paisley this offered. "We have been discussing the Dhryn life cycle and wish your thoughts, Mac," Kay informed her as she joined them.

"I'm not a xenobiologist," she cautioned. "I told you yesterday. My field is salmon."

"Nonsense. You are a trained observer, with a relevant background. Your insights would be most valuable."

No one at the Ministry had wanted them. Mac couldn't help but feel a little glow of satisfaction. Then she quelled it. "Valuable? Not without more data."

"At the Gathering, you should find the data you lack," Fourteen said. He seemed strangely subdued.

Mac took a closer look at him. "Are you feeling all right?"

"He received a message while you were saying your farewells. The news wasn't good."

"About the Dhryn," Mac guessed, sitting down. *The air wasn't this close,* she told herself, making herself breathe more slowly. "Tell me."

"You tell her," Fourteen said, covering his eyes.

Kay combed his facial hair with one hand. "We called them the Pouch People. They lived on a moon in the Osye System. Prespace technology, a peaceful, pleasant culture. The Osye were letting them develop with minimal cultural interference. Some trade. Farmers, for the most part."

"Harmless!" the Myg wailed softly.

Mac swallowed bile. "Go on," she said.

"There is nothing more to say. The Dhryn had come before.

The Pouch People were warned of the signs but had no defense, no ships. The Dhryn came again and consumed every molecule of organic matter. Their world is lifeless. They are gone."

Mac leaned forward, her elbows on her knees. "And the Dhryn. Did they stay?"

"No."

"Again," she whispered, chin in hand, tapping the side of her nose with one finger, deep in thought.

"What is it?"

Mac's finger stopped tapping. "After complete victory, they abandon a world suitable for their species. Why?"

Fourteen lowered his hands, wiping his eyelids as he did so. "They were afraid of being caught by the Osye."

"They had what they came for," Kay added.

Mac pursed her lips. "Or is it that they couldn't stop there? Not yet, anyway."

"What do you mean?"

She rested her artificial fingers on one end of the nearest table, then drew a line with her other hand from that point to the far side. "What if the Dhryn are on a journey," Mac mused slowly. "A journey with a purpose—a destination. They don't stay, because they can't stay. They haven't reached their final goal."

"Disturbing."

Mac sat up and gazed at Fourteen. "Yes, it is."

"If we knew that goal," Kay ventured, "we could predict where they will strike next."

She shook her head. "We already have evidence that the Dhryn are returning where they've been before, as if following a trail set by advance scouts. But from what you told me, there was only one Progenitor ship seen at Ascendis. That's a problem."

"Why?"

"Previous attacks—our only reports are of a few, scattered incidents. We don't know which of those were Dhryn for sure. And we can't know where else the Dhryn have been. Add to that? We don't know how many Dhryn there are. When I was on Haven, I saw the Progenitors leaving. It looked like dozens—but the Human ships reported more, at least three hundred."

"Why would only one attack at a time?" this from Kay.

Fourteen: "Where are the rest?"

Mac nodded at each question. "That's why we can't predict the attacks. If they are on a journey, a migration of sorts, all Dhryn should be making it. If only some are actively feeding—" she was proud of how the word came out without cracking, "—that implies the rest don't need to feed themselves yet, or are being supplied by others, for all we know by ships going off the main path. There's no pattern established."

"Our military strategists are plotting the Dhryn's most likely moves based on time-honored space tactics. Trisulians," Kay said almost smugly, "were once highly respected combatants."

"Ruthless invaders," Fourteen corrected. "Good thing you civilized yourselves or you'd have lost your transects."

Irrelevant, Mac caught herself thinking. "Nothing the Dhryn have done suggests they have some plan for conquest," she objected. "They don't occupy territory. They don't communicate or negotiate. They just—are."

The other two were silenced by this. Mac didn't blame them. She wasn't too happy about the idea of a space-faring aggressive species that wasn't behaving like one either.

In the hush, she could hear a shovel and gravel being poured. Mac turned to look out the screen.

Nik was back, working at the top of the path, making a great show of moving gravel from side to side. *An excuse to stay in earshot,* Mac decided. He was working in the full sun at the moment, his shirt tied on his head to shade his neck.

"What about the Myrokynay, the Ro, Mac? Can they predict where the Dhryn will strike next?"

Mac swiveled back to face her anxious companions. *Almost time for beer,* she thought. "I've seen no indication they can. They needed help to find the Dhryn Progenitors." *But not the Dhryn world,* she thought suddenly. They'd known where Haven was. They'd attacked it before. *The Ro were after the oomlings,* Brymn had said.

Why?

"If only we could talk to them . . . ask what they know . . . maybe we could have protected those already lost . . ." Fourteen covered his eyes, making a quiet clicking sound Mac hadn't heard from him before, like a cricket lost in the kitchen at night.

She sniffed, trying not to be obvious, then held her breath as long as she could, hoping the faint breeze through the screens would help. *He was definitely upset.*

Kay's eyestalks drooped. "The Ro ignore us."

Mac unzipped her upper pocket and pulled out the sheet of mem-paper. "Not always," she said very quietly, hoping her voice wouldn't carry. She tapped Fourteen on his knee to get his attention, then spread the page out so they all could see it.

"What is it?" Kay whispered, eyestalks bent down.

Fourteen bounced on his chair. "It's a message from the Ro, isn't it, Mac?" he said, with regrettable volume. Mac winced.

"We can't understand it," she whispered, doubting he'd take the hint. "Kay said you were good with numbers. Maybe it will make sense to—" Before the words left her mouth, Fourteen snatched up the mem-sheet and ran into the cabin. "—you," Mac finished.

Kay gave her shoulder a quick pat. "He may be annoying, but he isn't just good with numbers. He's one of the best cryptologists of any species. If anyone can make some sense of it, Fourteen can. If he can't, then someone at the Gathering surely will. Thank you, Mac. Thank you."

"Ah, Mac?" The air might be stifling warm, but that voice through the porch screen was only a fraction above absolute zero. "May I have a word with you, please? Now."

She closed her eyes for a second, then somehow smiled at Kay. "Why don't you grab us some beers, Kay, and make sure Fourteen has what he needs? I'll just go—" *see how angry Nik is,* "—see what Sam needs."

Feet crunching through gravel, then scuffing pine needles, Nik marched around the cabin to the outhouse. He opened the door and walked inside, leaving her to follow.

That angry, Mac told herself, and squared her shoulders. *Fine.* She was a member of the IU, now. Not that it seemed likely to help at this instant.

The outhouse, despite its name and practical function in wintertime, was primarily a workshop and storeroom. Stuffed owls stared down from their shelves, surveying the irregular stone floor crowded with barrels and boxes. One wall held a rack of tools, most older than Mac. The back wall had the door to the privy, within a forest of skis, poles, ice drills, hockey sticks, and snow shovels, while the remaining wall was taken up by the requisite wood stove. The only light, at the moment, came through the skylight Mac hadn't bothered to clean of pine needles and cobwebs. Its beams sloped down in a cascade of pale yellow dust, to cast four bright squares on the floor.

Nik stationed himself beside the stove, stiff and straight, eyes hooded in the relative gloom. His arms were folded across his chest, like armor.

"Before you spout 'threat to the species' at me, Mr. Trojanowski," Mac told him, standing straight herself, "consider who was given that message in the first place. Me. I'm the one Emily expects to figure it out—not you, not 'Sephe, not your experts. Me. And this is how I'm going to try. With Fourteen's help. With Kay's help. I'm a member of the IU now."

He gave a curt nod. "Getting Fourteen on it was brilliant, Mac. Couldn't have done better myself."

Brilliant? Mac, all set to defend her decision, with colorful language and a brandished hockey stick if necessary, was thrown off-balance. "Why drag me out here then?"

"I'm leaving. Now." Flat, neutral. "I won't be coming back."

It was like that first moment of her swim, skin hitting ice cold water, the shock driving the breath from her body. Mac fought to see anything of Nik's expression in the shadows; she couldn't. *Hiding, Mr. Spy?*

That, more than anything, convinced her.

Her heart started hammering. "You haven't finished the path."

It wasn't what she wanted to say. Should say. Couldn't.

"I know. I'm sorry."

Did he mean he knew what she hadn't *said, Em?* Mac refused to follow that path into complete incoherence.

"Mac, I don't have much time." She thought she heard a hint of regret. *Or imagined it.* "We have to talk before I go."

Go where? Why? Mac longed to demand answers, to protest . . .
And how, she asked herself, *could that be fair to either of them?*

"I'm listening," she said quietly, surrounded by memories and
dust.

The words came out staccato sharp, like some battlefield briefing. *There really wasn't time,* she thought, beginning to worry why.
"A name you need to know. Bernd Hollans. Career Ministry. Spent
the last two years seconded to Earthgov as adviser on Human-IU
trade. He's the one who persuaded the Secretary General to take
the investigation into the disappearances, the Chasm, seriously. Just
been appointed our voice in IU policy regarding the Dhryn and the
Ro."

"Making him your new boss?" she guessed. *Was Nik's sudden departure this Hollans' doing?* Better that, than any of the other options
she'd imagined.

Nik took a step forward; a beam of light struck his leg. The contrast turned the rest of him darker, deepened shadows. "He knows
my value," he said just as obscurely. "I know his. He'll make the
tough decisions. You won't like him, Mac, but don't let that fool
you. Hollans—he can be trusted."

Politicians. Something she usually avoided. *As for trust?* Mac
wrapped her arms around her middle. "What else?"

"The Trisulian rescue mission to Ascendis turned out to be
something else."

"What?" Mac frowned. "Kay told me they'd sent more ships to
retrieve Eeling refugees than any other species."

"Oh, they sent more ships, all right." Sharp and edged. "Settler
convoys. Ascendis may be ruined for the foreseeable future, but her
moons and their very lucrative refitting stations remain intact. As
do her transect connections. The Trisulian Ruling Council has petitioned for official recognition of the system as part of their hold-
ings and it's unlikely any will argue. Certainly not the few Eelings
left alive."

Mac's eyes widened with understanding. "Ravens."

"I don't see what—"

"Ravens survive winter by scavenging deer and elk carcasses,
Nik. They follow predators in order to find their kills."

"The Trisulians as ravens to the Dhryn?" Nik was silent for an instant, then said slowly, as if thinking out loud: "I want to say it's unlikely, but they've a history of snatching new territory by force. It almost cost them their transects. With the prospect of conveniently uninhabited worlds, complete with atmosphere, water, even most buildings and roads intact? All they'd need are some climate regulators to keep the first miners happy, long-term reclamation projects for agriculture. It would be tempting."

"If," Mac emphasized, "they learn to predict Dhryn movements. They'd have to know, in order to arrive in time to feed on the corpse first."

"Remind me not to use your phrasing in the discussions of the issue."

She didn't quite smile. "Is Kay involved in this? Is that why he's here?" *Really tired of betrayal, Em.*

"No reason to think so." Nik's voice lost some of its edge. "He's a minor official, good record if undistinguished, presently serving his species' contingent at the Gathering. Handles catering, runs errands, that sort of thing. I can't see an underling being privy to the Ruling Council's actions. He volunteered to approach you for the IU and was someone who could be spared, that's all."

She could feel his doubt. "That's not all, is it? You suspect Kay of something."

He hesitated, then shrugged, a shadow shifting its shape. She still couldn't see his face clearly. "It's my nature. Trisulians are fond of secrets. They like collecting information; knowing things—even trivia—before everyone else. Didn't surprise me to find Kay had offered to meet you. For someone like him, chances to learn or do something first must be rare. But I was puzzled why he'd invite Fourteen. They barely knew one another before coming here. Then you, Mac, showed me the reason."

For some reason her mind stuck on poodle. "I did?"

"The Ro message. If Fourteen translates it while still at the cabin—" He waited.

"Kay could learn what it said before anyone else," Mac finished. She began to pace, real hand rubbing at the false. "But how would he know I had such a message?" She stopped and whirled. *How could she have forgotten to tell him?* "Nik, the IU—"

"Has someone working for them at Base. We know."

Of course they knew, Mac told herself, feeling foolish. "It's 'Sephe, isn't it? She knew about Emily's message. You put her there in the first place—to help the IU reach me. Right?"

She could see him shake his head, barely make out the gleam of reflected light that marked his eyes. "I put her there, yes. But she's not the IU's informant—and before you ask, you don't want to know who it is."

Mac bristled. "I most certainly do."

"How many secrets do you want to carry around, Mac? Besides, you'll meet this person again. Think you can act normally if you know?"

"What's 'normally'?" Mac exclaimed in disbelief. "If you don't tell me, I'll have to suspect everyone I know."

He laughed. "Welcome to my world."

"You can keep it," Mac growled. In the ensuing silence, she listened to a trio of white-throated sparrows outside, contesting territory with song instead of subterfuge. *Lucky birds.* Finally she grumbled: "Okay. Don't tell me. If I knew, I'd probably chuck whoever it is in the ocean and be done."

"We'll be watching," Nik promised.

"You'd better." *When had leaving an unknown informant among her friends become a lesser evil?* The eyes of dead owls gazed at her. *Not helping,* she told them. "If it wasn't 'Sephe, how could Kay know about Em's message?"

"He didn't have to. We aren't the only ones who've been waiting for Emily to contact you, Mac. You wouldn't have had a moment's privacy on Earth if the Ministry hadn't stepped in and insisted you be left in peace. The Trisulians wouldn't be the only ones to believe you've been receiving such messages all along, keeping them to yourself."

"I have not!"

From his tone, he was amused by her protest, but all he said was: "To Kay, Mac, such secrecy would make perfect sense. And be an opportunity. Tell me. When I wasn't here, did Kay ask about Emily?"

In how many ways was she a fool? "Yes," Mac said, the word bitter in her mouth. "About our friendship, how close we are—were. It didn't make much sense at the time, but I went along. Tell me, Nik. Is there a memo about me at the consulate that says 'totally gullible,' or is it just obvious to any being who meets me?"

Nik took a step closer, the light playing over his face. *Regret. Something less definable.* "The only thing obvious about you, Mackenzie Connor," he informed her, "is your heart."

There was a conversation stopper. Mac could feel her cheeks flaming.

He had to notice, but went on as if he didn't. "Kay's only worry would be his ability to understand a message from the Ro. So he finds a cryptologist interested in a jaunt to Little Misty Lake. It's all a gamble, but one that could pay off. Looks like it has."

"And I thought funding committees were cutthroat," Mac muttered darkly.

"Don't take it personally, Mac." Nik took another step, and the light finally reached his eyes, their hazel dark with emotion. "Species advantage. Kay probably doesn't know about the Eeling System yet—but be prepared for him to approve when he does find out. And this is only the beginning. The Gathering—you'll have to tread very carefully. I don't have to warn you about alien motives, how easy it is to believe you understand those around you, how suddenly everything can change."

"I remember an earthquake," she said tightly.

"We've people going over every bit of that data, Mac. When I have an answer, I'll make sure you get it." Nik paused and studied her face, a frown starting to form between his brows. "This doesn't feel right."

"What?"

"Leaving."

It wasn't about leaving her, Mac thought. She knew him well enough by now to understand the source of his hesitation. It wasn't about what warmed his eyes when he really looked at her. *It was about trust.*

"Am I safe alone with them or not?" she asked bluntly. "I mean, other than the ever present risk of snoring, Fourteen's warped sense of humor, and alien bondage rituals."

Nik ached to say no. Mac could see it; part of her wanted to agree. *For reasons,* she admitted to herself, *that had nothing to do with aliens.* Then he pressed his lips together and gave her a reluctant nod. "Kay and Fourteen are accredited members of the IU, sent as your escorts. It's no crime to be interested in what the Ro have to say—we all are. You seem to be enjoying each other's company." He waited for Mac to say something. She didn't speak. "It still doesn't feel right," he finished, for the first time since they'd entered the outhouse showing a clear emotion—frustration.

On impulse, Mac tugged the shirt from Nik's head. Conscious of him watching her, she untied the knot turning it into a hat, then gave the garment a hard shake. Dust and a few dead flies joined the motes in the sunbeams. The beams flickered and brightened as if a cloud had gone by. "Here." She handed it back. "You'll want this on in the woods."

"Thanks." He pulled it over his shoulders. "Your ride should be here tomorrow, probably after the weather goes through. You're sure you'll be okay, Mac? I could arrange for someone to stop in tonight."

"Worry about the aliens," she told him. "I've hosted fund-raisers."

"There's that," he acknowledged solemnly, that dimple showing as he finished fastening his shirt. A truly serious look. "I hope Fourteen can do something with the message. We've had no luck."

Mac took a deep breath, that nightmare image of Emily—her voice, her face, her desperation—swelling up behind her eyes. "If he does find out what it says, what do I do about Kay?"

Nik shook his head. "Nothing. He has as much right to the information as any of us, Mac, and the immunity to do with it as he sees fit. Representatives of the IU, including Kay and Fourteen—and now you—are outside Ministry jurisdiction. We can—and will—follow him if he leaves, monitor any transmissions, delay him with bureaucracy to a point. But that's it. We can't stop him sending anything he wants to his government." A gleam of teeth that could only be described as wolfish. "Though the IU may smack his eyestalks afterward."

Nik's smile faded. "Just don't lose either of them in the bush. Or yourself. Okay? And, Mac?" He cupped one hand, then tipped it over, as if proving it was empty. "The message might not be from Emily at all. Don't get your hopes up."

Mac gave a helpless shrug. "I have to hope."

"I know." Nik opened his arms, very slightly, as if in invitation.

It was good-bye. Mac didn't move. She studied his face instead, compelled to memorize details: the patchy beard and tired lines of dust and sweat, the dark sweep of lashes and that unruly lock of hair over the forehead, the strength along jaw and throat.

"I watched you this morning," she confessed. "When you were chopping the root."

"Why do you think I was working so hard?" At her shocked look, he gave a quick, shameless grin. "Spy, remember?"

"Oh."

"Makes us even. I watched you sleep."

"There's that."

Another of those abruptly strained pauses. Mac had no idea what to do with it and concentrated on digging her toe into a crack in the stone floor.

Nik finally gave a quick nod. "I'd better go." He started for the door.

How do I say good-bye, Em? Mac tried to think of something, but he slowed and stopped before she could. *Maybe,* she told herself, *he was having the same problem.*

Which didn't bode well for their ability to converse.

"Mac. One last thing. In case I don't see you for a while."

Promising.

"What?" she prompted.

"I heard you tell Fourteen that the Ministry doesn't value your insights. I wanted to tell you. You were wrong," he said, gazing down at her, his eyes clouded. "Everything you know, everything you've postulated about the Dhryn? We take it very seriously, Mac. You have unique ideas—they may be important ones. That's why your office was monitored, your privacy violated. As much—

more—as we were waiting for Emily or the Ro, we wanted to hear you."

It hurt, even more than him leaving. "You could have asked, the way the IU did," Mac snapped. "We're on the same side."

"Yes." Nik's lips pressed together in an unhappy line, then he shrugged. "But we're not the same. Not anymore."

The owls appeared to lean closer. *Illusion,* Mac decided, just like the way there seemed no air left in the small room, despite the open door. "What do you mean?" she whispered.

"You still dream in Dhryn."

Another ambush. Mac stared at him. "That's why you were in my room last night. You were hoping I'd have a nightmare so you could—" her voice cracked. "So you could hear me."

"Yes. We had to know."

"Why?" Mac balled her hands into fists, but kept them still. *Not anger; despair.* "Why, Nik? Does it make me some kind of traitor to my kind? Is that it?"

"No one questions your loyalty." As she watched, he seemed to wrestle with some decision, then make it. "We've tried using the self-teach Emily made you for the Dhryn language on others—I've tried it myself. It doesn't work for anyone else, Mac. Worse, we can't make one that does, not for a Human brain. Yours doesn't copy. Existing vocabularies for the adult language lack syntax for the infrasound component and there are none for the *oomling* version. That self-teach was specific to you; what it did seems unique. We can't even predict what its full impact will be on you."

Damn you, Emily, Mac thought wearily. "What you're saying is that the Ministry, anyone in authority, doesn't trust me because they can't translate what I say in my sleep."

"It's not a matter of trust. The psych experts were clear that none of your personality, nothing of you, Mac, has been affected. It's only—well, some view anything you say about the Dhryn as potentially tainted. That doesn't mean it isn't valuable, but, to be frank, my superiors aren't confident having you as the source."

"Are you?"

He hesitated an instant too long.

Mac shook her head. "I see," she said.

"No, you don't 'see,' " Nik snapped, eyes flashing. "I fought to have you brought in as an analyst. I argued for weeks, went over the heads of my superiors, and came close to losing my job. Even though I knew about your nightmares, Mac; knew you were hurt and grieving, how much you wanted your life back, your fish, to get to work. I wouldn't let any of it matter more than learning about the Dhryn. But all I could get was the authorization to arrange surveillance, to send 'Sephe to stay near you, so we wouldn't lose anything you could tell us. Why do you think I helped the IU reach you? They can do what I couldn't. Get you working."

He rubbed his face, smearing dust, and wound up with a charmingly chagrined expression. "I still can't tell if I felt more frustrated or vindicated when I listened to you, sitting on a porch swing with a beer, make more sense than any 'expert' I've heard yet. We're all fools."

"No argument from me," Mac said. She licked her thumb and used it to repair a smear on his cheek, paying attention only to his skin and the dust. "That's better."

Nik caught her hand before she pulled it away. "Don't." Harsh and low. "Don't forgive me."

"For what?" Mac tried not to smile. "For being right? Spying on me all this time was a waste; I should have been working with you. Do you think there's been a day I haven't picked at the puzzle, tried to comprehend what's happening, make sense of it? You asked me if I ever let go, Nikolai. Well, here's the thing." She turned her hand in his so their fingers intertwined, and gripped as hard as she could. "I really don't. Not of Emily. Not of Brymn. Not of the questions we have to answer to find her and understand him." Mac searched his face then nodded to herself. "Not of you."

His fingers tightened in response. "I thought I warned you about getting close to anyone in this business."

Now she did smile. "I wasn't paying attention."

A perilous glitter in his eyes. "I thought you told Fourteen I was too old, Mackenzie Connor."

"Something to discuss when I don't have an alien in my kitchen," Mac said primly, pulling free. "Go. You have spy stuff to do." *Keep it light,* she warned herself. *Make it simple.*

But in answer, Nik cupped her face in his hands before she could step out of reach. "We're the worst fools of all," he told her, leaning so close the warm breath of each word was like a kiss against her mouth, his eyes burning into hers. "I can't promise not to hurt you, Mac, or those you care about. Not with what's at stake. Not with the Dhryn out there. I'll spend us both—use anyone I can. I must. You can't bind me."

"Do you really think I would?" Mac put her hands over his and gently loosened his hold, with a reluctance every cell in her body felt. Pretending to smooth his shirt gave her a safer reason to touch him. "The way I look at it, Nik," Mac explained, her voice husky but firm, "fools are the ones who wait for the universe to rearrange itself, then wonder why nothing ever happens." She lifted her eyes to his. "The wise give it a shove."

"Explaining why I ended up in the ocean," Nik recalled, then gave a crooked smile. "Okay. I'll leave. I don't suppose you'd promise to leave the universe alone until we see each other again."

She stuck out her tongue.

"I thought not." Nik leaned forward to touch his lips to her forehead. "Take care, Mac." Then he spun on his heel and left.

At the same instant, one of the sunbeams hitting the floor flickered again.

Startled, Mac glanced up at the skylight. Then stared. *Nothing.*

Suddenly afraid, she rushed to the door, but Nik was already out of sight among the trees. *Damn, he moved fast.*

She froze in place to listen, hearing only the pounding of her heart at first. Gradually, the distant scolding of a squirrel overlaid the faint buzz of uncounted hungry black flies, the drone of a passing beetle. Mac turned her head sharply at a rustling, most likely a sparrow, through a drift of pine needles beside the cabin.

Everything normal.

She shuddered, not reassured in the least.

- Encounter -

THERE IS NO advance warning of a ship about to arrive through a transect. In the bizarre universe of no-space physics, only the act of arriving can create the passage along a transect itself. You arrive at B, because you left A with the intention of arriving at B. Before and after this intention, there is no passage at all. Poets are frequently more at ease with the process than the astrophysicists responsible for it; the few who combine these skills can name their price in any system of the Interspecies Union.

There being no advance warning, management of a transect consists of controlling the approach path of all departing traffic, keeping it to the exterior of a cone of space funneling into each gate probability area—and charging the applicable tariffs and duties. Arriving traffic is granted the interior of that cone and each starship is expected to vacate that privileged space as quickly and expediently as its sublight drive permits, heading immediately, of course, to be assessed for the required arrival tax or fee.

This is the way transects are managed by every species of the IU, as set out in the agreements put in place by the Sinzi, who'd rediscovered the transect technology and made it their quest to share it with any species peaceful or at least law-abiding enough, to maintain their end. After all, when it came to instantaneous intersystem travel, the more destinations, the merrier.

However, the Sinzi being peaceful, practical, and fundamentally prone to cooperation—having several brains per adult body—it wasn't surprising they hadn't appreciated the full range of opportunities that would be presented by having doors to thousand of systems which couldn't be shut. Or even effectively watched.

Like the wide expanse of a river mouth which carries its assortment of vessels to ports on either side as well as out to sea, each transect gate area is large enough to accommodate vast numbers of ships at a time. Unlike boats on a river, who share the level plane of the water's surface, starships don't have to be aligned in any way to one another. There is only intention: coming in or going out.

While by treaty members of the IU shared responsibility for improper use of the transects, in reality warfare among systems belonging to the same species was typically overlooked, so long as it didn't impede the passage of other species' shipping. Moreover, the monitoring of smugglers, tax evaders, and other scoundrels was viewed as a system responsibility. This was not only practical considering the transects themselves, but also necessary given the variety of attitudes among species. As the saying went: one Sythian's pimp was another Frow's grocer.

The Imrya version was, naturally, more elegant, much longer, and constantly evolving through language forms to be trendy. But the gist remained the same. Species who wished to control certain elements within their space maintained patrols or a military fleet, or locked up their precious thirdborns. Whatever worked.

Until now, when the Imrya inserted their entire battle fleet, from mighty cruisers to slaved clusters of solitary fighters, within the whirling spiral of normal traffic moving to enter the Naralax Transect. Several enterprising merchants abandoned their original plans to exit the system altogether, choosing to sell their luxury wares directly to the hulking ships. Others dropped bribes to hurry themselves through the application process, hoping to avoid being too closely checked by a bored deck officer.

Every morning, a new analogy for the potential danger of this particular transect was shared. Today it was "Abyss in the Darkness."

Later, the poet responsible for those fateful words—a minor talent who'd had an admirer sneak three and a half dozen entries on her behalf into the command sequence—committed public suicide. It was considered a prideful gesture among Imrya, with its implication of having reached the pinnacle of success in one's field. The debate would rage for decades whether "Abyss in the Darkness" had been powerful enough in its syntax and subtlety to cause the disastrous events of that day. Regardless, the carapace of the poet, her fateful words inscribed along one edge, would sway in the wind with the thousands of others hung for posterity along the Immortals' Bridge. That those immortals' words couldn't actually be read from this honorable location was never mentioned.

The Imrya always had more words.

Perhaps the new analogy was more alarming than its predecessors. Perhaps the day itself was inauspicious, given the discontent throughout the Imrya fleet over missing the opening of the Playwright's Festival on the home world, an event that only took place every thirteen solar cycles and was claimed to usher in the next great phase of Imrya literary masterworks.

Or, perhaps, it was the startling clang of metal against the hull of an isolated, lonely scoutship, bits of debris dumped from a passing ship that seemed, for the merest instant, to be the silver-clad tentacles of a grappling Dhryn.

An instant is time enough for an alarm to be sent, but not for it to be rescinded. An instant is more than time enough for the wink of a ship to appear from the "Abyss in the Darkness." And it is exactly long enough for a well-trained, terrified fleet to open fire.

If the arrival had been a Dhryn Progenitor, with her cloud of horrific feeders, the carapaces of heroes would have hung alongside poets on the Immortals' Bridge.

But it was the vast Sinzi starliner, *Wonder's Progress II,* filled to capacity with twenty-five thousand, three hundred and fourteen souls, a mix of tourists, actors, and drama critics, members of the founding species of the Interspecies Union plus diplomats from a hundred worlds, en route to the Imrya's famed Festival.

To die with no more advance warning than they gave.

That which is Dhryn must pause the Journey.

Feeders, replete and heavy, return to cling to their carriers. The carriers rise from the empty husk of a world to link together, then rejoin the Progenitor. The Progenitor accepts what is brought, gracious as dawn to the day it brings.

Done with care; done with haste. Any pause is delay. Any delay is threat.

The Journey continues, to the relief of all that is Dhryn.

- 9 -

BETRAYAL AND BRAVERY

"HOW ABOUT FROM here?" Mac tilted her head back to admire the distant pile of sticks. "What do you think?"

Kay came to where she stood and brought his recorder up to his upper left eyestalk, peering through it in the direction she recommended. "So long as you are sure it won't fall on us, Mac," he fussed.

She laughed. "That nest's been up there since I was little, and likely before that. So long as the pine lasts, it will."

"Remarkable." The Trisulian took a few more images, using one hand to hold his small round device and his other arm held perpendicular to his body, as though having an eyestalk preoccupied affected his balance slightly.

Or maybe he thought the posture made him look artistic, Mac thought to herself, as always careful not to jump to conclusions about aliens. "Are you game to find the next?" she asked when he was satisfied.

"Lead on, O Guide."

"This way."

Mac followed faint memory and a fainter trail deeper into the woods north of the cabin. It had been easier than she'd hoped to keep both aliens occupied. When she'd returned to the cabin, she'd found Fourteen in the common room and Kay banished to the porch, where he was watching the other alien through the window. Meanwhile, Fourteen, having pushed the furniture and carpets against the walls, had begun arranging everything small and portable he could find in patterns on the floor. Completely oblivious to her or Kay, he scurried among the items on all fours like some demented carrion beetle, pushing and pulling each into new locations. The floor was already littered with utensils, plates, food containers, and Mac's childhood collection of porcelain frogs, all casting tiny distorted shadows in the sunlight coming through the porch.

Kay had agreed wholeheartedly—or whatever would be the corresponding body part for his kind—to Mac's suggestion they leave genius at work and hike out to the owls' nests to make the recordings she wanted.

Mac was satisfied. Fourteen was—presumably—working on Emily's message, her father would get his nest images after all, and, as per Nik's instructions, she was keeping the aliens out of trouble.

So long as she didn't get them both lost.

A trifling worry. Worst case, the bioamplifier in her bone marrow would locate them for anyone looking. *Not,* Mac told herself firmly, *that she would get lost.* A few years weren't going to change her forest beyond recognition.

Mac halted when the trail, a generous word for a slot of mud last used by a moose with a healthy digestive tract, took a steep drop. Steeper than she remembered. So steep, in fact, she could hold out her hand and almost touch the tops of the trees below. She stretched out to try.

"Is this the way, Mac?" In spite of his anxiety over plummeting nests, Kay didn't appear worried about a plummeting trail. Then again, he was a much better hiker than Mac had expected. His caftan, its variegated colors almost perfect camouflage in the shade-dappled forest, didn't snag on branches. *Certainly better on foot than paddling a canoe,* she grinned to herself. A little too good at times. Although because of Mac's height, Kay took two steps for each of hers and regularly bumped into her from behind.

"I don't think so," Mac said, backing away from what would be a challenging descent with ropes, let alone with a Trisulian on her heels. "Let's go around. That way."

Hiking—without getting lost—took a respectable amount of

concentration. Mac had gradually relaxed, able to push the rest of the universe—from vanishing spies to Dhryn—aside, for the moment at least. Besides, the maples and birch of the upper slopes were still unfurling flowers, not leaves. Their branches let through warmth and sunlight, sufficient to trigger a blaze of early blooming lilies and other wildflowers underfoot.

The black flies had even taken the afternoon off, much to Kay's relief. Mac didn't have the heart to warn him such reprieves were temporary until summer. Whenever they approached a meadow, Mac checked for bears, groggy from hibernation and likely to be with young, but the largest mammal they encountered was a porcupine, dozing in the crotch of an ancient apple tree.

They'd found two nests so far, both high, wide, and messy platforms originally built by eagles or ravens and preempted by pairs of great gray owls. No one was home. If owls still used them, the young would have fledged by now and be perching in neighboring trees.

The next nest wasn't the one Mac had been looking for, *not that they were lost,* but she was delighted to find it. A promising cavity beckoned in a towering stump, riven by lightning years ago. The rest of the tree lay in pieces at their feet. "Ah," she exclaimed triumphantly. "Pellets!" Sure enough, neat finger-length cylinders of compressed fur and tiny white bones lay tumbled among the logs beneath the cavity.

"Look." Mac picked a nice fresh one to show Kay.

"What is it?" he asked, an eyestalk bending closer. *Curiosity or a way to change focal length?* she wondered.

"A pellet. The indigestible remains of the owl's prey," explained Mac. "Likely from a Boreal Owl. Handy for research." She regarded the pellet fondly. "The bird just coughs it up." She began teasing the fur apart. "Yup. See? Vole bones."

"Usish!" Kay scrambled backward. "Get that away from me! Disgusting Human!"

It took Mac a fair amount of convincing, and a couple of threats, to get the Trisulian anywhere near the tree again. Once there, he stood like a statue, eyestalks riveted on the cavity as if on guard against falling pellets.

"C'mon," Mac coaxed. "The owls aren't active in the daytime. Besides, regurgitation is a normal function. You can't tell me you've never needed to remove something from your *douscent*. Same idea."

"I most certainly can," he huffed. "It's disgusting. Scandalous! I insist we return to the cabin this instant!"

She planted her feet. "After you've recorded it."

Kay whipped up his device, clicked it in the general direction of the tree, and started walking away as quickly as the terrain permitted. Following behind, Mac grinned and tucked the pellet into her pocket to examine later. *Not so much raven*, she judged, *as fussy old bachelor.*

It didn't take long for Mac to regret her glib reference to Kay's digestive pouch. He remained offended and silent. The trip back to the cabin took on the rigor of an endurance race. It helped that they were going mainly downhill, with their return path clearly marked by footprints—especially those in moose droppings. The race aspect was purely Kay, who not only appeared to know exactly where he was going, but couldn't get there—or perhaps it was away from her vomiting owls—fast enough.

Mac finally let him scurry off into the distance, dropping her pace back to a more reasonable amble. It was too hot to rush and she was too annoyed with his reaction to be particularly gracious. "By the time I'm back, Emily," she promised aloud, grabbing a sapling to help her clamber past a puddle, "I'll be civil. But honestly. Even sea cucumbers barf." She amused herself with visions of the dignified Trisulian attempting to deal with having dropped a knife or coffee cup into his precious *douscent*.

By the time Mac reached the last stretch of trail, the sun was low on the horizon. It would be bright out on the lake for a while yet, but under the pines the lighting was already growing dim. She didn't mind. This portion of the forest contained fond memories. There were a few more deadfalls, the closest of which she earmarked to raid for wood for a nice campfire if they stayed long enough. *And if the aliens liked fires.* The rest could shelter varying hares and ptarmigan. Her father's "owl feeding stations." The thought made her laugh.

A laugh that died on her lips as Mac entered the clearing behind the cabin and saw the kitchen door was open.

Not just open, but hanging at an angle from one hinge. The screen was shredded, as if by a bear's claws.

It wouldn't be the first time a famished spring bear took a walk through the kitchen. *It would be the first time it found aliens there.*

Mac broke into a run, feet soundless on the pine needles and soil, but making plenty of noise herself as she took the stairs two at a time. "Big Scary Human Coming!" she shouted as she rushed into the kitchen. "Fourteen! Kay!"

The kitchen was fine.

No mess.

No bear.

Mac looked back at the ruined screen and frowned. *How much of a temper did Kay have?* "You're going to pay for that," she vowed, walking into the common room. "The door wasn't locked. Oh . . ." Mac stopped with her hands on either side of the door-frame.

The Ro! Her first thought. But they left glistening slime with their destruction. No slime here. *Not the Ro, then.*

But there was destruction, of a sort. Mac picked her way into the room, eyes surveying everything, careful to touch nothing. One of the couches—two small tables. They'd been tipped over. *A struggle?* The organized, if bizarre, arrangements Fourteen had been creating were gone; the items he'd used swept into piles. Mac picked up a yellow piece of porcelain. A frog's leg. Not much broken otherwise. It was more as if the Myg's arrangements had been tidied, but in a rush. *Why?*

She searched the rest of the cabin, unsure why she stopped calling out the aliens' names. Fourteen's room first. The door was open. Mac peered in and snorted. No destruction; the Myg was about as tidy as a second-year Pred in June. Bedding was in a lump, there were clothes strewn all over the floor, and—Mac sniffed, then hurriedly closed the door. *She'd air the room out later.*

Kay's room was a pleasant surprise. The bed was immaculate; he might not have slept in it. *Well,* Mac thought reasonably, *for all she knew he slept on his hairy head.* No sign of clothing or baggage, not that she was sure he'd brought any personal belongings. He'd worn the same or identical garments every day.

Quickly, Mac checked the remaining rooms, then went out on the porch. Nothing. No note, no sign of either of them. She began to feel a sick certainty they'd left her behind, but why? *An emergency?* She checked the sky with an involuntary shudder. It couldn't have looked more normal, evening blue, curled wisps of high cloud harbingers of the rain scheduled to move through tomorrow.

Or had Nik been wrong about the two aliens? Like some bad spy vid, were Fourteen and Kay somehow traitors on a cosmic scale, their credentials fake, the envelope itself a forgery capable of fooling the Ministry's finest? Had their promise to take her to the Gathering, to work on the Dhryn, been nothing more than a ruse? Had they'd taken what they'd come to get? *Emily's message?*

Mac gave herself a shake. *She could be fooled, Em, but not Nik.* "Then there's the whole poodle plot," she told the forest, her lips twitching. "Quite the masterminds, those two."

Unfortunately, that brought her back to some emergency that had taken the two away—without her.

As for Nik? "Asks me to do one thing," she muttered darkly as she went down the steps to the path, intent on checking the cove. "Watch two aliens. How hard can that be?"

The sun was touching treetops on the far shore. Mac shaded her eyes to scan the lake. All of her canoes were either under the porch or leaning against the rocks behind her. The only movement she could see on the lake was a delirious pair of courting grebes running along the water, necks curled forward. *At least someone was having a good time,* Mac grumbled to herself.

She climbed back to the cabin. Nik had found time to repair the worst spot and Mac delayed to admire his work. Then she looked uphill and sighed. "If I don't fix that door, Em, I really will have four-footed guests for supper."

As for aliens? They could have been scared off by a bear. Or suddenly recalled by the IU, unable to wait for a slow Human.

Or were laughing at how easy it had been to fool them all.

Morose, Mac kicked at a root, missed, and sent a spray of fine grit off the path.

Rustle, rustle.

"Sorry," she called to whatever wildlife she'd offended.

One leg of the couch had snapped off. "Finally have a use for you," Mac told the truly dreadful ornamental box her brothers had kept trying to lose outside and her father had somehow kept retrieving. She righted the couch and shoved the box where the leg had been, turning it so the sneering clowns were out of view. "Perfect."

Mac tossed a cushion back in place, then dusted her hands, deciding to leave the piles for tomorrow. Everything would need to be washed—what wasn't chipped or broken. To be honest, she wasn't in the mood to discover how much remained of her collection.

They'd trashed her home. Left her behind.

Interstellar incidents had begun with less motivation.

She'd rehung the kitchen door as her first task, wiring the bottom hinge in place. It would do for now. The screen was ruined, but Mac found a board to tack over the opening for the night. No point making it easier on the black flies, who'd come out in droves once the air began to still.

What she wanted was for a certain spy to make an appearance.

"What I want, Em," Mac said with a firm nod, "is a beer. And supper. But the beer first." She went into the kitchen and pulled open the chiller. Small items were arranged on narrow shelves along the inside of the door. At first, she *tsked* with disappointment. "None left. Damn aliens." Then she spotted something promising on the lowermost shelf and bent to check. "Aha," Mac crowed. "Even cold." She began to close the door, then stopped, leaning her head to one side.

She'd heard something.

There.

A series of soft clicks, hardly louder than the snap of dragonfly wings.

It had come from the back of the chiller, behind the stacked boxes of alien provisions Russell had brought. *Which they hadn't bothered to take with them.*

Mac switched her grip on the beer bottle to turn it into a club, noticing her fingers were numb. *Cold wasn't the word.* She exhaled a plume of condensation. *Odd. She hadn't set the chiller to freezing.*

Bottle raised and ready, she peered over the boxes.

The Myg lay on the floor in a very Human fetal curl, eyes closed, his skin patched with frost. Dropping the bottle, Mac hurried to kneel beside him. He was cold to the touch, but not frozen solid. She started to give him a gentle shake, then saw the damage to the back of his head. "Oh, no," she whispered.

It had been a terrible blow. The skull itself was indented knuckle-deep along two parallel lines, the surrounding wisps of hair covered in pale green blood, already congealed. She couldn't tell if he was alive or dead.

Someone had tried very hard to make sure.

Forcing down her grief and anger, Mac concentrated on the task at hand. First, get him out of the chiller.

After a moment's consideration, she took hold of Fourteen's ankles and pulled. His body was rigid and stayed curled, but it slid along the floor. At least until the chiller door, where his hip stuck on the rim. She tried lifting him over it, but the alien was unexpectedly massive.

Think. How had Seung moved that shark by himself? "Wait here," Mac told the comatose—and probably dead—alien, feeling foolish. She ran to a bedroom for a blanket. It took a bit of effort to roll him over and slip the blanket underneath, but she managed. Then it was one strong pull to ease him over the rim and into the warmth of the kitchen.

Which was far enough, Mac realized grimly. If Fourteen was dead, she'd have to move his body back into the chiller for safekeeping. Nik or someone would want an autopsy. *Had there ever been an alien murdered on Earth before?* The paperwork alone boggled.

What sunlight was left sent beams along the floor of the common room, barely reaching into the kitchen. Mac turned on the lights and gathered her courage.

"You'd think," she told Fourteen as she examined him, "you people would learn not to visit me." The only other injuries she could find without disturbing his clothes were to his hands. Both were bruised and bloody. She couldn't rule out cracked bones. His left was clenched into a tight fist, as if holding something. Being as gentle as she could, Mac took his fist in her hands and turned it to see.

An eyestalk?

Kay.

"So," she said quietly, lowering Fourteen's fist. "While I took my sweet time coming back, you were fighting for your life." *In how many ways had she been a fool?* The Trisulian's headlong rush to the cabin had had nothing to do with alien squeamishness—he'd known he could outpace her on the trail, had doubtless calculated how far they'd have to hike to give him sufficient time to return and attack Fourteen before Mac could catch up. He'd planned this. Planned it all.

Wasn't that what murderers did?

"Here's hoping he failed," she told Fourteen softly. "But how do I know?"

Mac licked the back of her real hand and placed it in front of Fourteen's nose and mouth. The generous lips were slack and the tips of his white tongue protruded. She waited, but felt no moving air. "Not good." His thick eyelids wouldn't budge short of using pliers, so Mac pressed her ear to his chest instead. *Silence.*

She rocked back on her heels. "If you were me, and I were you, I'd be dead," she informed him, proud of her calm tone. Hearing it gave her more confidence anyway. "But you're not. Me, that is." Mac gave him a gentle poke. "You stopped bleeding, which isn't necessarily a good sign. But why would Kay waste time to put your corpse—not that I'm saying you're a corpse, Fourteen—in the chiller? I wasn't that far behind."

Mac stood and opened the chiller door. Her beer bottle had smashed open on the floor, the liquid already slush at the edges. She ignored the mess, going to the climate control. Not only was it set to minimum, but a bloody green handprint smeared the wall beside it. *Fourteen. But to try and turn it up, or had he turned it down?*

Hopefully, she'd be able to ask him. Mac cranked the temperature back to normal, then pulled the door closed again. Now that she looked for them, there were green smears on the kitchen floor leading from the common room. Not many. The number that might have been left by bleeding hands if Fourteen had dragged himself along.

Rustle . . . scritch, scritch.

A little early for a raccoon or skunk to be checking the kitchen door, but Mac didn't bother shooing the creature away. "Good thing I fixed it," she commented, going back to Fourteen. "Imagine what they'd think of you."

The flutter of dragonfly wings.

Much too early in the season for you, Mac thought with rising hope. "Fourteen. Can you hear me?"

Another series of those faint clicks. *She wasn't imagining it.* The sounds were coming from the Myg.

Mac wrinkled her nose and grinned with relief.

So was that smell.

She made Fourteen as comfortable as possible on the floor, pushing the table out of the way and slipping cushions from the common room under his head and feet. Rolled blankets supported the curl of his back. *Now to get help.*

Seconds later, Mac stared into the box where the cabin's receiver/transmitter had been. *Well,* she thought pragmatically, *it was still there, just in pieces.*

Fourteen had carried a standard-looking imp; Mac had watched him use it to send various messages yesterday. A quick search of Fourteen's clothes—he was back in the Little Misty Lake General Store sweatshirt but still the paisley shorts—turned up nothing that didn't seem permanently attached.

In the interests of being thorough, and an irrepressible curiosity, Mac did confirm his claim to no external genitalia.

She could canoe for help. That meant leaving Fourteen helpless for several hours. The novice canoe had a distress signal she could activate, if willing to paddle out and capsize it in deep water or run it into a rock. Again, leaving Fourteen alone too long.

The one time privacy wasn't a bonus. "If anyone's listening," Mac announced in a loud, clear voice as she walked to the door to the porch and looked out in the fading light, "I've a seriously injured Myg on my kitchen floor. Could be dead," she said honestly. "The Trisulian, Kay, tried to murder him. We need help. Anyone?"

Nik might have planted one of his toys in the cabin after all. *For once*, Mac decided, *she wouldn't mind*. "Where's a spy when you need one, Emily?"

Louder clicking.

Mac hurried back to the kitchen. Fourteen was still in his distressed curl, but she could swear an arm had moved from where she'd placed it. The warmth of the room might be helping—

Or she was imagining a dead alien was clicking and moving in her kitchen. "And the night's young, Em," Mac sighed.

Optimism was more useful. Acting on her hunch, Mac tossed a handful of towels in the sink, running hot water over them until they were soaked and steaming. After cooling them from scalding to hot, she began to apply the towels to Fourteen's shoulders and chest. She didn't attempt to wipe the blood from his head or hands. The clots were holding the wounds together. She placed the last towel around his neck.

Three soft clicks.

His fist eased open and the eyestalk rolled free with a clatter.

Clatter? Mac caught the thing before it went too far, holding it gingerly. "Well, I'll be . . ."

Up close, the eyestalk was clearly artificial, an elaborate hollow fake complete with pincerlike clamp at one end. The clamp presently contained a twisted gray lock of Trisulian hair. Fourteen must have yanked it free.

Mac touched the hair. It didn't feel real either.

Nik had commented on Kay's eyestalks, told her four were normal. "Now would be a good time to know why," she mused uneasily.

She added it to her growing list of questions and focused on her patient, replacing towels before they cooled too much. In between, she went through the first-aid kit she'd brought to the table. Nothing seemed worth trying.

A few minutes later, Fourteen suddenly and unmistakably moved again, straightening out with a ragged sigh. Mac held her breath and listened for his. Sure enough, as if the sigh had been the first, the Myg began taking shallow, labored breaths. She stripped off the last of the wet towels and tucked a thick quilt over him.

"See, Em? I wasn't wrong," Mac said rather smugly, sitting cross-legged on the floor. She kept one hand resting lightly on the Myg's chest, gratified to feel it continue to rise and fall, ever so slightly. "Not dead."

She'd sat like this with Brymn. Only instead of recovering, she'd witnessed the change in his body, felt it alter beneath her fingers, seen the horror in his fading eyes mirror her own as they both realized what he'd become—

And what it meant.

A pufferfish Dhryn, the feeder form. Green drops consuming a helpless woman, digesting her arm . . .

A tear splashed the back of her hand. Mac jerked in reaction, then gave an unsteady laugh at herself.

"Mumphfle . . ."

"Fourteen?" Mac kept her voice soft and low. He had to have an intense headache. Her eyes flicked to the ugly wound and she winced. *If any brains were left intact in his skull to feel it.* "It's Mac. You're . . ." *All right* seemed premature, given she'd thought him likely dead minutes ago. ". . . you're safe. He's gone."

His lips moved. She leaned down to listen. "Pardon?"

"IDIOT!"

Mac fell back in surprise.

"Idiot! Idiot. Id . . ." the word weakened with each repetition. Just as Mac was sure she was dealing with serious brain damage, Fourteen's eyes cracked open. "Not safe," he whispered in a thick but clearer voice. "It's still here. It will kill us both."

It? "What? The Ro?" Mac looked around her kitchen, seeing nothing out of the ordinary and certainly no slime. "There's nothing here but us, Fourteen."

"That Trisulian. THAT DEVIANT!" The shout brought on a spasm of painful coughs. Mac hurried to get Fourteen water, holding the cup to his lips and helping him drink.

"I've checked the cabin," she assured him. "Every room. We're alone. Tell me how to treat your injuries—"

"Then it's . . ." His damaged hand lifted toward the boarded-up kitchen door, gave a weak gesture.

"Outside?" Mac took a steadying breath. "Then whatever it is can stay there. Right now, I'm concerned with you. Kay tried to crush your skull, in case you haven't noticed."

"Not Kay."

That wasn't good news. "Someone else was here?"

"No."

He struggled to sit; Mac forced him down again. "You're not making sense, Fourteen. Stay still. Please."

The effort had cost him. Fourteen's already pale skin looked more green than beige. "Mac?" His small eyes fixed on her and she thought they showed surprise. "I thought you were dead."

"I thought you were." Mac's hands paused on the quilt she was settling around the alien's shoulders. "I see. You thought Kay had attacked me, too?"

"He came back alone." As if it was obvious.

She supposed it was and flushed. "I'm very sorry, Fourteen. This is my fault. I'd been warned about him—but not that he was dangerous. I didn't see any harm in letting him come back first. I thought you were—" She hesitated.

"Friends?" He coughed and raised a hand to his head. "Irrelevant. We remain in terrible danger, Mac. Listen to me."

Mac swallowed. "Kay's still here?"

"No. Yes. Irrelevant. This structure will not keep us safe. We must—" Fourteen's voice faded again. He waved urgently at the chiller. "In there."

"You were hiding," Mac realized.

"Like this." He touched the black fly disk on her belt. "It hunts by heat. My species enters torpor—sleeps—in the cold." A spasm of pain. "It couldn't find me."

"What hunts by—"

Rustle, rustle.

Bleeding hands grabbed Mac, pushed her toward the chiller door with unexpected strength. "Hurry!"

"That?" She resisted, careful not to hurt him. "Calm down, Fourteen. What you're hearing is local wildlife. A raccoon or squirrels in the rafters. They're just a nuisance."

He didn't look convinced. "We must hide until daylight. Then take a canoe—"

"Yes, tomorrow I'll paddle to the store and get some help. Meanwhile, let's work on getting you into a bed."

"No!" He pressed his lips together, then said: "If you won't go in the chiller, then close the door and we'll stay here. Leave on the lights. It doesn't see well in light."

Mac sighed. "What 'it'?"

"Kay."

"I thought you said he'd left."

"Yes. Deviant!" Fourteen coughed again and closed his eyes. "Please, Mac."

"Fine. We'll stay here tonight." By this point, she'd have done anything to calm him down. The head wound had reopened at one end of the gash. His breathing, never even, was more shallow than before. Mac closed the door to the common room. It didn't lock, but a chair wedged under the knob did the trick. The windows were already closed, but she checked the back door, feeling self-conscious. Her patch job was holding up.

Fourteen had watched her. He appeared more at ease now that she was taking precautions against "it." *Whatever "it" was, beyond his imagination.*

"Can I make you more comfortable?" she asked. "Is there anything I should do for your injuries?

"Irrelevant." Somehow the word was both tired and kind. "I have a thick skull."

Mac brought him a fresh cup of water anyway, and put it within reach. She went to a cupboard and pulled out the first self-heating meal she could find.

Scritch.

The sound of tiny claws on the outside of the kitchen door turned Mac's head, but sent Fourteen into an arm-waving, heel-drumming frenzy as he tried to get up and couldn't. Hurrying to him, Mac held him down until he stopped, then sniffed and sighed. "I'll go see what it is," she said, standing.

"No! No! Mac! No!"

She opened the door anyway.

Only to jump in fright as a lean raccoon scampered off the porch, equally startled.

"Damn aliens," Mac muttered under her breath. Furious at herself for taking Fourteen's babbling to heart, and quite thoroughly shaken, she stepped out on the landing.

Something heavy landed on the back of her head, grabbing her shoulders with what felt like teeth. Mac cried out and staggered, trying to pull it off. She felt hair come lose between her fingers. It wasn't hers.

A muscular writhing, then a blow against the top of her skull like a branch falling from a tree. Through tears of pain and blood, driven to her knees and half falling down the steps, Mac fought for a hold, some way to pull the thing from her. She felt it convulse again, as if coiling to strike. Remembering the parallel wounds on Fourteen's skull, Mac rolled and threw her head backward against the wood rail as hard as she could, trapping whatever it was.

One set of claws released her shoulder. Mac fumbled with her left hand, trying to grab the thing, and felt something bite and tear at her fingers. She only pushed harder, shoving those fingers deeper and deeper into what she devoutly hoped was a mouth. "Choke on that," she yelled. It spat her hand out and Mac threw herself against the wood again.

The weight on her head was gone as abruptly as it had arrived.
Rustle, rustle.

Hot blood poured down her face. Holding the railing with both hands, Mac searched the darkness beyond the light spilling down from the kitchen door. When nothing moved, she slowly rose to her feet, backing into that light step by cautious step.

A gleaming spot of red, a reflection from a solitary eye no taller than a raccoon, stared back at her from the shadow, as if in promise.

Then was gone.

"What was that thing?" Mac balanced the pack of no-longer-quite-frozen vegetables on her head and popped another painkiller. There were advantages to being besieged in a kitchen.

Fourteen sat at the table across from her, elbows on a cushion. He'd tried to come to her aid, but had barely managed to stand before Mac had bled her way into the cabin, shutting the door behind her and ramming a chair beneath its handle.

Now she understood his hands. The surface of her prosthetic hand was deeply scored; the ring finger had been snapped off at the joint. If she'd made a mistake and used her flesh and bone to fight off the creature, Mac was quite sure she'd be lying outside.

As it was, she had a probable concussion—hopefully nothing worse. Its first blow had glanced, tearing loose an appalling amount of scalp, but sparing her the full force, a force which would likely have crushed her skull.

She'd used skin patches from the first-aid kit to hold the gash together and stop the bleeding, more on the pinprick-sized holes in her shoulders—at least the ones she could reach. Her shirt was still damp but now with mostly water; she hadn't tried to get the blood out of her shorts.

"What was it? Kay." Fourteen smiled faintly at her scowl. He'd taken a couple of Human painkillers over her caution and was certainly looking better than she'd expected. *In all likelihood,* Mac thought, *better than she did.* "Trisulians keep their sex with them— their sex partners, to be precise. Each mature female accepts as many males as she can afford. They attach themselves to her body for the rest of their lives. She feeds them, they mate with her as she requires it. You have organisms with similar biologies on this world, as do we. Symbiosis?"

"Symbiosis." Mac used her damaged hand to pick up the artificial eyestalk. "They attach under the hair on his—her head," she guessed.

" 'His' head. Once a Trisulian possesses at least one male, the pronoun changes. Unless both are gone. Then he is a she again."

Meaning she should avoid pronoun issues. "So the eyestalks belong to the males?"

"Two are the females. One more for each male. Theirs are the eyes closed in daylight. Male Trisulians see only heat—infrared." Fourteen made a rude noise. "Kay was a deviant—removing an attached male to do his bidding, replacing him with that thing so no one would notice. It is something desperate criminals do, not civilized beings."

Mac did the math. "So there could be two of them out there?"

"No. Despite his greed, Kay was not willing to sacrifice both his symbionts." He indicated his own head wound. "But even one un-attached male is dangerous. They hunt for receptive females in the dark and use their external genitalia, a formidable armored club, to strike and kill rivals, defending the virtue of their prize. Males mature on Trisul Primus. Interested females let themselves be hunted through its jungles." Fourteen gave her that sly look. "It's all ter-ribly romantic—if you're Trisulian."

He must be on the mend. "I was clobbered by genitalia?" Mac al-most wished she'd had a look at the thing. "You're kidding."

He laughed, though weakly. "You are safe with me, Mac. Re-member, I have none!"

Rustle, scritch.

They both fell silent at the sounds from the closed back door. Sounds that had earlier tried the windows; once the door from the common room.

Mac cleared her throat and adjusted the cold pack on her head. "How intelligent are the males?"

"Idiots. Barely sentient. I believe a valid comparison to your Earth fauna would be a weasel. Something violent and persistent. And stupid. Luckily for me. Otherwise, it would have stayed to be sure I was dead, and not merely unconscious. But all it wants is to kill other males, attach, have sex forever."

"Yet controllable, at least to the extent that Kay could make it leave—him—and attack us."

He shrugged. "So it seems. Or maybe rejection has driven it mad and it blames us. All we can assume is that Kay knew his aban-doned paramour would do its utmost to kill us both."

Wonderful. Oversexed and overwrought. Mac tried to think through the pain and the cloud of post-adrenaline fatigue. "But why? Why would Kay want us dead?"

The Myg covered his eyes with his hands. "Because I'd finished the translation, Mac. When he learned what it said, Kay grew agi-tated, insisted his government had to have it before any other. I told him he was an idiot and we struggled. Here. The other room. It was a great battle. When he realized he couldn't win, he turned out the lights to allow his genitalia to find and kill me." He lowered his hands to peer at her. "But I was too smart for it."

"Yes, you were," Mac said soothingly, mind racing. *Emily's message.* Her own pain forgotten, she put down the cold pack and leaned forward eagerly, but carefully. "What was the translation?"

Fourteen rested his head in his hands. "Kay took my notes as well as your original," he said miserably. "I would show my work but I'd already swept up my cipher."

"You broke my frogs for nothing!" Mac punctuated this highly irrational statement by slamming her good hand on the table, an impulse she immediately regretted as the jolt made its way up her arm to pound between her ears.

Fourteen peered at her. "I could tell you what the message said," he offered.

Oh, for patience with the alien.

Mac composed herself. "Thank you, Fourteen. I'd very much like to hear Emily's message."

He began reciting a list of numbers in a monotone. Mac listened. The numbers kept coming. He paused for a drink of water. More numbers.

Finally, she had to interrupt. "Wasn't there a message? Some words?" Mac asked. *Something she could imagine was Emily's voice. "Hi Mac. Wish you were here. How're the salmon."*

"There is no need for words."

"I need words," she begged.

"But . . . there are none."

Mac dropped her face into her hands. *Gods, Emily,* she thought. *Couldn't you have done this one thing for me?*

"I understand, Mac. You want words from your friend. We are both idiots, are we not?"

Rustle, scritch.

She mumbled: "I can't believe you tried to talk me into sex with that."

"Good. Your sense of the absurd returns."

Mac laid her cheek along her arm and peered at Fourteen. "What do the numbers mean?"

"To me? Very little." His wide mouth stretched in a tired smile.

"But to those who know how to build signaling devices they will mean a great deal. They are communication settings. Adjustments. How to call for help against the Dhryn."

She lifted her head. "What are you saying?"

"Using this information, Mac, we can finally contact the Ro. The IU will be very pleased."

Scritch, scritch, THUD, *scritch, rustle.*

"Still after our heads, Fourteen," Mac commented after the noise subsided. *Going to need a new door at this rate.* "But why would Kay want this information for his species first?" Mac closed her eyes. "I know. Idiot. The Trisulians want to make some kind of deal with the Ro to protect themselves. Then they'll be safe to follow the Dhryn, like salvagers who follow a plague ship until its crew is safely dead. Adding planet after planet to a new Trisulian empire." *Kay didn't have to be a mastermind. Just ruthless enough to seize an opportunity.* She took the bag of nearly-thawed vegetables and threw them across the room, hard enough to break open and spatter mixed greens on the wall, kernels of corn bouncing on the floor. "How dare they!"

"We forestall them, Mac, if the IU contacts the Ro first. So that is what we must do."

You don't know the Ro, Mac almost said, then stopped herself in time. She didn't either, not really. And this wasn't the time to air her private grievances with their new allies.

If one ever came.

10

FLIGHT AND FRIENDSHIP

THE FLIGHT PATH TO THE COVE would be the worst part. Mac and Fourteen both knew it, without need to discuss his weakness or hers. As for leaving the safety of the kitchen? They'd hoped for strong sunlight to blind the lurking Trisulian, but dawn had lost itself in the gathering storm, right on cue.

Beneath the trees it might as well be dusk.

Mac had spent the night torn between wishing Nik had changed his mind and would soar up on a white lev and a more rational hope he had someone following Kay. Besides, how would even Nik suspect one of the little weasels, as she'd come to think of the male Trisulian, would be roaming the woods?

And how could you guard yourself against a sex-starved weasel with night vision and a hammer?

This being the unanswerable question of the moment, Mac resolutely ignored it.

"You ready?" she asked Fourteen, inspecting him carefully.

They both looked like death warmed over, she thought. Blood where it shouldn't be—neither having energy to spare for a change of clothes—and precious little of it in their cheeks. They tended to lean until they'd tip, overcorrect, then stumble into one another. But the best part, Mac decided, would be the look on Cat's face when they arrived at the store.

Given they arrived at the lake to start with.

"I'm ready," Fourteen said, making that faint click of distress as

Mac checked the tightness of his repeller belt for the third time. "I don't plan to swim to across the lake," he protested.

Time to share her final worry. "This isn't going to be like your last paddle, Fourteen," explained Mac, pushing hair from one eye. "The wind's gusty; waves are already white-capped. We could very well tip and that water is cold enough to put you back to sleep. This—" she patted the belt, "—will be all that stops you sinking like a rock."

"If I will be a hazard, Mac, you should leave me here."

They'd talked about this before, too. But the dawn had made its way into the kitchen through a ruined portion of the back door. While they'd slept—or more accurately passed out—sitting at the table, the little weasel had almost made its way inside. It wouldn't take much for it to succeed.

She wouldn't have risked Fourteen before. Now, she couldn't, not with the meaning of Emily's message in his head.

"I need you for ballast," Mac said. *Not altogether untrue.* "Let's go."

Pride had nothing to do with their progress from the cabin. More dizzy than not, Mac sat to skid down the steep sections, waiting for Fourteen to do the same. It had the added advantage of speed; *although,* she sighed inwardly when they reached level ground, *there'd definitely be gravel to remove.*

Even the cove had turned ugly, slapping at the beach with crisscrossing waves. The sky was the next best thing to sullen. Mac could see a dark band of rain on the other side of the lake. Spring had an edge in the north the weather regulators left alone.

"Wait here," she shouted over the wind and splash. Fourteen leaned on his paddle in answer.

The novice canoe—where they'd left it, but not how. Mac glared at the burned-edged holes along the hull. Doubtless the "rescue me" signal device was in need of more help than they were. Kay was thorough, she gave him that. *Probably all the catering.*

Her canoe rested beside it, untouched. It didn't have the toys of the novice, but she knew and trusted it. Mac reached down and flipped it over.

The Trisulian came with it, a grimy mop of snapping claws that just missed catching hold of her face, but snagged in her shirt.

So much for getting a good look at the thing. Eyestalk up and closed against the light, it curled like a scorpion over her chest, aiming an immense hornlike structure at her eyes. Mac couldn't move, couldn't raise her hands in time.

Smack!

The swing of a paddle blade in front of her nose freed Mac from the paralysis. She staggered back into someone's arms, knocking him down as well. She landed in a smelly heap of upset Myg and Human, squirming around to try and see.

Where was the damned weasel?

Then she saw it, a pile of broken claws and hair, like so much storm wrack washed ashore. It gave a last twitch and was still.

"What was that?" a horrified woman's voice. *How odd,* Mac thought, clinging to Fourteen, *that it wasn't hers.*

"Rabid skunk," a man replied in no uncertain terms. "First things first, Wendy. Help me get them up to the cabin."

It couldn't be.

Brain damage, Emily. That's what it is. Mac thought this very clever.

Until Oversight, in his familiar ill-fitting yellow rainsuit, leaned down and offered her his hand. "Hurry up, Norcoast. It's going to rain."

"How's that?"

"Better. Thank you."

Mac cradled a mug of hot cocoa in her hands, her feet and legs tucked up beneath her in the big chair, and watched Charles Mudge III deftly apply a field dressing to a Myg. In her father's cabin. On Little Misty Lake. Earth.

And in case she doubted the veracity of her senses, she had only to look in a mirror to see the Trisulian blood drying on her face, splattered there when Oversight had—

—*had saved her life.*

"May I help you wash up, Mac?"

She turned her eyes to Wendy's anxious ones and lifted her

cocoa a few millimeters. "Let me get this down first." *And have a chance of standing without falling over,* Mac promised herself.

Wendy nodded and sat in a neighboring chair. "Charlie's amazing, isn't he?" she said very quietly. "You should have seen him leap from the canoe, straight after that—" she hesitated.

"Skunk," Mac supplied helpfully. *Charlie?*

"Right. Skunk. I didn't know old guys could move like that."

By the slight stiffening of Oversight's shoulders, he'd overheard Wendy's comment. Mac smiled. "He's not old," she explained. "He just dresses that way."

This drew an indignant look. Mac lifted her mug again, this time in salute. "Welcome to Little Misty Lake, Oversight."

He made a noncommittal noise and went back to bandaging Fourteen's hands.

"We've contacted the authorities, Mac," Wendy went on. She'd half carried Mac up the slope, then gone back to help Oversight with Fourteen, who'd been near collapse. Quietly competent, making no comment about the state of the cabin—or its occupants— she'd sent a call for help, found her way around the kitchen to make hot drinks and sandwiches, and located the first aid gear for Oversight. The kind of person who radiated comfort and competence. Mac was mutely grateful.

Oversight, of course, was nothing of the sort. He finished with Fourteen, making sure the Myg was settled comfortably on the couch, then came over to glare down at Mac. "Authorities?" he barked. "Which ones will show up? Real police or your friends? You do realize it took every connection I had to get out of that ridiculous house arrest—"

"They aren't my—well, maybe some are," Mac corrected herself. "Let's hope it's them, Oversight. Sit." When he didn't, she sighed. "Please. We have to talk before they arrive. Wendy—I'm sorry to ask, but would you go out on the porch and watch for the lev? That path will be a minor river by now. Whoever comes might need help finding their way up."

"Sure, Mac." Wendy stood and shrugged on her coat. The wind was whipping rain against each wall of the cabin in turn from the sounds of it. The porch screens wouldn't be much protection. There was a deep rumble of thunder as well.

Oversight scowled and bent over Mac. "Hold still." She did, scowling back at him. He gently tilted her face toward one of the lights in the room, thumbs easing open her eyelids. Mac winced. "You know you have a concussion," this in a tone that implied she'd probably earned it.

Diagnosis complete, he sat where Wendy had been, pulling the chair toward Mac's until their knees almost touched. "At least we had the sense to beat the storm here. What were you thinking, trying to canoe in your condition?"

Mac took a sip of cocoa, feeling it warm her throat. "As I remember, I was thinking I was about to die."

He harrumphed, as if she'd embarrassed him. "I admit, Norcoast, I wasn't expecting to see a Trisulian male going for your head."

"You know what it was?" Mac was astonished.

"Of course." His round face creased in disapproval. "Didn't you? I took my share of xeno at university. Jokes about those walking gonads have been a standby of frosh parties for years."

Was she the only Human who hadn't studied aliens? Mac could hear Emily's answer to that. "Yes, I knew what it was." Then, because she hadn't said it yet, she did. "Wendy's right. You are fast for an old guy. Thank you, Oversight."

That look, the one saying he was set to be stubborn. "If you want to thank me, tell me what the hell's going on. I was flying over the Trust, cataloging earthquake damage, and see the pods being towed. I try to find out where, and lo, your staff's dispersed. You? Gone again without a word. Why?"

"I had no reason to stay," Mac ground out. "Norcoast's suspended all research until the pods are reanchored at the mouth of the Tannu River and the main systems are running."

"And you let them get away with that?"

Mac shrugged, her head instantly making her pay. "What should I have done, Oversight?" she asked wearily. "Chain myself to a pod?"

From his expression, Oversight thought this a perfectly reasonable notion, but he didn't pursue it. "At least your father had a good idea where you were this time," he said with considerable satisfaction. *Enjoying being a detective,* Mac judged. *There, Em, was a scary thought.* "What are you doing here, Norcoast? With him?" a nod to Fourteen "Like this?"

"You deserve to know," Mac agreed. She gazed at the man she'd fought with most of her professional career, over what they both loved. *Funny, how clear that could make a relationship.* "But be warned, Oversight. If I tell you—you'll be caught in it too."

"I am already. You're wasting time." He steepled his pudgy fingers and leaned back in the chair, regarding her with a placid, already-bored look Mac didn't believe for a second. "Get to the point, Norcoast."

Typical. Her lips twitched. "Fine. I've never been to the IU consulate, Oversight. Or New Zealand, for that matter. You were right. They were lies. I didn't make them up, but I was ordered to live with them."

"By your friends in black."

"Who work for the Ministry of Extra-Sol Human Affairs. The Secretary General himself enlisted me. You've heard of the Dhryn."

Fingers waved dismissively, then returned to their positioning. "Implausible hysterics."

"The Dhryn are deadly," Fourteen interjected, his eyes staying closed. "Everything you've heard about them in your news is true—and more. Idiot. The Chasm will be only the beginning of the devastation, unless they are stopped."

"He's right." Mac continued. "Last fall, a Dhryn—Brymn Las was his name—came to me at Norcoast. At that time, none of us—not even Brymn—knew the truth about his species."

"The media covered that—the first of his kind on Earth. I couldn't believe you'd let him interrupt your work."

Mac smiled into her cocoa. "You know me pretty well, Oversight." Her smile faded. "The Ministry asked me to help Brymn investigate some mysterious disappearances that seemed related." Her hands shook and she took a moment to cover it by drinking from her mug. "They were. That's when the trouble began."

"The incident at Base," Mudge frowned. "More lies, I take it."

"Yes. It wasn't sabotage or any 'Earth-First' protest. We were attacked by the Myrokynay, the Ro." Mac shifted into lecture mode. *Easier that way.* "No one alive knew they still existed except the Dhryn, who feared them. We—experts believe the Ro invented the transects in the first place, thousands of years before the Sinzi found the remnants of their technology in the Hift System."

"I know all that."

"What you don't know is that the Ro watched the Dhryn destroy the Chasm worlds. They've been hiding ever since, waiting for the Dhryn to stir again. To stop them."

"So they're the good guys."

Mac raised her eyes to his. Whatever he read there made him add: "Or not."

"The Ro's methods," Fourteen said for Mac, "are repugnant by the standards of cultures like yours and mine. They wanted Mac and her Dhryn companion to flee Earth, so they attacked the salmon research station with no regard for life. They used Mac to locate the Dhryn Progenitors, in order to attack them without warning. Even now, they use members of other species as their agents, altering their bodies with no-space technology."

"Including Em—Emily Mamani," Mac continued, finding her voice again. "She went with the Ro, to help them stop the Dhryn. To—to push me in the direction they wanted. She hasn't come back. Not yet. The rest—" she reached out with her mug blindly, trying to find a place for it. Mudge took it from her hand. "—Brymn thought I was in danger from the Ro, so he took me with him to his home world. Yes," Mac said, fully understanding the stunned look on Mudge's face, "I abandoned my research and went offworld. Amazing what a little carnage and kidnapping can do to a person.

"As a result," she finished, "I now speak and read Dhryn better than any Human language—and, I'm told, better than any other Human. So far as I know, I've spent more time with Dhryn than any other non-Dhryn being. I've even been semiadopted, I guess you could call it, as a Dhryn. All in time for the Dhryn, for my dear friend Brymn Las, to be revealed as the greatest threat civilization has ever faced." She showed him the remaining fingers of her new arm. "Did I mention surviving a Dhryn attack? And helping kill my friend?"

Mudge didn't say a word, staring at her as if she'd changed into something he couldn't recognize anymore.

She knew the feeling. Mac patted Oversight's knee. "Oh, it gets better. Our walk in the Trust the other day? A chance for Emily and the Ro to slip me a message that only Fourteen here has been able to translate. That earthquake? Deliberate. Someone, and I don't know who yet, making sure the Ro landing site wasn't explored by you, or I, or anyone else. And this?" Mac waved at Fourteen and gestured to her own cap of dried blood and first-aid patches. "One of the side effects of a threat to members of the Interspecies Union. Which does, you see, include us."

"You'll come with us, now, Dr. Connor."

Mac turned her head slowly, completely unsurprised to see the cabin porch filled with rain slicked black-visored troops, three more coming in the door, all with weapons not quite not aimed their way.

"Welcome to my world, Oversight," she told him.

"A sight to warm the hearts, *Lamisah* . . ."

Mac nodded. She didn't move, letting puppy-sized *oomlings* explore her lap and arms. Their white down quivered as they cooed to her, the sound itself low and soothing. Tiny hands, six from each, stroked her clothing, patted her cheeks, investigated her eyelashes. Each touch was feather soft.

They hadn't touched her.

"Our future . . ."

The cooing grew louder, gained an undersound that raised hairs on her skin, intensified her emotion. It came from everywhere around her, though there was nothing but precious, vulnerable *oomlings* as far as she could see, all reaching their tiny hands to her over the low walls of their pens.

But she'd only glimpsed the crèche from above.

"We haven't time to waste . . ."

Shadows passed overhead. The first green drops fell at a distance. The *oomlings* beneath cried out and crowded together, but there was no escape.

No. They weren't trying to escape. They were raising their faces, opening their rosebud mouths, calling eagerly for their share.

It hadn't been like this.

All but the ones in Mac's lap. They were changing—their down falling away from pulsating transparent flesh, their shape lost, eyes vanishing. They were rising from her hands into the air . . .

She screamed as drops fell from mouths that insisted, in their sweet cooing voices: "We told you to go, *Lamisah.* We warned you. Didn't we?"

The ground beneath shook as the Progenitor laughed . . .

"Promise to let me know the next time you feel so much as drowsy," Oversight warned Mac in no uncertain terms. "I'll sit with someone else."

"There isn't anyone else," she pointed out.

He couldn't argue, since they were alone in the rear compartment of a large transport lev. There had been three crowding the storm-tossed cove. Another had taken Fourteen. Mac presumed the third had been courteous enough to return Wendy Carlson to the Little Misty Lake General Store, where she'd have an interesting, if mysterious, tale to relate to Cat and Russell. A tale doubtless provided by one of their companions in black.

One day, Mac swore to herself, *she was going to park herself on the dock, shoo away the pelican, and tell the truth to everyone who stopped or paddled by.* Her head dropped back against the seat. *Maybe she should tell the pelican, too.* She wished she'd washed her face. The dried blood was itchy.

Mudge's movements disturbed her. "Can't you sit still for two minutes?" Mac complained.

He finished unbuckling his safety harness and turned to face her. Without asking, he grabbed her chin and tilted her face upward, checking her eyes again. "We've been in this thing over an hour. You need medical help."

Mac pushed his hand away. "I need sleep," she muttered irritably. "You keep waking me up."

"You keep screaming," he countered. "What do you expect?" Mudge stood, presumably to storm the door to the pilot's compartment where the large persons in black armor traveled—persons who'd refused to say anything more than "hurry" and "now." Mac caught his arm.

"Don't bother, Oversight. I'll be fine." He didn't look convinced. She was touched by his concern, but tugged a little harder. "Sit. I promise to do my best to stay awake until we get there. No more screaming."

He gave the sealed door another look, then sighed and sat down. *Probably remembering the "large" and "armored" part of their hosts.* "Get where?"

"Where?" Stealth vehicle with the latest tech or not, the lev vibrated in a way that didn't help her head. "Last time, Oversight," she managed to say, "I ended up in orbit."

Rather than alarmed, Mudge looked intrigued. "Really?"

It didn't help her stomach either. "Really." Mac leaned back and closed her eyes, pressing her lips together and breathing lightly through her nose.

He didn't take the hint. "I've a pilot's license, you know."

Ye gods. Oversight doing small talk. "Really."

"Really." Definite smugness to his tone. "My brother, Jeremy, designs golf courses. Travels more than a diplomat. Before I joined the Oversight Committee, I'd copilot his jumper. Racked up enough transect passages to go commercial, if I'd wanted."

Mac cracked open one eye to stare at Mudge. "You?" Realizing how this sounded about the same instant she drew an offended breath, she opened both eyes and added: "You seem so focused on Earth."

He seemed mollified. "I can understand why you'd get that impression, Norcoast. Certainly, the Trust has been my mission in life these past years. But I was first and foremost an explorer in my early days. Quite miss it, at times."

"I've never wanted to travel."

"Oh."

Could she be any less tactful? "Last time," Mac offered, "they brought me to a way station and we—Brymn and I—took a Dhryn ship from there."

"What was it like? Their ship?"

He was so interested, she felt guilty. *As well as nauseous.* Hopefully, Fourteen was faring better. "I didn't see more than my quarters and one corridor. A bit of the hold, I think. Sorry. The doors and walls weren't perpendicular. There was gravity and—" Mac paused, then finished reluctantly, "—not a drop of water." She fell silent. *Brymn had saved her then, too.*

"That was a brave thing to do."

"What? Oh, my going with the Dhryn?" Mac would have laughed if she could. "I'm not sure how brave it was. There didn't seem any other choice. Everything happened so quickly and he—they—" she fumbled "—the Ministry wanted me to go."

Too late. Over the years, Mudge had developed radar for exactly what she tried to avoid. "He? He who?"

Mac pinched the bridge of her nose between thumb and forefinger. It didn't stop the ache, but provided a welcome distraction. "The Ministry's liaison for Brymn, during his visit to Earth. He made the arrangements to get us offworld." *Now there was a distraction,* she thought. *Was Nik on this lev? Had he been one of the anonymous figures in black?*

"Doesn't 'he' have a name?"

Not if he hasn't shown himself, Mac decided. Not with this compartment undoubtedly monitored. Aloud: "Something complicated, eastern Europe-ish. Annoying civil servant type. You'd like him."

The lev picked that moment to swoop downward. "Someone's in a hurry to land," Mudge observed, refastening his harness and giving hers a test pull.

"Suits me," Mac said.

"What can we expect, Norcoast? One call and a small cell? Or just the cell."

He deserved to know, she decided, hearing the feather of understandable anxiety in Mudge's voice. *Not everything.* The IU's invitation was still in her pocket, but Mac had no idea what her status was anymore. She concentrated on picking the right words, annoyed with how difficult it seemed. "The Ministry has unusual powers right now, Oversight. 'Threat to the species,' that sort of thing. Odds are good this is about information. They'll have questions for us. Order us to keep silent or not bother. Send us home."

"Or?"

"Or we disappear, for as long as that threat exists and we're an added risk." Mac studied his face as the lev leveled out again. "I guess you're sorry you followed me."

His expression was set and pale. There were drops of sweat on his forehead, more beading his nose and upper lip. But he shook his head emphatically. "I'm sorry you didn't come to me with this—tell me what was happening."

"I couldn't tell my own father," Mac reminded him. "Besides," she added lightly, swaying with him as the lev did some more maneuvering, "I didn't think you'd—" *care* "—be interested."

He might have heard the word she didn't use. "I care about what affects the Wilderness Trust," his voice was as cold and hard as she'd ever heard it. "Because of you—because of what you brought to Castle Inlet—an entire ridge has been artificially stripped. Grant you, it's an opportunity to regenerate some of the rarer successional species—but we have sufficient natural disasters without your help. This is your fault, Norcoast. You were selfish. Thoughtless. You should have stayed away! You should never have come back!"

The last were shouts that echoed in the compartment, pounding inside her wounded head, every word horrid and familiar. Mac could hardly see past the tears welling up in her eyes. She turned and struck wildly at him. "Don't you tell me what I should have done!" she shouted back. "I know! I know!" Her face grew wet with more than tears. Warm blood ran down her left cheek. Some or all of the patches holding her torn scalp had ripped free. Blood entered her mouth, making her choke on the words: "I know!"

He had hold of her. "Stop," she heard him say in a shattered voice. "Stop, Norcoast. I didn't mean any of it. It isn't true. I'm sorry. I'm scared. I'm angry. I don't blame you. Of course I don't. The trees will grow back. You have to survive, too. Who—" she felt him press his hand against her head, trying to stem the bleeding, "—who else will I argue with?"

This last sounded so plaintive Mac laughed, though the sound was more gurgle than anything else. She swallowed the blood in her mouth and worked on steadying her breathing.

Later, for some reason she couldn't be sure how much later, other hands intruded. Other voices. "We've got her, sir." "This way, please." "Watch her head." Mac blinked and tried to focus, then gave up as the effort sent her stomach lurching toward her throat again. She was picked up—*must have missed the landing, Em*—and carried a short distance. Someone, or someones—*lost count of the hands, Em, wouldn't do on the dance floor*—put her on a firm flat surface that spun in slow, sickening circles—*or we're crashing, Em*—and it began to move as well.

The last thing Mac remembered clearly was Oversight's familiar voice. But it wasn't complaining about clumsy grad students or research proposals, or berating her about the fine print of a report.

It was shouting furiously: "Who's in charge here?" Then: "Stop! Where are you taking her? I demand to speak to someone in authority!"

She wished she could tell him what a bad idea that was.

11

ARRIVAL AND ADJUSTMENT

O NCE CONVINCED she was awake and not dreaming—*an uncomfortably full bladder always added that firm dose of reality*—Mac listened before she opened her eyes, trying to gain a sense of where she was before admitting to being there. *It worked in novels.* But this? Waves against rocks. A shorebird?

She couldn't be home again. Could she?

Mac peeked through her eyelashes. Bright enough for sunlight, or someone wanted her awake. Nothing for it. She had to open her eyes. *So much, Em, for peace.*

All that happened was being able to see the room around her. No sudden assault of words or people poking at her. *No pain or nausea either.* Mac sighed with relief and took a better look, turning her head cautiously on what felt like heated jelly.

The ocean sounds were coming through a pair of French doors, trimmed in white and ajar to frame a picture-perfect view of water, sky, and tumbled cloud. There was a terrace just outside the doors, complete with a table set with sun-touched flowers and chairs cushioned to match.

Mac investigated the strange pillow with one hand. Not fabric but something almost organic. Soft and soothing, it caressed the skin of her cheek as she rolled her head to look the other way, yet fully supported her shoulders and neck.

On the opposite wall, the room had a second pair of French doors, these closed and their windows frosted in intricate patterns as if to grant privacy. To the left was an arch into another, wider room, also, from what Mac could see, white. Between arch and doors stood a pedestal topped by a vase filled with pale, nodding roses.

On the other side of the arch, however, was a large lump of what appeared the same white jellylike substance as Mac's pillow, shaped something like a chair. In its midst, curled into a ball of yellow rainsuit, slept Charles Mudge III.

Now there was an unexpected development.

Careful to move quietly, Mac sat up and put her legs over the side of what was an elegant, if unusual bed. Her pillow was part of the mattress, the mattress itself having a pouch on top she'd mistaken for being between satin sheets. She stroked the surface, admiring the lustrous feel.

Her artificial hand still lacked a ring finger, but the rest of her, Mac discovered, had been washed and dressed in a long, sleeveless gown, again white, which might have been made from the same stuff as the bed. Light and incredibly comfortable, the fabric was generating warmth along her shoulders and upper back, as if detecting the small ache she felt there.

Speaking of aches. Mac decided against exploring her head wound by feel, and stood, cautiously, in search of the washroom.

The floor was another delight. She glanced down, startled to find cool sand—or its counterpart—oozing between her toes. She didn't need to tiptoe to move silently past Mudge.

The area beyond the arch resembled a sitting room from a Human home, in that it held four more of the large lump-chairs, gathered in the center around a low, rectangular table. *But the table?* Mac walked over to it, going to her knees in the sand to have a better look. It was as if a slice of the undersea world had been transported here. The effect was so real, with no signs of a boundary between water and air, that she hesitated to touch it. Finally, she did, feeling a hard slickness under her fingertips her eyes insisted wasn't there.

It didn't fool the school of bright coral fish who swam to investigate her fingers. They stopped just short, then flashed as one in a tight turn, swimming into the protecting fronds of an anemone.

The depth—she could see an improbable three, perhaps four meters down, as if the table went through the floor and sunlight followed, yet her hands told her the table ended above the sand,
sitting on six round feet.

"You're coming home with me," Mac promised the table.

One wall of the sitting room was window, looking to sea. The
rest were unornamented, finished in plain white, as if designed to
urge the eye outward. She dug her toes in the sand, seeing no footprints but hers. *Designed by whom?*

The washroom itself was through a door on the far wall. It featured reassuringly Human plumbing, with water, as well as a tall s-
shaped curl of perfectly reflective material surrounding a similarly
shaped podium. The function was obvious, but Mac felt painfully
self-conscious climbing into the elaborate thing just to check her
head.

"Could have been worse, Em," she decided. A wide swathe of
hair above her left ear had been replaced by a kind of bandaging
she'd never seen before. Similar to her skin, but with a bubbled texture. She could touch it, even put pressure on it, without pain.

Mac tried to coax a couple of curls to lie over the gap. They
sprang back to their original position as if insulted. *Hair could be so
opinionated.*

She considered the rest, looking over her shoulder. The gown,
simple as it was, was more elegant than anything she'd worn in
years, clinging, as the expression went, in all the right places. To
Emily's despair, Mac usually went for functional and clean. Or The
Suit.

That didn't mean she was unaware of the potential of other types
of clothing. Or that she didn't approve of what she saw at the moment.

Would he?

Interesting if totally unhelpful question. Mac grinned at the serious look she caught on her own face. "It's only a nightgown,"
she reminded herself.

Her eyes followed the exposed line of shoulder and upper arm
to where flesh ended in pale blue, like the porcelain of a doll.

If she'd wanted to hide it, she'd have gone for the cosmetic skin, not this strong and useful material. *It had saved her life*. Mac traced the marks gouged into the wrist and back of the hand with her fingers, grateful and troubled at the same time.

"Does it cause pain?"

It was quicker to glance in the mirror than whirl to find the source of the soft-voiced question. Mac found herself looking into a face beside her own, a face that was a study in bone and angle, as aesthetic as the rooms. She had no doubt she was looking at their creator—or rightful inhabitant. "No," she answered and turned. "Hello. I'm Mackenzie Connor."

Sinzi. There could be no mistaking a member of the first sentient alien species to make contact with humanity. Any child would recognize those upswept shoulders, rising higher than the top of the head; every history book held images of their tall, straight forms, standing like sapling trees among smaller, rounder Humans. And every biology text rapturously described those two great complex eyes, comprised of a pair for each individual consciousness within the body, and speculated on the psychology of being many in one. For the Sinzi were the only group mind yet encountered.

Mac stepped down from the podium. The Sinzi courteously bent her long neck, for the graceful shape of the shoulders was feminine, to keep their eyes at the same level. Mac could see herself in a dozen topaz reflections. *Six minds*. Not unusual, but as far as she knew more than average. "We know who you are, Dr. Connor, and are enriched by your presence."

She couldn't remember if a Sinzi referred to him or herself in the plural, or if "we" meant more nearby. *Must read more*, Mac promised herself. "Thank you. I appreciate the care . . ." she hesitated. *What was Sinzi protocol?* All Mac could remember at the moment was that they were polite. *But one species' "polite" was another's "insult."* And among the species of the IU, the Sinzi were the next best thing to royalty.

The Sinzi made a gracious gesture with her fingertips. Humans had originally mistaken the fingers for tentacles, apparently amusing the Sinzi representative. The aliens had true hands anatomically more similar to those of whales or bats, than primates. Their arms had been reduced to a series of joints within the upper shoulder complex, fingers beginning at that point and extending below the waist. Each of the three fingers per "hand" was the diameter of a human thumb, with such strong bones and joints that they appeared skeletal rather than flesh. The nail at the fingertip was thick and functional.

Far from elongated bony claws, the fingers were sleek and flexible, capable of subtle moments of extraordinary precision. This Sinzi had coated the upper third of her fingers with delicate rings of silver metal, sparking light each time a joint flexed. She wore a shift identical to Mac's, simple and as white as her skin. On her curveless body, it fell in straight pleats to the floor, brushing the sand and the tops of her long toes, four of which pointed forward and two behind, to act as heels.

"You may call me Anchen, Dr. Connor," the Sinzi said. *"Me" answered the pronoun question,* Mac thought, fascinated as Anchen turned her head as though to bring particular eyes into closer focus on her. "While your injuries are not serious, I would recommend you spend the next period of time resting and regaining your strength. There was significant blood loss. Please stay here until you feel able to join your fellows. No one expects otherwise."

"Mac, please. My fellows? I don't understand."

"The Gathering, Mac."

The Gathering? They'd been transported by agents from the Ministry of Extra-Sol Human Affairs; she'd swear to it. The same people who hadn't wanted her to receive that invitation, but . . . Nik had implied accepting would put her under IU jurisdiction, not Human.

Yet Humans had brought her here. *Okay. Where,* thought Mac a little desperately, *was here?*

"Anchen, where am I? What is this place? Am I on Earth?"

The thin-lipped Sinzi mouth was triangular, but quite flexible. Anchen demonstrated that by forming a pleasant, albeit it toothless, smile. "My apologies, Mac. I realize the Gathering is being held secretly, for security, but I thought you knew. These are part of my apartments within the residence wing of the Interspecies Union Consular Complex. Definitely on Earth. New Zealand, southern hemisphere, to be precise. It is the consulate's honor to

host the delegates who gather to share their knowledge of the
Dhryn."

Mac frowned. "Humans brought me here. Didn't they?"

"Yes, of course. The consulate has always relied upon your government for transportation. Any movement of non-Humans on
Earth continues to attract attention, Mac, and your species has a
limitless curiosity under normal circumstances. I'm sure any un-
predicted traffic over your world would be noticed, given the ten-
sions of the times." *An understatement.*

Well, she was into it now. Feeling her way around the concept,
Mac said, "What do I do in this Gathering? Has it started? Where
do I go?"

"The Gathering has been underway for some time, Mac, but we
continue to add new delegates such as yourself. Please, rest. You
will have full access to all information and sessions which have
taken place over the past weeks, and meet the others as soon as you
are fit."

"I'm fit now, Anchen." Beyond eager, Mac came within a breath
of asking for access to reading material, then changed her mind.
Learned the hard way, Em. Check the fine print. "Anchen, I'll need
my things, from Norcoast. And to contact my family and friends—
let them know I'm all right." *Even if she couldn't tell the whole truth.*
In Mac's firm opinion, one mysterious disappearance was enough
for a lifetime.

"I will look into appropriate arrangements." It wasn't a re-
sounding yes, but it wasn't no either. *And no one would miss her for
a couple of weeks, anyway,* Mac reminded herself. "In the meantime,
I advise you to more fully recuperate," the Sinzi bowed, a complex
and graceful movement Mac didn't even attempt to emulate. "You
and the other delegates face a daunting task."

Mac nodded. *Daunting covered it.*

She'd been ready to go into space, to work on some alien world.

Instead, she was in the one place in Human-settled space where
Humans held no power at all. Where they were only permitted on
business for the IU.

Where she was the alien.

After showing Mac how to contact consular staff with any needs, which involved nothing more difficult than pressing her hand any-where on a wall and asking out loud, Anchen left as swiftly and silently as she'd arrived. Mac watched the sea life for a while—an admirable selection of local fauna she would have believed no more than images suspended inside the table, except for the convincing way those animals with eyes reacted to her presence. It begged the question: could they see her because they really were in the room or were they able to see her because she was an image sent to where they really were?

There was headache potential, she decided, *if it wasn't enough a weasel had tried to split hers open with his gonads.* Mac grinned to herself. Which would make one of those stories to tell Emily. One day.

Time to deal with Oversight.

Back in the bedroom, Mac found Mudge, to all outward signs, still asleep in his raincoat. *And if she believed that?* She sat on the bed, briefly startled by its ability to immediately form to her body. "That can't be comfortable, Oversight," she observed.

Silence. Then, a faint hoarse whisper: "You'd be surprised." He didn't move. She might be talking to a stuffed yellow ball. Wearing boots. "Are we alone now?"

"I doubt it."

More silence, then a slightly mortified: "I didn't see any 'bots."

The innocence of those used to legal surveillance, obvious and fa-miliar. "I was going to order lunch." Mac glanced at the long rays of sunlight on the terrace. "Breakfast," she amended.

"You're sure? Bother." Mudge unfolded with a groan, pulling off his raincoat. Beneath, his shirt was wrinkled and sweat-stained. He glared at the room as if its crisp surfaces were to blame for his condition. "And it's supper. New Zealand. We arrived around mid-night local time and you've been out of it for almost fifteen hours. It's now four in the afternoon. Fall, by the way, not spring. Nippy." He rubbed his eyes and peered at her. "And tomorrow, not today."

Mac snorted. "I can do the conversions, Oversight. Don't tell me you've been in that chair the entire time."

"No." His tone did not encourage curiosity. Nor did his expression, with its classic Mudge-stubborn clench to the jaw.

She ignored both. "What happened?"

"It's not important. Order the food. I haven't eaten since getting here."

Mac smoothed the fabric over her knees. "I can wait."

"You can—" he started to bluster, then grimaced. "And you would, too. Very well." He slid lower in the jelly-chair, heels digging lines into the sand of the floor. "After they carried you out of the lev, they tried to leave me in it." Mudge stretched his hands over his head. "I didn't agree," he said simply.

Which doubtless meant numerous threats to contact authorities of every ilk, all delivered at significant volume. She had heard some of it. Mac shook her head in wonder. "And that worked?"

"No. They locked me in the hold and ignored me for quite some time. Luckily, someone already at the consulate who knew me heard I was being forced to leave against my will. He straightened your friends out in a hurry, found out where you'd been taken, brought me along. So here I am."

Leaving Mac with two pressing questions. One Mudge couldn't answer. *Why had that someone helped him stay where the IU was hosting a very secret meeting?* One he could. "Why didn't you go?" she asked.

His round face reddened. "How can you ask me that, Norcoast?" Mudge objected gruffly. He got to his feet and shook his finger at the light fixture hanging from the ceiling. "Think I'd let you carry her off to who knows where, hurt and unconscious?" he told it. "Think I'd take a chance you meant to finish the job the Trisulian started?" He looked back to Mac, his eyes round with distress. "What kind of old friend would do that?"

Old friend? There was a novel interpretation of fourteen years of conflict. *It had led to a certain depth of mutual understanding,* Mac conceded. But not to expect Mudge to stand up for her as though she was part of his Wilderness Trust. *Proving him a better friend than some,* her inner voice whispered.

It didn't matter. Couldn't matter. Mac fought the warmth of having someone think of her first, aware above all else that Mudge didn't belong here. It wasn't just the IU. She could hear Nik's warning: *"Don't let anyone close."* It wasn't meant for her protection alone. Mudge could have been safely, if angrily, on his way back to house arrest by now.

Of course, then she'd be without a friend.

"I suppose hugging is out of the question," Mac said, smiling at his alarmed look. "Thought so. Supper do?"

Despite her good intentions, which included regaining her strength as quickly as possible, supper was wasted on Mac. Her stomach rebelled the instant the steaming platters arrived— brought by courteous staff of some humanoid-type species she didn't know, clad in pale yellow uniforms. They set it out on the table on the terrace, where Mac spent the meal watching enviously as Mudge ate his portion, then accepted most of hers.

"Splendid," he informed her when done, wiping his lips and sipping the last of his wine. "You're sure you don't want anything else?"

Mac assessed the status of the few spoonfuls of soup she'd forced down. *Uncertain.* "Quite sure." She gazed into the distance, estimating there wasn't much time until full sunset. The view was of water, with perhaps the hint of islands on the horizon. She'd taken a quick dizzying look over the rail to confirm they were on land. A great granite cliff, to be exact, sheer enough that incoming waves struck and rose in gouts of foam. *She'd have to check the tides.* This building was a white curved tower, four stories high as Humans measured, the curve another s-bend like the mirror, following the edge of the cliff. These rooms were on what Mac estimated was the third floor, though she assumed the building extended below ground, into the rock itself.

She was no closer to knowing what to do about Mudge, Mac admitted to herself. Nik might help, but she'd have to wait for him to contact her. His people had brought them here, presumably willingly, so he either knew where she was, or would find out. *Didn't mean she'd hear from him anytime soon.*

Or at all.

"What do you know about the consulate—this place?" Mac asked Mudge, not hopeful.

He surprised her. "I applied for a job here once, so I made sure I was pretty familiar with it."

"Let me guess," she smiled. "Shuttle pilot."

"I was young, Norcoast. Alien worlds sounded more interesting. What I know isn't up-to-date, though."

"Tell me about it. Anything," Mac pressed. She'd learned to value knowing her surroundings.

According to Mudge, who tended to describe things with as many numbers as possible, the consulate occupied a stretch of coast five kilometers long and three wide, along the southwestern edge of New Zealand's South Island, occupying the tip of one of many fjords that fingered the Tasman Sea. No roads or walking trails led here. The only docking facilities were for consular traffic, and those only by air. The complex itself had grown over time into a sprawl of connected buildings, a few Human-built, most contributed by those handful of species interested in a more substantial presence on Earth, the rest being the original constructions of the Sinzi themselves.

The nearest Human habitation was the town of Te Anau, the hub for those seeking the vast wilderness preserved along the coast, the Te Wāhipounamu. Accustomed to tourists tramping through in all seasons, few residents took much notice of the consulate or its visitors. In fact, local New Zealanders were so accustomed to aliens wandering their streets that most shop signs were in both English and Instella.

There had been many obvious reasons for setting the consulate here: a temperate climate, if you didn't mind meters of rain per year; nearby mountain ranges offering microclimates from lush forest to desert to snowpack; even the lease arrangement between New Zealand and the Ministry of Extra-Sol Human Affairs, who acted as titular landlord to the IU. Less obviously, the area was off the beaten track and sparsely populated, making it easier to isolate alien from Human and vice versa. And, though no one said it out loud, if anything nonterrestrial was released and spread, it wouldn't be the first time New Zealand had had to deal with foreign biologies.

Mudge stopped, rubbing his face self-consciously. "You let me talk too much, Norcoast."

Mac gestured to her head. "With this? I'm more than happy to listen to someone else. Interesting stuff. Thanks, Oversight."

He harrumphed, managing to sound pleased. "Did I mention the trout fishing? It's quite famous here. I'd assume at least some visitors to the consulate indulge."

Mac contemplated a fast-flowing stream filled with aliens in paisley shorts and fly-fishing hats. "It wouldn't surprise me," she chuckled, "but it might the trout."

"Norcoast. I know you should rest, but . . ." She recognized that anxious wrinkle between his eyes. Mudge was preparing to fuss over something.

Warily. "But what?"

"Why did they bring us here? Why the consulate?"

Right to the heart of it. Again, typical. Not that Mac had ever had reason to doubt Mudge's intelligence. He probably knew as much about the research underway at Base as she did.

Lie or evade, Em?

Evade, Mac decided. It wasn't a moral choice—her head was too fuzzy to attempt anything as profoundly complicated as falsehood. "The IU must have questions about Emily's message—and the Trisulian, Kay." Or not-Kay. *Once-Kay?* Mac wasn't sure how one referred to an abandoned symbiont.

"But they didn't bring you here for questioning after the Chasm."

"No," Mac answered, wondering where Mudge was going with this. "The IU had people on the ship that brought me back. I answered their questions—" *for days on end, hazed with grief and pain, repeating the same details over and over and over,* "—and they have copies of everything I know. I'm sure the Ministry kept them informed since." Easy to picture Nikolai Trojanowski in this place, delivering the latest recordings of her dreams into Anchen's long fingers. Mac shivered.

She hadn't intended it as a distraction, but it worked. "You're getting cold," Mudge noted with a scowl. "Let's go inside."

"I'm warm enough," said Mac truthfully. The terrace floor was warm underfoot; she suspected it generated heat to combat the chill of evening. As for herself, the Sinzi's gown was either insulating or warming; regardless, it kept the skin it sheltered at a comfortable temperature. "I like it out here." *It was home,* she thought, the familiar scent of salt and seaweed, the tireless argument of wave against stone so normal she felt as though her bones had melted into the chair. *Probably couldn't stand if I wanted to, Em.*

Mudge muttered under his breath and then went inside for a moment, returning with his raincoat. "The blanket's part of the bed," he explained, putting the coat over Mac's shoulders despite her protest.

It was heavy and somewhat redolent, but it did feel good on her bare arms. *Almost as good as the gesture itself.* Mac looked up at Mudge. "Thank you."

He harrumphed again, but a fleeting smile escaped before he sat again himself. "There's something going on here, Norcoast," he insisted, earnest and determined. "Something other than normal consulate business. When we came in, you probably didn't notice, the pilot hovered for some time—my guess is there was traffic landing ahead of us. I've kept watch most of the day and there was a steady flow of incoming levs with very few departures this morning."

After their arrival? Not good, Em. "They entertain," Mac said, aware how flimsy it sounded. "Really big supper parties. Famous for it." He didn't need to respond; Mudge's face, she'd often thought, might have been set on skeptical at birth. *Or else she brought that out in him.* "What else have you seen?"

Mudge's expression went from skeptical to grim. "The security here. I'm no expert, but it's as though they expect to be attacked at any minute. They even searched me. I will spare you the details, Norcoast, but I have," this with the gusto of one truly offended, "written a memo."

She didn't doubt it. Mac tucked herself more snugly in his raincoat. "It might have been better if you'd left when they gave you the chance. You still can." *Maybe,* Mac added, honest with herself at least.

"Not without you." *Stubborn as his trees.*

Don't make promises. Mac made herself smile. "You make it sound as though I'm in some kind of danger here." Light, confident. "Nothing could be farther from the truth. They've taken care of me, offered their hospitality. As for being here, meeting the Sinzi? What an amazing opportunity! I intend to take full advantage of it. It's that, or fix the cabin door and wait for Base to be running again. I think there's no—what?"

He'd puffed out his cheeks, now adding a frown just shy of thunderous. "Tell me it's the concussion."

"Too much?" Mac pulled a face herself. "The bit about the door, wasn't it? A little over the top, I know."

"This is no joking matter, Norcoast! They wouldn't let me contact anyone outside the consulate. I'm sure they won't let you either. That's hardly benign."

"No," Mac sighed. "But since the Dhryn, it's become business-as-usual, Oversight."

He put both elbows on the table and leaned forward, eyes harder than Mac had ever seen before. "I'll tell you what I think is going on, Norcoast. I think there's some kind of secret meeting being held here, something the IU doesn't want the rest of Earth to know about. I think those incoming levs are bringing others like you, who've had some experience with the Dhryn. You've been coerced—kidnapped—and you're trying to protect me by not telling me the truth."

Now he'd done it.

Mac closed her eyes, unable to decide if she'd let anything slip or if Mudge had put his foot in it all alone, estimating how long it was going to take for someone in authority to show up on the terrace. *Not long.*

"Well?" he demanded hoarsely.

She looked at him. "What do you want me to say, Oversight? That your usual blend of mistrust and cleverness just cost you the chance to leave here anytime soon? That you should have stayed in

Vancouver? That you should have repotted that damned aloe plant by now?"

Sure enough, over his shoulder Mac saw the doors to the bedroom open, helmeted figures in all-black uniforms following those in yellow. "I wasn't kidnapped. I was invited," she told Mudge in an urgent, low voice as the others approached. "Don't you understand? Working with these people is the only way I can do anything, the only hope I have. It could be the only hope any of us have. Yes, I've tried to keep you out of it—for your own good—"

Too late.

They'd lined up behind Mudge, four who appeared identical to the Ministry agents she'd seen before, visors down, plus three consular staff. Only now realizing he was essentially surrounded, Mudge lunged to his feet, his eyes wide.

"Would you come with us please, Mr. Mudge?" Respectful, proper. *Somehow looming over the poor man spoiled the effect,* Mac thought resentfully. "Dr. Connor needs her rest."

"Dr. Connor," she informed the one who'd spoken, "wants to know where you are taking her friend and colleague. And how to reach him there."

One of the yellow-clad humanoids, consular staff, bowed so deeply Mac had an excellent view of how her short bristly hair was trimmed in tidy brown spirals from crown to the base of her neck. *Not that she cared at the moment.* "To his quarters, Dr. Connor. You will have ample opportunity to visit tomorrow, I assure you. But Noad, your physician, left firm instructions as to rest. Please. We must insist."

"Noad?" Mac didn't recall the name. Then again, she didn't recall being seen by a physician either.

"It's okay, Norcoast," said Mudge, making a valiant effort to take this in stride.

"It is not okay." Mac rose to her feet, taking off Mudge's raincoat and folding it carefully as she spoke. Her voice was the one she reserved for negligent students and unreliable skim salespersons. Mudge probably recognized it too, given their history. "I will not let these—these people—push you around. You came to help me." She put the raincoat on the table, her hands flat on top. The gesture nicely covered the need to hold on to the table in order to stay on her feet. "Oversight can stay right here. There's plenty of room."

The consular staff began whispering among themselves in another language, as if she'd proposed something scandalous. Three of the four in black turned their visor-covered faces toward the one who'd spoken to her. Their leader? *Good to know.* Mac kept her eyes on that one, standing as straight as she could. The cool sea breeze tugged at her hair and gown, but she ignored it. The pounding above her eye was another matter. *Any minute now, Em, she was going to throw something or throw up.*

"Well?"

"Such an arrangement would not be acceptable to our hosts." Before Mac could protest, the Ministry agent continued: "But there's an apartment across the hall. Will that be close enough, Dr. Connor?"

She caught Mudge's look of relief out the corner of her eye. She shared it, but waited for the rest. Concessions from such people always involved something in return. Sure enough, the agent held out his hand for Mudge's raincoat. To pass it to him—or perhaps her, given the armor—Mac would have to lift her hands from the table.

Something she couldn't do without falling on her face.

Mr. Ministry Agent could wait forever before she'd ask for help on those terms.

He appeared prepared to do so.

Stalemate. *At least until she passed out.*

Then Mac noticed his left forefinger tapping the side of his holster.

"Across the hall would be perfect. It's good night, then, Oversight," she said cheerfully, sitting down and shoving the raincoat across the table. "Talk to you in the morning."

Mudge took his coat, giving her a puzzled look. "In the morning, Norcoast."

"But I'll talk to you now," Mac said, pointing at the agent who'd tapped.

The cant of his helmet shifted and he gave a signal to the others. Without a word, the remaining agents and three consular staff escorted Mudge through her bedroom and out the door, although Mudge looked back at the last minute as if about to object. Mac waved reassuringly.

They were alone. Mac could see her reflection in his helmet. She looked rather smug. " 'Sephe told me you were short-staffed, but this?" said Mac, shaking her head. "You can take that thing off, Sing-li Jones. I know it's you."

"Hi, Mac." Jones tucked the now-pointless headgear under one arm, then took a seat, shifting to accommodate his weaponry. His expression was more rueful than embarrassed. "How are you doing? That's—" he looked at her scalp, "nasty."

"What I'm doing is wondering why all the hardware, the secrecy, here. I thought you cooperated with the consulate."

He tipped his head toward the now-empty bedroom. "Your friend."

"Oversight?" Mac said in disbelief. "Don't tell me you suspect him of anything other than being difficult."

"You know I can't tell you things like that, Mac."

She waited.

Jones' caramel skin blushed nicely. "I don't know," he qualified. "Our orders were to keep him under surveillance and intercede before he found out more than he should about the present situation. Which, by the way, he seems to have done without any help."

"He's annoying that way," Mac agreed. "But the gear?"

"Just staying anonymous." He grinned. "It works with most people, Mac. Trust me."

Trust him? The words were like cold water on her skin, but Mac made herself smile. "It's nice to see a familiar face. Although I suppose I can't ask you any questions."

Jones' forefinger tapped the table, then stopped. "Everything back at Base is as you left it," he offered. "Including, by the way, your fish heads and barnacles. Pretty slick, Mac. Zimmerman still can't believe we fell for it."

She tilted her head. "That's okay. Neither can I."

He smiled comfortably, but didn't admit a thing. *She hadn't expected he would.* "Last I heard, they were on schedule for the move. There hasn't been much media attention."

"You need bodies for that," Mac said. She gathered herself with an effort Jones noticed.

"You look about to fall on your face, Mac."

"Oh, not quite yet. First, help me out here." She smiled at the sudden caution in his eyes. "Don't worry, it's nothing compromising. I'm under the IU now, remember? Not your responsibility."

"Maybe not the Ministry's. We still watch your back."

"We" implying she would recognize others without their helmets, Mac realized, but didn't press him. She acknowledged the words with a grateful nod, then said frankly: "I need my things."

Jones' eyes narrowed in suspicion. "What things this time?"

"My imp, clothes, records from my office. Anything else would be appreciated. No one knows how long this Gathering will take. I asked Anchen, about my stuff, but . . ." She gave an expressive shrug. "It didn't sound promising."

"Because Pod Three's sealed and being towed," he pointed out.

"I know. Not to forget security systems . . ." Mac let her voice trail off.

"Oh, let's not forget those."

She held his eyes with hers. "Sing-li, you know I wouldn't be asking if it wasn't important. I've files on my imp that aren't in Norcoast's main system: my research on the Dhryn, on what we're here to accomplish. There are references, notes in my office I want here. I can't wait weeks or more until Base is set up and running again."

"I'll have to consult, Mac."

"Consult all you want," she told him, then added with abrupt ferocity: "You asked me to trust you, Sing-li. I trust you to know if I find out Pod Three was capsized and ruined so your people could fetch my underwear—"

"Mac. Mercy. Please." He held up both hands. "It won't come to that, believe me. We've been keeping watch on the pods; we've people on the hauler. Give me a day."

Mac drew a breath that shuddered and caught in her throat. She nodded, mute.

He put on his helmet, the man she knew disappearing behind the visor. But his voice was the same, warm with concern. "Now. Bed for you. And no arguments."

She accepted his help, a strong arm, but when they were standing beside the bed, she squeezed it once and let go. "Good night,
Sing-li. And thanks."

Mac stayed standing until the door closed. Only then did she
collapse on the most comfortable bed on the planet, not bothering
to do more than close her eyes.

For once, she didn't dream.

- Encounter -

The sacred caves were, as they had always been, ancient, hallowed, and worn. They were, as they had always been, shelter to all who sought protection from the elements or war; source of gods' comfort for those in need or grief.

Now, for the first time in recorded history, disaster had struck and the sacred caves were empty. Oh, they had sheltered the people. They had taken in the terrified flocks and foodstuffs, accommodated what belongings could be carried. They had even accepted the wild things, driven from the fields.

But shelter did not mean safety.

The green flood had greedily followed them inside, chased them deeper underground. It surged through every water-carved channel, licked away the life that dug its hopeless claws into wall and ledge, that clung to the stones called godstooth and howled for the pity of gods.

Had he, Oah, Primelord, not howled loudest for his people? Had he not sought the highest point in the cave, the secret shelf where gods would endure only those who ruled? Had his mighty voice not been loud enough to drown out the screaming and be heard at last?

But the gods did not mean to save them.

Instead, they'd sent ghouls to drift through the silent caves, unmindful of the darkness. Oah, Primelord, had cowered like any milk-thieving runt at their coming, had panted like a mother in birth pain as one after the other brushed against the stone below his hiding place, had felt the bones along his spine rise in horror at their—drinking.

When all was still, Oah, Primelord, waited in the dark, nostrils burning with acrid remnants of what he didn't know.

When all was still and his body weakening from hunger and thirst, Oah, Primelord, waited in the dark, pressed against the stone that should have saved them.

When all was still and his body failed him, Oah died in the dark, Primelord and last of his kind.

It does not matter if it this is the wrong place or the wrong time.

That which is Dhryn hunts for the Taste, but cannot find it.

Perhaps others have come before. Perhaps the scouts mistook the path. Perhaps technology failed.

None of this matters.

The Progenitor must survive to continue the Great Journey.

That which is Dhryn turns to the *oomlings*.

There is no future but now.

- 12 -

WONDERS AND WOUNDS

HOLDING ON TIGHT, Mac bent as far as she could over the delicately wrought, but strong—*hopefully*—railing, trying to see past the outer wall of the white building. *There*. To the north, the building ended where the cliff continued its upward climb, a climb staggered by hanging valleys filled with green forest and braided with waterfalls that plunged to the sea. The sea itself was unusually deep here. She longed for a chance to dive it. However, first things first. Mac hunted for anything that didn't belong. *Ah. Might be a landing field,* she told herself, squinting at a flat patch of lighter green within the nearest indentation in the rock.

Or cricket pitch. It was New Zealand.

"Careful!"

The warning startled Mac into losing her grip and she had an unpleasantly intense perspective on the sheer drop to rock and froth before grabbing hold again. With a heave, she pulled herself back on the terrace and whirled to glare at the new arrival. "I was being careful—"

She stopped and grinned. "Fourteen!"

"You did not appear careful. Idiot. It would be a waste to fall from this height so soon after breakfast."

Mac laughed. "Glad to see you, too. How are the head and hands?"

"Mygs heal quickly." He held up his hands and she was aston-ished to see only fine green lines where there had been scrapes and gashes. "My head? All better. Unless I bump it. Which I attempt not to do."

He looked better. *In fact,* her eyes narrowed, *the Myg looked very different.* Gone were the ill-fitting Human clothes, replaced by a set of finely tooled leather plates made into pants and vest. Beneath the vest was a tailored red shirt, generous sleeves widest at the elbows and caught at the cuffs. There was a red gemstone at his throat and another hanging from one ear. Three small black imp cases hung from a strap across his chest. Black polished boots and a wig of immaculately groomed silver-gray hair completed the transformation from clumsy tourist to—

—*to someone important,* Mac decided, pinning down the change. *Maybe a touch reminiscent of a pirate from old vids, Em, but a classy one.* Not that she'd point that out.

It was, of course, not the clothes alone or the posture that went with them. His eyes were still mere glints within those fleshy lids, but Mac thought the lines of his face had altered, as if he acknowledged a weight of responsibility.

Given why they were here, she wasn't surprised. "I didn't think of a wig," Mac told him lightly, taking one of the chairs at the little table and waving him to the other. "Looks good."

"Irrelevant," he grumbled as he sat. "It's been the fashion since my grandsires' day. You'd think the transects would have freed us from tradition—instead, we now export it as part of our identity. Bah."

She brushed her fingers across her patch of bare scalp. "There are advantages."

Opening one of the cases on his strap, Fourteen brought out what indeed looked like an imp and put it on the table between them, after first scowling at the vase of flowers as though they took up valuable space. "Irrelevant. You do not need a wig and your head is intact. The Sinzi-ra has done us a great service with her care." He busied himself with a second imp.

" 'Sinzi-ra,' " Mac repeated. "Is that Anchen's title?"

Fourteen didn't look up from the confusion of overlapping workscreens he'd set hovering parallel to the tabletop. "No. It's what she is. She is the Sinzi contingent to this consulate."

"So she's a physician."

"Noad is a physician, yes. A fine one."

"Another Sinzi."

That sly look. "You Humans are a pleasant species, but hardly important or annoying enough to require the attention of more than one." Fourteen grinned at Mac's expression. "Yes, Mac, I will explain. The name any Sinzi gives to a member of another species is a composite of the initials of the names of the consciousnesses within that body. It saves confusion for those less familiar with their ways. Noad is one of these consciousnesses—an expert in xeno-medicine." He plucked a bright orange flower petal and laid it in front of Mac. "The others are Atcho, Casmii, Hone, Econa, and Nifa. Atcho is the consulate administrator. Efficient and very thorough. Don't break anything." Another petal, beside the first. "Casmii is a member of the IU's judicial council. A powerful voice. Econa and Nifa are both scientists whose specialties have to deal with this planet of yours in some way. If you let them ask you questions, they'll never give you a moment's peace. Hone is a transect engineer. A bit young, if you ask me, for such responsibility." A petal joined the group for each name, until there was a tight circle of six, their bases touching. "Sinzi-ra Anchen."

Talking to one alien was fraught with interspecies' confusion. *This?* The potential for disaster made Mac gulp. "How do I know which one's speaking to me?"

A tall shadow crossed their table. "If it is necessary to identify an individual mind," Anchen said, "for clarity or proof of intent, that identification is provided. Otherwise, all who are awake and participatory speak as one."

Fourteen scrambled to his feet. "I meant no disrespect, Sinzi-ra."

"The effort to understand one another is never disrespectful. Quite the contrary, Arslithissiangee Yip the Fourteenth." Anchen's head lowered in what seemed a bow. "I am honored."

Mac had remained seated, regarding the Sinzi with a mix of awe and regret. Few Humans met this species face-to-face; she hadn't been wrong to tell Mudge it was the opportunity of a lifetime. But regret won. She wasn't here to explore their differences. She was here concerning another species altogether. "If you've come to see if I'm fit to join the others this morning, Anchen, I am."

"Are you?" The alien's fingers swayed as if the light, but growing sea breeze had the power to move them. *Indecision,* Mac guessed, then wasn't sure why she thought so. "I find it unlikely you are free of pain so soon."

"It's nothing—I mean, there isn't enough pain to impair my ability to work," qualified Mac. If ever she needed to express herself clearly and accurately, it was now, in this place, where the shortcuts of Human conversation were likely to be pitfalls.

"The in-depth sessions are in the afternoon. Every morning, there is a greeting arena. It would be appropriate for you to attend. Several others arrived yesterday as well, so you will not be the only newcomers." Anchen gestured expansively. "Although you and Arslithissiangee Yip the Fourteenth are the only ones who join us courtesy of the Myrokynay."

Mac's blood ran cold. "The Ro are here?" she asked, schooling her voice.

Anchen didn't laugh, but something about her posture suggested amusement to Mac. "No. And we do not yet have the ability to invite them, much as we wish." A more sober note to her voice, a gesture toward Fourteen. "The message you brought us only proves the difficulty. Its coding was so complex few could have deciphered it. An achievement of note. And yes, the results suggest its purpose—all agree—but the requirements to implement this signal? A puzzle we are not close to solving." Her fingers bent upward at their lowermost joint. *A shrug?* Mac wondered. "If this is the Myrokynay attempting clarity, it could take years to attain true conversation."

A pause. "Thus we start with basics," Anchen continued. "Their presence has been confirmed on this world before; it was Human ingenuity which disabled the Myrokynay's stealth technology during the attack on the Dhryn home world. It is our assumption they will continue their interest in Earth—our hope they will acknowledge this gathering and its purpose although to us, so far, the Myrokynay have been silent. But you, they contacted. And you," a lift of a white-clawed fingertip at Fourteen, "were able to decipher the meaning of this contact. There is deep significance within your combination."

Which meant . . . ? Mac filed the Sinzi's cryptic statement to mull over later. "Then it's time to get to work," she said hopefully, then paused. Today, Anchen's upper fingers shone with golden rings, but she wore another of the simple white gowns, twin to Mac's. Perhaps the garment was "significant," too.

The problem was, Mac's own belongings had yet to appear. *There were worse things than walking around in a nightgown, Em.* Mac grimaced inwardly. *Like meeting a roomful of strangers while walking around in a nightgown.*

Rings caught and shattered light as Anchen gestured to the doors and beyond to Mac's rooms. "In that case, I trust you will find suitable attire among the selection of Human clothing we've provided, while you await your own things. If not, please contact the staff or myself."

"Thank you." Mac let out a sigh of relief, adding before she thought: "Mind reading must be a Sinzi trait."

"Mac!" This exclamation, plus Fourteen's shocked look, drew Mac to her feet, fumbling to apologize, not that she knew why or how. "Just kidding," probably didn't cut it. *Or was there something about being multiple minds in one body that made the very concept of shared thoughts repugnant to Sinzi?*

Fortunately for interspecies' relations, Anchen merely smiled. "We take great pride in anticipating the needs of our guests. I am gratified to have 'guessed' yours so well."

"You are a superb host. My thanks," Mac said sincerely. "I'm grateful to have other clothes for the Gathering."

"You do mean to attend today, then." At Mac's confident nod, the Sinzi's shoulders shuddered, the motion traveling down every finger so her rings flashed in sequence. *Acceptance?* Mac guessed. It could as easily be just a random shudder, and Mac could almost hear her great-aunt, who was fond of strange old rhymes, saying: "Cat walked over your grave." "You do not have the thick skull of a Myg," noted Anchen, luckily not telepathic. "I request you return to your quarters at once if you experience any significant pain or dizziness."

"I will."

Anchen bowed and turned to leave. Mac slipped around the

table to intercept her. The Sinzi's head twisted to bring her lower sets of eyes directly to bear. "I see there is something further," she acknowledged before Mac could utter a word. "Let me 'guess' again. You wish to know the status of your companion, Charles Mudge III."

"Yes, please."

"He's here?" Fourteen stood and joined them. "How did that happen?"

Mac snorted. "Very quickly, as you may remember."

"He saved Mac's life, Sinzi-ra Anchen," the Myg told her. "I, for one, place a high value on that."

"As do we all, Arslithissiangee Yip the Fourteenth. What is your wish for him, Mac?"

She glanced at Fourteen, who nodded encouragingly as if they'd discussed the issue beforehand. *That obvious, was she?* "My wish, Anchen, is that Oversight—Mudge—be offered the chance to stay and contribute to the Gathering. He's—" *a minor stretch here,* "—been essential to my work over the years. I believe he'd be an asset." And she did. *In his annoying, pinpoint-every-flaw, way.*

"And if he chooses not to stay?"

Mac imagined Mudge working at his desk, completely oblivious to the row of black-visored guards behind him. *That wasn't the problem.* "He would be at risk," she admitted. "There could be others, like Kay, interested in any information about the Dhryn and the Ro. He'd need protection. He wouldn't like it." *Any more than she had.*

"Among those gathered is a Human-ra of diverse and as yet un-productive individuals," said Anchen, no readable expression on the sculpted contours of her long face. "It is my understanding you are accustomed to coordinating such a research group. If you wish to undertake that responsibility, I will look into ways Charles Mudge III can be included."

Blackmail—very civil and reasonable—blackmail. *Was Mudge worth it?* Mac didn't hesitate. "I agree, of course. I'll let him know." Then, more as a test than anything else: "If I think of any-one else who might be of help, what should I do?"

"By all means, let me know at once, Mac. I will consider every suggestion." If there was a hint of irony in the voice, Mac was willing to ignore it. "If there is nothing else? Then I will leave you to your preparations, Mac. Arslithissiangee Yip the Fourteenth." Her long-toed feet made virtually no sound on the tiled terrace, less on the sand.

Fourteen went back to the table. "Idiot."

"Me?" Mac joined him, eyeing the complex of workscreens still displayed over the pair of imps he'd laid out. "Why?"

He gave his vest a proud tug. "You didn't check the clothing before she left. What if it doesn't fit?"

She grinned. "Irrelevant. I'll walk beside you and no one will notice me." Fourteen barked his laugh. "So what's all this?" asked Mac, waving at the displays but careful to keep her fingers out of them.

"This," he slid one of the imps closer to her, "is for you. I accessed your messages—oh, don't rumple your face. I didn't read them."

"I didn't rumple—" Mac began.

Another laugh. "I've loaded it with schematics for the consulate— at least those areas for which the Sinzi provide schematics. You will find the latest list of attendees—again, those the Sinzi wish known to all, as well as some information about each. Our number is presently four hundred and thirteen beings. I counted Anchen as one. Hmm. Four hundred and twenty-three, if you count the Nerban translators who travel with each of the Umlar delegates. Their mouthparts can't handle Instella. Idiots refuse to use appliances."

Never put a Nerban and a Frow in the same taxi . . . Mac shook off the memory of Emily's voice. "Any external genitalia I should know about?"

That sly look. "Didn't you bring your drugs?"

She grinned. "I see you're back to normal. Thanks for this." Mac picked up the imp. She turned it over in her hands. Not much to see on the outside. A palm-length dark cylinder, stubbier than the Human version, but otherwise plain. She spotted what should be the activation pad and looked inquiringly at Fourteen.

"Your first entry locks in your code," he assured her. "Do it once, then repeat."

Automatically, Mac tapped in the code from her imp at Base. She almost changed her mind, then shrugged and repeated it. *Odds were good she'd forget a new one anyway.*

The workscreen was crisper than hers, but either the Myg used the Human interface or he'd preset this one to suit her vision. *And hers,* Mac admitted to herself, *had been in the water more than a few times, let alone its trips with her through no-space to the Dhryn worlds.* Mac put the device on the table, then drew a finger through its display to lift it to vertical from horizontal. No problem accessing the data Fourteen had provided. Mac held her breath.

The consulate schematics were visual representations of rooms and corridors. Furniture was absent—reasonable enough, furniture was often moved—but there were symbols showing each room's function floating within it. Mac was entranced. Someone, more likely several someones, had gone to a great deal of trouble to design symbolic representations of functions not necessarily shared— or done the same way—by different species. The washroom symbol alone was a masterpiece of tactful suggestion.

The rest?

Text. Text. Text. None of it more legible than the IU's letter. Mac poked through the 'screen until she found the audio option. A selection began reading itself to her. *In Fourteen's distinctive, somewhat gravelly voice.* Stopping it, she looked through the display at him. The Myg appeared remarkably smug. "My entire family adores my reading voice," he proclaimed.

"No offense, but since I'm neither a relative nor a Myg, how do I change it?"

His generous lips actually pouted. *As likely mimicry as a shared expression,* Mac decided. "We'd need a recording of another voice. Does it matter? Who uses audio anyway?"

She hadn't told him about having trouble reading. Or Kay. Or Mudge. Or anyone who didn't already know or have to know, for that matter.

It had been possible to hide it at Base, where Mac knew everything and everyone.

Here?

She needed help.

Might as well start asking now.

"I suffered more damage than losing an arm and hand, last fall." As she spoke, Mac focused on the display, finding a visual list of delegates and starting to scroll through their faces—or what corresponded to a face. "My language center was affected. You heard me telling Oversight that I can speak and read Dhryn. That's true. What I didn't tell him—" Mac considered the possibility others were listening and nodded to herself. *They'd have to take her as she was. Bent. A bit scuffed. But capable.* "—I didn't tell him it's now very difficult for me to read anything else. I can muddle through English and Instella. Sometimes. Others, the words fragment in front of my eyes." She was startled by her own face in the list and closed the display. "So you see, it does matter. I find it less—frustrating—if it's my voice reading to me."

"Who have you consulted about this? Other than Humans."

Mac blinked at Fourteen. He seemed serious. "Who else would I consult?" *The Ro?* "Besides, with all that happened—is happening—my own government wasn't about to let me wander too far."

"They no longer have jurisdiction over you. Discuss this problem with Noad. The Sinzi, as you might gather, are exceptional neurologists."

There was an idea that qualified as terrifying, Em. "I'll think about it." Mac stood. "First things first. I need to get ready to meet the masses, Fourteen, not to mention talk to Oversight." *A conversation she wasn't looking forward to.*

"I will help you choose appropriate clothing."

Mr. Paisley Shorts? Mac shook her head. "Out. I can manage. I need you to check in with Oversight—make sure he's ready for this. Please."

"Of course." Fourteen stood, then gave a bow from the waist, deep and prolonged. When he straightened, Mac was surprised to see moisture beading his thick eyelids, and his mouth working with some emotion. "What's wrong?" she asked.

"Noad has assured me that, with my wounds, I would not have survived that night alone. I'd set the temperature too low in my panic; I was too weak to voluntarily awake from torpor. By warming me, you saved my life."

"Lucky guess, believe me."

"It was not a guess when you continued to protect my life with yours, even when injured yourself. You could have left immediately. You could have left in the morning and sought safety for yourself. You didn't." He stopped and placed both hands over his eyes. "I, Arslithissiangee Yip the Fourteenth, cannot thank you, Mackenzie Connor of Little Misty Lake, for saving my valued life," he said formally, lowering his hands again to look at her. "Twice."

"I don't need—"

He frowned at her and she closed her mouth. *Not done.*

Hands over his eyes. "I, Arslithissiangee Yip the Fourteenth, can only offer my firstborn offspring to you, Mackenzie Connor of Little Misty Lake, in return for saving my valued life."

Mac's eyes widened in shock. "No, I—"

Hands down. Another, sterner look. She closed her mouth again.

Hands up. "But since I, Arslithissiangee Yip the Fourteenth, have not yet produced an offspring and do not, in fact, ever intend to do so unless forced by my grandsires or in a weak moment under the influence of illicit drugs, I can only offer you my allegiance, flesh, mind, and spirit, so long as I may live, in return for saving my valued life."

Mac waited.

Hands down. "That's all of it," advised Fourteen, sounding normal again. "Tradition. Sorry about that."

She lifted one eyebrow. "A simple 'thank you' would have sufficed."

The Myg tucked his imp back in its case. "Idiot," he commented fondly. "Of course not. Within my sect, only ethical acts can move a lineage into the highest possible *strobis*. You do know the word?" Mac shook her head. "The closest Instella equivalent is 'class.' Irrelevant. To all Myg, *strobis* is the measure of a life's value to the whole. Actions determine that value. We act according to the allegiances we hold, to ideals, to others of our kind, very rarely to an alien. Allegiance must flow toward greater value; it is thus not given lightly." That sly look. "Though there is a recent trend, much deplored by my grandsires, to offer allegiance to favorite sports teams."

In a Human, thought Mac, *she'd assume he was trying to lighten the moment.* For her sake or his? Regardless of species, this was obviously a significant commitment for the Myg.

She just wasn't sure what to do about it.

Fourteen reached out and tapped her nose. "It was a joke."

"I got that," Mac said dryly. "I'm honored, Fourteen, by your allegiance. I don't see how I deserve it."

"Irrelevant. It's for me to give, not you to deserve. Enough. Traditions waste time. I try to tell my grandsires, but they never listen to me. You, Mac, must dress. I will go and see if the valued Mudge has done the same."

"Tell him I'll be right over."

After Mac closed the doors behind Fourteen, she ran her fingers along what felt to be painted wood and frosted glass. No guarantees about the materials, but the style was vintage Human. Nice to be reminded the transfer of culture and knowledge went both ways.

She took out her new imp and sank into the jelly-chair. *Messages.* Setting her 'screen hovering above her, Mac hunted until she found the very short list. Three—she squinted—likely meeting announcements. One that seemed intended for someone named Recko San. Mac deleted that, having enough to struggle with as it was. And one more.

The source was marked 'personal,' with no return. A recording, not text. Her hand trembled slightly as she activated it.

"Hello, Mac." Nik's voice.

She stopped it immediately.

Coward.

Emily's judgment or her own?

Mac restarted the recording. "Hello, Mac. The complete text of your letter from the IU follows. I've indicated the clauses I feel you need to pay particular attention to, but the overall gist is that you've accepted citizenship within the IU for the purposes and duration of the Gathering. Within that framework, you are protected and governed by intersystem law . . ."

Eyes closed, Mac lay back in the chair to listen, feet tucked up. His voice flowed over her, as intimate a caress as the warm waves that kissed her toes in summer. The words didn't matter, not right now. She'd pay attention to meanings later. For now, she relaxed and let herself own this, own the sounds that had left his mouth, come from his throat, sounds meant for her.

All too soon, it was done. Mac resisted the temptation to listen again. Instead, she put away her imp and went to stand where she could see the distant horizon, a line of deepest blue against the sky, a hint of cloud marring its edge. She wrapped her arms around herself. It could be land. She'd have to see a map to know for sure.

As for Fourteen?

Here we go again, Em, she thought.

If she'd understood Fourteen correctly, an alien she'd come to view as a friend had just sworn to be her ally for life. It was a promise that didn't always work out well.

Her lips moved silently. *"Lamisah."*

As daunting settings went, Mac decided, the consulate's "greeting arena" wasn't as bad as say, the busy loading docks of an orbiting way station.

The noise level and utter confusion to the unfamiliar was, however, even worse.

"Where do we go from here?" Mudge shouted in her ear.

Mac pointed helplessly at Fourteen, who was pushing his way though the throng clogging the ramp. "Follow him."

"I still haven't agreed to all this, Norcoast," another shout.

She nodded. Mudge had been predictably reluctant to commit himself. This was, after all, the man who routinely took six long months to renew a research proposal he'd approved for the previous three years' running. Accepting an invitation to leave his work and join an alien conference? She'd allow him a little time for that decision, even if the outcome was, as far as she was concerned, never in doubt. With Oversight, a push always produced the opposite reaction.

That he was willing to come along this morning without being dragged was, Mac judged, a significant accomplishment for their first day. Given the Ministry somehow had him under surveillance, probably a device in his clothing, she only hoped Mudge would watch his tongue.

Suggesting he do so? She shuddered at the likely consequences.

The consulate's greeting arena wasn't a room or hall. They'd followed Fourteen outside to where a sequence of gardens connected the protected east side of the complex to the true wilderness of the mountains behind, manicured slopes merging into the massive upward steps of the rising hills. The plantings had the tired, proud look of fall, more seed heads than buds, those leaves intending to drop rattling and loose on the trees. The air was warmer than crisp, but not by much. The building itself protected them from the rising wind, but if the sun hadn't been shining, they'd all need coats.

Those without a natural version, anyway. "This," Mac decided after her first incredulous look at the host of beings spread over the patio below them, "is a caterer's nightmare."

There were so many different aliens milling in front of them, and so many different types of the same aliens, Mac didn't attempt to dredge up the names of any she might have studied. *It's a masquerade ball, Em.* With her and Mudge the only ones not in costume, from their viewpoint anyway.

Although she was well-dressed. Mac smoothed the front of the jacket that had been one of the choices hanging on the rack she'd found in the sitting room. Midnight blue, knee-length, tailored to perfection. With, she was delighted to discover, pockets. There'd been pants to match, flat shoes, and everything else, including a comb, to make her comfortable—and ready for inspection.

Her clothes from the cabin lay clean and folded on a counter in the washroom itself. She'd found the invitation from the IU in her shirt where she'd stuffed it, no worse for whatever laundry technique the consulate staff used. Or they'd taken the envelope out and replaced it. The owl pellet was gone. *Just as well.*

Mac patted her left jacket pocket. Both envelope and the imp from Fourteen were there.

An elbow dug into her back. "He's getting ahead of us," Mudge fussed. Mac barely avoided stepping on someone's flipper but stayed in place.

"Don't worry. I still see him. Hang on," she ordered.

The central consular building, itself a mammoth warren of halls and varied internal environments, sprawled behind them. Where they stood, at the top of the ramp leading to the gardens, was high enough to afford a good view of the grounds.

Although it had seemed a kaleidoscope of moving, fragmented colors, Mac gradually made sense of what she was seeing. The main arena was a sunken patio, irregular in shape and bordered by stately trees to the left and right. Several shaded paths led off to either side. Farthest from them was a set of broad terraces cut from the granite, rising like giant stairs to another garden above this one. The result was a bowllike space, capable of holding, barely, what appeared to be far more than four hundred and something delegates.

Within that space were three main clusters of activity. The first, to the left, focused around a series of clear bubblelike structures. *Ah,* Mac decided, intrigued. *Non-oxy-breathers.* Clever.

The next was in the center, around a series of curved, elaborate fountains. Mac took a closer look. The fountains themselves overflowed with delegates.

Made sense. There were several aquatic species in the IU. *First group she wanted to meet,* Mac decided.

Last and the most popular area, judging by the sea of heads, was near the first terrace, to the right. Mac didn't need to glimpse the long tables in the shade of the trees to know this was where food and beverages were being provided. She smiled. *Never met an academic who couldn't find the bar, Em.*

The noise—and the smell—at close range? Mac began to suspect at least one reason the Sinzi held these mass meetings outside.

"There he is, Norcoast. He's waving to us. Can we go now?"

Looking ahead at the crowd, Mac put her arm through Mudge's. "Lead on."

After making their way through a bewildering mixture of body forms, they reached Fourteen, who was standing under the first of the great trees. Mac noticed Mudge sneaking looks into its branches, despite the truly fascinating aliens to every side, muttering to himself: "Silver beech. Southern species . . . bigger than the ones I saw in Argentina. More podocarps—rimu, I'd say—aha!" Mudge tugged at her arm and exclaimed. "Tui!"

Mac guessed this wasn't a sneeze. "Pardon?"

"Look, up there."

Obediently, she craned her neck back. The lowermost branch, just above a group of intensely debating delegates, contained a fairly large, albeit nondescript bird, with white feathers at its throat. "Tui?" she guessed.

"Shhh. Listen."

As that seemed improbable, given the volume from all sides, Mac shook her head, but tried anyway. Nothing. Then, she noticed delegates under the bird suddenly looking up as well, which in their case, being Frow, meant unfolding their neck ridges and leaning left.

Then she heard it and grinned. The bird was mimicking Frow laughter, something like rattling coins in a bucket. The delegates were not impressed.

Welcome to Earth.

"Trees. Birds. Idiots. Wasting time," Fourteen said impatiently. "Come. The first of those you should meet is over there."

At that moment, a large group of brown-cloaked furry somethings stampeded by everyone else, as if it had been announced the bar was about to close for the day. Doing her best not to be swept along, trampled, or pushed into the already testy Frow, Mac dodged to one side.

When she looked for her companions, both Mudge and Fourteen had managed to get themselves lost in the crowd.

When opportunity walks in the door, Em, Mac grinned. It wasn't that far to the fountains, which were roughly in the direction the Myg had indicated anyway. Winding her way between beings whose reaction to her varied from polite acknowledgment to oblivious, she moved as quickly as seemed inoffensive. With luck, she'd meet some of the aquatics.

As if to thwart her, the crowd thickened until Mac had to slow down to avoid stepping on anything attached to someone who'd be offended. Finally forced to stop, she stretched to her full height, trying to see a better way. Hats, fleece, antennae, feathers, lumps. The few Human heads looked out of place.

One of those heads turned with familiar grace.

For an instant, a heartbeat, it was as if the world went silent, the pushing of others against her meant nothing, and Mac saw only dark eyes set against smooth olive skin.

It couldn't be.

"Emily?"

A tall, shaggy Sthlynii stepped in front of Mac, blocking her view. She tried to move around him, but he grabbed her arm. "Sooooo," the vowels extended in emphasis. "Yooouuu aaaareeee heeereeee!"

"Excuse me," Mac said, twisting frantically, but somehow resisting the urge to kick a fellow delegate. "Please. Let go. I have to see someone! I have to go!"

"Aaaas beeffoorreee yooouuuu weeent, leeaaaviiiing oooonlyy thee deeaad."

"I don't know what you're talking about. Let go of me!" This time, Mac did kick, with force enough to hurt her toes, if not to impress the larger alien. Around them, the crowd suddenly fell still. *Not the first impression she'd hoped to make.* Somehow, she composed herself. "Do I know you, sir?"

"You should, Connor."

Mac turned to face a short, no longer chubby Human, his skin and hair pigment-free. The name and context snapped into place. "Lyle. Lyle Kanaci." The ruined Dhryn home world. The archaeological team who had sheltered her—and Brymn—during the sandstorm. *Of course, they'd be here.* She had so many questions for them—but first, Emily! She pulled at her arm. "Tell him to let go!"

"Therin. Be civil. Remember our host."

Rubbing her arm, Mac realized she recognized every face, or equivalent, surrounding her. Two Cey, their expressions impossible to read. Therin, now flanked by three more of his kind, their tentacled mouths disturbing to watch. The rest of the circle, Humans, including Lyle.

In contrast to the aliens, the Human faces expressed their feelings a little too well. Mac had never seen such disgust and anger, never had loathing directed at her before. Her mouth went dry.

This was what it felt like, to be the target of a mob. She knew better than to move. She couldn't imagine what to say that wouldn't ignite the violence in their eyes.

Why was the one thing Mac did understand.

For she had brought a Dhryn into their camp and he had killed one of their own, digesting her alive as she'd lain helpless and injured. They'd all heard her screams.

She still dreamed them.

"Mac. There you are." Those around her fell back, giving way to the tall, graceful form of the Sinzi. "I see you've found the Human-ra I told you about, including these, their research companions," Anchen said, fingers rising to encompass them all. "Excellent. I know your group will produce fine results."

She was wrong.

It couldn't have been Emily.

Mac sipped the drink she'd been handed without tasting it, eyes hunting through the crowd, seeing only what wasn't there.

There were dozens of other Humans, not to mention humanoidlike aliens. Consular staff, diplomats, other delegates. Tall women with dark eyes and olive skin weren't uncommon.

These morning outdoor gatherings were designed to attract the Ro. There'd been no sign of them.

Every security guard and staff member, likely most of the delegates, would know Emily Mamani's face.

It couldn't have been her. Yet . . .

"Had enough?"

"Of what, Oversight?" she answered wearily. "This—" a lift of her water glass, "—or them?" The archaeologists had remained in their tight defensive huddle since Anchen's poorly timed announcement. Mac had only to look their way to be seared by glares from everyone capable of glaring.

"Of pretending your head doesn't hurt."

She didn't bother lying to him. "It doesn't matter. I can't leave." *Not when there was any chance Emily really had been here, had looked at her, was waiting.*

Fourteen poured two glasses of wine into his mouth simultaneously, then belched. *Apparently,* Mac thought, *clothes weren't everything.* "You will have to—all delegates are to report to their assigned research areas this afternoon. Charlie is right, you need a rest. And they—" the Myg deliberately didn't look around, "—promise to be a challenge."

"Charlie?" Mac glanced at Oversight.

"Please don't," that worthy said with a shudder. "It wouldn't sound right coming from you, Norcoast." An expert in glaring himself, Mudge had been trading a few with the archaeologists. "As far as I'm concerned," indignantly and not for the first time, "you can't work with those people."

"I can," Mac disagreed, quietly, but firmly. "And I will. If they know anything of use to me, I want it. If they have anything to offer, I want it. Everything else—anything else—I'll deal with my own way."

He harrumphed, giving her that look. "Well, I'm staying to help you. Someone has to—you can't expect Fourteen here to know the depths of academic depravity our kind is capable of."

A second bright spot on a very dark morning, Mac thought. She raised her glass in a toast to both of her supporters. "I appreciate that."

A low hum vibrated through the air and underfoot. Fourteen caught Mac's eye before she could ask. "A request for attention. The Sinzi-ra is going to make an announcement."

The sounds of conversation and movement dropped away like magic, leaving only the wind in the treetops. "Thank you, Delegates." Anchen's voice came from everywhere, not loud, but impossible to miss. "As we have done each day since the Gathering began, let us give the Myrokynay the chance to join us and share their knowledge of our common peril that all may survive it. A moment of silence, please."

Every being Mac could see aimed its head, eyes, or whatevers at the sky, as if that was the most likely place to find Ro. She could tell them otherwise. *But it was an impressive display.* Hundreds of such diverse life-forms, all intent on one result. Would the Ro pay attention?

The Tui decided to practice its Frow laughter again. *Entirely too appropriate*, Mac thought grimly.

The voice began again, drowning out the bird. "Our new arrivals have been assigned to existing research teams. Provide requests for additional equipment and other needs to any member of the consular staff at the earliest opportunities. Record all findings and results for review and assessment.

"As of this moment, the IU confirms three worlds lost to the Dhryn. We fear more have been consumed. It is up to you to end this."

The semi-party atmosphere of the greeting arena vanished as if it had never existed, replaced by subdued tones and purposeful movement. Everyone seemed to know where to go. Consular staff appeared and began to remove tables. The bubble tents for the non-oxy-breathers rolled away, presumably self-propelled. Some of the aquatics from the fountains donned helmets, walking or slithering away. Others, to Mac's frustration, slipped away down large drains before she had a good look.

Maybe tomorrow, she thought wistfully.

"Where to now, Norcoast?"

"Where?" Mac eyed the huge building presently being restocked with aliens. *Not there.* Not yet. "Why don't you both go ahead—see what you can find out about our research colleagues and facilities?" she suggested.

Fourteen didn't look happy. Mudge, on the other hand, positively glowed. *Definitely had the detective bug, Em.* "What about you?" the Myg asked her.

"Don't worry. I'll meet you there." Mac drew out her imp. "Got a map." She made a gentle shooing motion with her hands. "I'm fine. I need a few minutes alone, that's all. Here." Here being the garden around them.

As more and more left, the place was revealing its true self, an outdoor palace of magnificent proportions, shaped by growing things and stone, bordered by widely spaced trees whose dappled shade enticed the explorer. Birds who couldn't compete with the crowds like the Tuis had begun to flit about, adding their song and chatter to the restored babble of fountains. Fat pigeons waddled the patio, cooing as they hunted dropped olives and bits of pastry amid the litter of leaf and seed case.

One wandered by them, making its methodical, unhurried way down the path of shredded bark and moss that led under the trees, away from the patio. That was enough for Mac. "See you in a while," she announced.

She half expected one or the other of her companions to follow. She'd been reasonably certain one of the many yellow-garbed consular staff would object to pigeon pursuit, or at least send her off with the rest.

But no one followed or objected. The pigeon left the path on its own business. And after those initial dozen or so steps, Mac slowed her pace, answering both her mood and the thumping of her skull.

Had it been Emily?

Should she have called out—told someone?

"More likely the little weasel knocked something loose, Em," Mac only half joked as she walked.

Not a wild forest, she decided, but designed for the peace and contemplation one could provide. Mac grew absorbed in the patterns and textures, admired the skills of those who coaxed living things to remain tame, while showing off their natural beauty. Ferns swept alongside the path like still-life rivers. In openings, groves of miniature conifers guarded pale roses. And everywhere birds. High above, in the canopies. In the shrubs, busy at their business. Perched and watching her with bright, distracted eyes.

The path was lined with white benches, some designed for anatomies Mac couldn't imagine. She found one that suited hers and sat.

But not to rest.

After looking around to be sure she was alone, and not daring to hope, Mac folded her hands on her lap. "Here I am, Em."

Nothing stirred that didn't belong.

"Short of stealing a lev and heading out to sea, this is the best I can do."

Nothing.

"Your mother said you always were difficult," Mac said, her voice thick. She coughed to clear it. "In case you don't know everything, Em, I'm here to work with other Dhryn experts for the IU. I tell you though, what they really want is to talk to your—to the Ro. If you can arrange that, first beer's on me. And the next ten. Mind you, after that I'm probably broke. No one's talked about paying me here. I suppose I'm out of a job at Base. I know. I could have asked. You're the practical one. You should have reminded me."

The sunbeams cutting across the straight, tall trunks were the only answer.

Mac drew up one leg and put her chin on her knee, watching what appeared to be an extraordinarily large cricket, disturbed by her arrival, as it pushed its way through a pile of twigs. If she picked it up, it would almost fill her hands, real and artificial. "You probably aren't here, Em," she went on. "But I've been talking to you when I knew you weren't, so talking to you when you 'probably' aren't is a step closer to sane, don't you think?" She paused. "Sane's overrated, in my opinion. But still. There's perception."

The insect, free of the twigs, stroked its long antennae through the air at her before marching under a nearby bush.

"Would it be so hard to answer me back, Em?" Mac turned her face so her cheek rested on her knee, let her eyes trace the textures of chipped bark and fallen leaf. "Won't they let you? You, who can charm grant funding from a stone? You know what to say. Tell the Ro we're on the same side. Tell them we're sorry about that misunderstanding at Haven—we're only Human, right? Make a joke. Beg. Bribe. Whatever it takes. Whatever they understand. Spout prime numbers."

Mac closed her eyes, seeing the familiar, graceful turn of a head. "Don't worry, Em," she whispered. "I won't let go. I'll wait."

ACCUSATION AND ANSWER

THERE WASN'T SAND on the floor, but the expansive curved room assigned to her research group had all the other hallmarks Mac had come to expect of Sinzi design: clean lines, light, unornamented walls, and abundant windows overlooking the patio—presently revealing the shadows of gathering clouds. Not to mention comfortable chairs—although these were better suited to being moved from conference table to console than the giant jelly-chairs in her room.

The room also possessed all the hallmarks of a bad start to a field season: too-quiet staff; resentful looks; everyone sitting as far apart as possible. Worst of all, no one already at work. They'd waited for her. Even Fourteen and Mudge greeted her with somber looks.

Not a good sign.

Assessment completed with that one glance, Mac strode through the door. "Good afternoon." Without waiting for a response, she went straight to the table in the center and leaned on her knuckles, gazing around the room from face to sullen face, or reasonable facsimile, as she spoke.

"Yes," Mac said, her voice ringing out. "I brought Brymn Las to your camp. No, I did not kill your friend. Yes, Brymn changed into the deadly form of his kind. No, we didn't know that would happen or we wouldn't have come to you in the first place. And yes, for his sake as well as for the sake of the friend you lost, and for the millions dying as we waste time with what can't be changed," she drew a deep breath and gave them all her most intense "get on with it" glare, "I will have every single thing you've learned, suspected, or outright guessed about the Dhryn from you. In return, I promise you not a moment's peace. But I will give you everything I know. Together, we may have a chance to stop them. Do we understand one another?"

Fourteen put up his hand. "The waste of time is this group. Studying the past is irrelevant."

Mac hid a smile as the archaeologists leaped to their feet, at least four shouting at once. She did enjoy the passion.

But not the way Lyle Kanaci was looking at her. He was ignoring the others. His eyes burned and his jaw was clenched tight enough to hurt.

"I see." She propped a hip on the table edge and stared right back at him. "We don't understand one another."

The silence following those words had an ugly quality to it. Those who'd stood, sat. No one moved otherwise.

"Oh, we understand you have 'special' knowledge about the Dhryn," Kanaci spat. "What we don't understand, Connor, is why you aren't still in jail and why we have to put up with having you here."

"In jail?" If Mac's eyebrows rose any higher, her forehead would hurt. *Too late.* "Pardon?"

Therin, if she'd identified the Sthlynii correctly, spoke up. His voice surprised her, the words as crisp and clear as anyone's. Mac was distracted by the thought that the elongated vowels he'd hissed at her earlier had been some kind of vocal threat display, an intimidation. *Which only worked if the one being intimidated knows the rules.*

"We saw them take you away under guard after helping your *friend* kill Myriam—before you could attack the rest of uuuus! Saaaaaaw yoooouuuu!"

So. Mac nodded, gesturing to a flustered Mudge to keep seated and quiet. She pulled up her left sleeve and flexed her hand. The ceramic pseudo-flesh caught the light, returning its strange hue, more blue-pink than flesh. "This is why they rushed me away," she corrected, keeping her voice matter-of-fact. *They had a long way to go here, and no time for mistakes.* "I'd been injured as well. There are people at the consulate who can testify to that—you don't need to take my word for it."

"As if we would!" Surly, then louder. "Liar! Murderer!"

"Anchen will make sure you get the facts." Her calm invocation of the Sinzi-ra's name seemed to startle them. *Good*, Mac thought grimly. *About time they realized she had support from higher up.* She hoped it was true. "Brymn couldn't help but attack me," she continued. "He'd lost all reason by that point in his metamorphosis. As for my being under arrest?" She didn't have to force a laugh. "I don't know where you got that idea. I went straight back to work until being invited here."

"What work? We tried to find you." This from another of the Humans, a dour-faced individual Mac remembered only as one of the non-scientists in the original group. "We couldn't."

"What were you using? Only my name?" He gave a reluctant nod. Mac felt sympathetic. Mackenzie Connor, in Sol System and throughout the colonies, must turn up hundreds of times. *Hundreds of thousands.* "Remember something under Norcoast Salmon Research Facility?"

Lyle frowned. "Yes, but . . ." his eyes widened. "That's you? The Earth-based fish biologist?"

There was a moment of bedlam, most shocked and none flattering. Mac waited it out, tapping the table with one finger. Therin's voice won; not by volume, the others deferred when he spoke. *Good to know, Em.* "Lies!" the alien exclaimed. "You're a criminal working with the Dhryn—a murderer! They'd have us believe—these twooo, theee staaaff here—you're an experienced science administrator?" He made a rude noise that fluttered his mouth tentacles.

"Oh, that I am," Mac replied coldly. "I've helped run Base—the Norcoast facility—for fourteen years. Ask Oversight here. Check government records. My life isn't a secret. You just didn't see it."

Before Mudge could make his contribution—something he seemed adamantly determined to do, being on his feet with a fist in the air—Lyle leaned forward and shouted. "Then what the hell were you doing on the Dhryn home world, Dr. Connor?"

"Mac." She waved Mudge down a second time before he obeyed, and finally took a chair herself. The ordinary act stopped some of the background muttering, but not all. Mac ignored it, concentrating on Lyle. He led them as much now, in this room, as he had during the sandstorm. She chose her words with care, aware the moment was fragile, and said quietly. "I was looking for the truth."

"What truth? The Dhryn's? Yours? I doubt it's ours." Murmurs of agreement.

"There's only one truth." Mac's eyes traveled from person to person as she spoke, making sure she had the attention of all twenty-seven. "The problem is finding all of it. If anyone understands the danger of extrapolating from partial evidence, it's you. Everything we think we know so far? Fragments. Pieces. We can't use them; we can't even see where they belong. We must find the connections to put those fragments together. Into one truth. The truth."

"First time I've heard the word since we've been here." This from a gray-haired woman sitting between the two Cey. "No one at this Gathering of the Sinzi's is talking about truth. We're supposed to build a weapon or dream up some strategy to destroy the Dhryn. Not exactly what our lot's qualified to do."

There was a smattering of laughter at this. Mac felt some of the tension leave her spine. *Not all.* She raised her prosthetic arm again. "No one," she emphasized, "wants to be eaten alive. Or see the life of a world stripped bare. But we, all of us here, know some new weapon, even if it does wipe out an entire species and end the threat, isn't an answer. We need understand how something like the Dhryn came to exist, learn where they came from, what might happen in the future. We need the truth."

"We've been singing that song to deaf ears since arriving." Another voice. More nods.

"Then don't waste your breath. Let's get to work." She looked at Lyle Kanaci. He gave her the barest of nods, his eyes guarded. *Good enough.* Mac rose to her feet. "I'll need to talk to you individually to find out your fields and areas of strength. Yes," to those exchanging puzzled looks, "I have the conference list, but I'd rather hear what you want me to know. While I'm doing that, give Oversight here, Charles Mudge III," she introduced quickly, hoping his glower didn't scare anyone off, "a list of whatever you need. It can be data, people, equipment. Anything relevant; I don't need to approve it. For once in our lives, budget is not the issue. Time is." This induced another, happier round of murmuring. Mac raised her voice to be heard over it. "Last, but not least. While all this is going on, I'd like you to turn your attention to a particular aspect of salmon biology."

Silence again, but this time incredulous. Mudge and Fourteen looked as dumbfounded as the rest.

Mac didn't smile. "Most species of salmon live out their lives around a single imperative, folks. A hardwired need to leave where they are and go somewhere else, no matter what's in their way, in order to survive as a species. Migration."

She could identify the bright lights in the room by the way they took the word and absorbed it like a blow. Some turned immediately to colleagues. A few sat without moving. There were the inevitable individuals who still looked as though they thought she was certifiable.

They could be right, Em.

But most were giving off that indefinable energy that, among scientists at least, meant a new paradigm had begun to take hold, a new framework was shifting conclusions and inferences. These were researchers who dealt in vast stretches of time, in cycles. Mac had thought they might be the ones to appreciate the significance.

If the Dhryn had ever been a migratory species, there should be evidence from their planet of origin.

If the Dhryn still answered that call, these researchers might already possess clues as to where and why.

Mac met Fourteen's eyes across the table, quite sure he'd told Anchen her supposition about the Dhryn being on a journey. This group who had been studying the Dhryn home world were the best choice to investigate that possibility. So her working with them now had nothing to do with her qualifications as an administrator or even her history with them. With a deftness Kammie Noyo would appreciate, the Sinzi had put Mac where she had to be.

Refreshing, that.

"I will personally check your story and credentials before doing anything else, Dr. Connor," Therin said loudly, cutting through the chatter.

"Great idea," Mac beamed at the Sthlynii. "And it's Mac. Don't take too long. Meanwhile . . ." she pointed to someone at random and crooked her finger. "You. Let's grab a couple of chairs and that corner, shall we?" Without looking to see if she was being obeyed, Mac left the table and began pushing her own chair closer to the window.

Hands took over the job. Mudge. "I hope you know what you're doing, Norcoast," he whispered over his shoulder to her. "They aren't convinced—not by a long shot."

"Got you to stay, didn't I?" she whispered back, lips twitching. "Give them time. They made a mistake. At least they're listening."

He harrumphed, then was pulled away by a boisterous Cey eager to know how soon she could receive a . . . Mac didn't bother trying to make sense of the name of the device or whatever, but it sounded expensive. *She'd thought the lure of a wide-open budget would help get things moving.*

"Mac."

She positioned her chair and turned, not surprised to see it was Lyle, not the person she'd indicated, pulling his chair up beside hers.

They faced each other, with their respective pieces of furniture in hand like jousting knights waiting mounts, for a ridiculous length of time. Just as Mac was about to give in and sit anyway, he said very quietly, as if each word had to be forced out: "Myriam Myers. The woman who died. She was my wife, Connor. I've been hunting you, as best I could from the Chasm, ever since. Now, I . . ." His pale eyes glistened.

Mac gestured to the other chair and dropped into her own as he sat, pulling out her imp as though they were about to exchange data. Her hands trembled. "Now," she finished for him, equally softly, "you don't know what to do or think. You feel empty. Cheated. Lost."

"Yes." He looked up at her, having slumped to rest his elbows on his knees. "How did you—"

"It's a three-pint story."

A hint of a smile. "Haven't heard that in a while."

Mac shrugged. "I'm an anachronism. Either that, or I don't get out much. But I will tell you everything that's happened, Lyle. If we're going to work together, you'll need that."

He sat a little straighter. "I needed this as well." A nod to the rest of the large room, where everyone was now standing in small groups to talk. Except for the line that had formed behind where Mudge had taken a seat at the table, his workscreen already up. "We've been here two days, Mac. No one's felt necessary until now. Oh, the IU promised to quarantine the Dhryn home world while we're here, preserve our excavations. But they have their own people there and no one's said when we go back. No one's given us any direction what to do here."

"Not to mention you heard a Dr. Connor was taking charge. No wonder you were ready to hang me from the nearest tree this morning."

"Not quite." His pigmentless skin blushed, beginning as rosy dots on either cheek and a band low on neck, the colors rushing together. "But that wasn't our best moment. Now it looks like we jumped to conclusions, maybe ignored data that led elsewhere. It's a shameful thing. I'm sorry."

"Keep your doubts about me until you've checked my side of things for yourself. All I expect now is that you listen with an open mind."

"Fair enough." Lyle's eyes flicked to Mac's head. "That a three-pint story, too?"

"A misadventure with external genitalia!" supplied Fourteen helpfully, coming to stand beside Mac. "So Human." He squinted at Lyle. "Oh. You're Human, too. Couldn't tell. No offense."

"None taken." The archaeologist almost smiled. "Sounds like a story worth hearing."

Mac glared at Fourteen, who took advantage of his thick eyelids to pretend not to see her. "It had its moments," she said to Lyle. "But first—"

"But irrelevant. First, Mac," Fourteen interrupted, "you are wanted." Mac followed his gesture to the doorway, where a pair of consular staff stood waiting.

"Is it an emergency? The Dhryn attacking? Any sign of the Ro?" *Of Emily?*

"They say Sinzi-ra wishes you to return to your quarters and rest."

"Then please advise her I'll do so in—" Mac did a quick calculation. Five minutes an interview—if no one was long-winded, which was unlikely, so half would go ten—twenty-four researchers left to meet. "Three hours. Plus. Make it four."

"But, Mac—"

She finally caught and held Fourteen's small eyes. "I could take five if you keep delaying me."

"Very well." From his tone, Mac might have asked him to do more dishes.

As he walked away, Lyle half smiled. "If I needed more proof you run a research station in the middle of nowhere, there it is."

"What's that?"

"You're used to doing things yourself."

"You know what they say, Lyle," Mac said primly, smoothing the fabric of her lovely blue jacket over her thighs, "about doing something right. Now, who should I speak with next?"

As he stood to call someone over, Mac looked past and saw Fourteen arguing with the staff, who were not looking at all happy.

And sometimes, Em, she smiled to herself, *it wasn't about doing it right. It was about setting rules.*

Either this room and all it represented was hers, or it wasn't.

She intended it to be hers.

There was nothing quite as soothing as sand to tired Human feet, Mac decided as she kicked off her shoes that night. She lay back in the jelly-chair and dug in her toes, head back and eyes closed. Her scalp throbbed, her stomach was beyond empty, and she thought it likely she'd fall asleep before being able to stand again.

Haven't felt this good in months, Em.

Every member of the group—she'd dubbed them the Origins Team—was exceptional. No surprise, given they'd organized, funded, and established an independent research camp on one of the lifeless Chasm worlds. *Not bad.* Mind you, a significant proportion of those funds came from private donors they preferred not to name, but Mac had no problem with generosity, so long as there weren't strings attached.

Lyle Kanaci? She put her teeth together and whistled tunelessly. Brilliant, determined, responsible, obsessed. An asset she'd invite to Norcoast in an instant, if only he was as interested in living things as he was in what they built and left behind. He'd expressed the doubts Mac found many of the Origins Team shared—what could they contribute here? Even more frustrating, they'd been forced to suspend much of their work to help set up the influx of new researchers to the Dhryn world.

The new arrivals, all sponsored by the IU, hadn't been asked to attend the Gathering in person; their findings and data were being fed here. Mac was well aware her group considered their invitation a sign their independent research was in jeopardy.

It probably was.

"Are you in pain?"

Mac opened her eyes and sat up as quickly as the amorous chair allowed. "Anchen. I'm sorry. I didn't hear you come in." *She never did.*

The room was dimly lit. The Sinzi was little more than a pale, slender silhouette against the dark night sky that showed through the terrace doors. "It is I who must remember not to startle my guests, Mac. May I examine your wound, please." It wasn't a question.

Mac stood and let the Sinzi explore her bandaged scalp. The alien used her fingertips, gently pressing in various spots until Mac winced cooperatively. "Very good," Anchen assured her. "The regeneration of your skin should be complete soon. We'll be able to remove the covering shortly." A pause, her touch lingering on Mac's forehead. "Do you wish treatment for pain?"

"I just need some supper and a night's sleep, thank you."

Anchen spoke one word: "Attend." The lights brightened and

Mac stifled a yawn as a trolley of food floated through the open doors into her room, guided by another of the staff. She didn't think she'd seen the same one twice.

"Once more, you anticipate my every need," Mac said gratefully.

"As is always my intent. Now I wish you to anticipate mine."

Mac, who'd found the energy to follow her supper into the sitting room, stopped and looked over her shoulder at the taller alien. "I'm afraid I don't have your skill at anticipation, Anchen," she said, stalling. What did the Sinzi want? *Hopefully nothing that involved a body part.* "What can I do for you?"

The Sinzi produced an imp, white and more disk-shaped than Mac's or Fourteen's. "I visit the team leaders each night to record their impressions and insights for the IU. I need yours, if you please."

Mac was afraid her relief was obvious. *Still . . . there were over thirty separate research teams.* "How do you get any sleep?" she asked involuntarily.

Anchen looked amused. "At this moment, four of my 'selves' are asleep, Mac."

"Oh. Of course." *Handy.* "Why the imp?" she asked, thinking of the light fixture Mudge had suspected. "Isn't the room monitored?"

Anchen's head snapped up to an impressive height. "It is not. We could not host honored delegates from the IU here if they had the slightest reason to doubt their privacy."

Her vehemence was convincing. Mac felt a twinge of guilt. Sing-li must have hidden some Ministry snooper of his own on Oversight—an abuse of consular protocol Mac doubted the Sinzi would tolerate. *If she found out.*

So, how close together did Humans stick?

Mac's stomach chose that moment to gurgle. Loudly.

Being in charge of a consulate on Earth led to certain understandings. Anchen lowered her head and lifted three fingers in the direction of Mac's supper. "You can provide this information while you eat."

Refusing didn't seem an option, but Mac went for a gracious, "Then please join me, Anchen."

"I would be honored."

They each took one of the jelly-chairs, the attendant arranging the floating trolley at Mac's side. Before Mac could offer to share, Anchen reached to the table between them, aglow with fish, sponges, and anemones. Her fingertip pointed at a bristling shrimp, marching delicately over a coral.

"I saw that one earlier—" Mac began, then closed her mouth as the attendant extended a small rod into a long silver implement which he deftly stabbed into the table. The tip instantly adhered to the small animal and the attendant smoothly withdrew both implement and now motionless shrimp, proffering both to Anchen.

Without a drop of water hitting the sand.

"I'm impressed," Mac said as Anchen delicately but efficiently used her nails to peel shell and pluck appendages, putting these in a small bowl provided by the attendant before consuming the remaining morsel of flesh in one tidy mouthful.

Mac looked at the table, where the sea life seemed completely unconcerned, and scratched her own fingernail along the top. Hard and solid. A parrot fish tried to nibble her finger before diving deeper. "Okay. I have to know how you did that."

Anchen beckoned to the attendant. He bowed to Mac and said: "The table is both menu and larder for the Sinzi-ra, who consumes only fresh marine life."

Mac raised an eyebrow. "Preference or physiology? If you don't mind the question."

The Sinzi smiled, cleaning her fingertips on a cloth the attendant had exchanged for the bowl. "Assuredly I do not. It is both, Mac. On Earth, these delicious organisms are also the most easily digested by my species. In addition, I find the movements of these beautiful creatures to be soothing as well as appetizing, so there are tables like this in several locations in the consulate. Do you enjoy them as well?"

"Very much. Soothing always. And several are very tasty." Still perplexed, Mac studied the table. "But—the water appears deeper than it can be. And how did you catch the shrimp and pull it through the table?" This to the attendant. "Trust me, I know what it's like trying to net something in water."

The attendant looked to Anchen, who lifted two fingers. *Grant-*

ing permission, Mac decided. "The table is more than a convenience for the Sinzi-ra," he explained. "It is a demonstration of a
brand new technology the Sinzi is offering to qualified members of
the Interspecies Union. This—" he indicated the table, "—is not a
tank filled with water and living things. It is an access gate, permanently opened to another, much larger tank." He showed Mac the
slim featureless rod, collapsing it. "This device acts much the way
the navigation array on a starship does when it stipulates a destination through a transect, creating a pathway. In this case, the destination is an object in the tank. The connection is instantaneous and
the object, the shrimp Anchen favored, can be retrieved."

She'd been tapping the outside of a transect through no-space.

Mac lifted her fingers from the table.

"It is an accomplishment in which we take great pride," noted
Anchen. "However, there remain serious constraints. It takes a
constant input of power to maintain—we have been permitted to
draw directly upon the geothermal energy beneath this building.
More significantly, there is an impact on the living things within the
tank. They appear normal and thriving, do they not? So far as we
can determine, they come to no harm entering or existing in what
is essentially a fixed bubble of no-space. Once inside, however, they
cannot be removed alive."

Emily.

Perhaps the Sinzi interpreted Mac's look of horror as one of awe.
Or understood all too well. "How to survive upon exit is among the
most important of the many questions we have for the Myrokynay," she said. "We Sinzi have but built on the fragments they left
thousands of years ago." Fingers cascaded, rings flashed light. "We
do our best—yet how pitiful our efforts must seem to them. From
your own account and those of others, now the Myrokynay can
form transects at need, live themselves within no-space, pass freely
into this reality. While we achieve shrimp snacks, using as much
power as this entire complex."

Pitiful? Mac stared at the table, with its imprisoned life. She
wasn't so sure. Many living things staked out territories, defended
what they viewed as theirs; Humans could do it with a look. *What
would the Ro think of the Sinzi's shrimp, Em?* Would they have the

proud attitude of parents who see their children strive to exceed them? Or might they see trespass—a challenge to their supremacy over no-space itself from those who still walked planets?

Mac shivered. "You want a great deal more than help with the Dhryn."

"Of course," with that lift of the head indicating surprise. "In our wildest imaginings, we never expected to find the creators of the transects still lived. To work with them? To learn from them? The Sinzi aspire only to be worthy."

"If I were you," Mac said dryly, "I'd aspire to find out what they'll want in return and be sure you can afford it."

Anchen's head tilted to bring another set of eyes closer to Mac. *Whose attention did she have now?* "First contact is by its very nature doomed to misunderstandings, Mac." Her voice was gentle but firm. "We can only proceed in this by stepping from known to known. The Dhryn feared the Myrokynay. For good reason, since the Myrokynay tried to destroy their Progenitors before they could launch their ships. All we know about the Dhryn is that they pose a devastating and terrifying threat to life. Surely the Myrokynay, who possess knowledge and technology far beyond any other species within the Interspecies Union, know more. We need them as allies. We will pay their price, if one is asked."

This was the being who represented the IU on Earth. *Nothing she says, Em,* Mac told herself uneasily, *would be less than policy for all.*

Still, she couldn't keep completely silent. "I urge caution in every dealing with the Ro, Anchen. We know even less about them than about the Dhryn."

"An insight of value, Mac, which is why you are here." Anchen brought out her imp and put it on the table. "Please, if you are ready, eat your meal and share any thoughts you have from your first day." She made motions with her fingers, implying a workscreen in existence over the device, but Mac couldn't see one—unless that shimmer when she tilted her head marked a portion. *Differing visual range? Interesting.*

If things hadn't gone so well today—*after that appalling start,* Mac admitted—she might have been stuck with nothing to tell the

Sinzi, but as it was, her food grew cold as she described the potential of her group of researchers. "I wouldn't be surprised," she finished, waving her fork in emphasis, "to have interesting results as early as tomorrow."

The Sinzi had listened without comment until now. "Why do you expect this, Mac? They had nothing to contribute yesterday, beyond what was recorded about the death of their fellow scientists. Today, they have requested data on you, not on the Dhryn."

"The information about me will restore trust. As for my expectations?" Mac tilted her head, trying to decide which of Anchen's paired eyes were most intent on her. "They don't know what they know," she said at last. "It's about context, Anchen. I've given them a new one. I think it will shake some things loose."

"Ah yes. Migration. You believe the Dhryn are on such a journey. That their motive may be biological. That they act, at least in part, out of instinct rather than conscious plan. A novel approach."

Fourteen had made a full report, Mac smiled to herself. Aloud: "Believe? No. Not yet. I simply see value to assessing what we know about the Dhryn in those terms. That could be the prejudice of my own specialization. I admit that. But consider this, Anchen. At least since the Chasm, Dhryn Progenitors have outlawed the study of living things, including their own physiology. Why?"

"Is this an important question?"

"Any question we can't answer about the Dhryn is an important question."

The Sinzi lifted her fingers, touching them tip to tip to form a hollow ball before her complex eyes. "I concur, Mac. I will share your insights with the other delegates in hopes of granting them a new 'context.' " She lowered her fingers and smiled. "I am personally gratified by your behavior with the Human-ra since this morning. You exceeded the expectations of some of myselves for you, and those were already high."

Given the time of night, and a mind this side of putty, Mac wisely avoided trying to understand that, accepting the implied compliment. "The Human-ra—" *the term must be loose enough,* she decided, *to include Kanaci's non-Human colleagues,* "—lacked the information it required about me. I've begun to rectify that. Call it a misunderstanding during first contact. We have a common purpose, after all."

"We do. Ah. I am reminded." *By what,* Mac wondered. *One of the group minds?* A deft finger stroke through empty air, away from where Mac had assumed the invisible-to-her workscreen hung. *Separate 'screens for each mind?* "There is a query for you. It comes from the team correlating our data on the Myrokynay."

"Me? I don't have anything new to add to my original statements," Mac reminded the Sinzi. "And I made those when things were fresher in my mind."

"We have your very useful information, Mac. This query concerns a more esoteric interpretation of your experience. Yes. I see it is posed in mathematical terms which, while elegant and succinct, do not translate into Instella. If you will permit me to approximate?" At Mac's nod, she continued: "Did you observe anything about Emily Mamani implying the passage of biological time in no-space?"

"Biological time." While several possibilities came to mind, Mac chose not to guess. "I don't understand."

"The state of being alive is postulated to require time that at least appears to move linearly, from what was to what is, thus permitting growth and metabolism to take place in sequenced steps. There are other modes of time which do not support this state. Within our tank," a gesture to the glittering fish, "there is movement and thus the impression of biological time, is there not? We are divided in interpretation. Is this true biological time or its echo, since what passes for life here is, in real space, already dead?"

Mac gamely attempted to wrap her brain around the philosophical connections between linear time and death, other than the one being at the end of the line. After a moment, she gave a helpless shrug. "I'm sorry, Anchen. Salmon researcher, not physicist. What's the point to this?"

"If we accept that the Myrokynay truly live within no-space, the answers to questions of time have significance to our hope for mutual understanding."

"If they live in time as we do," Mac narrowed her eyes, "they're like us. I get that part. But as opposed to what?"

"Some other state of being." The Sinzi brought two fingertips closer and closer together as if to touch, only to have them miss each other at the last instant. "An alarming possibility, Mac. You and your fellow Humans experience misunderstandings, as does any species within itself, despite shared biology and history. Negotiations between IU species involves more effort to sort through unintended confusion than all other deterrents to agreement combined. This, despite a shared language and technology." Anchen shuddered, her hundreds of tiny rings tinkling. "Imagine the difficulty communicating with beings who don't share the very experience of life itself with us."

They'd have a better chance explaining Trisulian sex to a salmon through a straw. Mac became acutely conscious of her heart beating, the air passing in and out of her nostrils, the way her head ached. A body plan reasonably similar to the Sinzi's. The same ability to exchange complex ideas. "Puts my problems with the Origins Team into perspective," she said at last. "I wouldn't worry too much yet. After all, Emily's managed to deal with the Ro."

Anchen's small mouth formed a smile. "A comforting observation to end the day." Putting away her imp, the Sinzi rose from the jelly-chair without a wasted motion. Mac stood up as well, feeling as though she flopped in every direction possible before finding level ground. "Good night, Mac, and thank you for your insights. I will return tomorrow evening—late again, I assume."

Mac smiled. "Good thing you sleep in shifts, Anchen."

By early the next morning, the now officially named Origins Team was well underway. They skipped the mill and swill, as Mac called it, in the garden in favor of getting to work. Not to mention being set out as mass enticement for the Ro was the last thing she felt like doing, no matter how determined the Sinzi. Fourteen showed his approval by showing up sans wig and in those paisley shorts, clean at least. As for the others, it hadn't hurt that she'd arranged for breakfast to be served here, then refused to let the staff clean up, knowing perfectly well they'd be grazing the leftovers before lunch.

The room itself had a completely different look from yesterday.

The research consoles had been moved into five clusters, Lyle suggesting those to be included in each. The big conference table had been shoved against one wall to provide the expanse of empty floor space archaeologists apparently required. Mac didn't ask.

Fourteen had brought in three large tables of his own, setting these up in a u-shape so he had his back to the window—Mac presumed so he could see what everyone else was doing, curiosity being one of the Myg's traits. Each time she looked at what he himself was doing, there were more small objects scattered over the tables, each new acquisition placed with the rapt concentration of a chess master. Objects like other people's writing implements, combs, and buttons. And a shoe.

She'd better send around a memo, Mac decided.

Mudge had taken a corner for himself, adding a desk. He'd stayed up most of the night, by the bags under his eyes, managing to send their initial supply requests through in time for the first arrivals to accompany the catering staff.

It had been a toss-up which had been more warmly received, coffee or image extrapolation wands. *Whatever they were.*

Mac wandered over to Mudge, leaning on the wall behind him to survey the bustle, mug in hand.

"Do you," he asked acerbically, "have the slightest idea what they're doing?"

"Not a clue." She took a sip and sighed contentedly. *Cold already.* "How about you?"

"I've placed requisitions for equipment I didn't even know existed, let alone how it could possibly be used by—by archaeologists!"

Mac smiled down at him. "They aren't all archaeologists."

"Don't," he growled, "get me started."

There was now a curtained-off section of the room, behind which the author of the ever-popular "Chasm Ghouls: They Exist and Talk to Me" and his trio of followers were apparently conducting chats with the departed. "Here I shared a sandstorm with the famous man and didn't even know it," Mac mused.

"I wish I didn't."

"We're all talking to the dead here," she pointed out, taking another sip. "I don't care who gives me the answers."

"You've never settled for other people's before, Norcoast."

Mac half smiled. "I've never asked these questions before."

Mudge fussed with his workscreen. "Kirby and To'o are qualified climatologists, but according to your list, we need a xenopaleoecologist."

"I know. Fourteen's working on it. Says he knows one."

"There's another thing. Why is a cryptologist working with us? We have translators." He consulted his workscreen. "An even dozen. There must be other groups who could use him."

She could see the Myg from here; he'd abandoned his object arranging and was deep in conversation with Lyle. "Probably. But he's attached himself to—" *me,* she almost said, "—us for now and no one's objected. He may come in handy."

Especially if Emily tried to send her another message. Something Mac was quite sure had occurred to the Sinzi, and whomever else was in charge.

"Mac, do you have a minute?"

The question, asked in that hesitant "don't know you yet" tone, was so familiar, Mac was smiling before she turned to answer it. "Of course."

It was To'o, the Cey climatologist. Or Da'a, the other Cey. They dressed like twins, and Mac hadn't seen enough of their species to pick out the physical features that distinguished individuals. *Or,* she told herself honestly, *she couldn't get past the heavy wrinkles of their faces.* The dark brown, pebble-textured skin hung in great, limp folds, starting with small ones at the top of the head to free-swinging cascades by the elbows. It was as if each Cey wore another organism like a veil.

For all she knew, they did. Mac shuddered, thinking of the Trisulian symbionts. She'd been very happy not to have to converse with another of that species quite yet.

The problem wasn't that the folds were ugly—*okay,* Mac confessed, *grotesque came to mind*—but the ones on the face itself gave each Cey a perpetually miserable look, as if nauseous. It might have helped if they'd had less Human-like features between the folds.

"If you'll come?"

Quite sure she'd been staring, Mac waved the Cey to proceed her.

Moments later, Mac seriously considered finding a wrinkle to kiss. "This is—this is splendid work, To'o, Kirby. I hadn't expected anything so soon."

Kirby, Human male and probably no older than most of Mac's first-year grad students, grinned up at her from his seat at the console. "It wasn't soon. We'd looked into longer cyclic events with respect to climate for over two Earth years. The research didn't point us anywhere, so we moved on to another topic. Till you. I have to admit, yesterday I thought you were nuts, Mac."

"I get that," she replied absently, leaning over the display with one hand on the console for support. "Why were you looking at cyclic events in the first place?"

To'o replied, "My home world experiences long-term climatic shifts, though none so dramatic as this world's. When you mentioned migration, Kirby and I began to reexamine our old data, looking specifically at the livability of the northern hemisphere relative to the south. We had some more recent data as well from the IU's team back on Myriam."

" 'Myriam?' "

The two exchanged guilty looks. "Sorry. Slipped out," To'o said quickly. "We're not supposed to call it that here."

Mac had no idea of the protocol involved in naming planets—especially planets doubtless named by those who'd evolved there. *Still.* She shot a troubled glance at Lyle, preoccupied with his work, then looked back to the climatologists.

Who were, just like her grad students, holding their breath.

"You named the Dhryn home world after his wife?" she asked, keeping her voice steady but low. "She died there."

"We all agreed." Kirby shrugged. "Lyle's—well, he felt she'd have liked it. And we renamed our research station after Nicli Lee. She died in the storm."

"We keep saying their names, that way," To'o volunteered. "It's important to speak of those we've lost—not to forget them."

She could hardly disagree. "It's shorter than 'Dhryn Home World'," she commented, tacit approval. "Now, what did you want to show me?"

Kirby took over. "We'd collected data on the Dhryn System, including planetary orbits, solar intensity, and so forth. You have to keep in mind we went to—" he seemed at a loss for the name.

"Myriam," Mac helped without thinking. *Damn. She knew better than to encourage this.*

But his smile was so heartfelt and sincere Mac knew she'd committed herself for good. *Another memo,* she sighed inwardly, *so the Sinzi-ra isn't perplexed by reports on planet 'Myriam.'* Kirby had continued, meanwhile. "We went to Myriam to answer questions about the destruction occurring throughout the Chasm. Our initial results showed climate change wasn't implicated, although plenty took place following. Last few months, To'o and I were pretty much left to predicting sandstorms." He surveyed their display with possessive pride. "Wobbly little orbit, isn't it?"

"One way to put it." Mac traced the line without letting her finger invade the active portion of the image. "It doesn't take much," she murmured. "How would this affect the planet?"

"We'll have to do more detailed models," explained To'o, "but my preliminary estimate is that before whatever happened to cause the Chasm-effect, Myriam cycled through polar desertification every five hundred plus orbits."

"At the same time as one pole baked dry, the opposite pole may have experienced near ice age conditions," Kirby offered. "We're not sure. It's a tight orbit. Might have been enough solar radiation transmitted throughout the atmosphere to keep the entire planet above freezing. If so, it would likely have been very wet in temperate zones, ocean currents would have shifted, upper air movements be affected." His voice conveyed awe. "Frankly, an Earth-type seasonal change would have been trivial compared to this. I don't know how a culture would cope."

"More to the point," Mac said, straightening, "how would life?"

"You said migration—but can this fit the bill?" Kirby sounded doubtful suddenly. "I'm no biologist, but aren't migrations annual? Running from winter, that sort of thing. Five hundred year cycles?" He shook his head. "I dunno, Mac."

Mac didn't quite smile. "Nothing is that simple. There are species on Earth, like my salmon, who only migrate when their bodies are ready to reproduce, however many years that takes. There are others whose individuals never complete a migration, having generations born, reproduce, then die as steps along that journey. Look at us," Mac put a hand on Kirby and To'o's shoulder, feeling the differences in the joints beneath her fingers. "If there's anything biologists have learned, it's that life offers a variety of ways to get the job done. Survival first."

"We'll get on a model for you," To'o offered. "Should let us infer what conditions existed over evolutionary time lines."

"I look forward to it. Good work, you two."

Mac left the climatologists and began wandering the large room, listening to conversations and the hum of equipment. There were no looks of condemnation today. If anything, there were a few more sympathetic smiles than she liked, each of which she had to acknowledge with a polite nod.

Anchen's doing. During breakfast, Mac learned that last night the Sinzi had sent everyone a copy of the report the consulate had received on her experiences with the Dhryn. She'd held a faint hope not all had taken the time to read it, but, from the looks now—and given their original attitude toward her—it seemed everyone had.

Personally, while Mac had planned to give her colleagues any information that might trigger a connection or produce an idea, she hadn't planned to share every detail of the events themselves. *Not going to guess, Em, what these people think now.*

She supposed she should relax and be grateful her team no longer believed she'd been imprisoned as a murderous traitor to her kind.

"Someone die?"

At the sound of Fourteen's voice, Mac started, then smiled and shook her head. "Sorry. Just thinking."

"Idiot."

"Probably. Did you want something? I was going to talk to Lyle."

"Talk to me first. Outside."

He wasn't happy about something. Mac gave a discreet sniff, detecting nothing but mint. Without argument, she followed Fourteen from the Origins room out to the Sinzi version of a corridor, which consisted of a broad ramplike balcony that wound around a central opening, eventually reaching every floor of the building. A few pigeons perched on the edges, taking full advantage of the practice of wide-open doors every morning. Mac presumed they'd find their way out again or be fed. *Then again,* she thought, amused, *maybe they'd be fed to some of the delegates.*

"Well?" asked Mac when they were out of earshot of the room. "Quickly, please, Fourteen. I'd like to get back."

"Your Dhryn, Brymn Las. You said he'd published work on the Chasm, correct?"

"Yes, of course." She frowned. "What's this about?"

"Significant work?"

"Yes," Mac said again. "I believe some are considered definitive on the subject. Core texts. Why?"

The Myg's answer sent her marching straight back into the research room, straight to Lyle Kanaci. He looked up as Mac approached, then stood with alarm as her expression registered.

Good, Mac thought. Despite an overwhelming urge to shout and tear hair, not necessarily hers, she toned her voice to quiet fury. "How dare you refuse to use the work of the foremost expert on Chasm archaeology?"

Lyle's face settled into stubborn lines. Silence spread in ripples from them. *So much for subtle, Em.* "You lost your wife," she snapped. "Are you willing to lose everyone in this room—everyone and everything alive on this planet—the same way?"

He opened his mouth, face ashen. Mac quelled whatever he was about to say with a sharp upward gesture of her hand. "Use your grief and rage however you want," she continued just as angrily, meaning them all to hear. "But don't let it blind you. Don't ever let it *think* for you."

She took a ragged breath. "Brymn spent his life seeking the truth about what destroyed the worlds of the Chasm. I hope none of us ever feels how he must have felt, to learn it was his own kind, to have his own body betray everything he believed." Mac's eyes never left Lyle's. "I will not permit his life's work to be lost or ignored. How dare you . . ." She lost her voice somewhere in fury, then regained it. "I will supply complete sets of Brymn's work to everyone on the Origins Team. If you or anyone is unwilling to use it, find somewhere else to be. I won't work with you."

Without waiting for an answer, Mac spun on her heel and left.

"No one left."

Mac's fingers tightened their grip on the terrace railing, but she gave no other indication she'd doubted the outcome. "Lyle?"

"Staying, Norcoast, but not happy." Mudge leaned on his elbows beside her, shaking his head. He reached out to touch the invisible barrier protecting them both from the blustery northwest wind and the driving rain it carried. "He'll be looking for flaws in the Dhryn's research, questioning every piece of data, suspecting hidden motives. Could be difficult."

She turned her head to grin at him. "Sounds familiar."

Mudge pretended to be shocked. "If you are implying a comparison to my annual reviews, the word you want is 'thorough.'"

"Not 'obsessive'?" she chuckled, then relented. "Thanks for bringing me the news. I knew the consulate had everything I needed. It's already been sent to their imps and consoles. Now all I have to do is unpack."

"Your belongings arrived?"

In a manner of speaking. Mac straightened. "Let me show you."

She led Mudge back through her bedroom and the sitting room, to where a new door had appeared—or rather been revealed, since Mac didn't doubt it had always been there—since she'd left this morning. She pushed it open and waved Mudge to precede her. "Watch your head," she cautioned as she followed.

Behind the door was, for lack of a better term, the Sinzi version of a closet. It was more like a warehouse. Larger than the sitting room, but with a floor constructed of the same weatherproof material as the terrace, the closet had no window on the outer wall. Instead, that wall was sectioned and fitted with a mechanism to both open and extend its panels into what Mac assumed was a landing pad for a t-lev. A rope of bright light ran along the junction of walls and ceiling.

The three inner walls, other than the entranceway, were studded with hooks, as was the ceiling. From each hook hung a large bag, roughly the length of a Human being, but varying in width. There were dozens, the ones from the ceiling swaying gently.

"When I first saw this, I thought it was a Sinzi nursery," Mac said. Mudge, who'd gone to the center of the closet and was poking at a bag above his head, quickly withdrew his hand. "It isn't," Mac laughed. She grabbed a strap attached to a bag hanging near the door, using it to pull down both bag and hook. The assembly paused where she stopped it, and Mac tugged open the bag, stepping to one side as she did.

Boxes and boots tumbled out on the floor. Her boots, still caked with mud from the pod roof. Mac regarded them fondly. *Such a homey touch in an alien closet.*

"You mentioned the word 'thorough,' Oversight?" Mac flung her arm at the bags on every side. "This would appear to be an example. They must have—" she paused to grunt with the effort of pulling down two more bags at once, "—brought everything that wasn't attached."

Mudge helped her free the bags' contents. Sure enough, they were shortly surrounded by a mix of sweaters, wooden salmon, and an eclectic variety of lab equipment. "Wrong—some things were attached," he offered, holding up the end support of Mac's desk for inspection.

She shook her head in astonishment. Sing-li, or whoever he'd sent, was a literal sort.

The floor was soon littered with the contents of Mac's office and lab. Nothing was in order, but it was all intact. They began taking turns moving items to the other room to leave space for more. On one such trip, Mac returned to find Mudge hurriedly closing the bag he'd just brought down from the ceiling. "What is it?" she asked, curious. He hadn't flinched when her underwear had come flying out past his head.

"Stuffed llama. With sunglasses." Mudge gave her a wide-eyed look. "Is that yours?"

Emily's things. "Of course. I don't need it now. Please close it up, Oversight." Mac looked up at the rest of the bags hanging from the ceiling.

They had *brought everything.*

He looked, too. "Let's stop here," he suggested reasonably, arms limp at his sides. Sweat beaded his forehead and cheeks. The bags had held heavy equipment as well as pressed leaves. "You can't need all of this immediately. You probably don't need any," this opinion with a scowl at her curtain beads, piled around his feet. "We should get back to the team."

"I want to give them some time to go over Brymn's material without me breathing down their necks. Or whatevers." Mac kept digging through a stack of promising reference works. They'd been near her desk. Her desk had had her imp. *Mind you, dismantling her desk hadn't helped in using it as a locator.* The parts were spread among fifteen bags so far. "Have to find my imp," she insisted.

"You have one."

"That?" Mac shook her head, burrowing deeper. Inside a bag she'd thought empty was a small assortment of objects, difficult to see and too deep to reach. She half climbed inside. "One of Fourteen's," she said, voice muffled by fabric. "I want mine."

It wasn't just her voice that was muffled. She could barely make out Mudge saying something. "Can't hear you," she muttered, feeling the end of a promising cylinder. "Aha!" *Sample bottle.* Mac put it down and leaned in farther.

Another voice answered Mudge's, deeper and familiar.

Mac squirmed out of the bag, hands clutching whatever they'd last grabbed, and half staggered to her feet. A guest?

In her closet?

"Norcoast, meet my friend at the consulate, Stefan Young, the one who helped arrange for me to stay. We've known each other for years." Mudge beamed, his hand on the shoulder of the man he was introducing. "Stefan stopped by to see how I was doing. Stefan, this is Dr. Mackenzie Connor."

The suit and cravat were immaculate. The glasses gleamed. The brown hair was neatly trimmed above the collar, the skin of cheek and chin free of beard. Perhaps the smile was a bit forced, the eyes caught by her bandaged scalp.

But otherwise, Mac decided, *Nikolai Trojanowski appeared in fine form.*

"Hello, Dr. Connor."

- Encounter -

THE GREAT JOURNEY must continue. That which is Dhryn cannot falter. All that is Dhryn must move.

That which is Dhryn . . . *starves*.

That which is Dhryn remembers this place, knows its *Taste,* rushes forward.

Then stops. There is not enough here to sustain the Journey. That which is Dhryn cannot afford waste of effort.

But it is the way of the Great Journey, that all must follow the Taste.

That which is Dhryn . . . moves.

"Did you check the L-array, David? It's been acting up."

"Yes, Mom, I checked the L-array."

The woman alone in the operations booth winced at the patience in his tone. "Asked already, have I?"

"Twice, but who's counting?"

"Obviously you. A little respect for your commander, young man, if you please, or I'll make you wait to park your shuttle until Maggie's brought the freighter up."

"Fine by me. Sooner I park, the sooner I'm back cleaning tubes." A pause. "Just kidding, Mom."

"I know. C'mon in. You should be in time for supper. Thanks for the check, David."

"Shuttle coming in, Commander Mom."

His laugh lingered, warming ops. Even so, her eyes wandering ceaselessly over the remote feeds, Anita Brukman lost her smile.

She couldn't ask often enough. They couldn't be careful enough.

They'd survived once—if surviving was blowing clear of the station as her seals dissolved and hatches breached to vacuum—if surviving was listening to the desperate, futile struggles of those too late to escape pods or shuttles—if surviving was returning to make repairs and go back to the work and ship out ore as if everyone else who should be there, be part of your life forever . . . wasn't gone.

Anita drew a deep breath and relaxed her shoulders. They'd survived and they were careful. Fact was, the station was close to shipping at sixty percent capacity again, or would be once Maggie's freighter was filled and on her way. A tribute to Human determination, the company rep called it. Bonuses all around by tour's end.

As if fate heard her, two-thirds of the remote feeds flared red at once.

The com crackled with overlapping shouts: "Incoming!" "Dhryn everywhere." "They're heading for the station!"

Then, one voice, with a calmness that made her proud: "Mom, get to the shuttle bay. I'm coming for you."

"It's too late, David," Anita said gently. "Go. Everyone in a ship. Go."

Seals began to breach. A claxon would sound as long as air carried it.

"Mom."

"David." Anita put her hand on the cold metal of the station wall and closed her eyes.

"I love you," she told him.

One last time.

- 14 -

ACQUAINTANCE AND ANGUISH

"THIS ISN'T A SOCIAL call, Charles," Stefan/Nik informed them both. He'd acquired a faint accent Mac couldn't place; it changed his voice significantly. *More annoying spy stuff, Em.* She frowned, mind racing with questions, none pleasant, about 'Stefan's' connection to Mudge. But he didn't give her time to say anything at all. "Dr. Connor, I'm to escort you to reception. There's someone to see you. Please come with me."

Mac's hands lost their grip, the objects in them falling to the floor with a clatter. She couldn't help the hope.

She couldn't utter it.

Mudge harrumphed. "Dr. Mamani?" he asked, for her sake. *A kindness.* "Is she here?"

Even through the glasses, Mac could read the flash of pity in those hazel eyes. "No," she answered, for him.

To recover, she bent to pick up what she'd dropped. Another sample bottle, this filled with salmon otoliths from three years ago, a hairbrush she didn't use anymore, and . . . her imp. *Well, Em,* Mac told herself, feeling hollow, *something positive.* She clutched it in her hand and tossed the other items back in the bag.

"Dr. Connor. If you'd come with me, please? We're pressed for time."

"Yes, of course," she said quietly. Mudge puffed out his cheeks and Mac shook her head at him. "You should get back to the group."

A disapproving look. "What about all this?"

Mac held up her imp. "Now it can wait. Thanks for your help, Oversight. I'll check in later."

Mudge patted Stefan/Nik on the shoulder. "You're in good hands, Norcoast." To Nik, "Make sure she gets lunch, Stefan. Something nourishing."

This, Mac decided, *was too bizarre for words.* Both Nik and Mudge had some explaining to do.

It wasn't going to be now. Nik was already out of the closet and through the sitting room, walking so quickly Mac was reasonably sure he'd have sand in his shoes. With a last look and an apologetic shrug at Mudge, who was stepping his way free of her beads, Mac followed.

She caught up with Nik as he led the way down the corridor ramp to the nearest lift. The suit disguised any tension in his shoulders or posture—*convenient, that*—but she felt it coming in waves from him anyway. *Something wasn't right.*

Mac grimaced. *Nothing new there, Em.*

Once in the lift, Nik waited for the door to close. The Sinzi-built device responded to voice or an input pad with five choices, corresponding to the four aboveground floors and the roof. He didn't use any of these, instead placing his hand flat on the wall beside the pad and pressing it there. "This will work for you as well, Dr. Connor," he said, still with the accent. The lift began to drop. There was no sensation, but lights coursed down the sides to indicate movement, a brief ring of green announcing every floor. Three. Two. One.

" 'Stefan?' " she commented, watching the lights.

"Long story."

"I'll bet."

They kept going. The flashes reflected from Nik's glasses as he looked at her, hiding his expression.

She'd been sure there was a basement. *Just never planned to go there, Em.*

They kept going, floors blinking by so rapidly Mac lost count at seven below ground.

They kept going.

Finally, Nik removed his hand and the lift stopped.

"Reception?" Mac asked dubiously as the doors opened on a white, featureless corridor, flat and long.

"In a sense. Please hurry."

Hurry? Mac swallowed and kept up with Nik, giving a little hop every three steps to match his longer ones.

The corridor ended at another, perpendicular to the first. A figure stepped out from the left in front of them. With astonishing quickness, Nik pushed her to that wall and down, using the effort to dodge right and to the floor himself, his hand swinging up to aim before Mac knew he'd drawn his palm-sized weapon.

And before she had time to be more than shocked, Nik was putting his weapon away again. "What happened to patience?" he asked, accent gone.

It was a Trisulian. Mac automatically counted eyestalks—*two upper, no lower*—as the being answered: "Patience, my good Nikolai, is a virtue without value at this time. Dr. Connor. Forgive my partner's deplorable reflexes. Are you all right?"

Partner? One hand on the wall, Mac rose to her feet. By the feel, she'd have a bruise on her shoulder, another on her hip. As for her head? *Bah.* "Mac. And yes, I'm fine, thanks." She couldn't help herself. "Partner?"

Nik gestured to the alien. "Meet Cinder. Who usually knows better than to surprise me." This with a glare.

An eyestalk coyly bent in his direction. "You haven't shot me yet."

"Day's young."

"I thought we were in a hurry," Mac commented dryly.

Nik gave her the strangest look before he nodded brusquely, motioning her to follow the Trisulian.

Recognizing the look, Mac felt a chill as she obeyed. *Why sympathy, Em? Who or what was waiting for her?*

Whatever it was, it was well-protected. They took the left corridor as it gradually bent to the right. *Following the cliff and coastline, not the building,* Mac deduced. Along the way, Nik and Cinder escorted her through three checkpoints, set equidistant along the plain white hall, the last two within sight of each other.

The checkpoints appeared an afterthought. At each, a member of the consular staff waited at a table set to block half the width of the corridor. The remaining gap was guarded by an assortment of aliens, also in the yellow consular uniform, but with armor showing beneath—those who didn't have their own natural version. After the second of these pauses, during which the staff courteously inquired after their needs and clearances, questions Nik answered for her, Mac decided the choice of guards wasn't completely random. No two of the same species were present at one checkpoint. *IU policy?* she wondered as they passed the third. *To prevent collusion— or share some risk?*

Beyond the third checkpoint, the corridor took a sharper bend, widened into a bulb, and came to an end. They stood in front of a choice of three ordinary-looking doors. Mac was a little disappointed, having geared herself for a more spectacular destination.

"Wait here, Mac," Nik ordered. He gave her another of those disconcerting looks, seemed to hesitate, then went with Cinder through the first door to the right. Mac peered past them, seeing nothing but more white walls. Another corridor? They closed the door before she could be sure.

Well, Em, this is an anticlimax. Mac put her shoulders against the nearest wall, tipping her head back to rest it on something solid. It was, to put it mildly, throbbing. Somehow she didn't think Anchen—*or would it be the physician mind, Noad?*—would consider being violently slammed to the floor as proper care of a concussion. *Spies.*

Mac closed her eyes. Odd. The throbbing had a second component, out of sync with her heartbeat, *elevated*, or breathing, *steady*. She concentrated, turning her head slightly. The bare part of her scalp happened to touch the wall. Through that contact, the throbbing developed a fascinating, singsong pattern. It wasn't sound, Mac decided, not as she could hear.

But it had meaning.

Mac straightened, her eyes wide. Without hesitation, she went to the middle door, the one closest to her, and shoved it open.

The smell caught her first. She covered her nose, staring at the shape huddled at the far end of the cage. For that was the only feature of the rectangular, white room: a floor-to-ceiling enclosure of vertical white bars each the width of her hand, set her shoulder-width apart. The cage filled half of the floor space, away from any wall by several meters. Within was nothing but the shape, motion-less, naked, and blue.

It was as if her blood congealed within her veins, leaving noth-ing but a lump of flesh incapable of movement, of feeling. *Oh, not incapable of feeling,* Mac realized. Emotions surged through her, battering at her senses. Blinding rage. Betrayal, deep and sour. Fear like a chorus that sang along every nerve. *How had she dared lecture Lyle?*

Suddenly. Unexpectedly. A whisper of hope.

Shaking, Mac clung to it, desperate to clear her mind, to think. *No time for gut reactions,* she pleaded with herself.

She began to hear her own breathing again, deep and ragged, feel her hands, clenched into aching fists. There was sweat running down her sides.

Hope. Opportunity. She focused on those.

Mac reached down and took off her shoes. Barefoot, she could feel the vibrations through the floor. The hairs on her arm and neck rose. *Distress.*

She walked around the cage until she was as close as possible to the shape, then sank to the floor herself, balancing on the balls of her feet, and nodded.

Dhryn.

Even huddled in its misery, she couldn't mistake that rubbery blue skin, dotted with weeping pits of darker blue. No mistaking the three pairs of shoulders either, or the massive, podlike feet. There were wounds, marked by more dark blue liquid. It was smeared over much of the cage floor, as were other stains.

Mac hugged herself.

The *oomling* tongue, the Dhryn language spoken by those too young—or unable—to produce and hear the deeper infrasound—came to her with sickening ease, as if more natural than her own. "Who are you?"

A once-powerful arm pushed against the floor, then another. One after the other, each slipped and lay flaccid.

Conscious, then.

Mac stood and walked around to the other side of the cage.

She hadn't expected to be relieved his eyes were closed behind their marblelike lids, that she'd unconsciously stiffened in anticipation. *Fool,* she told herself.

"I am Mackenzie Wini—" her voice failed and Mac coughed to free it, starting again. "Mackenzie Winifred Elizabeth Wright Connor—" after a hesitation, she finished, "—Sol is all my name."

His hands scrabbled at the floor, as if the Dhryn tried to rise and couldn't.

She understood. Manners dictated he rise and accept her name with a clap of all six hands. *Three hands,* Mac realized, as the last arm, middle left, moved into view. Its wrist ended in a fresh scar. *Grathnu.* Dhryn sought all their lives to sacrifice their hands to their Progenitor. It was a mark of Her greatest favor. Mac suspected it was also a contribution to the gene pool, allowed only the most worthy.

But three? This was no ordinary Dhryn.

Emily had warned her—the Ro claimed a wounded Dhryn was dangerous. Brymn had transformed only after being injured in the sandstorm, but not after giving up his hand. *Does it matter how severe the damage, Em, or did the Ro lie to you?* It wasn't the first time she'd asked herself that troubling question. An answer this living Dhryn could provide. *It would be the last one.*

Mac shuddered. "Don't try to move," she said. "Who are you?" The face shifted on the floor, shadows changing beneath the thick ridges that overhung the closed eyes, where they played over the curved rises of skin-covered bone sculpting nose and ears. The small mouth was tight and fixed. *Pain.* Mac felt the vibration of complaint through her feet.

The eyes snapped open, their huge pupils black and lustrous, like figure eights on their sides. The oval iris of yellow filled the rest. She'd seen it warm. Now it was a cold, accusing gold.

With the eyes and changing light, despite the scars and sunken appearance, Mac suddenly knew who this was. "Parymn Ne Sa," she whispered.

"—Las."

So it had been *grathnu* and not more violence from his keepers. Numb, Mac repeated his full name. "Parymn Ne Sa Las. Honored. I take the name Parymn Ne Sa Las into my keeping." She clapped her hands together. His eye coverings winked blue. *Acknowledgment.*

This was not a Dhryn who traveled, before his entire species had taken flight. This had been the Progenitor's officer and gatekeeper, the same Progenitor with whom Brymn—and Mac herself, though with hair not hand—had committed *grathnu*. More, Brymn had called Parymn Ne Sa an *erumisah,* one who is able to make decisions.

Not an ordinary Dhryn at all, Em.

Mac knelt, not daring to touch the bars. "What are you doing here?"

"I was sent to talk to you."

"Me?" She rocked back on her haunches and began shaking her head. "No. No. There are people in authority—important people. I—" *study salmon.*

Parymn managed to raise his head and first shoulders to better look at her. She could see his flexible seventh limb now, curled out of the way, its scissorlike fingers tucked under an elbow. "They are not-Dhryn," he gasped out, then sank to the floor again. "You are Dhryn," more quietly but with as much effort. "Unlikely . . . as that appears . . . to me."

"Oh, dear," Mac said in Instella.

A touch on her shoulder. She startled from under it, rising and turning to put her back to the bars.

Nik let his arm fall to his side. Mac searched his face, but it was like a mask, fixed and expressionless.

And he wasn't alone. Others walked around the cage to array themselves on either side of him, all confronting her: the Trisulian, Cinder, hands combing the mane over her face; another Human, older, male, and in a brown suit almost twin to Nik's; a scaled humanoid Mac couldn't identify, with a dainty beaked mouth and feathered crest; and a stout Imrya, carapace dark with age spots, her hands clutching what looked like an unusually ornate recording device. Two of the consular staff remained by the door.

Last, but not least by any measure, the Sinzi-ra herself, regal in

her white gown and long silvered fingers. "You were right, Nikolai," Anchen said. "I see you can communicate with our visitor,
Mac. Most gratifying."

"Visitor," she echoed incredulously. Mac felt vibration through
the soles of her feet as the Dhryn subvocalized. She couldn't understand it. *Perhaps it wasn't words at all, Em, but a moan.* "Well,
you haven't taken very good care of him."

Anchen lifted two fingers. One of the staff members stepped forward. "What have I done wrong, Dr. Connor? I cared satisfactorily
for the Honorable Delegate from Haven during his stay with us.
This individual has proved more, forgive any impertinence, challenging a guest, but I have followed every established protocol for
his species."

She'd forgotten Brymn had been here. Mac blinked. Finally, she
managed to ask: "Do you want him to live or not?"

Nik shifted involuntarily, but said in a noncommittal voice. "It's
preferable."

"To start with, they—" Mac pointed at the yellow-clad staff,
"—shouldn't wear that color near him. Why doesn't he have furniture and clothes? He looks to be starving."

His wounds? *That was territory she didn't dare tread, Em.*

"Your concern is admirable but misplaced, Mac," responded Anchen, making a calming gesture with her long fingers. "Our guest
was originally provided with civilized accommodations. He tore
them to shreds, along with his clothing. He refuses food." Again,
as if able to read Mac's thoughts, *or,* Mac judged, *with the awareness of a superb negotiator,* the Sinzi went on: "The wounds you see?
Self-inflicted. We've done our utmost to keep him healthy and
comfortable. It is our in own interest as well as his. But he has rejected all of our efforts. We feared he was attempting to die."

The floor vibrated more intensely. "*Oomling* language," Mac
hissed in Dhryn.

Sure enough. "Mackenzie Winifred Elizabeth Wright Connor
Sol," Parymn almost bellowed. "These are not-Dhryn! You must
not interact with them!"

"What did he say?" Nik, quietly.

"He's not happy," Mac summarized, then frowned. "You said the teach-sets weren't working, but surely you've servo translators."

"They function without adequate success, thus your cooperation is most essential," said the beaked alien, in precise, feather-edged Instella. He/she/it lifted his/her/its elbows, the other Human moving to avoid those sharp ends. "We predict our current technology capable of reliable translation of no better than twenty percent—"

The other Human broke in: "He hasn't said a word to translate until now—"

"Mackenzie Winifred Elizabeth Wright Connor Sol! You must desist!" Parymn's bellow faded into a desperate whisper.

Mac shot Nik a look and he nodded reassuringly. She turned to the Dhryn. "It's all right, Parymn Ne Sa Las. It is—" she tried to think how to calm him, "—it is my task among Dhryn, to speak with those who come to you like this."

Faint. "I do not understand. How can it be so? They can talk?" It was almost plaintive.

Save her from cloistered Dhryn, Em, Mac sighed to herself, the problem yawning like a pit before her feet. Brymn had warned her that the Haven Dhryn, those who stayed on their world, avoided contact or information about other places or other life. Why should they care about what would never matter to them? She'd seen it for herself. "That which is Dhryn" was enough.

Not anymore. Not for Parymn, if he was to survive. No doubt the others here were anxious for the answers to a long list of questions. No doubt everyone from physiologists to weapons designers would be eager for the answers his living body could provide.

Em, why did it have to be a Dhryn she knew?

Mac planned to sit down and have a talk with herself, a long one, later. Likely with something stronger than beer.

In the meantime, how to solve this? "Think of them as Dhryn," she ventured.

He closed his eyes. *Rejection.* "Only the Progenitor decides what is Dhryn."

There was the rub, Em. The Progenitor—any of them—wasn't here. *She hoped.* Things wouldn't be this calm if a Progenitor's ship, with its millions of feeder Dhryn, were in Sol System, or orbiting Earth. She'd dreamed it often enough. There'd be alarms, news, panic, running for shelters, for ships . . .

Nik had urged her to hurry.

Mac licked her lips. "Are they here?" she asked without turning from the Dhryn, proud she sounded so matter-of-fact about nightmare.

"Just him," Nik answered.

She shuddered with relief, closing her eyes for an instant.

"Do not . . ." Parymn began weakly, ending with a handless arm flailing.

Mac looked over her shoulder. *A mistake*—they were all staring at her, waiting for something worthwhile. "He's upset," she stated the obvious, then went back to Parymn. "You said the Progenitor sent you to talk to me. Why? What about?"

"You must not . . . interact with the not-Dhryn. I forbid it." Weaker. She wasn't sure how conscious he was—or perhaps he wouldn't tell her anything more while not-Dhryn were present.

This particular Dhryn, his upbringing, was the problem. The Progenitor Mac had met on Haven had been fully aware of other species, curious, in fact, to meet Mac, an alien, in person. The Dhryn had accepted membership within the IU, had their gate to the Naralax Transect, although not-Dhryn traffic was forbidden to their home system and Haven. They'd maintained colonies in other systems to take overflow population, those colonies freely conducting trade with other species. Brymn himself had been fluent in Human languages as well as Instella, although he'd been, she'd freely admit, unusual for any species.

"The Progenitor values the abilities of all Dhryn," Mac began cautiously. *Interspecies communication, Em, is carpeted quicksand. With hair-trigger wasps on top.* "Is this not so?"

The eye coverings opened again. "All that is Dhryn must serve." Stronger, with that familiar sarcastic note. *Good.*

"So the Progenitor must value my ability to talk to the not-Dhryn." She rephrased hastily: "She sees that ability as having use to Her, to all that is Dhryn. Thus I must use my ability. For all that is Dhryn." *Stop now,* she told herself.

His tiny lips pursed, then moved in and out a few times as if hunting teeth no longer there.

Just when Mac was about to try another tack, Parymn's lips formed a tight smile. "Your reasoning would have more impact if you weren't talking like an *oomling*." Mac felt a thrumming in the floor as the Dhryn added what he knew she couldn't hear. By her estimate, adults used infrasound for more than a third of their vocabulary and most of its emotional overtone.

Even Brymn had had difficulty with the concept of their differing auditory ranges. He'd been willing to try, at least.

Parymn Ne Sa Las, Mac knew without any doubt, *would not.*

"You understand me well enough, Parymn Ne Sa Las. Do you understand them?" she gestured to the others, still silent and waiting. When he gave her a baleful look, she nodded. "I do. So you are to talk to me and the Progenitor needs me to talk to them. All that is Dhryn needs me to talk to them. Will you permit it or not?"

A final vibration through the floor. Another unhappy look. "I somehow doubt, Mackenzie Winifred Elizabeth Wright Connor Sol, that you require my permission."

She crouched lower. "I ask your cooperation, Parymn Ne Sa Las."

He considered so long, eyes almost closed, that Mac feared this time he was unconscious. Then: "You have it. For now."

"Thank you." She stood, giving her sweater a tug to straighten it. "First order of business—to look after you, Parymn Ne Sa Las. Why did you—" Mac stopped there. *On second thought, she probably didn't want to know why Parymn had attacked the furniture.* Doubtless something alien and complicated about not-Dhryn upholstery. "To serve the Progenitor," she said instead, "you must look and behave with pride, as an *erumisah*. Even among the not-Dhryn."

"That is so." His hands fluttered along his skin, explored patches of congealing fluids. "Bathe. I must bathe."

"I'll make arrangements. What else?"

"Clothing." Fingers trailed along his eye ridges and his mouth turned down. Mac added cosmetics to her mental list.

"What else? Food?"

His eyes closed again. *Rejection.*

It was a beginning, Mac decided. She turned back to her observers and made herself smile.

Anchen's fingers rose and fell, the silver rings making a waterfall of light down her sides. *Approval? Or aggravation at the delay.* Mac wasn't about to guess. "What was said?" the Sinzi asked her.

"Every word?"

The beaked alien leaned forward, her body quivering. *Eagerness? Or a chill,* Mac thought. "Yes, we will need every word, every nuance." The Imrya, still silent, lifted her recorder in agreement.

"In-depth analysis can be done later," the other Human snapped. "We don't have time to waste. The gist, Dr. Connor. Summarize."

"Summarize." *Mr. Brown Suit had something up his* . . . Mac raised her eyebrow and caught Nik's cautionary look. *Fine.* "To start with, this isn't just any Dhryn. I can't imagine how he got here, but this is Parymn Ne Sa Las. I met him on Haven. He's a decision-maker, someone who speaks for his Progenitor. He's the closest thing to an ambassador the Dhryn could have sent us."

This raised eyebrows and elbows, as well as promoted an almost frantic moment of facial grooming by the Trisulian. Only Anchen seemed unaffected by the news. And Nik, who Mac doubted would show his reaction to an explosion unintentionally.

"How he came to be here, I can tell you, Dr. Connor," the beaked alien offered. "Our patrol stopped a starship, no larger than one of our single-pilot vessels. It contained him alone and was operating on a preprogrammed path to our world, N'not'k. He wore no clothes, was already damaged, and would not communicate with us. He grew increasingly agitated by our attempts to do so. We brought him to the IU consulate, where our Sinzi-ra had no better luck with him, but understood the significance of the artifact within his ship, that it was a message indicating he should be brought here, to the Gathering."

"To Earth," Anchen corrected gently. "I would show Mac the artifact, if you please."

One of the staff went over to a wall and pressed on a particular spot. A drawer opened from the wall and he reached in, pulling out a bag identical to those in Mac's closet, but a fraction of the size.

Mac's eyes widened as she saw the black velvetlike lining of the drawer before it closed again, then gave the rest of the white wall a suspicious look. *Had that lining been of the fabric the Dhryn used to hide from the Ro?* She wouldn't be surprised.

The Sinzi opened the bag, passing its contents to Mac.

Mac took what at first glance seemed a plain disk of some gray metallic substance, cool at first, then warming to the touch. She lifted it within the curve of her thumb and forefinger. Held in better light, there was a dense spiral marking one side. No, Mac realized, rubbing her thumb over it lightly, the spiral was formed by something inlaid into the metal. At what could be compass points were small raised areas, three intact, the fourth hollowed as if something had been removed from it.

As "artifacts" went, this one was neither old nor beautiful. Mac looked at Nik, who gave a tiny shrug, then back to the Sinzi. "What is it?"

"A biological sample, Dr. Connor. A sample of you, in fact." A finger reached over Mac's shoulder, the pointed tip of its nail tracing the spiral. Another feathered one of Mac's curls. "If removed, you would recognize this part by its pigmentation, perhaps. Or its length might be sufficient."

"A hair," Mac breathed, eyes wide. "Mine." From the braid she'd given in *grathnu* to the Progenitor on Haven. She'd thought it would have been digested or discarded long before now.

The nail tip touched one of the raised dots. "Beneath each of these, a single intact epithelial cell. One was removed for analysis. Your genetic code was, of course, in the report sent to all IU consulates and officials."

"Of course," Mac said faintly. The cells would have come from the skin of her scalp or hands; probably thousands had been lodged in the braid, given how she'd habitually fussed with it.

"Make no mistake. This was prepared by someone who not only knew exactly which biological materials would bring you and this Parymn Ne Sa Las into contact, but that we would be capable of interpreting and acting on this—message. Succinct, practical. It speaks the language of science rather than species, yet acknowledges shared individual experience." The Sinzi took the disk from Mac. "I remain impressed."

"You promised we wouldn't waste time, Anchen, time we don't have." This, predictably, from the man Mac had now dubbed "Mr. Brown Suit." "It doesn't matter how he came here! What we need to know is why! What does he want?"

As the latter part of this appeared directed at Mac, she chose to answer. "Access to a sonic shower," she informed him, "though we'll have to take off the safeties and set it to cook pie. Several bands of silk this wide." She held out her arms. "About four meters long. Any solid color but yellow. Jellied mushrooms. Lipstick and eye liner. Assorted shades." She fastened her best "don't mess with me" glare on him. "He can barely talk in this condition, let alone think to answer questions."

Mr. Brown Suit took an abrupt step toward Mac, his face red and mouth working. The consular staff followed, as if alarmed, but Nik put himself in front of Mac first. "Sir. This is why Dr. Connor is here," he told the other in a low urgent voice that nonetheless carried perfectly. *I'm right here!* Mac frowned at Nik's back, quite willing to scrap on her own behalf. "She's our only chance to make use of this resource; the IU has graciously granted us access to her expertise. Let her work."

The other shoved Nik aside—that Nik allowed it told Mac a great deal about who Mr. Brown Suit probably was—but didn't come any closer to where Mac stood, barefoot and still. "Do it," he told her, pale eyes drilling into hers. "But do it knowing Humans joined the list of confirmed Dhryn targets last night. A helpless refining station. Families—" His voice broke on the word. "Do it knowing the Secretary General of the Ministry has declared humanity under imminent threat. From them." He didn't need to raise his voice. He didn't need to point to the Dhryn.

Threat to the species, Mac said to herself, ashamed she'd taken offense. *Where on that scale do any of us fall, Em?*

"Whatever Parymn Ne Sa Las requires will be arranged immediately," Anchen promised; Mac didn't doubt her in the least. She gestured to the ceiling and Mac paid attention to the clusters of vidbots for the first time. *Too used to them everywhere else on Earth,* she realized with some irony, *to notice.* "There are monitoring devices throughout this room; staff will await your needs. Simply ask.

We will prepare our questions." She began to leave, her long fingers sweeping the other Human, Imrya, and beaked alien with her, leaving Nik and the two staff.

"Oh, no. Wait! Anchen, please." Mac stopped short of lunging for one of those fingers. "I can't stay here. I've work to do with my team." She glanced at the huddled Dhryn. "Now more than ever."

"Now, this is your work."

"Yes. No. Not all of it. The Dhryn don't understand themselves. Don't you see—no matter what he can tell us, we'll have to learn more." Mac took a deep breath and said firmly: "Your word I'll be allowed to spend part of every day working on the origins problem."

"Nonsense." Mr. Brown Suit again. "Questioning him is the only priority."

And she thought a righteous Mudge could set her blood boiling. "I'll be free to come and go," Mac added, forcing the words between her teeth. "Four hours a day with my research team, when I choose."

"Absolutely not!" "Three and you sleep here."

The words overlapped, but it was Anchen's counteroffer that silenced the Human's protest.

Outranked and knows it. Mac ignored him, sure she was right, that what she wanted was important. "Three, I sleep in my own room, and I can consult with my people at any time no matter where I am." She took a gamble and quoted the alien's own words about her work with the Myg. "There is deep significance within our combination."

"How so?"

How? Mac hadn't actually expected to explain. *Note to self, Em. Never gamble with alien terminology.* Her lack of answer stretched toward awkward.

"Clearly, Anchen, there has developed an interwoven circularity of purpose," Nik stated.

There has? Mac wisely kept her mouth shut. If anyone knew the Sinzi-ra, it should be the liaison she'd requested most often. She hoped.

"Elaborate."

"Between Kanaci, Mac's team, and Mac herself, their work weaves into the goals of the IU and their member species, while involving an additional circularity of accomplishment from the present with that of the past, in order to resolve mutual debts, a resolution, I might add, which may well produce future gain for all." *Nik sounded confident,* Mac acknowledged, even if what he said made no sense to her at all.

What mattered was that it made sense to the Sinzi, whose shoulders rose as she pointed a white-clawed fingertip at Mac. "I am corrected. My thanks, Nikolai. You may begin on the basis you wish, Mac, to fully take advantage of these opportunities afforded us by your combinations. Be aware," she added, "failure to produce meaningful insights swiftly will require modifications."

Mac nodded, then caught the eyes of Mr. Brown Suit with her own. "We're here to prevent more tragedies," she said quietly, the words for him. "That's all that matters. You'll have your answers as soon as possible. I give you my word."

His scowl faded, replaced by something akin to respect. "Dr. Connor," he said, then turned to leave with Anchen and the other aliens.

Their departure roused Parymn. "Mackenzie Winifred Elizabeth Wright Connor Sol . . . what has happened?"

She'd wait till he was better to stop that full-name business. Try to, anyway. This wasn't amiable Brymn . . .

. . . *who'd consumed Lyle's wife and her arm.* Mac shivered, just slightly.

Nik noticed. "Concussions are nothing to fool with," he said, frowning down at her. His eyes explored the wound. "If you need to rest—"

Mac raised her hand to stop him, answering Parymn first. "They've gone to bring what we need to help you recover your strength."

"*Nie rugorath sa nie a nai.*" A Dhryn is robust or a Dhryn is not.

"You don't have the luxury of that belief here, Parymn Ne Sa Las," Mac snapped. "The Progenitor has given you a task and you must not fail. You will accept care."

He lay back. *She'd take that as agreement.*

"He's not in good shape," she told the others—*who knew how many others, Em,* Mac corrected, remembering the room was monitored.

"We're here to help, Mac," Nik assured her.

"You'll stay?" She closed her mouth too late, hearing the relief in her voice. *So what?* Anyone listening would assume she was pleased to have a familiar face—and species—to help. Nik?

Oh, he knew. A flash of warmth from those hazel eyes, the hint of a dimple. Nothing more, but that was enough. *It wasn't as though a weight had lifted,* Mac decided, *but more as though someone else had taken a share from her shoulders.*

"What do we do first?" This from Cinder.

Mac felt herself coming back to normal, as normal as possible under the circumstances, but she'd take it. She swept the Trisulian with a critical look, seeing what she hadn't before. He—*she,* Mac corrected, *since no male symbionts were present*—was taller than Kay by a considerable amount, closer to Mac's own height, though shorter than Nik. Instead of Kay's caftan, a clothing choice perhaps for his work when not concealing unattached weasels, Cinder's limbs were wrapped in tight ribbons of black, while her stocky torso was covered by a brown-red shift, belted at both waists. The lower belt was festooned with gadgets, some of which were probably weapons, if she was in Nik's line of work. The upper belt simply held the fabric together over the opening to her *douscent.* The hair cascading over Cinder's entire head was a fine shiny brown, almost Human, and matched the skin showing on her hands.

Nik's partner. *She'd like to know about that.*

First things first. "We do something about his living conditions, starting with this cage," Mac decided. "Where's the door?"

Cinder pointed to the ceiling.

Mac snorted. "That's ridiculous—how am I supposed to get in?"

"You don't." Nik's voice had such an edge that Cinder bent an eyestalk his way.

"Not until it's clean, I'm not," Mac agreed. She didn't give him time to argue the point. "What are the options? For this room," she added quickly.

"We can make any modifications you require, Dr. Connor," said one of the staff.

Mac considered the two of them. One male, one female. *Maybe.* With some discreet padding, they could pass as Human on a dark night, doubtless the reason they were the species chosen to work at the IU's Earth consulate.

She spared an instant to wonder about that. Were they chosen to provide "familiar" faces to visiting Humans? Hands suited to the local technology? Or were they to help acclimate other, less humanoid species to the body plan before leaving the consulate to visit Earth. *Probably all three.* She respected the Sinzi's thorough dedication to hospitality.

Meanwhile, those faces looking back at her bore identical expressions of what would be bright, willing attention, if they'd really been Human faces. "What are your names?" Mac asked.

Bright and willing changed to guarded and stubborn. "We are consular staff," one said, as if Mac were confused. The male.

"I know that. I want to know what to call you."

They exchanged quick looks. "Staff," the female said.

Nik made a muffled sound. Mac didn't bother glaring at him. "I have no wish to offend, but I need to be able to refer to you as individuals."

Another exchange of looks. "Call me One," said the male.

"Two," said the female. Then both gave her pleased smiles.

Whatever worked, Em . . . Mac nodded. "Thank you. Now, please change into something that isn't yellow. It alarms Dhryn."

"Yellow?" Two repeated, sounding puzzled.

Cinder volunteered: "Xiphodians are polychromatic. They do not see color as Humans do. Or Trisulians, for that matter."

So they likely saw ultraviolet. *Made sense.* Mac was entranced by the notion of the all-white Sinzi decor covered in staff memos. *Or rude comments about guests with fewer visual receptors.* She focused on business. "Cinder, would you look after this please?"

"Of course, Mac. Staff?" The three left the room.

A room empty but for the Dhryn in his misery, herself, and Nik.

Watching Parymn, Mac stole a look at the spy, and caught him watching her, by his expression finding something amusing in all this. "What is it?" she asked.

"You do realize this is the second time I've brought you a Dhryn?"

Mac grinned. "Some guys bring pizza." That drew a smile. She savored it for a moment, then nodded at Parymn, who had opened his eyes to study them. "I had to persuade him it was all right for me to talk to you—to any of you. Home world Dhryn like Parymn don't view other species as civilized. No. Nik, that's not the right word. I'm not sure what is," she finished, frustrated.

"It's a starting point." To Nik's credit, he didn't appear to take offense at Parymn's opinion—a reminder she was in the presence of someone with far more experience comprehending the non-Human.

Not just a comfort—an asset. One Mac suddenly appreciated. "He's here because the Progenitor sent him to talk to me," she explained. "That's exactly how he put it: to talk to me. I've convinced him that She would also want me to talk to you, to not-Dhryn."

"About what?"

"We hadn't got to that part yet." She tightened her lips, then nodded. In Dhryn: "Parymn Ne Sa Las, what does the Progenitor want you to say to me?"

"We . . . are to talk, Mackenzie Winifred . . . Elizabeth Wright Connor Sol."

She crouched down, pitched her voice lower in hopes it made it easier for him to hear. "I know. But about what?"

"The Progenitor . . . searches for . . ." His voice disappeared into vibration.

"Searches for what?" Mac urged. "Please try, Parymn Ne Sa Las."

With abrupt clarity:

"The truth—the truth about ourselves."

As if that last effort had been too much, Parymn's eyes closed.

"The Honored Delegate Brymn did not ask for such treatment."

"Brymn Las," Mac corrected automatically. "And he was trying to fit in, so of course he didn't ask for special treatment. Trust me. A sonic shower. Will that clean the floor as well?" There were dried and drying smears of Dhryn blood everywhere.

"At the requested setting, yes. But Brymn Las did not—"

"You can do it, can't you?" she challenged the pair. Nik, watching the exchange, rubbed a hand over his chin as if to hide a smile.

One and Two traded offended looks. They stood side by side, a matched set in Dhryn-neutral pink. *Not the time to ask if they liked whatever color that appeared to their eyes.* "We will make all of the arrangements you've requested, Mac," answered Two stiffly. "We suggest you occupy yourselves elsewhere for an hour."

"Or be crisped," Mac said jovially. She reassured herself with a last look at Parymn's thick, rubbery hide and a memory of the hazards of Dhryn "bathing." "Good. Then I'm off to check on my team."

Nik nodded at the door. "There's fresh coffee—and a com link. You'll want to be here when he's ready for questioning." She scowled and he gave her that too-innocent look. "Or not."

Coffee and a few moments' peace and quiet, versus retracing her steps and plunging—for too brief a time—back into the turmoil she'd deliberately stirred behind her.

Coffee with Nik *and a few moments' peace and quiet,* versus confronting a host of testy archaeologists who'd doubtless noticed Fourteen's predilection for acquiring small objects by now. She winced. *Forgot the memo.*

Mac noticed the dimple deepening in Nik's cheek and scowled again. *Just enough to let him know it was her idea.*

"Coffee works."

15

DISCLOSURES AND DILEMMA

"I ADMIT I WAS EXPECTING something—smaller. And damp." Mac gave the subject of basements another moment's serious consideration. "Maybe a troll," she said finally.

To be truthful, while she'd assumed there was something beneath the consular complex, Mac had leaned toward wine cellars and seasonal storage, with perhaps accommodations suited to those aliens who liked it small, damp, and dark. A vault or two seemed reasonable to protect whatever precious goods might be moving on or off Earth with guests.

Basements were good for such things.

There was, she acknowledged with an inward shudder, *a dungeon of sorts.*

But the reality, behind door number three, was—*like walking into one of Emily's favorite thriller vids.*

Having been in the Progenitor's vast cavern, Mac would have scoffed at the suggestion she'd ever again be impressed by a large room in a basement, even a very large room in a very odd basement.

Until Nik opened the third and final door at the corridor's end, the one beside Parymn's cell, the one she blithely assumed would simply lead to another corridor or room, and, as promised, coffee.

It didn't. *And she was.*

"Impressive, isn't it?" Nik said into her ear.

Mac grunted, too busy struggling to grasp it all.

Straight ahead was easy, almost ordinary: a floor, although it widened to the right like a great fan until ending at the far curve of a wall. It was bounded by one other wall, this Mac touched with her right hand. She looked up, captivated by how this wall rose not to a ceiling, but to meet another floor, set back from the first; above it, another, and another, stretching up and away like a staircase.

To her left, the floor dropped away. Mac walked to the unprotected edge and looked down. *Another floor below this one, and another.*

It was as if they stood on the steps of a giant pyramid buried underground, only revealed here.

There was more. The pyramid's partner, mirror image, rose across a gulf between the two. Mac could see figures moving about on a floor at the same height as this one—but so distant she couldn't have shouted and been heard. There was, she realized belatedly, a third series of steps ahead. She turned. The tiny door they'd used came through a wall that was itself part of a step.

The pyramids re-formed in her imagination to a well, sunk deep underground, she and Nik mere droplets on bricks near the bottom. Like the building aboveground, she realized, hollow within, floors linked by a central spiral ramp as well as lifts. *As if the Sinzi valued open space above all.*

Space filled with light. The white walls and floors almost glowed. Mac craned back her head to see the distant ceiling, squinting to make out a familiar pattern edged in brightness. *The patio!* The tiles were allowing sunlight through. She couldn't find any tree roots hanging down. *Neat trick.*

This space was filled with life. Everywhere she looked, Mac saw purposeful movement. Raftlike platforms laden with passengers and cargo sedately crossed the space between the steps, as many moving vertically as horizontally. Some hung in midair, overhead or below, grouped into workspaces or forming bridges from side to side.

The steps themselves, each forming immense "rooms" of their own filled with labyrinths of equipment, were connected by lifts along their walls. The nearest sighed to a stop beside Mac, as if in invitation. Along the wall itself were doors, implying a maze of rooms beyond all this.

And the space sang. Granted it was the drone of voices and machines, rising and falling, punctuated by the occasional metallic clang or whoop. But song nonetheless. There had to be hundreds of beings working here. *Answering one question, Em.* Mac drew a quick breath. "So this is where they've been hiding."

"Who?"

"The other researchers from the Gathering. Mudge and I went over the consulate schematics Fourteen gave me. We couldn't figure out where the Sinzi had put everyone."

"Yes, but hardly hiding." Nik chuckled. "Several teams are down here to make use of the equipment."

"What equipment?" Mac gave him an uneasy look. "Why is all this here, Nik? What are these beings doing?"

He smiled. "Coffee first."

" 'The truth.' " Nik handed Mac her coffee and took one himself, shaking his head. "I didn't expect that from our visitor."

They'd taken the lift to the next step up, Nik leading the way to what was, if not a lounge, a reasonable facsimile. Like the eye of a storm, benches made a circle of calm around a tall water-touched sculpture of—*well, she wasn't sure, but if three Sinzi finger-wrestled, this could be the result.* The sculpture's base provided unobtrusive storage for beverages and snacks, watched over by another of the ubiquitous consular staff, only too eager to provide whatever they'd like.

The rest of the area was a bustle of activity. Doors opening and closing. Consoles and other equipment communing with their operators. Platforms docking and undocking all along the edge, so the floor space and those on it constantly morphed around her. *Like a termite mound,* Mac decided, *where everyone else knew what to do.*

For her part, she'd asked for coffee, hoping to gather her thoughts.

The coffee, Em, she'd got.

Mac's thoughts were another matter entirely. She had enough questions about this place and what was done here to set her head spinning. *But she did know one thing.* The Ministry of Extra-Sol Human Affairs was well aware of what the Sinzi-ra kept in her basement.

Nik knew this place.

More. He was at home here, the way she felt among the pods of Base and the rivers of Castle Inlet. His body posture had subtly altered, losing that tiny "ignore me" slouch, regaining his true height. His movements lost none of their suppleness, but gained confidence, as if here he finally shed a camouflage intended to make outsiders underestimate his abilities, misjudge his strength. This was the real Nikolai Trojanowski, the version she'd only caught in glimpses.

Albeit yummy ones.

Scowling at her seemingly infinite ability to focus on the trivial, Mac raised her hand to their surroundings. "Speaking of truth— this is where you really work, isn't it."

He didn't bother denying it. She was pleased—unless that meant she was so deeply into all this now it couldn't matter what else she learned. *Not the most comforting thought.*

"This is the Atrium. The IU shares its facilities with us," Nik informed her, one arm outstretched along the back of the bench. His eyes darted about, rarely still. *Checking on things,* Mac guessed, the same compulsion she always felt when walking into a lab or waking up at a field station. "There's one in every consulate, with a Sinzi administrator. Some of what's done here is to monitor the transects—the Sinzi are devoted to maintaining the flow of traffic. The upper levels are where any technology proposed for import or export is given a final assessment by their people and ours."

Mac looked up with some alarm. "Is that safe?"

"Safety tests are done in orbit or on the Moon," he assured her, the corner of his mouth twitching as if he tried not to smile at her reaction. *Wise man, Em.* "Here they look at other factors. Economics, appeal. As often as not what's a good idea for one species simply won't interact as hoped with the technology base or culture of another. You don't know until you tinker with it."

"But you," Mac persisted, "do something else. When not escorting tourists or pestering innocent biologists, that is."

"True enough. Most of my time is spent right there." Nik pointed to the opposite side, indicating an area up a step from their level. Mac couldn't see anything distinct about it, unless she counted the three platforms presently attached, and more lined up to do so. "Telematics center," he explained. "Sends and receives information over long distances."

Mac was quite sure the 'long' in this instance referred to very long distances indeed. She also guessed moving information was only one step. Every iota of data must be translated as necessary, then analyzed, compiled, and stored. Within the Interspecies Union, information would be the currency of value to all.

"Looks busy," she observed.

"It is."

Something in his voice caught her attention. "That's where they're working on Emily's message, isn't it? Doing whatever it is the Ro want them to do." A chill fingered her spine.

Nik didn't deny it. "Off-limits, Mac." Clear warning.

She didn't argue, busy looking for Fourteen.

"Mac."

A few possibilities—none in paisley. "Is it off-limits to you, too?" she wondered aloud.

"Why?"

Surprised, Mac glanced at Nik. "I like to know things."

"That I've noticed." Nik lowered his head, but she could see the curve of his lips as he lifted his mug and sipped. "Hollans and I have access," he said finally. "I can't take you there; he could. Want me to ask?"

"No, thanks." *She could imagine* that *conversation.* Mac shifted around on the bench. "You work there—doing what?"

"Whatever needs to be done." She frowned at him and Nik smiled. "It's the truth. There's no job description for what I do, Mac. I'm one of the links between the Sinzi-ra and the Ministry, between the IU and Human interests both on and off Earth. Most of my time I spend analyzing the information flow, what matters to whom, basically observing the workings of the IU for us. Every so often," a chuckle, "I have to interpret us for the IU. Or escort aliens around the home planet." A shadow crossed his face. "I'd retired from anything more intense until the Dhryn."

A reminder of the topic at hand, Em. "You said the Sinzi monitor the transects—watch traffic through the gates—" Mac swallowed, then went on. "They must have data on the Dhryn attacks."

Nik's face sobered. "Some. But system-to-system communication obeys real space physics. Even where there's a facility like this, information has to be transmitted to a ship before it enters a transect gate—or someone has to have the presence of mind to prepare and launch a self-guiding com packet. When the Dhryn swarm through a gate, the result has been utter chaos. People trying to escape, defend themselves. They aren't making observations. While on Ascendis?" He paused, eyes darkening. "The Dhryn penetrated and destroyed that consulate as easily as everything else."

The Atrium wasn't a refuge for scholars—it was a cup from which the feeders would drink.

Mac hunched her shoulders. "You must have something," she insisted.

"Data's coming in—late and in pieces. Whatever we have is put together for the experts. So far, though, it looks as though the Dhryn attack at random, then leave the moment their target is devastated. What is it?" this as Mac began shaking her head.

"I don't understand what the Dhryn are doing," she said fiercely. "It makes no sense."

"To us," Nik corrected.

Mac shook her head again. "No. Not just to us. It doesn't make sense for the Dhryn. I realize I don't know as much as everyone here about aliens—okay, anyone here or most people on this planet," she rushed to say before he could. "But grant me that I know a fair bit about living things and how they evolve. There's something here we're not seeing. Something besides the Ro."

The hair rose on her arm and neck at the thought of them. She couldn't help it.

Nik didn't dismiss her. He didn't agree either; Mac could see it in his slight frown. "Your old friend should be able to explain," he suggested, pointing over her shoulder.

Mac turned. She hadn't paid particular attention to any one area yet, too busy comprehending the overall scale of the place. Even so, there was no excuse not to have noticed they'd sat within meters of where One and Two were busy working on— "That's the ceiling of Parymn's cell," she concluded, quickly estimating the distance from the small door they'd entered on the step below this.

The staff were directing the transfer of crates from a platform docked beside them through a pair of larger, open doors. Through those doors . . . more crates blocked Mac's view of the section of floor where she presumed the access to Parymn's cell was located. *A secret in plain sight,* she thought with wonder. *Why not? Everyone here was focused on their work, their problem to be solved.* She'd have missed it, and she knew.

The area Mac could see was two, possibly three times larger than that of the cell beneath it, bounded by a complex of what she presumed was monitoring equipment. An assortment of beings in lab coats paid rapt attention to their devices or each other.

While the two standing on either side of the open doors paid attention to everything else. Familiar black armor, engaged in very familiar looming. "Who's here?" Mac asked, waving a greeting at them. Sure enough, one nodded back. By his height, she guessed Selkirk. She swung herself back around on the bench to face Nik. "Or is that a secret?"

Nik took a slow sip of his coffee, eyeing her over the rim of his cup. "I suppose if I don't tell you, you'll find out for yourself anyway."

Mac grinned. "Exactly."

"We've six in gear within the consulate itself. Four you know from Base. One, Tucker Cavendish, you met—briefly—at the way station. And Judy Rozzell. She was at the Ro landing site. I believe," he added pensively, "Charlie dented her visor."

"What about 'Sephe?"

"Busy teaching a course, I'm told. Corrupted by evil statisticians."

"Which would be your fault," Mac pointed out. *A relief, to know the capable agent was with Kammie, John, and the rest who'd gone to the university.*

She curled one leg under her, leaning back. The noise was loud but constant, reminding her of waves babbling their way through beach pebbles. Just as easy, after a while, to push to the background. Mac rolled her head, stretching the kinks from her neck, then sniffed at her coffee. *Still too hot.* The Sinzi mug must be self-warming.

"Want some ice?"

He surprised her into a laugh. "And here I'd hoped you'd missed something in my dossier." *Which really wasn't funny,* Mac decided, losing her smile.

"There's a great deal about you that's not in any record, Mac." Nik's raised brow and dimple dared her to ask.

Emily would.

Mac deliberately turned back to the subject at hand. "We can't assume," she cautioned, "that Parymn knows about the attacks committed by other Dhryn."

"Agreed. But I believe his Progenitor knows. Why else contact you?"

Mac nodded as she blew steam from her coffee. She thought out loud: "Nik, the N'not'k were on the Ministry's list of previous Dhryn attacks—a balloon ship lost, wasn't it? But instead of a second, more devastating attack, the pattern everywhere else, the Progenitor sends in one ship—Parymn's. Why?" Mac answered her own question. "She somehow knew they wouldn't shoot first—and that they'd understand the message. Or realize it was a message. Which leads to another why. Bah."

"That one I can guess." Nik's smile was crooked. "Unlike the rest of us," he lifted his mug and used it to indicate the varied species working around them, "the N'not'k are obligate pacifists. To travel their space, incoming ships have to disarm—even Sinzi. So if there's one species in the IU who wouldn't destroy a Dhryn ship on sight, who couldn't, it's the N'not'k."

Implying the Progenitor, this one at least, knows a great deal about the IU. Aloud, Mac settled for an acknowledging: "Oh."

"Leading us back to other whys. Why him? Why you?"

"What 'truth.' " Mac got to her feet, and Nik followed suit, looking his question. "I should go back upstairs while I can," she answered.

"Don't worry. Anchen will keep her word." Mac's turn to raise her eyebrow. Nik smiled and motioned her to sit. "Circular combinations, remember?"

"I admit, that was slick," Mac commented. *Truth, Em? She wasn't ready to leave*. Parymn, the bench, or him.

Nik mimed a small bow as they both sat again. "Part of the job, Dr. Connor."

As if sitting was a signal, the attendant hurried to refill their coffees. Mac protected hers, studying Nik. When the attendant moved away, she asked: "Is this a good time to add to my dossier on you?"

"It's never a good time."

Which wasn't outright refusal. "Oversight and 'Stefan.' What's their story?"

"That?" Nik took off his suit coat and laid it on the bench, easing back on the seat as though preparing to rest awhile. "Nothing for you to bristle about."

"I never bristle," Mac protested. He raised an eyebrow. *Fine*. "Okay. Much. So explain."

"Regular procedure, Mac. We had to do background checks on Norcoast—and you, Dr. Connor—before the IU would allow Brymn to visit. First Dhryn on Earth, unlikely mission, that sort of thing. The Sinzi-ra, as you may have noticed, believes in anticipation." At Mac's nod, he went on: "Some at the Ministry are content to go through channels in order to—"

"Snoop," she finished when he paused for a word.

"Precisely. I prefer to make contact, engage in conversation, ask a few casual questions of acquaintances. That sort of thing. But in your case, I ran into a small problem."

"Base," Mac grinned. "Not the easiest place to drop in and visit."

"Not without gaining your immediate attention." He made it a compliment.

"But—Oversight?" Mac made a face. "He's the most meticulous, stubborn, paranoid . . . to start with, I can't see him letting a stranger waltz into his office." *Though the thought of Mr. Spy stuck with the aloe for a few hours had a certain justice, Em.*

Nik stretched like a cat. "My dear Dr. Connor," he said in his "Stefan" accent. "A member of the Wilderness Trust Awards Committee is always, always welcome, especially when what that member really wants is to hear the down and dirty about that scandalous salmon researcher Mackenzie Connor and her appalling treatment of the Castle Inlet Trust. Over supper at his favorite restaurant, of course."

Meaning Mudge gossiped about her over beer and pierogies. "You are a sneaky and dangerous individual, completely without conscience," Mac told him. "I'll have to warn Oversight about you— or 'Stefan.' "

"Want to know what he said about you?"

"Spare me."

"You sure?" His eyes glittered behind their lenses. "There were juicy bits."

"I'm quite sure. What I want to know is how you explained being here—that had to be a shock."

A smug look. "Not really. Mudge is well aware of ongoing talks between the awards committee and the consulate regarding the allocation of a substantial portion of its leased and unused coastline to the Te Wāhipounamu Wilderness Trust lands. He's been writing in support of it for years. When he saw me, I didn't have to say a thing—he immediately assumed I was working on that negotiation. Wished me luck, in fact. It's always best," Nik grinned, "to let others make the lie for you."

Which left only one question, Mac thought, loath to ask it and risk ending his honesty, see the return of the spy. As she hesitated, his eyes narrowed. *Damn, he was observant.* "Oversight should have gone home," she said, resigning herself to whatever happened. "Why did you help him stay?"

"Why?" Nik reached out to gently touch the side of her head, below the swathe of bandage. "He was there. When I wasn't." Suddenly, there was nothing gentle in his look; nothing calm in the lines around his mouth.

Just like that, even here in this busy room, he could make her believe no one else existed, scatter her thoughts into this strangely urgent confusion, a confusion that wanted to spread elsewhere.

The man had the worst *timing, Em.*

For some reason, the notion made Mac duck her head and smile. "Fourteen did warn me about external genitalia," she said lightly, looking up. "Guess I should have paid attention."

The hazel eyes were still dark, the lips pressed together. Mac wanted to say other things: how she'd spent half that night glad he was safe; how she'd spent the other half equally convinced he'd changed his mind and come back, that she'd find him in the morning, lying within reach of her steps, his head shattered among last year's pine needles.

"He must have been desperate—or insane," Nik said grimly. "I know the species, Mac. It never occurred to me any Trisulian would risk their symbiont. It would be like you or I ripping off an arm to use as a club. Worse." He collected himself. "I didn't get the tracking report until morning. Kay was picked up by a lev and taken to the Baffin spaceport. A Trisulian courier ship with diplomatic clearance was sitting at a way station—another stood ready to enter the Naralax immediately, which it did after receiving his transmission." Nik nodded, more to himself than her. "With what he's delivered to his government, our Kay will get his moment of glory. Mind you, he'll also be arrested for deviance."

Nik continued, saying again: "I didn't realize Kay would go to such extremes just for a head start with the Ro message. I shouldn't have left you alone with him."

"If I'd realized what that furry excuse for a gonad could do," vowed Mac, "I'd have taken the cast iron skillet with me down to the lake."

"No, thanks." Nik's lips curved into something easier. "Hard enough to explain a paddle to the Trisulian ambassador. I'd rather not involve cooking utensils."

"I see your point." Mac smiled at him. "It worked out well," she offered. "Oversight seems willing to stay. He'll be—" she almost said 'a comfort' and stopped herself in time, "—useful."

"Useful." That dimple beside Nik's mouth.

This time, Mac let herself bristle. "We're not friends," she insisted, wondering who she was trying to convince. "He's—annoying."

"As long as he's useful. And stays quick with a paddle." This last wasn't amused. "You're the only one who can talk to Parymn. That puts you at risk."

"Oh, no," Mac objected, sitting back and cradling her coffee. "I'm not going to start looking over my shoulder, here of all places. This is an academic conference. A secret academic conference. With—" she freed one hand to wave wildly at the atrium, "—this! Our guys in black. You!"

She regretted the last when Nik's face darkened with shame. "Me. Where was I when you were attacked in your own cabin? When an earthquake almost drowned you?"

"We'll concede the weasel," Mac quipped, trying to ease the moment. "But you couldn't have predicted the earthquake. Right?"

"No." His lenses caught the light, hiding his eyes. "They gave us no warning."

"They? You found out who caused it?" she breathed, leaning forward. "Wait. If it wasn't the Ministry . . ." Mac narrowed her eyes. "I knew it. The damn R—"

Nik's finger was across her lips before the word could come out. "Not here," he said very quietly. His fingertip stroked her lower lip before leaving it, as if he used the intimacy to add weight to the warning.

A warning the Ro could well be here, with them, and they'd never know.

Mac shivered. Maybe someone here, a level above, on one of the hovering platforms, behind a wall, was close to penetrating the Ro's stealth technology, would make it possible to detect the thinning of reality when the aliens used no-space to defeat the senses and devices of other species, make it possible to yank them into real space. Surely the IU would be fools not to work on at least a defensive weapon. *Surely the Sinzi-ra was not a fool.*

Unfortunately, Mac was equally sure they'd see the Ro only when the Ro wanted them to, and not before.

She thought of the ruined hillside and coast, the lives lost, and began to shake with rage as much as fear. *Couldn't you have picked—safer—allies, Em?*

"Mac."

Nik's voice drew her back into herself and this room, made her remember the mug in her hands, the bench beneath her. "How can we work with them?" Mac demanded, keeping her voice to a harsh whisper. "If they'd do this? If they'd do what they did before? How can we dare?"

If she'd wanted reassurance, there was none in his grim face. "I'm no happier than you are," he said, again very quietly. "But it was an impressive demonstration of power—listen, Mac—" when she would have objected to that description, probably loudly. "I'm just letting you know that's the way the earthquake damage's being seen—by Human eyes as well as others." He paused, as if waiting for her comment.

There were no words, Em, Mac thought with disgust, waving him to continue.

Nik pressed his lips together, then went on. "With no success against the Dhryn, the strain is showing on the IU itself," he told her. "The Sinzi have their fingers full. A coalition of newer species has petitioned to have their transects cut off from the rest. Then there's nonsense like the Trisulians taking advantage of utter misery." His voice deepened. "It's going to get worse. More transect connections are being made all the time, Mac, at every edge of the IU. That can't be stopped without threatening the entire system, even though it adds new, unknowing systems to the reach of the Dhryn. The Sinzi—we all need the hope of a strong ally, Mac, even a ruthless one, to hold everyone together." A curt nod drew Mac's attention to the telematics center, with its knot of researchers huddled around. "Unfortunately, it's a hope waiting on a miracle. Transmit a signal into no-space?" His lips twisted as if over a bad taste. "No one's convinced it can be done. I'm told the Myrokynay's instructions, if not interpreted correctly, are as likely to ruin the entire communications array as retune it."

Mac jerked her thumb toward Parymn's cell. "If you want the Ro that badly, put him on the roof."

"It's been proposed," Nik said matter-of-factly. "So has putting him in a suit and dragging him through transects like a worm on a hook. Both risk the most potentially valuable resource we've got at the moment. Some of us have prevailed otherwise—for now."

She wrinkled her nose. "I take it 'us' includes you, Anchen, Elbows, and Mr. Obnoxious in the Brown Suit. Bernd Hollans," she added.

Nik leaned back and hooked both hands around one knee. "Oh, I knew you two would hit it off."

"With sparks," Mac confessed, half apologizing. "But he wasn't hearing me."

"He's everything you think he is, Mac, but cut him some slack." Nik half shrugged. "Hollans' job is to provide humanity's help to the IU, while making sure nothing puts Earth and humanity in special danger. Thankless from all sides. Having the Dhryn brought to this consulate was over his protest. He wanted you taken from Sol System instead."

Mac said quietly: "I would have gone."

"I know." His eyes glowed with warmth. "But the Sinzi-ra wasn't budging. Neither was 'Elbows,' better known as Dr. Genny P'tool, the N'not'k. Genny is—" Nik hesitated.

"Is what?" Mac prompted.

"Her people enjoy a special closeness to the Sinzi. Genny herself is not only of high rank within her government, but has been mentor to Hone for many years, one of Anchen's selves. She's considered one of the IU's leading no-space theorists. And . . . there is one other thing you should know, Mac. Since it might come up." Nik let go of his knee, sitting straighter. "It's a little personal."

"Personal?" Mac grinned at him. "Let me guess. This important, brainy alien has a crush on you."

He actually blushed.

She'd been kidding. "Oh. Well. Any chance of you two . . . ?" Mac waggled her fingers suggestively.

That earned her one of those warm and dangerous looks.

"Guess not." Mac tilted her head at him. *Fun was fun, but . . .* "I can't argue with her taste," she admitted, smiling.

"What about taste?" Cinder asked, wandering into their oasis at exactly the wrong moment.

Or exactly right one, Em. They weren't alone. They had vital tasks to perform. Mac told herself the sensible things, sure Nik was doing the same.

It would help, she thought wryly, *if he'd stop looking at her like that.*

Cinder sat on the opposite bench, eyestalks forward with obvious interest. "Lunch? Or something else?"

Mac turned and forced a bright smile. "Nik was about to tell me how you two came to be partners," she improvised.

"Now there's a story worth telling." The Trisulian waved away the staff who'd hurried up, pot in hand. "Where shall I begin?"

"Don't," Nik said flatly.

"Nik . . ." Mac stopped. He'd tensed, from the fingers around his knee to the muscle jumping along his jaw. *New topic,* she decided, filing the first for another time. "What about Trisulian males?"

Nik's tension disappeared in a burst of surprised laughter. Cinder, on the other hand, began combing her front hair furiously, apparently struggling for composure.

Oh, dear. "I take it that was inappropriate," Mac concluded, looking from one to the other. "Sorry."

Cinder relaxed, her hands dropping to her lap. "The Unbonded—females—may only discuss such things in private. Girl talk—isn't that the Human expression, Nik? Maybe later, Mac, you and I can compare notes about our opposite sexes?"

The biologist in Mac rose to the bait. "I'd be delighted." Nik's expression turned to one of comical dismay. *Not buying it, Em,* Mac thought. Both of them were trying to distract her.

Not likely.

Not when her guts were churning just sitting this close to a Trisulian.

Mac took an appreciative swallow of now-cold coffee, weighing the chances of offending both Nik and his partner. It didn't matter. *She was who she was, Em. Honest, yes. Subtle?*

Not so much.

So. "If we can't trust your species, Cinder, why should I trust you?"

Nik merely tilted his head, the light hitting his glasses and hiding his eyes. Cinder's hands stayed calm and quiet in her lap. "Good question. All I can say is that—like you, Mac—I'm here as a member of the IU. I'm not bound by the policies of my kind, which I believe lack *nimscent*. Nik—the word?"

"Nimscent," Nik told Mac, "is an expression meaning 'future thinking.' Its lack implies going after a short-term gain in a way that may jeopardize ultimate success. Risk-taking." He reached over the low table and smacked the Trisulian affectionately on one leather-wrapped knee. "Don't worry, Mac. Cinder's okay."

Friendship? Trust. Nik should know better.

Abruptly weary, Mac wondered if she'd ever see them as a source of strength again, and not a trap.

Dismayed by her own reaction, she did her best to smile cheerfully at both of them. It must have been a miserable effort because a worried crease appeared between Nik's eyebrows and even the Trisulian bent a concerned eyestalk her way.

"Excuse me, Dr. Connor."

It was One, wearing a long white coat over his yellow uniform. Mac looked at him with relief. "Yes?"

"The Dhryn is ready."

Nik and Cinder stood to accompany her, the former giving her a small nod of encouragement, still with that worried frown.

Well, Em, Mac told herself as she stood, *there'd been coffee.*

"Parymn Ne Sa Las."

"This was your doing, Mackenzie Winifred Elizabeth Wright Connor Sol?"

Mac walked around the two sides of the cage left with bars, astonished. "Not alone," she said. The other two sides of what had been the cage were now walls, one with a door leading into a biological accommodation, complete with smaller sonic shower, and the other featuring a pulldown cot, Dhryn-sized. The nearer barred side had developed a door, her size.

Not bad for an hour.

The Dhryn hadn't recovered. She could see it in the way he listed as he sat. It likely didn't help that he had no hands on his lowermost arms, so had to balance himself on the stubs of his wrists.

But, like his accommodations, he'd improved immeasurably in that short time, even without *hathis,* the comalike Dhryn healing sleep. The floor was clean, and so was his skin, glowing its rich blue. With the ooze removed, Mac could see his wounds were regular, as though he'd used the sharpened fingers of his seventh arm to carve thin stripes along his midriff and over one shoulder. None of the wounds looked dangerous. Most were days old and healing.

None, her eyes narrowed, *appeared older than the severed wrist, his latest act of* grathnu.

Completing the picture, Parymn's body was wrapped in bands of white silk. He'd had trouble doing it; the layers weren't perfectly aligned. It didn't matter. When you were used to clothing, wearing it went a long way toward restoring confidence.

That was the real difference, Em, Mac cautioned herself. He might be weak, but Parymn was again every bit the stern, formal *erumisah* she remembered from Haven, the one who'd warned her about the impossibility of her succeeding as a Dhryn.

"I wish to be returned to my own chambers."

"Your chambers?" Mac echoed, with a puzzled frown. "These are your chambers, Parymn Ne Sa Las—"

"Of course not." His great black pupils dilated further. *Stress?* "My chambers adjoin the Progenitor's. I do not know where this place might be or how I got here. Nor—" a scowl, "—why not-Dhryn have been permitted on Haven, but I rely upon the Progenitors to have good reason."

He wasn't aware of leaving his world, Em, Mac told herself, amazed. *Or he chose not to believe it.*

An attitude she fully understood.

"You must stay here," she said.

Parymn Ne Sa Las pursed his small lips and stared at Mac for a moment. But he didn't press the point, saying instead: "Then you will express my desire for warmer air to the not-Dhryn."

Definitely back in form, decided Mac. "So now you believe they can talk."

He'd folded his arms just so. "Now I believe they can hear you," he qualified. "Have you come to talk to me, Mackenzie Winifred Elizabeth Wright Connor Sol?"

Mac gestured to Two, who brought forward a tray of jiggling black tubes. They'd had her data on the Dhryn diet and no trouble reproducing something comparable—only in stopping Parymn from throwing it.

"If you eat."

"If you do."

Oh, in fine form—Mac smiled. "Of course." At her signal, Two brought the tray to her, a finger discreetly indicating the nearer cylinder. Mac deftly pulled it free, tipping its contents into her mouth. "Delicious." Which was true, considering what she'd consumed was a fruit jelly.

The Dhryn's turn. Mac didn't look at Nik as she took the tray from Two and walked to the new door in the side of the cage. Mr. Trojanowski had made his objections to the door known, strenuously, and now stood close by it. His hand was in his pocket, doubtless with a weapon already in his palm.

She didn't, Mac shivered inwardly, *really mind.* Not that she needed to fear Parymn. Not in this incarnation, anyway. Memories were what chilled her blood as she stepped inside his enclosure, door snicking locked behind, then walked close enough to bend down and place the tray on the floor within his reach, sitting, despite Nik's hiss of displeasure, on the floor herself.

"Eat," she said. The rest of the tubes contained a fungal concoction that should, the dietitians said, help alleviate the nutritional cost of days spent fasting.

One arm unfolded, but instead of reaching for the tray, Parymn's hand shot toward her head. Mac forced herself to remain still as his fingers, three in number and arranged much like petals on a flower, roughly explored her scalp. "What is this?"

Dhryn didn't have a word for bandage. " 'A Dhryn is robust or a

Dhryn is not,' " she quoted, amazed her voice didn't shake. Behind, she heard the door close for a second time. Nik must have
started through, then backed off as he realized the Dhryn meant
no harm.

"True." His hand left her and found one of the cylinders. Mac
concealed her relief as he sucked it empty, then went for a second.
"These are adequate. Ask the not-Dhryn for—" and he rattled off
a series of dishes.

"I'll see what they can do, *Erumisah*," she said doubtfully, having recognized only the first.

He was on his third tube. Adult Dhryn didn't experience hunger
until they were shown food, Mac remembered. That being the
case, Parymn's new appetite had at least days, possibly more, of
starvation to overcome.

"You said the Progenitor seeks the truth," Mac began carefully.
"The truth about what?"

Parymn put down his fourth empty; his hand was markedly
slower going after the fifth and last. "Where is Brymn Las?"

Mac pressed her real hand against the floor, keeping her voice
steady. "Brymn Las Flowered into his final form, then—"

"Stop." Parymn's eyes could be very cold. "This is nonsense. He
would not have done so. What are you talking about?"

"His body underwent its final transformation," Mac explained,
searching for the right words. "It wasn't the Wasting."

Parymn flinched at this—no Dhryn willingly acknowledged that
type of death, where the body failed its change and withered. Suf-
ferers were shunned and left to die alone, preferably in the dark.

"Brymn Las," Mac continued with difficulty, "became one of
those who serve the Progenitor." She lifted both hands, fluttering
them as if in flight.

"That is not possible."

"I assure you it is. I was there. He was—damaged—in a storm.
Then he began to change." She fought to control her voice, to be
careful what she revealed. "He didn't survive very long after that.
I was there—at the end."

"No!" Parymn threw the final cylinder across the room as he staggered to his feet. "None of this is possible!" He towered over her.

"It's okay," Mac called in Instella, knowing Nik would react. Then, in Dhryn, as steadily as she could: "Sit, Parymn Ne Sa Las. Perhaps this is part of the truth the Progenitor seeks. Please. Calm yourself and sit."

He obeyed—*probably,* Mac thought, *more because he was about to collapse than due to her urging.* "Talk to me," she suggested. "Tell me why you say what I saw with my own eyes is impossible."

Parymn wrapped his free arms around his middle and rocked gently. Mac could feel thrums of distress through the floor. "He could not have changed yet. Even if he had . . . our final form is known to Her," he whispered. "During *grathnu,* she tastes what we will be. I carry that knowledge. Brymn Las . . ." His eyes winked open and closed repeatedly, their blue covers flashing like strobes. "I had to learn his fate. Brymn Las was to be one of the glorious ones. Not—not mere hands and mouths—a mindless, servile beast. He was to be one of our lights, our guides to the Return. Our future." He rocked harder. "It is impossible. Impossible. Impossible."

"Brymn . . . a Progenitor?" Involuntarily, Mac's hand rose to her mouth, as if to hold in the word. "What—what could have gone wrong?" She grabbed the Dhryn's nearest elbow, gave it a sharp tug. "Parymn Ne Sa Las. Please. That's not what happened. I swear it to you. Is there anything that can change the final form? Could the Progenitor have been wrong?"

"IMPOSSIBLE!" His arm flung outward, sending Mac skidding across the floor.

She rolled to her hands and knees, reassuring Nik and the others with a look, then stood, rubbing one hip. *Not good for the head either,* she told herself, shaking off a wave of dizziness. *Should have seen that coming, Em.*

Parymn was huddled on the floor again. Stepping over the remains of the tray and its contents, Mac knelt by his head. She rested her hand on his shoulder. His skin was warm and dry; it quivered at her touch as if to shake her off. "I will find this truth for the Progenitor," she promised. "I will learn what happened to Brymn Las. Rest, Parymn Ne Sa Las."

Mac collected the tubes and tray, then went to the cage door.

Nik opened it for her, his face pale and set. *He'd trusted her judgment.* Grateful, she held out her hand and Nik took it in his, using that hold to draw her from the cage. Someone else, One, took the tray.

"Are you injured, Mac?" Cinder asked, eyestalks bent forward at her.

"From that?" she forced a chuckle, but didn't let go of Nik. "Parymn wasn't trying to hurt me—just get rid of me. He's a little shaky at the moment. I went a bit farther than I should."

"What did you find out?"

For a fleeting moment, Mac had the unsettling impression that worlds upon worlds of beings suddenly hushed, waiting for her answer to Nik's question. *Foolish, Em?*

Still, for all she knew, the Sinzi were *broadcasting what was viewed from this room.*

"Mac?"

Brymn. She couldn't talk about him, not yet, not here, not to all those listening.

Not when she didn't understand.

"Are you sure you're all right?" Quieter, with an undertone of concern.

If Brymn Las should have Flowered into a Progenitor—how was it possible that he'd changed into the feeder form instead?

"Mac," sharper.

Mac gave Nik a smile. "Sorry. I was trying to remember the names of the foods Parymn wanted. He's on the mend. We should have a good session once he's rested a bit more." She looked at those she could see, One, Two, and Cinder, and thought of those she couldn't, then deliberately put weight on her hand in Nik's, as if needing his support.

"Time for you to rest as well," he said immediately. "I'll take you upstairs."

"Mr. Hollans awaits your report, Nik," Two disagreed.

One added: "We will escort Mac to her rooms."

Two continued: "And discuss with her the importance of absolute discretion."

Mac snorted and Nik smiled. "No need for that," he informed both staff before she could make an acid comment.

She squeezed Nik's hand once, then released it, letting her eyes say what she couldn't. "Then I'll see you later, Mr. Trojanowski."

But it was the huddled Dhryn she glanced back to see before the door closed between them.

And the question he'd given her was what kept her silent during the trip back to the surface.

Why had Brymn transformed at all?

- Encounter -

THAT WHICH IS DHRYN has followed the Taste, followed the path.
There is harmony. Concordance. The Great Journey must be completed.
That which is Dhryn resists change.
That which is Dhryn resists . . . resists . . . resists . . .
. . . succumbs. Obedience to the Call is the Way as well.
Change.
That which is Dhryn follows the new path.

At night, even without moonlight, jungles aren't quiet. This one was no exception, although the babble of voices was an addition that startled most inhabitants into hiding.

It attracted others.

Movement began, high in the canopy. Stealthy, cautious movement. The kind that let one watch for rivals as well as predators.

Not that predators were allowed here. This was, after all, a civilized jungle, with wide paths to prevent the snagging of fine cloth on a rough branch; paved, to protect expensive shoes. It even boasted landing fields, so visitors needn't exhaust themselves reaching . . . here.

The voices were closer. There was laughter. The sort of nervous laughter that meant some weren't sure being here was such a good idea. Maybe some weren't as ready as others. It wouldn't matter.

Movement reached the tree trunks, became a climb downward. Always careful. Always ready.

Always . . . hungry.

A rival came too close. The battle joined, loud and urgent. The voices were silenced by it; footsteps ceased.

Movement continued.

As if only now realizing the nature of this place and their purpose in it, the voices began again, but lower, more . . . eager. The need to be here, in the dark, had supplanted any other.

The voices drifted apart, not to seek, but to be found.

The movement became quicker, came from every direction. Battle raged at each trespass, but more kept coming. The hunger was upon them all.

The jungle night rang with startled cries of ecstasy.

Until the rain began to fall.

And the cries became screams.

Then silence.

16

CONUNDRUM AND CHANGE

MAC SHOOED One and Two from her bedroom, feeling as if she was back at Base and dealing with overly helpful grad students. Despite Nik's assurance, they'd been unable to resist "briefing" her on the Sinzi's requirements for secrecy all the way to her quarters. Only those approved by the Sinzi-ra could know about the Dhryn. Only information assessed by the Sinzi-ra could be passed along to those who knew about the Dhryn. And so on.

Rubbing her throbbing temples, Mac avoided so much as a look at the extraordinary bed, walking through to the sitting room with the intention of splashing water on her face, then heading down to meet her team. *New questions to ask; hard ones.*

But two steps into what had been the sitting room, Mac stopped. "Oh my," she whispered.

The Sinzi's fish table was still there, its improbable contents moving in and out of rays of sunlight that didn't match those shining through the windows. The jelly-chairs remained, and the sand on the floor.

Everything else was hers.

Her desk, reassembled complete with clutter, was in front of the rain-streaked window, her chair where she liked it. There were new shelves on one wall, white, but filled with her things. The silly screen stood guard by the curved Sinzi mirror, complete with an old sweater tossed over it, while salmon . . .

Salmon hung everywhere. Wood glowed where light caught an

edge. Potent lines of black and red outlined fins, eyes, and gave meaning. Their shadows schooled across the white walls and ceilings, oblivious to gravity, intent on life.

Her salmon.

"You're early!" Mudge gasped as he came out of the closet and saw her. He was carrying an armload of beads which he promptly dropped on his feet. As he bent to retrieve his burden, he muttered something she couldn't hear over the rattle and clank of the beads.

"You did this?" Mac asked incredulously.

Feet rescued, Mudge fumbled the beads into a mass against his chest and stood looking at her with charming despair. His hair, what there was, was sweat-soaked to his scalp, and he was out of breath. "Ah. Norcoast. Back so soon. How was your meeting?"

"You did this?" she repeated.

He gave an offended-sounding *harrumph* and actually scowled at her. "You'd left a mess in there." A jerk of his head to the closet behind him came close to freeing the beads again. "And we have to do something with these," he said anxiously, struggling to contain the noisy things.

Mac didn't know whether to laugh or burst into tears. As either reaction would no doubt embarrass her benefactor, she merely blinked a couple of times and asked: "What did you have in mind?"

It turned out that he wanted them on the terrace. Mac followed Mudge outside, and helped hold the mass of beads while he climbed on chairs and affixed the end of each strand above the French doors. She was impressed. He'd obtained some type of glue from the staff that was delivered by spray. It seemed to hold well. *Probably need a chisel to get them off again,* Mac judged.

Her hair danced against her face in the light breeze allowed through the Sinzi's screen. The air was cool enough Mac was glad of her jacket. *Better than the basement,* she thought. "Why outside?" she asked him, passing up the next strand.

Mudge glanced down at her, one hand pressed against the door for support. He'd already left a series of sweaty palm prints on the glass—or whatever the transparent material was. The staff would not be pleased. They obsessed about her footprints in the sand, raking them away every time she left. *As if a person could float to the washroom.* "Outside?" he repeated. "Where else do you expect the Ro to come from—the basement?"

As this was far too close to her own notions for comfort, Mac wisely shut up and kept helping.

"That's the last of them," Mudge said with distinct pride as he stepped down from the chair a few moments later. Mac managed to save both from tipping over. The chair was more grateful, Mudge shaking her hand free with an annoyed *harrumph*.

The strands weren't evenly spaced. They didn't even all hang straight down, a couple having a decided list. They did, however, thoroughly fill the space left when the doors opened. The noise-makers within the beads were heavy enough they wouldn't sound at the harmless touch of a sea breeze.

It would take a body trying to push past them, or a hand trying to move them aside, to sound the alarm.

When they finished, instead of "Thank you," Mac merely asked: "You hungry, Oversight?"

But she wouldn't forget. What Mudge had done was an act of friendship as pure and real as anything she'd have expected from Emily.

Nik had known, when she had not.

"You're late."

"Lunch meeting. Anything come up?" As she waited for Lyle to open his imp—*implying something had*—Mac let her eyes wander the Origins' room, noticing nothing unusual, unless she counted a second Myg. "Who's that?" she asked.

Lyle glanced up. "Who? Oh. Ueen-something. Nope, Uneen-something. Unensela, that's it. I have an awful memory for Myg names. All the vowels. She's your xenopaleoecologist."

"Just Unensela . . .no number?" Mac asked.

"Number?" His pale eyes crinkled at the corners with amusement. "You were expecting a number? She's female."

Would every single Human she'd meet here know more about aliens than she did? Mac asked herself with exasperation. "Any good?"

"Your friend thinks so. Hasn't been more than three steps away since she arrived."

Sure enough, Fourteen was hovering behind his fellow Myg like Lee used to hover around Emily—until that worthy would send him on an errand or four. "This Unensela better know her stuff," Mac muttered under her breath.

She brought her attention back to the archaeologist, who was, rightly, wondering why she wasn't looking at the display hovering between them over the conference table. He'd commandeered it as a very large desk, shoving what appeared the remains of the communal lunch to one end. "Sorry. What am I looking at, Lyle?"

"This is from Sergio's most recent assays of Dhryn ceramics from the ruins on their home world. I've correlated them against the references you gave us yesterday—Brymn Las' work—and the results are, well, you can see it's quite remarkable."

Mac dutifully examined the complex three-dimensional chart, then turned back to Lyle. "Salmon," she reminded him. "I know ceramics are in tiles and mugs, that's it. Tell me what this means."

"Biologist." He had the gall to grin at her, then put his hand inside the chart, pulling at a serpentine mass until it expanded to reveal more, to Mac, incomprehensible detail. "Ceramics is an entire field of engineering. You can build a civilization around it. Several in the IU have. Dhryn were very good ceramic engineers. Were," he emphasized. "A long time ago, over a relatively short period of time, ceramics virtually disappear from their technology. There's a massive switch to other materials. Plastics. Metals. Spun glass. Microgravity crystals. Now your friend didn't have access to our fieldwork. All he had to go on were artifacts from within the Chasm purported to be Dhryn. From before the event. None were ceramic, Mac. None."

"Imports," Mac guessed. "You're thinking the change in the Dhryn materials came when the Dhryn home system was first opened to others by a transect. New technology arrives, better than the old. We see it here."

Lyle bit his lip and closed the display with a quick gesture. "No, we don't. Here we take alien technology and blend it with the best or most popular of our own. Half the time, no one remembers what came first, but you can find the roots if you look. This? The Dhryn abandoned everything they had and replaced it. That's not a natural pattern, Mac."

"The Haven Dhryn had tile mosaics on their buildings." *Lovely ones,* she remembered, *as well as outright jokes on passersby.*

"Alien technology, Mac. Sergio's already determined the Dhryn imported their ceramics from other species after joining the IU."

"Give me a time line." A moment later, Mac stared at the resulting display. "That's . . . old."

Lyle leaned so close to the display that millennia played over his pale cheekbones. "We estimate the Chasm was home to a thriving interspecies culture like the IU when our particular ancestors had pointed noses and hunted bugs."

"Connected by transects made by the Ro."

A few more had come up to listen. One volunteered: "We don't know that."

Another: "Of course they were. The Chasm transects were reactivated when the Sinzi re-initialized the Naralax Transect from the Hift System."

"All of them?" Mac asked, curious. "What if some were destroyed—or connected in other ways?"

"The Sinzi sent probes designed to generate random destinations into every transect they encountered, Mac, probes that could multiply and send copies of themselves through any additional gates. All returned to their starting point in the Hift. The Chasm transects form a closed network. Everyone knows that."

Everyone? Mac didn't protest.

"Why?" She frowned at the now larger half circle of researchers.

"That's how many systems were ready for the technology," someone offered.

Mac held her hands up, palms together, fingertips touching. "I meant, why a bottle?"

Mutters of "Bottle?" "What bottle?" "What's she talking about?" went around the group.

With a look to get Lyle's permission, Mac replaced his imp with hers and set the screen high enough so that all could see it. She pulled up a map of the Tannu River watershed. "If I wanted to count all of the salmon born and ready to migrate from every one of these lakes and streams, I could wait here." She pointed to the mouth of the Tannu, where it opened into the Castle Inlet. "It's like a bottle, with only one opening. So is the Chasm, if I understand you correctly. Why build something with only one opening? Control over what moves in or out."

"But the Dhryn were already inside," Lyle protested.

"Yes," Mac agreed. "They were."

A buzz of conversation started around the edges of the now-complete group, much of it involving jargon that didn't translate in Instella or any language Mac knew. A pair sat at one end of the table to argue with each other. She waited.

The Sthlynii, Therin, had sat beside her. Sure enough, he found an inconsistency. "If there was only one 'opening' to the Chasm, and it led only to the Hift System, how did the Dhryn escape? You said they claimed to be pursued by the Myrokynay until they found a hiding place in the Haven System. But how did they get there?"

"I'm not sure even the Progenitors know," Mac said.

"Sublight?" this from one of the Chasm Ghoul followers.

"They'd still be in transit," from Therin, with disapproval. "We're talking no more than three thousand years."

"The IU connected the Naralax Transect to the Dhryn's new home," observed Lyle. No frowns or remarks followed, a testament, Mac judged, to the respect the Sinzi had earned with their care in choosing new species to invite into the union.

If any other species had let the Dhryn out of their system, there would have been blame enough to start wars.

"I don't know about you," one of the Humans looked around at the rest, "but I really don't like the idea that the Dhryn ships might have the capability to form their own passages."

"We haven't seen it," Therin said calmly.

"Yet."

"If they could do it, they wouldn't risk using transects."

"What if they do?"

The room filled with speculation. Mac let it go a while, finding and meeting Lyle's eyes. She waited until she saw them widen with comprehension, then she stood to get everyone's attention. When they were quiet, she asked: "What is a planetary system without a transect?"

Lyle didn't hesitate: "A sealed bottle."

"A sealed bottle that can sustain life," Mac elaborated. "The Dhryn didn't escape, folks. They were preserved."

All that could be heard was breathing, some of it rather odd to Human ears. That, and a shuffle of feet.

Followed by a cheerful bellow from the back row: "My colleague warned me you were full of surprises, Dr. Connor. Glad to see it's true." There was an abrupt parting of the line—Mac suspected a shove—and the new Myg made her way forward, Fourteen predictably behind. "Preserved, is it? By who? And why?"

"Who is obvious." This from one of the wrinkled Cey. "The only species with that level of no-space technology are the Myrokynay."

The female Myg, Unensela, seemed the only one not shocked by this bold statement. Unensela and her—Mac blinked—her family.

The Myg was built so much like Fourteen she'd have had trouble telling the two apart, if it weren't that Unensela's hair was short, sparse, and black, compared to his short, sparse, and red. Their features were a match as well, though Unensela was wearing color on cheeks, forehead, and lips. All the same shade of vivid fuchsia. She wore a crisp white lab coat, open at the front apparently to supply a view for her offspring.

There were six looking out at the moment, each about the size of a half grown kitten and, as far as Mac could tell, identical to one another and their mother. Naked, they clung with hands and feet to a harness Unensela wore under her coat. Their necks were flexible enough to allow them to stare over their shoulders with huge brown eyes that reminded Mac of Sam's irresistible beagle, who had successfully haunted so many supper tables.

Unensela, meanwhile, was peering under her thickened pink eyelids at the Cey. "Idiot," she proclaimed. "Why would the Myrokynay ferry the Dhryn to a new home and keep them there?"

"A prison," shouted someone else. There was a chorus of "yes, aye, has to be," and species-appropriate nods. "What else could you do with them?"

"What they'd do to us."

Everyone looked at Lyle after he spoke. He was standing now, too, his cheeks suffused with red. There were a few nods, some quick, some reluctant. With the exception of six Myg children, everyone listening understood what he meant.

Genocide.

Mac coughed. "Fortunately," she said, "we're not being asked to make that decision. We're being asked to provide answers to help those who must."

"We don't have the power of the Myrokynay." "We need to contact them." "Get their help!"

"In this room—" Mac stopped and raised her voice to be heard over the bedlam. "In this room, our job is to understand why the Dhryn are acting as they are." She lowered her voice back to normal as they began listening. "Where they came from. Origins. Focus on that, people. There are plenty of experts here working on other aspects of this problem—and its solution. Have you seen the daily reports from the Sinzi-ra?"

Mudge was the only one who nodded brusquely at this. Mac wasn't surprised. Of course he paid attention to everything going on, read every scrap of information. Even the deluge of information synthesized by Anchen for dispersal.

They'd have to talk, she decided. *Meanwhile . . .*

"If you have ideas how to contact the Ro, give them to any member of the consulate staff on your own time. My time, you are on my questions. Is that understood? Let's get back to work."

As they exchanged wary looks and sorted themselves out, grabbing lunch remains on the way, the Myg stepped up to Mac. "Well? What questions do you have for me?" Unensela demanded. "This is a bunch of irrelevant archaeologists." One of her children started to wail and she patted it absently. "And idiots."

At least she didn't point at the ghoul chasers, Mac thought. There was sufficient tension in the room as it was.

"I promised you a famous xenopaleoecologist, did I not, Mac?" Fourteen pushed himself forward. A sly tilt of his head. "Is she not thoroughly splendid?"

Unensela ignored him. "Well?"

"I want you to work with To'o and Kirby," Mac said, choosing to ignore Fourteen for the moment as well. *So long as he doesn't start drooling over her console, Emily.* "They'll provide you with what climatological information we have. I believe Oversight has obtained scans from cores into the planet itself."

Mudge, who'd stayed tucked behind his corner desk during all this, gave a start at the sound of his name. "Scans? Scans?" He realized he was repeating himself and shut up with a nod.

"From those," Mac continued, "I need you to tell me if there have been significant and predictable biome shifts. And why. As soon as you can. Tomorrow, if possible."

Unensela's hands patted offspring at random, her attention firmly on Mac. "A challenge, Dr. Connor. Interesting."

"Mac. And welcome to the team. All of you," she added, gazing into a dozen limpid eyes. "As for you, Fourteen?" Mac had every intention of assigning him a task at the other end of the room, if necessary.

"I have my task." The Myg held up his hands. "Yours are irrelevant," he said. "I continue to help the idiots downstairs interpret my perfectly clear translation. Helpless without my genius." This last directed at Unensela, who seemed to make a point of being preoccupied with her offspring.

Mac opened her mouth, not that she was sure what was about to come out of it beyond a question concerning the usefulness of a stolen shoe to a genius, when a shout drew everyone's attention, including hers, to the door. "Dr. Connor! Dr. Connor!"

She stared at—yes, it was Two, back in her yellow uniform. Consular staff, in her admittedly limited experience, never shouted, much less burst into rooms. "Dr. Connor. You must come with me immediately!" Two insisted loudly. Mac glanced at Lyle, then Mudge. Both men nodded back to her, Mudge with an anxious frown.

"I'll be back later," Mac promised the room at large, following the obviously impatient Two out the door.

Out in the hall, everything seemed normal enough. A few delegates walking about. A non-oxy breather hummed down the ramp in his/her/its/their bubble. *No sign of panic.* "What is it?" Mac demanded, controlling the impulse to check over her shoulder first. "Is he awake? Is there a crisis?"

"No, Mac." Two's voice had returned to its normal dignified calm. "Please excuse my abruptness, but we were briefed this was the most efficient way to extricate one Human from a group."

Mac stared at Two in disbelief. "In a life-or-death emergency, maybe. You startled everyone in that room! Including me!"

"My apologies." Somehow, the voice lacked sincerity. Mac harbored a sudden dark suspicion about what the staff on an alien planet did for fun.

"Where are we going?"

"The Sinzi-ra wishes to hear your daily insights."

Before they entered the lift, Mac checked the light streaming down from above. "It's not evening. Isn't this a bit early?"

"I was not given the Sinzi-ra's reason for the change in schedule, Mac." Two's hand paused at the control. "Would you like me to use the com system to inquire?"

Aliens. Mac leaned a shoulder against the wall of the lift. "No. Just take me up."

The Sinzi-ra was waiting in Mac's apartment, playing with salmon. Mac assumed it was play, although she was willing to believe there could be other motivation for Anchen to use her long fingers to poke a series of the statues into motion. *Distraction, perhaps.*

"I'm here," Mac announced. Two had left her at the doors.

"Ah, Mac. Thank you for coming." Anchen's fingers dropped gracefully to her sides. The salmon swayed back and forth, slower each time. Their shadows had elongated as the sun dropped lower, giving them an urgent look. "I see you've obtained your belongings."

"Yes, although I hadn't expected everything." Mac gestured to the room. "I hope you don't mind all this. I would have asked first, but . . ."

"But your friend wished you comfortable. It is understandable." The Sinzi took one of the jelly-chairs. She'd come alone this time. "I trust you don't feel you require these additional security measures."

"The beads?" Mac smiled without mirth. "They've become a habit."

"Ah." Anchen drew out her imp, waving it in the air like a wand before laying it on the table. A ragged tooth barracuda within the table targeted the device, then ignored it. "Shall we begin? First, please, come here. I wish to remove your bandage."

Mac sat cross-legged in the sand beside the Sinzi's chair, waiting patiently as the alien's fingertips feathered over her scalp. She felt a sudden coolness. "Excellent," Anchen pronounced. "See for yourself."

"It's healed remarkably well. Thank you," Mac told Anchen a moment later, trying not to grin as she ran her fingers over scalp that was now intact, instead of torn. No pain or tightness. *But there was—* "Excuse me, Anchen, but why is my hair growing in like this?" Mac felt the fine silky stuff. It looked as though she had a pale c-shaped stripe along the side of her head. *Not the fashion this decade, Em.*

"The regeneration process starts with biologically young cells," explained Anchen. "They will mature quite quickly. By the end of this week, you should see no difference. If you wish, a staff member can apply coloration to this portion immediately."

Baby hair? Mac wrapped some around a finger, forming a curl. "This is fine. I'd forgotten I started blonde." Her eyes met the Sinzi's in the mirror and she came to a decision. "There is—I have another injury."

"*Alexia.* Word blindness. Yes. I know."

"You know." *She shouldn't feel surprised,* Mac scolded herself. The Sinzi and the Ministry had shared their data about her. "Good. Then you're probably aware it's beyond our physicians. Can you help me?"

Anchen moved aside to let Mac step down to the sand. "Can our medical science repair the damage done to the areas of your brain involved in language? Of course." Then she shook her head. The gesture looked forced, unnatural, as if the Sinzi had learned it in order to communicate with Humans. "But the process would risk your ability to communicate with our guest, Mac. Until the situation changes, all we dare do is begin to retrain your reading centers—your greatest need at the moment, I assume. I will provide materials to help you. Practice when you are rested. Be patient."

As if she had a choice, Mac thought grimly. "I understand, Sinzira. I won't say I like it."

"Nor I, Mac. It is a compromise—in this case one that burdens you most. You have my sympathy."

With a sigh, Mac nodded to the chairs. "Shall I give you my report? There's quite a bit."

"And I have much to tell you. There has been another attack."

"Who?"

The Sinzi didn't answer until she'd sat, Mac following suit. The alien activated her imp. Mac squinted, but again could see no more than a glimmer. "The Trisulians have suffered a terrible loss."

Mac closed her eyes briefly, then opened them again. "Their males?" she asked, sure of the answer.

"Yes. Word arrived within the hour. Trisul Primus was consumed by the Dhryn. How did you guess?"

"It's where the Trisulians are most vulnerable. But what I don't understand," Mac added aloud, but to herself, "is how that helps the Dhryn." Mac drew both feet up on the chair and hugged her knees.

"It did not. They paid dearly for the attack. The Progenitor's ship and all Dhryn in the system were destroyed—thankfully in time to save the remaining populated planets: Secondus and Tierce."

"So the Ro came to their aid?" Mac felt a surge of relief. "The message from Emily? It worked?" *This time, Em, she'd wanted to be wrong about so much.*

Anchen paired her fingertips. A cautious, slow movement. "It remains unclear whether the Myrokynay were involved and, if so, to what extent. The Trisulian Ruling Council has never been forthcoming in matters of strategy—understandable when you consider their unfortunate history with neighboring systems." She aimed her lower eyes at Mac. "If they received help from the Myrokynay, I admit being astonished the Trisulians were able to reconfigure their technology so quickly upon receipt of the instructions in the stolen message. It is a feat our experts have yet to accomplish."

"Perhaps they were already close to such a device themselves."

A graceful tilt of the head. "It could help explain Kay's willingness to commit violence—a last piece of the puzzle, an advantage within reach." Anchen's fingers rippled from shoulder to tip. "Perhaps they had reason to anticipate a Dhryn attack."

"Or provoked one."

"An insight, Mac?"

Mac shrugged. "I'm no strategist. But the Trisulians were resettling the Eeling System. They hoped to find a way to be first in line to take advantage—that word again—of the other devastated systems. Not every predator will tolerate a scavenger on its kill."

The Sinzi's fingers shot into the air as if avoiding something offensive, their rings, silver today, sliding toward her shoulders. *Like a melodramatic willow,* Mac thought. "You believe the Dhryn continue to watch their victims? How? Is this what our guest told you?"

"No, Anchen." The jelly-chair rewarded every posture but sitting up straight. Still, Mac made the effort. "I was only speculating why the Trisulians might have been a target for the Dhryn. I have no evidence, no reason for saying so. Forgive me if I distressed you."

"The search for truth is worth any distress," Anchen said feebly. One by one, her fingers gracefully slipped back down, each quivering as it moved, the whole process mesmerizing, as though the Sinzi hypnotized herself—and Mac—into a measure of peace. "But another subject would be easier at this moment. Perhaps insights about our guest? You've done wonders anticipating his needs."

Our guest. "Insights," Mac repeated, staring down at the Sinzi's imp. *On the record,* she reminded herself, unsure why she felt impelled to caution. *Same side, Em. Still* . . . "Anchen, should we speak freely here?" She gestured to the room.

The Sinzi aimed all of her eyes at Mac. "We have privacy here, Mac." She touched fingertip to her imp. "But no secrets from fellows within the IU," she said calmly. "Particularly this Gathering."

Other than a room lined with the Dhryn cloaking material, complete with Dhryn. Mac's lips twisted wryly. She understood the need for that discretion. There probably wasn't a single researcher here who wouldn't want to see the Dhryn—or, her blood chilled, *worse.*

The Sinzi read her expression with practiced ease. *Unsettling,* Mac decided, *when she couldn't do the same.* "I admit the inconsistency, Mac. The situation calls for some information to be—delayed. All will be recorded and shared. To those working on physiology, we have provided data; there was no need to specify its source. Nor do we see a need for experimentation or invasive tests at this time. Your interrogation of Parymn Ne Sa Las comes first. What results do you have?"

Mac gazed into multiple reflections of herself in alien eyes, feeling twisted inside, as though her lunch expressed an opinion. "Very little yet, Anchen. He's come to talk on behalf of his Progenitor. She wants to learn the truth."

"About what?" the other asked reasonably.

"We didn't get that far. Parymn's unaccustomed to alien lifeforms. He's had trouble adjusting."

"A poor choice of ambassadors."

Was he? Mac frowned thoughtfully. "It would seem so," she agreed at last. "Parymn did have a question of his own for me. He wanted to know what happened to Brymn Las." Her voice held, steady and sure. *You'd be proud, Em.* "When I told him, he didn't believe me at first. He still might not."

"How is this significant?"

"I don't know," Mac admitted. "But the transformation to the—feeder form—is the point at which individual Dhryn become a threat. We should find out as much as we can about it."

"I concur. Is there anything more?"

Something went wrong. Brymn was to be a Progenitor. Mac, grateful she hadn't said the words aloud, gathered herself. "Yes. I think we should be careful how literally we take what Parymn tells us. I have doubts about his ability to—" she hunted for the right word, "—reconcile his worldview with ours. What he thinks he knows? Very little may be of use."

"Is he insane?"

Mac blinked. "I'm not qualified to say—"

"Give me an opinion, Mac," Anchen insisted. "We have already seen him be self-destructive. Is he sane for what you know of his kind?"

"He's angry. Frightened. Resentful. Who wouldn't be?" Mac paused to consider, watching fish swim inside the impossible table. "Otherwise? I honestly don't know, Anchen. I'll need to talk with him more first."

"You are a remarkable being, Dr. Mackenzie Connor."

Surprised, Mac looked up at the Sinzi. "I am?"

"There are few within this building I would trust near our guest, even if they had the courage to step within his cell. Fewer still I would trust to act as interpreter, under such dire and unhappy circumstances, even if they had the ability. Yet you, with what has happened, all you have endured, continue to act with clarity and compassion." The Sinzi bowed. "Remarkable and rare. I deeply cherish our connection."

"Thank you, Sinzi-ra. I cherish it as well." Mac sighed. "All I can I do is try my best. I hope that's going to be enough."

A shrug that set rings sparkling. "So do we all."

Mac made her way to Parymn's cell, having grabbed a bag of supplies before leaving her room. She'd also moved the information she wanted from the imp Fourteen had given her into her own—along with an astounding number of messages from other attendees of the Gathering, all collected within the last twenty-four hours. *Which was what being named head of anything really meant, Em.*

Needing only one hand to control the lift, Mac set her imp so the list hovered in front of her, the flashing lift lights a minor distraction. She pushed the device into the waistband of her pants to free her left hand. Now to attempt to organize the mess.

Sorting by priority didn't help, since almost all were marked "urgent!"

Trust academics, even alien ones. "Some things never change," Mac muttered out loud. By source, then. She found and pulled aside those from her group and the Sinzi. She looked at the rest rather helplessly, then forwarded them to Mudge with one sweep of her hand.

What were friends for? she grinned to herself.

The door whooshed open on the white corridor.

Mac took a deep breath and closed the display. As before, the corridor was empty and featureless, like the inside of a throat. She found herself reluctant to step from the lift, started to reach for the controls to close the doors. *As if she could stay here, Em,* she scolded herself. Settling the bag over her shoulders, and her imagination with it, Mac started walking.

At each of the three guard stations, she was stopped while beings of varied species examined her small bag. Mac wasn't sure what they were looking for—or in one instance, sniffing—considering she was one of the "assets" being protected by their presence. *Bored,* she decided.

Faced with the three doors again, Mac looked wistfully at the one which led to the vastness of the Atrium, then went toward Parymn's. She hesitated, looking over her shoulder. She was still alone. No obvious surveillance. Her eyes were drawn to the door Nik and Cinder had gone through first.

What was behind it?

"Probably nothing," she assured herself, again turning toward Parymn's.

Then again, Em, she'd never have guessed what was behind the other two.

That did it. Mac left her bag on the floor by the door she should go through and went briskly to the one she likely shouldn't.

It wasn't locked. No alarms sounded when she pushed it open. At first, Mac was disappointed. Another white corridor, this time offering only one large door before turning right and heading into a perspective-turning distance. It sloped downward at the same time, like the hallways above ground.

" 'In for a penny,' " Mac whispered to herself, pushing against the large door.

Instead of swinging forward, this door reacted by sliding to one side, disappearing into the wall. Sunlight, dappled and moved by water, lay across Mac's toes. It was an invitation she took without hesitation.

"Oh," she breathed as she walked inside.

The impossible table in her room was a window here, to this place. A block of ocean, for it could be nothing less, stretched three times her height and wide enough to vanish into shadows on either side. Sunlight, either brought from the surface or feigned, cut through the water in great beams. Fish of every possible color and form slipped in and out of them, alone, in schools, flashes of life wheeling above the corals, oblivious to anything but themselves. Shrimp scurried everywhere, antennae flicking in the currents, too busy to hide despite being on everything's menu. Including the Sinzi's.

Mac laid her palms flat against the transparent hardness of the tank wall, stopping short of pressing her nose to it. The floor of this room wasn't the bottom. She could make out the edge of the coral shelf, slim dark shadows below that marking where barracuda and shark loitered.

No-space. Remembering, Mac took her hands away and swallowed uneasily. Remarkable, that she could see inside it from here. *If she was.* Now that she wasn't transfixed by the marine life in front of her, she noticed the steady throbbing of the floor and paid attention to the writhing mass of machinery overhead that started halfway up the wall behind her. The hairs rose on her arm and neck. She gave the imprisoned fish a sympathetic look. Trapped forever, like insects in amber. But trapped alive.

Was Emily?

"Mac?" Cinder walked out of the darkness to the right of the door. "What are you doing here?" She didn't appear pleased.

"Got lost," Mac said, not surprised her voice was higher-pitched than usual. Her heart was racing, too. *Was there some memo she'd missed about scaring her today?* "This is quite the setup," she added.

"The fish?" Caught in sunbeams, the Trisulian looked as agitated as she sounded, stroking her facial hair, her eyestalks shifting in jerky movements. "I suppose so."

Then Mac understood. "The Sinzi-ra told me about—about Trisul Primus."

As if she'd somehow used a weapon, Cinder folded at both waists, collapsing to the floor. Mac hurried to crouch beside her, unsure how to offer comfort. *If it was even possible.* "Cinder," she said gently. "I'm so sorry. Is there anything I can do?"

She hadn't expected an answer, but the other pressed something small, round, and cold into Mac's palm. "Take this." Muffled.

It was a weapon, identical to the one Nik produced at need.

Mac wanted to drop it. Instead, she put it into the pocket of her jacket.

"This, too." Cinder's hand shook as she pulled a sheathed blade from her boot.

"I—" Mac didn't know what to say.

"One of *them* so close. In reach. I can't think straight. Don't trust myself. Not yet. *Usish!* Take it! Please."

Mac obeyed, putting the knife with the weapon. "Should I get someone—Nik?" she offered.

"No!" Then, quieter but a hoarse undertone. "No, thank you, Mac. I must collect myself before I see a male. This is—I am—It's unseemly." Cinder's hands clenched in her hair, round knuckles white. "You are unmated, are you not?"

By Trisulian standards? "Yes."

A sigh, closer to a moan. "Yet you—you have that future. Thanks to his kind, the *usishishi* Dhryn—there are no mates for my generation, Mac. Can you understand? Oh, our kind will survive. There will be a new jungle. When all are satisfied it is safe to do so, those already bonded will impregnate themselves. They will give birth in its warmth, take their daughters home with them, leave their sons to grow. Sons who will be ready when those daughters are ripe. Our kind will survive," she repeated in a dull whisper. "But I . . . I will be forever alone and incomplete."

There had to be options. "Forgive my ignorance, Cinder," Mac began with care. "I only want to help. I've heard a female Trisulian can bond with more than one male. I've seen a male removed from his mate." *At close range.* "So wouldn't it be possible for your people to—redistribute—" *what a crude word* "—the males you have? To share?"

"Deviance." The word wasn't harsh, it was chill, matter-of-fact. "You could say waste. Or murder. All fit. You see, Mac, bonding is permanent. There is a—I don't know the word in Instella—a body part of the male which becomes part of the female's flesh. Insertion of it is—I'm told," Cinder corrected herself softly, wistfully, "a moment of the most exquisite rapture my kind can know. To remove a male severs him from this part. He can't mate again. He lives on, impotent." Eyestalks steadied as Cinder looked directly up at Mac, her rust-brown hair catching sunlight. "As must I."

Mac hesitated, then asked: "Must every female take a mate?"

"No. Some choose to remain alone, for control over their lives. I might have been one of them . . . now, I have no other choice." Cinder pressed her hands over her lower waist. "Fertility, for us, is a matter of mere minutes, its occurrence unpredictable." *Hence the value of symbiotic males,* Mac couldn't help thinking. "Three cycles in a life is exceptional. Most, only once. So it is expected that one allows pregnancy whenever possible, regardless of career or situation." She began rising to her feet, moving as if wounded. "You must think me lacking in *nimscent*—grieving for myself at a time like this. I am shamed."

"Nonsense." Mac offered her hand to help Cinder straighten. "We were going to have some girl talk," she said, but not lightly.

"Thank you." Cinder squeezed her hand then released it. "I feel able to be around others now—just not—would you—I—"

Mac patted her pocket. "I'll hang on to these for a while," she suggested.

The Trisulian shuddered, her hair quivering from forehead to chest, but didn't disagree. "I should return to my post," she said instead.

And would probably appreciate a little space from empathic Humans, Mac decided. "Would it be all right if I watch the fish for a while?" she asked. "A moment or two, not long. Thought I saw a sand shark."

One eyestalk regarded the tank at that angle suggesting anxiety. "Glad it's in there," Cinder said, her voice close to normal again. "Don't stay long, Mac." With that, she left.

Once the door closed, Mac walked to the right, looking for—there, a mass of wiring, looping down through some kind of clamp. Standing on tiptoe, she took Cinder's weapon and knife and pushed both as far back in the mass as her arm could reach.

Keeping the deadly things in her pocket hadn't been an option.

"Trained spy, target in a box, and me holding the hardware," Mac summed up for the fish. If the grief-stricken Trisulian doubted her self-restraint that much, what was to say she wouldn't lose it? Then what was she, Mac, supposed to do? Fight her off? Throw herself in front of the Dhryn?

"No winners, Em," Mac sighed. "Like all of this."

Time to get back to Parymn and hunt answers. But she couldn't help one last look at the Sinzi's living larder.

Odd. Mac walked along the tank, following the coral as it built up from the depths, then rose to her shoulder height and more. Anemones bent under what appeared natural wave motion, finger-like extensions hoping for unwary swimmers.

She leaned closer, staring at what had caught her eye.

There. The play of light and shade over the irregular coral had disguised the damage from the doorway.

The living coral was colorful, each hollow containing its tiny organism, like so much shrimp-beaded concrete. Mac's fingers traced the lines where living coral had been dug out and pushed aside, or peeled back, as if someone had used the tines of a large fork to remove it.

Her hand dropped to her side as Mac took slow, careful steps back.

She'd seen such marks before.

They'd scarred the moss carpeting Mudge's mountainside. She'd followed them as if they were footprints. For all she or anyone knew, they could be, since their makers showed themselves to no one.

Mac felt the door at her back. The occupants of the tank looked completely normal. *If she didn't know—if she hadn't seen—*

She threw herself around, yanking open the door and running out as if chased.

"Whoa, Mac. What's wrong?" Nik's voice jumped from surprised to urgent.

"The Ro," she gasped, pointing behind her. "In there."

"And I'm telling you, Mr. Trojanowski, unless you want to order a diver to commit suicide over some broken coral, there's nothing more we can do."

Putting down her bottle of water, Mac glared at the speaker, an unnamed, overdressed, vaguely bovine alien. He/she/it had arrived with a small army of scan techs and their equipment. And, as far as she was concerned, a supremely unhelpful contempt for Human powers of observation. Particularly hers.

Granted, they'd aimed their devices at the marks she'd found, and everywhere else in the tank, for over an hour. An hour during which Mac had leaned against this wall to wait and watch. An hour during which Nik, who had taken her very seriously indeed, had arranged for guards—sans armor, in case the Ro took offense, but armed nonetheless.

One of those guards wandered over to Mac as Nik and the alien began a heated argument over monitoring equipment to leave in the room, the alien, predictably, opting for none. "Didn't you get your stuff, Mac?" he asked, taking up some wall space of his own.

"Hi, Sing-li." Mac looked up at the tall man. "Yes, thank you. More than I imagined, in fact. Nice work."

"Good. You had me worried."

She lifted a brow. "I did? Why?"

"Didn't think you'd willingly stay dressed like that."

Mac stood away from the wall to stare at him. "Why—" then she grinned. "I don't wear coveralls all the time, you know."

"Could have fooled us."

"Obviously not," she said, shaking her head. "Let's say this place is a little intimidating for my usual gear. Besides," she held out her arms to show off the well-tailored jacket, "this came with the room."

He grinned back. "Goes with the hair."

Self-consciously, Mac ran her fingers through the downlike stuff where her wound had been. "Thanks. I think." She put her back to the wall again, companionably close to Sing-li. "Nice to see a friend."

"Nice to see you, too, Mac. But here?" He lowered his voice. "This is pretty intense stuff. The Sinzi don't let many Humans see it."

"Trust me," Mac said fervently, "I didn't ask for the privilege." *Unless one counted sneaking in, but she didn't see any point going into detail.*

Battle of wills resolved, Nik approached them, leaving the alien to complain, loudly, but wisely in something other than Instella. "Jones?" he asked, giving the other man a searching look. "What are you doing here?"

"Just checking on our Mac," the guard said with a nod. "I'll get back to my post."

" 'Our Mac,' " Nik repeated, raising an eyebrow at her.

"He's from Base," she explained.

That almost drew a smile. "You can't just adopt my field operatives, Mac."

She shrugged, then wrapped her arms around herself to stop the motion from becoming a shiver. "Nik, I know what I saw."

Nik's eyes grew shadowed. He looked over his shoulder at the tank, where the alien's staff were busy setting up their devices, then back to her. "The marks look the same to me, too, given the difference in material. But scratches in coral aren't enough—especially in there. It could be coincidence."

" 'In there' they should be more than enough!" Trying to keep her voice down, Mac only succeeded in producing an impassioned growl. "The Ro live in no-space, Nik."

"And seem to move around in normal space just fine. Why hang out in a bowl of fish?"

"It's more than that—and you know it. The Sinzi built this thing. That means it could be new to the Ro. We've no idea what that might mean."

Nik held up his hands. It wasn't quite surrender. "I know I've done all I can, Mac. You need to go. He's awake." One of his hands gestured a summons. "Jones?"

"Still here."

"New orders. Please accompany 'our Mac' to her destination. Stay at the door until relieved by me personally, or she comes out." Nik considered the other man, then added so quietly Mac could barely hear. "She's in your care, Sing-li. Priority One."

"Priority One," Jones echoed, his lips tightening. The look he sent Mac was worried. "Something I should know, Nik?"

"Right now—only that there may be a threat. Full gear when

you get the opportunity. Meanwhile, don't take chances. Any doubt—act first and I'll back you." Nik reached out and fluffed her newly grown hair. "Oh, and trust Mac."

"Thanks," she said dryly.

"Don't mention it. Are we clear, Sing-li?"

"Crystal, Nik."

With her new nursemaid looming at her side, Mac headed for Parymn's cell, Nik remaining behind to supervise. She wasn't sure if she felt frustrated they hadn't found incontrovertible evidence of the Ro, or relieved.

In either case, she was glad of Sing-li's substantial presence. The empty white corridors of the consulate were no impediment to creatures able to hide in plain sight.

Her bag still sat beside the door. Mac picked it up, then hesitated before entering. "Do you want me to have them bring you a chair?" she asked.

Sing-li, who'd already stationed himself to one side, shook his head. "I'm used to being on my feet," he assured her. "Worked way station customs before this." His finger tapped the large weapon he carried. "I'll be here if you need me."

"That's good to know," she told him, meaning it.

Then Mac went into the room, closing the door behind her.

To be immediately greeted by a bellowed: "Where have you been, Mackenzie Winifred Elizabeth Wright Connor Sol?"

Someone was definitely on the mend, she thought, hoping the door was soundproof. The floor wasn't. The Dhryn, on his feet, arms folded, was broadcasting in the lower ranges as well. *Probably something disparaging about her eating habits,* Mac decided.

There was no one else in the room, unless you counted those watching and recording. Mac preferred to ignore that aspect as much as possible. She dug into her bag, producing a handful of small rings she'd found among her belongings. They were for banding ravens and their golden shine was to help an observer spot them, but she trusted Parymn Ne Sa Las wouldn't know the difference. "I brought you something, *Erumisah*," Mac told him, opening the cell door and walking inside. "Here."

He took the rings in his hand, eyes cold, then turned his palm downward so they dropped and danced on the floor. "I want to be released from this place. Now."

Mac didn't bother bringing out the "cosmetics" she'd found in the Sinzi washroom. "This is the only room protected from the Ro," she snapped.

Brymn had shrieked and tried to run at that name. *There had been,* Mac recalled quite vividly, *a moment of alien hysterics.* But Parymn was made of sterner stuff. He merely tightened his arms as if their folding was somehow a defense against his kind's greatest fear. "You are sure, Mackenzie Winifred Elizabeth Wright Connor Sol?"

"Yes."

Magnanimously, as if granting her a favor, "Then I will stay."

Someone had added a boldly striped carpet in every color but yellow to the cell's furnishings, along with a Human-suited stool. Mac made a mental note to ask for a proper chair, but perched on it anyway. Her feet didn't quite touch the floor—*of course*—but there was a rung to support them. Parymn sat as well.

Mac took a quick breath, then blew it out between pursed lips. *Where to start?* She hoped Nik would arrive soon. This "interrogation" business was well over her head. Emily would be better at it.

Her stool. Her alien. Mac settled herself. "What truth does the Progenitor seek, Parymn Ne Sa Las?"

"I do not wish to think of it." The pat Dhryn phrase for a forbidden topic.

A little soon for that. Mac frowned. "Where is the Progenitor?"

"I do not wish to think of it."

Was it because she'd invoked the Ro? Or was Parymn being honest with her? *In either case, Em, not helpful.*

"*Erumisah,* you were the one sent by the Progenitor to talk to me. You must answer my questions."

Parymn drew himself up, clearly offended. "I must do nothing."

Mac opened her mouth to argue. At that same instant, Parymn's seventh hand slipped out from the others, striking at his upper shoulder like a snake, leaving a blue gash behind. "Aieee!" he cried, rocking back and forth, his eyes wide and staring. "No! No!"

"What's wrong?" she demanded, dismayed. *Was he going mad?*
Another strike, another gash. Another cry of anguish.

Mac gripped the stool. "Parymn—stop it!" She almost called for
help. *Almost.*

The blue-stained hand hovered before the Dhryn's eyes, as if
controlled by something else. He spoke, the words monotonous
and low, like a chant. "I am become . . . I am become . . . I am become . . ."

Become what? Mac leaned forward—afraid but fascinated. It was
the way she felt whenever a grizzly came so close it crossed that
line, the line beyond which she knew she had no chance to run and
she had to wait on its motives, not hers, her life held by no more
than skin. But to be there, to see such a creature, to be part of its
world . . . "Become what?" she breathed.

"No! I am Parymn Ne Sa Las!" A strike, a gash. "I am Parymn
Ne Sa!" Another. His white silk was soaking up fluid, growing
streaked with blue. "I am Parymn Ne!" Drops flew everywhere as
a slash opened one cheek, staining the carpet as the Dhryn chanted
more quickly, urgently. "I am Parymn! No! I am become—" A
pause. The seventh arm slipped back to its resting place. His entire
body seemed to adjust itself, as if relaxing into a more comfortable
fit.

Then, "I am the Vessel."

17

TRANSFORMATION AND TRIAL

MAYBE ANCHEN was right, and the Dhryn insane. Mac began calculating the distance to the cell door. "The Vessel?" she repeated.

"Yes." Parymn's voice—it had changed somehow, becoming higher-pitched, smoother, *familiar*.

Mac stared. "Who—who are you?"

"I am the Vessel," the Dhryn said again, gently. His small lips formed a smile. "Greetings, Mackenzie Winifred Elizabeth Wright Connor Sol. You have done well."

It couldn't be. But it was. "Thank you—Progenitor," Mac acknowledged. "It is you, isn't it?"

A graceful, somehow feminine gesture of three hands. "In a limited sense. I gifted Parymn Ne Sa Las with a minute portion of myself. This is our way, when one Progenitor must travel to another, to exchange information, to debate or discuss. Are you troubled by this?"

The Progenitor's body filled a cavern—it was a world unto itself, covered with a dust made of new life, enriched by blue ponds replenished by feeder-Dhryn. Yet her face had been like Parymn's, golden-eyed, expressive. Mac swallowed hard. "What of Parymn Ne Sa Las?"

The lips turned downward, the great eyes winked closed, then open. "*Grathnu.* He will be remembered as Parymn Ne Sa Las Marsu. These names will be inscribed in the corridor of my ship." The Dhryn clapped two hands together.

His protests, the tearing of his own flesh. She'd watched Parymn sacrifice himself, here and now, and done nothing. *Alien ways,* Mac chided herself. Who was she to denounce them? *Hard enough to follow without a game plan, Em.*

"It was an honor to know him," she said, at a loss for anything more.

The Dhryn—Mac couldn't think of another name yet—folded his arms again in that intricate pattern. "We have little time, *Lamisah.* What has happened since I was sent? Have you heard from others? Has the Great Journey begun?"

"Mac." From behind—with her. Human and anxious. "Are you all right? What's going on?"

"Your pardon," Mac told the Dhryn, then turned to look up at Nik. He was flushed, as though he'd run some distance and quickly—doubtless alerted by some watcher that the Dhryn was slicing himself, with her in range. "Not now," she urged. "Things have become—complicated." *There was an understatement, Em.*

Tense. Sharp. "You've his blood on your face."

Mac wiped her cheek, looked down at her blue-coated fingers in surprise. "I'll clean up later," she assured him. "We're fine."

"Fine!" Nik took her arm in a tight grip, as if preparing to pull her from the stool by force if necessary. "He's losing it again." Urgent and low. "You aren't safe in here!"

"I'm safer here than out there," she retorted, giving her arm an impatient tug to free it. "Let go of me, Nik. I know what I'm doing."

"You haven't proved that to me," fiercely. "The Dhryn's changed. Something's different about him. We need the med team in here—"

He was good, Em. To recognize the switch from Parymn to the Vessel from body language and tone? Mac was impressed.

Not that it was saving time.

She grimaced. "I don't suppose if I asked you to trust me, to just leave us alone, you'd do it."

"I trust you to be stubborn," he replied, eyes dark behind their lenses. "To take chances with your own safety. Not a good combination, Mac. You're too valuable to risk."

She made a rude noise. "I'm valuable only when I'm doing the job you're interfering with, Mr. Trojanowski."

"You know better than that."

Mac shrugged, her own temper keeping her from anything more gracious. "There's no need for concern—or a med team. This—" she nodded at the wounded Dhryn, who was waiting, if not patiently, then at least quietly, "—is normal." *Not the word she'd initially planned.*

"In what possible way is cutting your own flesh normal?"

She lifted one eyebrow, considering the question. Had the cuts been Parymn's futile protest against the coming death of his personality, or the Vessel's cue to emerge and take over? Or was the self-damage completely unconnected—the body's involuntary reaction to the very odd things happening in the Dhryn's mind? "I've no idea," Mac said at last, keeping it honest. "The psychologists can work out the details later, but essentially the person who came here, who spoke to me earlier today, has been—replaced—by another personality. Nik, I watched Parymn Ne Sa Las sacrifice himself. It's *grathnu,* but of the mind, not the flesh. He acquired the name 'Marsu.' "

It spoke volumes to his experience with the non-Human that Nik's first reaction wasn't the scorn or disbelief Mac half expected. "Then who is this?" he asked.

"I'm not sure 'who' is the right way to put it," she countered. "Because Dhryn Progenitors can't physically visit one another, they imbue one of their *erumisah,* a decision-maker like Parymn, with something of themselves, their personality. I can't begin to guess the mechanism—for all I know, *erumisah* grow so used to their Progenitor's way of thinking, they somehow switch to it and abandon their own. It doesn't matter now. This Dhryn," Mac nodded to the silent alien, "is now such a Vessel. From what I've learned— which isn't much yet—I believe he is meant to convey information from his Progenitor. He's able to carry on a conversation that's consistent with what I remember of his Progenitor's nature and wishes. He's very much Her, in a way I can't explain, Nik."

"A living message," he said, a look of awe on his face. "A biological, preprogrammed, interactive message. Remarkable."

"And impatient," Mac nudged. "Can I get back to talking with him now?"

"Yes. Yes, of course." Nik studied the Dhryn, seeming distracted. *It was,* Mac judged, *a reasonable reaction.*

Then the Dhryn hooted softly. "I see he should know better than to argue with you, my *lamisah.*"

Feeling as if she moved in slow motion, Mac swiveled her head to meet a pair of golden eyes. "You understood what we said?" she asked in disbelief, careful to speak Dhryn. "The language of the not-Dhryn?"

A regal nod. "Of course. A Progenitor must not rely on translation, *Lamisah.*"

A rock and a hard place moment, Em, Mac told herself. Aloud, in Dhryn: "Do you trust me?"

"You are Dhryn. Of course I trust you, Mackenzie Winifred Elizabeth Wright Connor Sol."

More like a crossing the chasm on a swaying cable bridge moment, Mac thought, *an old, decrepit, untrustworthy bridge.*

Nik stood so close she could feel his body heat, a possibly insane Dhryn bled at her feet, and her backside was all but paralyzed from the uncomfortable stool.

She had to decide. Now.

The Ro. They were here, or they were coming. Mac felt it in her bones. The situation wasn't stable or safe. And if Anchen or the Ministry learned anyone could talk to their guest, anyone at all, Mac would be back upstairs, waiting. On the outside.

No. Not again.

Mac gave herself a shake. *Decision made.* Until she had the answers she was after, *until she had Emily,* this Dhryn was hers alone. No one, not the Sinzi-ra, not even Nik, was going to get in the way.

"Vessel, give no sign that you understand anything but what I say in Dhryn. Please. They will take me away from you."

"I would not permit it."

Mac shook her head. "You wouldn't have a choice. Trust me. And—" she added, struck by a sudden, better thought. "Trust this Human, Nikolai Piotr Trojanowski. If ever he comes to you alone and says my name, speak to him in his language. Consider him as your *lamisah* as well. Will you do this for me?"

A clap. "I take the name Nikolai Piotr Trojanowski into my keeping. An honor. Of course, I will do what you say. This is, my *lamisah*, a strange and unsettling place."

"Yes," Mac agreed. "It is." She climbed down from the stool. "Stay if you wish, Nik," she told him calmly, in Instella, careful not to look at him. *Em always said she had the worst face for poker.* "You might want to grab a chair, though. I've a feeling this is going to take a while." She sat cross-legged on the carpet in front of the Dhryn, avoiding the spots of blood.

That neutral voice. "If you're staying, so am I." She felt, more than saw, Nik sit beside her on the floor.

The Dhryn towered over them both, his great yellow eyes warm and curious. *Amazing how like the Progenitor's his every expression had become,* Mac thought with awe. On impulse, she held out her hand. Immediately, the Vessel put his into it. The opposing fingers, three in total, were as warm, rubbery, and muscular as Mac remembered. Brymn's hand had been thus. The fingers gripped, very gently, then withdrew. "We have no time," the Dhryn reminded Mac.

She nodded, swallowing hard. "Yes. I'm sorry. Vessel. Is that what I should call you?"

"It is what I am."

"You want to know what happened since you were sent. There's no easy way to say it. Other Progenitors have destroyed inhabited worlds, taken all life from them."

The Dhryn frowned. "This cannot be."

"It is," Mac said earnestly. "You must believe me. Millions—billions of not-Dhryn have died already."

He reared up, giving her a suspicious look. "Why would we do such a thing?" Then, more kindly: "I see that you are confused, *Lamisah*. The not-Dhryn kill one another. Dhryn do not take life."

Confused covered it from all sides, she thought and turned to Nik. "He doesn't believe me, that other Dhryn have been attacking worlds. I'm trying to explain, but—"

His eyes were guarded as he looked to the Dhryn and back to her. "How specific do you want to be?"

"There's no time to waste."

"In that case—here." Nik pulled out his imp and activated its 'screen, setting a display to hover at eye level in front of the Dhryn.

Ships appearing at a transect. A confusion of attackers and defenders. Mac could barely make out which was which, except that the Dhryn seemed intent above all on reaching the planet, squandering tactical advantage in order to drop their smaller ships—that appalling number of smaller ships—ships that produced a green rain—

Mac wanted to close her eyes but couldn't. The images were fragmented, nightmarish. Most were brief, as if the ships doing the observing were under assault themselves.

"Aiieeeeee!" The Vessel's cry bounced around the room. He surged to his feet, backing away from the images, hands out as if to block them. "Aieeeeeee!"

Turning off his screen, Nik looked at Mac. "We can't assume it's shock—it could be his reaction to the Dhryn ships being destroyed."

She scowled back. "I know Her—him—better than that."

"Careful, Mac."

Rather than argue, Mac shrugged and switched back to the *oomling* tongue. "This is what has happened. It's still happening, in other systems. That's why we're all here, Vessel. Why you're here. To try and stop more loss of life."

"This not the Way." With an undertone of despair. "I don't understand."

She'd been afraid of that. "Neither do we," Mac admitted. "What should be the Way?"

"The Way?" A calmer, but puzzled look. "All that is Dhryn answers the Call. Then the Great Journey takes us Home. All that is Dhryn must move."

"Why?" Mac held her breath. "Why do you move now?"

"I do not," the Dhryn answered. *Was he being literal?* Mac worried. Then: "I believe—I hope—that others—do not. We must resist this Call if we are to survive."

"What Call?" Without thought, Mac reached for Nik's hand and found it. He didn't interrupt or ask why. "Whose?"

The question sent the Dhryn rocking back and forth, arms

wrapped around his middle. Blue kept flowing from the gashes, and Mac worried how much he could spare. "We do not know," he said finally. "The oldest stories passed from Progenitor to Progenitor tell of a time when the Call came over generations of *oomlings,* that new Dhryn were born readied for it; able to grow stronger, larger in preparation. The urge to move would then spread through a line-age like breathing into a body. Inevitable, natural. The Great Jour-ney would spend all but the Progenitors, who would await the future, remembering the Way home again. So the stories say."

"That's not what's happening now."

"No, *Lamisah.* I fear what is happening now is not only the deaths of others, but of all that is Dhryn."

"Is this why you told me to run?" Mac remembered that mo-ment when she and Brymn had balanced on the palm of the Prog-enitor and heard Her horrified warning. "You said my species should run before the gates between worlds closed again."

"As we ran to Haven," the Vessel said, a reverberation in the floor attesting to some emotion. "Were it not for the great buried ships that awaited us, to shelter us from the rain, to feed us, all that is Dhryn would have perished as the rest."

The rest? *Hundreds of other species. Entire worlds, scoured to dust.* Mac swallowed. Suddenly, their differences overwhelmed her, the blue skin, the bony ridged face, the arms, maimed and moving rest-lessly. Even the smell. If it hadn't been for the solid, so-Human, pres-ence at her side, she might not have dared go on: "You mean the other species in the Chasm. Did the Dhryn consume them, too?"

"Dhryn do not consume other life. It is not the Way."

Around to that again. Mac frowned. It wasn't that the Dhryn defined life as only including themselves. Brymn Las had certainly understood there were other living things, that other worlds than Haven were homes.

In the pause, the grip on her hand tightened a fraction. "Mac."

She glanced sideways at him. "It's still complicated."

"That was Dhryn, Mac."

Blushing, she took a moment to be sure what she was about to speak. "Sorry, Nik," in English. "It's still complicated."

"I understand that. But we need something tangible, a place to start. Ask if this Dhryn, the Vessel, can help us communicate with others. Arrange negotiations."

Doubtful, Mac nodded. "Vessel," she began, "we'd like to speak to the other Dhryn—"

"How?"

"That's what we'd like you to tell us."

A lift and fall of six arms. "Within a lineage, only *erumisah* may speak to their Progenitor without invitation. You have not yet committed sufficient *grathnu* to be so elevated, my *lamisah*. And only a Vessel may approach another Progenitor."

Mac repeated this, in English, to Nik. He nodded thoughtfully. "What about the colonial Dhryn, those who lived away from Haven and the Progenitors? They were accustomed to com systems—many traded freely within the systems of other IU species."

She hurried to translate. The Vessel gave a soft sigh. "The great ships launched without their return. They have no Progenitors to guide them. They are lost, Mackenzie Winifred Elizabeth Wright Connor Sol."

"Lost as in dead—or lost as in they've become a separate faction?" Nik responded when he heard this.

"Do you want me to ask?" Mac said, rubbing her temple.

He gave her a worried look. "English."

It had sounded right. "It's getting harder to keep it all straight," she confessed in that tongue, ashamed.

"You're doing fine, Mac. You aren't trained for this." Nik shook his head. "I'd like to give you a break, but . . ."

"I know." Mac stretched her arms and spine. "I'm okay. Do you want the question about factions?"

"No. We'll deal with that later. It's the Progenitor ships we need to stop. Try and get a time frame. How long do we have between attacks?"

Good question. Mac nodded. "Vessel—" she paused to be sure what language her tongue was shaping.

"The great ships were not prepared for the Great Journey," the Dhryn answered—too soon, Mac realized. *Nik didn't miss a thing; he wouldn't miss this.* Sure enough, he was sitting straighter, starting to frown.

Damn.

This time, she grabbed for his hand deliberately. "I know what I'm doing," she insisted, trying to convey the same message through look, words, and touch. *Trust me. Be patient*.

His fingers squeezed hers again, twice, before letting go. She'd have been more relieved if his face hadn't worn its patented 'spy on the prowl' expression.

Later would be soon enough. Mac turned to the Vessel. "What does that mean—the ships weren't prepared?"

"Before my time, we broke with the tradition of keeping each ship ready to depart. We believed it a meaningless duplication to have food production in every ship, when there were new, more modern facilities above ground. So most was centralized in a few key locations. If the Progenitor is not producing *oomlings*, and adults fast, it is possible to go for a considerable time without a new source. But . . . that which is Dhryn must not starve."

"Nik," Mac translated quickly, her mouth dry, "the Dhryn can't grow their food, not on every ship. They'll need an outside source. Given their numbers—probably often."

His lips pressed into a grim line. "Noted. How many per ship? Weaponry? Insystem speed? We need details—as much as you can get."

Before the Vessel could open his mouth again—and confirm Nik's growing suspicions, Mac said quickly: "Don't answer his questions. Not yet. We need to talk about the Call, first. Was it the Ro?"

"The Ro? The Ro are the Enemy, Mackenzie Winifred Elizabeth Wright Connor Sol." A humoring tone, as if she were young and lost. "They do not Call the Dhryn. They steal and terrorize our *oomlings*. They wish us gone. As, I fear, do all not-Dhryn. Including this one." An arm ending in a stump pointed at Nik.

"What we wish is not to be food for Dhryn," Mac snapped back.

"I do not consume not-Dhryn," the Vessel replied. "Others do not."

"You saw for yourself. Dhryn are doing this."

"Aiieeeee! Yes, but I do not understand." More rocking. "Do not speak of it."

"For now. The *oomlings*," Mac circled back. "Why would the Ro go to such effort to steal them? If they wanted to harm you, they could have destroyed Haven any time they wished."

"To threaten the *oomlings* is to threaten all that is Dhryn." The tone flat and with a hint of threat itself.

Nik heard it and reacted. "What's wrong, Mac?"

"Nothing," she snapped, then waved an apology. To the Vessel: "Why do some Dhryn consume other species and other Dhryn do not?"

"I do not know. In the Great Journey, all that is Dhryn must follow the Taste."

"Scouts," Mac crowed triumphantly. "I was right! The disappearances earlier—they were caused by Dhryn scouts, weren't they? They were collecting the Taste of what was on various worlds, bringing it back to the Progenitors. Those that digest and feed—" somehow, she didn't shudder.

"Impossible."

"What do you mean?"

"The mouths and hands of the Dhryn must stay with the Progenitor. They do not exist elsewhere. They have no purpose elsewhere."

"Then how do you find the Taste to follow?" Mac asked, thinking it a reasonable question.

The Dhryn's mouth turned downward at the edges. *Disapproval*. "The Taste is not found. It is that which the Progenitor requires on the Great Journey. All that is Dhryn then follows the Taste."

Mac sighed. Somewhere, she was convinced, buried in the mythic, convoluted language, there had to be a greater truth than she was hearing, some clue. "Vessel, I—"

She was interrupted by Nik, as he rose to his feet. "We need to talk. Now." He stood, looking down at her.

"I'm going to consult with my companion," Mac told the Dhryn as she stood, too. "Don't react to what we say to one another. It is important."

"As you wish, *Lamisah*."

Nik led her a few steps from the Dhryn, but didn't leave the cell, as she'd expected. "What's going on, Mac?" he demanded in a low, urgent voice.

"We're a little stuck on aspects that seemed to be fixed in Dhryn myth. I'm getting stuck," Mac corrected. "Maybe you can help me—"

"Forget that. What did he say about weapons, deployments, their ships?"

"The Vessel?" Flustered, Mac blurted: "He doesn't know things like that. I'm trying to find out what's controlling the Dhryn. Where they go. Why—"

"You didn't ask, did you?" Nik didn't let her finish, a new edge to every word. "Mac, that information's crucial. There are worlds filled with beings needing help now. All the rest—the whys, the past—we don't have time for your curiosity!" He took a deep breath, as if tamping down his temper. "From now on, I want you to translate for me. Word for word. Nothing more."

It hurt, seeing his anger, knowing she was the cause.

Couldn't be allowed to matter, Em.

"I can't do that," Mac told him levelly. "You aren't asking the right questions."

His eyes, now stone-cold, flicked up to the vidbots and down again. *As if she'd forget their audience.* "You study salmon, Dr. Connor. I'd like to hear how that makes you an expert in the gathering of strategic information."

"What strategic information?" she fumed, losing her own temper. "The Dhryn are being led around the universe like a hungry bear following a bait bucket. What would you ask the bear, Nik? How long his claws are? How sharp his teeth? His ultimate intentions toward fish heads?"

Mac watched as it hit him, gave the tiniest possible nod as Nik's eyes widened, felt a dizzying wave of relief when he didn't say it out loud, as he realized the consequences if the Ro could somehow hear. *He sees the real question,* she thought triumphantly.

Who's carrying the bait?

Then his eyes narrowed again. "It doesn't matter what theories you're investigating. We need that information. Either you ask what I want you to, now, or we'll find another way." From his grim expression, she knew exactly what he meant. *He'd tell others the Vessel understood Instella.*

"You can't!" Mac gasped. "Not now. I'm close. I know I am."

"Close to what? You can't make decisions for the IU, Mac." Trying another tactic, Nik put his hands on her shoulders, bent to look into her eyes. Quietly: "There'll be time later for your questions, Mac. Please."

Unfortunately, it wasn't a tactic all understood.

A bellow rattled the metal stool. "Release my *lamisah!*" The Dhryn rushed toward them, his head lowered in threat, three hands rising as if to reach for Nik.

Everything happened so fast Mac was never sure of the order. Nik shoved her aside, but she managed to twist from that force, using its momentum to half fall toward the angry alien. Nik was shouting something she didn't hear—likely frustrated and directed at her—but Mac was intent on only one thing.

Sure enough, the Dhryn coughed.

She slapped her hand over his mouth and pressed it there as hard as she could, shouting herself.

"Stop, *Lamisah*! He wasn't hurting me!"

The sideways figure-eight pupils of the Dhryn dilated, as if to encompass her so close. His three hands had automatically grabbed to stop her from colliding with him. She winced at their tight hold—*there'd be bruises*—but didn't release her own. She said more calmly: "It's okay, Vessel."

She could feel his muscles ease. The convulsive retch already underway subsided. Still, enough acid spurted between the Dhryn's lips to dissolve most of the pseudoskin from the palm of her hand. *So much for stirring acid,* Mac thought inanely. She was careful not to touch any of it with clothing or flesh as she let go and backed away.

"Careful!" Mac admonished as an equally powerful Human hand took hold of her and pulled. *More bruises,* she thought fatalistically. She held her acid-coated fingers as far from Nik as she could. Drips hit the carpet, sending up smoky plumes. "It would help," she snapped, as he released her, "if you both calmed down." For the benefit of watchers, she repeated it in the *oomling* tongue.

Almost casually, Nik dropped something from his palm into his pocket. His face was pale and set; a muscle jumped along his jaw. *He'd been about to kill the Vessel,* she realized numbly. *To save her.*

"Don't get close." His warning to Mac; he should have listened. She could see the bleak awareness in his eyes, the shame of letting his emotions make a choice. They both knew the Dhryn had to live, even if it killed her before his eyes.

He wouldn't make the same mistake again. She saw that, too, and acknowledged it with a half smile.

"Lami-sah . . ." The alien's voice was weak. Mac turned even as he stumbled. Nik reached out to support him before he fell. The Dhryn flinched, but couldn't avoid him, letting the Human guide him to a sitting posture.

"Nik meant no harm to me, Vessel. None to you. Please. Don't worry." Mac used her real hand to stroke the Vessel's forehead, feeling the shivers coursing through his body. A body, she realized, that had been through a great deal, especially for a Dhryn as old as Parymn must have been. She looked at Nik: "He needs rest."

Their eyes met over the Dhryn's blood-slicked back. "So do you," Nik agreed. "And to clean up that hand. I'll give you both as much as I can. Half an hour, hopefully more."

" 'A Dhryn is robust, or a Dhryn is not,' " she quoted, giving Nik a nod of agreement.

But, as she listened to the Vessel's labored breathing, Mac hoped she was wrong.

- Encounter -

That which is Dhryn accepts the Great Journey.
  That which is Dhryn must *move*. It is the Way.
  The path changes more often now. It is the Way as well.
  As before, the Call is heard. Irresistible . . . dominant . . . *urgent*.
  That which is Dhryn must obey.
  It is survival.

18

MEETING AND MAYHEM

"I TOLD YOU to run, *Lamisah*. Why did you stay?" Kindly. As though fond.

Those had been the words.

She'd answer, but her mouth was sealed.

She'd run, but her limbs were wrapped in a net. Mac struggled, feeling the bonds around her tightening, feeling them *burn*. Tears ran down her cheeks, tears of helpless rage.

"You never learn, do you, Mac?" *Emily*. "Trust. Friendship. Coin of the realm, dear girl. Nothing more. Survival's what counts."

Hard to breathe. Mac lunged out with her bound feet, trying to find a target.

"Getting late, Mac. You really should run. It's the only choice you have."

Light, sudden, blinding, from everywhere at once. Reflecting from the hard silver of tiny ships. Thousands upon thousands.

Mac fought for freedom even as the rain began to fall, even as her feet dissolved, her legs, her . . .

"I told you to run, *Lamisah*."

Jerking awake, Mac rested her forehead against the back of the Sinzi shower, letting the water from three jets pound her shoulder blades, letting the steam and roar keep the universe at bay for a few minutes more.

She hadn't meant to fall asleep.

Even less to dream.

Mac turned, letting the water hit her face. The Dhryn's blood and acid was gone; the nightmare wouldn't wash away. *Something she knew full well.*

"Time to get back, Em," she said, licking drops from her lips as she hit the control to start the dryer. "Wonder what time it is." Late, for sure.

Nik and Sing-li had brought her here, back to the Atrium. A swift, dizzying ride up three steps on a platform, a choice of rooms to suit any body plan. Staff, of course, ready to offer her whatever she might need. A jelly-chair, a table with sandwiches, juice. This shower. *She wasn't the only one who worked late down here,* Mac thought. She'd spend some time huddled over her workscreen, trying to catch up while the Dhryn rested, listening to notes from her team. When she'd begun to feel sleepy, she'd stopped trying to pull sense from fragments of disparate information, and went for a shower to wake up.

That hadn't worked.

Dry, she pulled on her clothes. The staff had performed their discreet magic again. There'd been blood on the beautiful jacket, acid damage to a sleeve, but while she'd showered, it had been replaced by another, this time red. What mattered was her imp was in its pocket. Mac dropped into the chair, pushing still-damp curls from her forehead, and checked for messages.

Nothing new. "I've been cut off, have I?" she muttered, closing her 'screen and pocketing the device. "We'll see about that—in the morning."

One more minute. Mac leaned her head back, careful to keep her eyes open and fixed on the ceiling, breathing slow and steady through her nostrils.

Not surprisingly, given her past experience with such things, that was when a quiet knock sounded on the door, followed by the door cracking open. "Mac?"

Sing-li. Doubtless looming outside since she'd arrived. "She's not here," she told him.

"You dressed?" he asked, coming in anyway. He'd changed into full armor, but left his visor open.

It let her see his face, now set in sober lines, so she swallowed what she'd intended to say. She sat up. "What is it?"

"The Sinzi-ra wants your report—now."

"Here?" Mac lifted her eyebrows.

"No. There's a meeting of the Admin council for the Gathering underway. The major players. She wants you to report to all of them."

"I hate meetings," Mac informed him. *Especially when she didn't know what to say.*

Sing-li's teeth flashed in a quick smile. "I remember. But I can't see you skipping out of this one, Mac. We'd better hurry. They're waiting for you."

"I'm sure they are."

"Oh, Mac? Nik sent you this." Sing-li held out a long supple glove. Mac took it with a nod, pulling it over the now-exposed workings of her left hand and wrist.

As gestures went, she thought with an inward smile, *it wasn't bad.*

Her guide led the way. Rather than a platform, he took her via three lifts to the level with the door they'd used, then through that door to the corridor. Once there, Mac hesitated outside the Dhryn's room. "I should check on—things."

Sing-li shook his head. "He's asleep—or unconscious. Nik said to tell you you'll be notified."

Answering the question of whether her companion was kept fully briefed, Mac told herself.

They took the door to the next corridor where two guards, neither Human, now stood watch on either side of the entrance to the tank room. Mac restrained a shudder as she passed it, moving closer to Sing-li. They turned right with the corridor.

Another series of plain doors. The place was a maze of featureless white. *Or was it?* "Just a minute," Mac said, stopping. "I want to try something." She reached into her bag and took out her imp.

"Mac, you don't want to be late. There's no time for this."

"There's always time for a quick experiment, Sing-li," she assured him absently, setting up her 'screen to show a chromatic display of the walls in front of them. With a slide of her fingers, Mac removed the filtering from the display.

Silvery ghosts, representing ultraviolet reflections, appeared over the normal image. The white walls were aglow with symbols and images. Portraits, schematics, a few rather nice landscapes. And each door in sight had a label. Not Instella, but definitely a script. "Thought so," Mac exclaimed with satisfaction. This was only an approximation. *One thing for sure.* The world of the Sinzi and her staff was neither plain nor white.

Sing-li stepped into the area she was imaging. His initials glowed on his chest and Mac nodded her understanding. "I take it the Sinzi-ra doesn't like faceless strangers."

"Bad as you, Mac," he agreed, grinning. "As for the walls? You could have asked for a look." He tapped his visor meaningfully with a finger.

Mac put away her imp. "I prefer to experiment," she informed him. "Which one?" She waved at the doors.

It was the third. Sing-li opened it for her, but remained outside as she stepped through, taking his post.

"Greetings, Mac," from Anchen, rising from her seat at the head of a long, well-populated table.

There was always, Mac thought glumly, *a long, well-populated table.*

The Sinzi's fingers indicated the position opposite her, at the far end. There was a second empty seat, halfway up one side. *Neutral turf.* Mac eyed it longingly, but obediently took her place at center stage.

She'd like a moment to take notes on who sat where. Hard enough to keep twenty-five Humans straight, let alone assorted sapients. Her eyes went to Nik, at Anchen's left. He gave her a comforting look. *One ally.* He faced the N'Not'k, Genny P'tool. Mac spared an instant to wonder if she'd try footsies with him under the table. *Probably not. The ambience was pretty far into stress range.* Bernd Hollans sat midway down the right side, facing the empty seat. An Imrya, likely the one who'd accompanied Anchen to Parymn's cell, was at his side, taking notes already. No other Humans, not that Mac expected more. Two beings in full environment suits. She'd love a closer look, but they were near Nik.

Cinder sat to Mac's left. *Perhaps another ally. Perhaps a complication.* Mac gave her a nod and received one in return.

The rest were strangers. She had to assume they represented the innermost circle of the Interspecies Union. Those who had set up this Gathering.

Those would decide the fate of the Dhryn.

She was so out of her depth, she might as well be in the Sinzi's tank, Mac thought despairingly.

The room itself was square, with four doors set opposite the ends of the table. No ornament visible to Mac's eyes. No other furnishings. The lack drew her eyes back to that last, empty seat.

Mac glanced at Nik. He'd followed her look and now gave an almost imperceptible shrug. *Didn't know either.*

"Are you ready to give us your latest report on the Dhryn, Mac?"

For once, Mac would have preferred "Dr. Connor," which at least sounded reputable. "Yes, Sinzi-ra."

Anchen gestured to the empty seat. "Our remaining participant will join us shortly. Implementation of the Myrokynay's instructions is going very well at last. I'm sure none of us wish to delay it."

Nods, a few grunts, and one of the suited figures pounded the table with a heavy fist. Mac hoped she'd remember how each indicated agreement. Not that she expected much to what she had to say.

"Mac?"

Automatically, she stood up again, resting her fingertips on the table. Real and artificial. The table felt the same to both. Mac pondered the significance of that as she collected herself. "Parymn Ne Sa Las is dead," she said. No one moved or spoke, waiting for her to clarify. This wasn't a group who startled easily. *Good.* "His personality has been replaced."

"By whose?" Anchen prompted, her head tilted to one side as if one of her minds was more keenly interested than the others. Noad the physician, Mac guessed.

Time to make her first choice, Mac told herself. If there were Ro hiding in this room, listening to what was said, dare she risk the truth? But would Nik contradict her if she lied? Had he already given his report? *She hated thinking like a spy even more than meetings.* "His personality has been superseded by another's, called the Vessel. The Vessel is a messenger from a Progenitor, in this case, the one I met on Haven. In practical terms, he is the Progenitor, as She was before Parymn Ne Sa Las Marsu accepted his—fate."

Even the IU's representatives had to mutter among themselves about this. Mac gave them a moment, glancing at Nik for his reaction. Nothing showed beyond the glint of his lenses.

"Continue," Anchen said, silencing the rest. "What does this 'biological message' say?"

"The Progenitor—this particular Progenitor—took damage to her ship during the Ro assault on Haven. She's in hiding. The Vessel doesn't know where—"

"As if it would tell us!"

Mac looked at who'd interrupted. "Dhryn has no word for lie, Mr. Hollans. The Vessel's sole function is to communicate as accurately and completely as possible. That information wasn't supplied for obvious reasons." She looked to the rest. "The Progenitor has a question for us, for the Interspecies Union. She wants to know what's happening to her species."

Someone on the left. "She doesn't know?"

Another moment of choice. Mac licked her lips and nodded to herself. "She knows they have begun what she calls the 'Great Journey.' As far as I could determine, this journey is something cyclic, a shared compulsion, but it hasn't occurred in living memory. The Dhryn weren't expecting it—they hadn't prepared. She doesn't know why they've embarked on it now, only that they have."

A shiver of gold-clad fingers. "Where are they going?"

"Home." Mac held up her hand to stop any questions. "Which doesn't help, I realize. I don't know where the Dhryn 'home' is, if it isn't their world of origin. The Vessel doesn't appear to have that information—maybe the Progenitor Herself doesn't know. However, my team has uncovered evidence supporting an hypothesis that the Dhryn might have been a migratory species. This Great Journey could be just that. In which case—"

"Migration, is it?" a low bass rumble from an alien to Mac's right. "We have beasts who migrate on our planet. They respect no boundary, no law. You cannot train them to avoid farmland. We build fences to protect our crops. When those do not work, we are forced to destroy any herd that trespasses."

Another delegate: "We could dismantle the transects, lock the Dhryn into one system. Trap them."

"Sacrificing the life in that system!" bellowed another. "Whose will you pick? Mine?"

Worse than Preds scrapping over pizza. Mac rapped on the table with her gloved knuckles. The strange sound got their attention. "I wasn't finished," she told them.

"Please continue, Mac." Anchen's eyes took in all those at the table. "There will be no more outbursts."

"If the Dhryn's Great Journey is impelled by a migratory drive," Mac proposed, "it is an adaptation that has helped them survive on a planet, one planet. There, they had a destination—a 'Home'—where they could take advantage of drastic changes in their environment. None of that applies to a space-faring civilization. There's no reason to believe the Dhryn have a real destination anymore, that there is a 'Home' for them to seek.

"If they are responding to an innate drive," she continued, "it may simply compel them to keep moving and moving until their ships fail or they run out of supplies. No matter which happens first, the Dhryn will starve and die." Mac paused. When no one offered comment, she continued: "As that will likely be after they've consumed as many worlds of the IU as they can reach, the Dhryn migration must be stopped as quickly as possible."

"By killing them all!"

"How?" Nik spoke for the first time, face impassive but his voice rising above the muttering. "We don't know where they are, let alone where they are going. If I understand what you're saying, Mac, they could begin picking targets at random. How will we find them then?"

"The Dhryn didn't expect this," Mac reminded them. Another choice that wasn't. *She had to try.* "The Progenitor wants to know why it is happening. Migratory behavior is stimulated to begin by certain cues. And ends. If something outside the Dhryn started them moving—provided that Call—maybe something outside the Dhryn can stop them."

"The assault on their world set them off—that's what started it," offered Hollans. "What we need to do is reach the Myrokynay. They can find the Dhryn—end this."

Another chorus of agreement—from all but Nik, who was watching her.

Brymn hadn't been ready to transform. But he had. *He had.*

The Ro had lied.

Had they done more than that?

"We don't know if that was the stimulus," Mac countered, feeling sweat trickling down her shirt. "After all, there were Dhryn attacks, perhaps by scouts, before the assault on Haven. We need to look more closely."

"The Myrokynay will stop the Dhryn. You have their word."

That voice!

With a wordless cry, Mac was in motion before her eyes fully comprehended what they saw, rushing toward the tall, slim, *familiar* figure standing in the now open doorway behind the N'not'k. She was only dimly aware of Nik surging to his feet, of the excited rumble of voices . . . *None of it mattered.*

"Emily!"

But the face which turned in answer was the image from the Ro message: cheeks sunken, eyes like dark pits, skin cracked and shadowed. Her hair hung limp and dull with filth. Her body? A skeleton, barely filling its mockery of clothing. And the clothing? Torn and ragged, its rents going deeper than fabric, revealing tears in her flesh that held nothing but space and wheeling stars.

Mac didn't hesitate, arms out to gather in her friend.

But the face turned away.

The body walked to the final empty seat at the table, sitting as if nothing and no one else existed.

"The Myrokynay will be gratified you have completed the signaling device," Emily stated in that clear, dead voice. "They will respond to your messages through that medium, and through myself."

She couldn't breathe.

Anchen made a graceful gesture. "It was only with your assistance that we were successful, Dr. Mamani. You have our gratitude."

As if from a great distance, Mac heard her own voice, strange and broken. "Emily—Em? It's me. It's Mac."

Hollans said something; she couldn't hear it, didn't know if it was impatient or kind. Someone, it was Nik, took her arm, gently but firmly, and led her from the room.

Once outside, Mac came to her senses. She whirled and tried to go back. Nik stopped her. "Not now, Mac. Please," he pleaded.

Sing-li hovered. "What's wrong?"

"It's Emily! Didn't you see her?" Mac demanded, struggling wildly against Nik's grip. She freed one hand and struck at his face. He caught the blow, holding her wrist. "She needs a doctor—help me, Sing-li!"

"Nik?" Sing-li was frowning. "What's all this? Dr. Mamani?"

Mac threw her weight back, tried to break free. Nik held on. "Stop it, Mac. Stop! Gods, will you let it go a minute? I don't want to hurt you."

The desperate tone penetrated, when the words meant nothing. Mac shuddered and stood still. "It was Emily."

"I know. I saw. Something's terribly wrong with her. We'll get help—but we can't interrupt them. We can't force her. She's still connected to the Ro, to no-space. Do you understand me, Mac? We have to wait."

Mac stared up at Nik, eyes swimming with tears. "She didn't know me."

He gathered her in his arms like something inexpressibly fragile. "We'll get Emily back," he promised, lips against her hair. "She's alive, Mac. She's here. On Earth. It's a start."

"They've taken too much of her," Mac whispered.

Nik heard. "Let the medical team worry about that." He lifted her chin so Mac had to look at him. "You study salmon, remember?"

"Do I?"

"That's the rumor." Ignoring an interested Sing-li, Nik bent and kissed her on the mouth, once, very soundly. Mac's eyes widened until she felt like an owl. "Go to your quarters, Mac," he said gently.

It was all Mac could do not to look at that door, knowing who was behind it. "I'm in the IU now, not a citizen of Sol, of Earth. You told me I can't—I can't ask for help. But, Nik, I—"

He didn't let her finish. "You don't need to ask. I'll keep an eye on our Dr. Mamani and find out what I can." A flash of something dangerous in his eyes. "Including why her return was kept from the Ministry until now. I don't like surprises, especially from allies." Nik paused. "But, Mac, I'm asking you a favor in return. Please. Go."

She gave in. "You be careful."

"I will. Sing-li?"

"I've got her."

Feeling remarkably like an unwanted parcel—which was infinitely better than feeling like an unwanted friend—Mac let Sing-li escort her to the lift.

"No."

Mac narrowed her eyes. " 'No,' as in you think you can stop me?"

" 'No,' as in you aren't going anywhere without me."

She made an exasperated sound. "You can stand by the door. You like that."

Sing-li looked anything but willing to negotiate. He tapped his weapon. "No."

"Fine." Mac knocked on Mudge's door. "But he's not going to like having you wake him up, too."

"I'll take my chances, Mac."

The left hand door to Mudge's quarters opened a crack. Mac waved at a bleary eyeball.

"Norcoast? What—?" Mudge opened the door the rest of the

way. He wore, Mac noted, managing not to smile, one of the Sinzi's elegant nightgowns.

"May we come in?" she asked.

"We?" Mudge glared at the Ministry guard. "Certainly not. It's three A.M!"

Ignoring his protest, Mac started walking inside. "I know. Hence the chaperon," she told him. "The Sinzi-ra doesn't approve of fraternization."

Blushing furiously, Mudge moved out of the way. Mac and Sing-li followed. "At least let me put something on," their host muttered, hurrying to the other room as fast as he could move through the sand. To his closet, to be exact, closing the door behind him.

Mac studied the place, curious. Sure enough, the room was the mirror-image of hers, right to its impossible table of fish. She noted the arrangement of anemone and corals—same view as hers as well. Feeling slightly foolish, she went to the washroom and grabbed the wrap and extra nightgown she expected would be there. *Not going to explain,* she vowed, aware of Sing-li's rapt attention as she used the garments to cover the table.

But his attention wasn't concerning her compulsion to redecorate. "So, Mac. How long have you and Nik been—?"

Mac's look dared him to continue. Sing-li wisely resumed his task of silent looming. *Something,* she realized, *being in black armor allowed a large Human to do rather well.*

Nik had wanted her back in her room. Mac herself wanted nothing more than her jelly-bed and some time to think—or blissful oblivion. But there wasn't time.

Besides, why should Mudge sleep when she was still awake?

"Now," Mudge blustered, "what's so important it can't wait till dawn at least?" As he said this walking out of a closet, it was less impressive than he'd likely hoped.

"Sit down, Oversight." Mac did the same, but perched close to the edge of the jelly-chair. If she sank into it, she'd likely spend what was left of the night here. "I wanted to be the one to tell you. Emily Mamani's back. She's here, at the consulate."

Mudge knew her face a little too well. "Something's wrong with her."

"Yes. She's been altered by the Ro again. Much more. Physically. Maybe mentally. I don't know the extent of it. She's—" Mac looked up and said in a shaky voice: "—I don't think she's Emily anymore, Oversight."

He harrumphed. Twice. Then: "She's been living with something stranger than any of us can imagine. Give her time to remember herself, her friends."

"That's the rub. There isn't time." Mac waved Sing-li to the other seat. He obeyed, lifting off his helmet. "Oversight, this is Sing-li Jones, from Base. Sing-li, who can hear us right now?" she asked him.

Sing-li raised an eyebrow, but didn't bother with denials. He pulled out his imp. "The transmitter on Mr. Mudge feeds directly to this—nowhere else. Unless something warrants an immediate report, I bundle the recordings and send them to main for analysis and file when I go off shift."

Before Oversight could do more than turn red and begin to sputter, Mac nodded. "Good. Stop recording, on my authority."

Sing-li didn't hesitate. He stood and went to Mudge, who twisted around in alarm. "Oh, hold still," Mac told him.

"This might sting a bit, sir." Sing-li peeled a fingernail-sized patch of what had seemed skin from the back of Mudge's neck. "There."

The look on Mudge's face promised an abundance of pithy memos, once the situation permitted such ordinary means of retribution.

Mac resisted the temptation to feel her own neck. "Do I have one?"

"Not to my knowledge. You're aware of the bioamplifier in your tissues." Mac nodded. "It's concentrated enough of your DNA signature to let us pinpoint your location with reasonable accuracy." Sing-li paused thoughtfully. "Unless you're in a null gravity field."

"Not planning on it," Mac assured him, waving him back to his seat. Then she leaned forward to put her elbows on her knees, studying both men. "I've reached certain conclusions about our situation here," she said. "If I'm wrong? At worst, I'll be sent home as a nuisance. If I'm right?" She pressed her lips together then continued. "If I'm right, and we do nothing about it, the next blow to strike the IU will fall here, at this Gathering, at Earth. And soon."

Sing-li tensed. "So that's why Nik wants me to stick like glue. In that case, you're the logical first target, Mac. We should get you out of here." He started to rise.

"Relax." She gave him a faint smile. "I appreciate your concern and his, Sing-li, but I'm not what's important. It's what I know and what I suspect. I have things to tell you both. I won't risk being the only one who knows outside the Sinzi-ra's inner circle. I can't, for all our sakes."

The two men exchanged grim looks. They understood what she was asking. "Get to it, Norcoast," Mudge grumbled.

"First. There's a Dhryn in the basement of this building, sent by the Progenitor I met on Haven to talk to me."

"About what?" asked Mudge.

"What's happened to their species. They don't understand any more than we do. Oh, there's no doubt the Dhryn are attacking planets. That they're a horrific threat to other living things. But what's the advantage to the Dhryn? I haven't found one—not to the Dhryn. Which made me ask my own question. Are the Dhryn the hands or—" Mac indicated the weapon strapped to Sing-li's leg, "—the tools in someone else's hands?"

You can't be serious," Mudge said, eyes wide. "An entire sentient species?"

Sing-li's lips thinned. "You think the Dhryn are being used as a weapon."

"I think they were made to be one. I think they've been used before, to annihilate the civilizations in the Chasm, then put away in a bottle until needed again."

"By the Ro?"

"By the Ro," Mac nodded. "And who shows up when we finally have our own source of information about the Dhryn? The Ro's puppet: Emily Mamani. Just like she did before, when Brymn came to us." She gave a short, bitter laugh. "You'd think I'd have figured it out sooner, having had practice."

"Guesswork, Norcoast," Mudge pointed out. "Even if you had hard evidence—which you don't, I might add—your feelings about the Ro are no secret. Who here will believe you? They're doing everything they can to welcome the Ro, not defend against them." He brought out his own imp. "I've gone over the messages and daily summaries. Teams are working feverishly on new weapons— mining the transect gates was thankfully abandoned. Dhryn detectors; predictions of where they'll attack next; three groups working on the Dhryn acids and how to create shields—none going well, by the way. Four others preparing defensive simulations. Ten spending their time on evacuation logistics and worst case scenarios—most productive of the lot, if you ask me. And a significant investment in Ro psychology—most of their work," he sighed, "makes the ravings of your ghoul chasers sound sane."

"The Origins Team, Oversight," Mac told him. "We're close. I can feel it. Unensela has findings about the vegetation and ecology that may prove a Dhryn migratory pattern. Others have discovered evidence of outside tampering with Dhryn technological development. All we need is the missing piece—what, if anything, happened to the Dhryn themselves, their physiology." Mac's enthusiasm faded. "And time. Emily helped get the Ro signaling device up and running ahead of schedule. It's on right now, begging for their help with the Dhryn." She paused to rub her eyes with the back of one hand, then was startled by the feel of glove instead of skin. "Believe me, I'd give anything to be wrong. I keep hoping I am. But the Dhryn—everything I know tells me they couldn't have come to exist on their own. And if that's true? The rest makes too much sense to dare ignore."

"What do you want us to do?" This from Sing-li.

Mac looked to Mudge. "You have the room assignments for the members of the team, right?" He nodded. "Wake everyone up. Start with Lyle Kanaci—he can help with the rest. We have work to do."

A familiar scowl. "And where will you be?"

"I'll join you as soon as I can," Mac promised. "We'll wake up Fourteen on the way—I want to talk to him first." She turned to Sing-li. "We should—"

"I don't think so," interrupted Mudge, giving the larger, younger man a disdainful look. "You need protection. I should go with you."

Snooping was one thing; risking himself was another. "You're a fearsome administrator, Oversight," she said gratefully but firmly. "Unusually deft with a paddle, I'll grant you. But I'd better stick with the professional with the large weapon, don't you think?"

He harrumphed. "A P917-multiphasic pulse pistol—pardon, P915, I'd thought it was the newer model—is no substitute for experience."

Sing-li raised his eyebrow again, but didn't say anything; Mac, less tactful, grinned. "Experience?" *He had to be kidding.*

Mudge put on outraged dignity the way anyone else put on a coat. "Experience with you, Norcoast. And your propensity for dashing off on a whim to find trouble."

"I do not—" Mac reconsidered. "I don't try to find trouble," she temporized.

"Don't worry, Mr. Mudge," Sing-li reassured him. "I lived with her at Base for six months. We all know the signs."

Mac's head snapped around. "What signs? Signs of wh—" She stopped, startled.

What was that?

Mac held up her hand for silence, listening, her mouth dry. *There.* She lunged forward and swept the covering from the table.

Clear water and fish exploded into a writhing mass of sediments and broken coral, as whatever had been closest to the glass fled into the depths.

Sing-li had surged to his feet with her and now stood, his pistol drawn and ready, although somewhat nonplussed to be aiming it at a piece of furniture. Mudge, who'd managed to jump right over his jelly-chair, peered over the top of its dubious shelter. "What—what was that?" he gasped.

Heart still hammering in her ears, Mac said fiercely: "That, my dear Oversight, is what happens when guesswork meets evidence. The Ro." *Were they aquatic?* she caught herself wondering for the first time. *Did they rejoice in the seawater tank, or was the liquid inimical to them? Did they prefer the same mixture of gases she breathed?*

What could you breathe in no-space?

You know, Emily, Mac thought grimly. She'd like to believe her friend would answer questions. *She'd also like to be standing beside the Tannu River right now.*

The probability of either was the same.

"There are tables like this everywhere," began Sing-li, worry creasing his forehead. "Can the Ro exit into rooms through them?"

Staring at the table, Mac resisted the impulse to duck behind her own chair. "Let's not wait and find out. Can you reach Nik, discreetly, without using the consulate's system?"

"Who's Nik? Mudge demanded. Mac silenced him with a look.

"Sure." Sing-li pulled out something like an imp. "What do you want me to tell him?"

"Have him meet us in the Origins Room as soon as he can." She looked from Mudge to Sing-li. "Let's move, gentlemen."

At this hour, the residential corridors of the IU consulate were deserted, lights dimmed to night levels, everyone asleep or at least quiet. Mac was reminded of the times Emily had talked her into staying out late, late enough they'd have to sneak back into the Pods to avoid waking other researchers. Of course, then, the consequence of discovery had been a continuation of festivities till dawn in someone's quarters, with Mac doing her best to excuse herself and Emily all for it.

Tonight, she was with Sing-li, who managed to turn walking into something ominous and silent. Tonight, Emily was the one person Mac didn't want to encounter, hard as that was to admit.

Tonight, dawn wasn't a sure thing.

Technically, Fourteen's quarters were the floor above hers, but the Sinzi's ramplike corridor wound its way from level to level steeply here, making it faster to walk than take the lift. Mac found herself moving quicker as well, stretching her strides to match Sing-li's longer legs, almost breaking into a run.

Running out of time, she fussed to herself and hoped Fourteen wasn't a sound sleeper.

"Here," Sing-li said quietly, stopping in front of the next set of double doors. "We shouldn't wake the neighbors."

"Wait a moment." Mac leaned her head against the door. "He snores," she explained. "Loudly." *Nothing*. She reached for the door handle. The consulate didn't lock doors, presumably to allow staff discreet access at any time. *Or to encourage clandestine activity?* Mac thought inanely. Who knew what went on after-hours here?

A large hand got to the handle first and the Ministry agent gave her a gentle nudge to one side with his shoulder. "My job," he informed her.

"Go ahead," she agreed, but stayed close by.

Sing-li opened the door. No lights, as expected. "Fourteen?" Mac called out as they stepped inside.

Nothing.

"Something's wrong," her companion said abruptly. At that instant Mac realized her feet weren't walking on sand, but through jelly. "Stay back."

Sing-li hit the lights.

The room before them was in ruins. The Sinzi's jelly furnishings, both bed and chair, were slashed apart, their contents—*light blue,* Mac observed numbly—staining the sand. Glistening trails of slime crisscrossed everywhere she looked: walls, ceiling, and floor. Where the slime touched sand, that material was already hardening into a crust.

"Fourteen!" Mac shouted, bolting for the other room.

Sing-li made a grab for her but missed. "Mac! Wait!" He pounded after her through the arch, cursing under his breath, only catching up when she staggered to a stop before a pile of ripped clothing.

"It isn't—him," she managed to say. *No body.* Just the pile beside the table, the only intact furnishing left in the Myg's quarters. Sing-li, weapon drawn, quickly checked the closet and washroom, then came back to her, shaking his head. "The terrace," she whispered, and he went into the other room, coming back a moment later.

"Clear," he told her. "No evidence of a struggle—no blood."

"That doesn't mean they didn't take him," she ground out. Just then, something about the pile of clothing caught Mac's eye. It seemed different, somehow.

"Sing-li," she hissed as she bent and teased the top layer free, wincing at the cold stickiness of slime on her fingers. Most of the material was Fourteen's fine leather, ripped to ribbons, every edge jagged as if the damage had been caused by serrated knives.

Or teeth.

The pile beneath *shifted*. Just a bit, but enough to make Mac drop to her knees and pull more urgently at the mass. Sing-li, muttering various dark things under his breath, loomed at her shoulder, weapon ready.

The last lump of slime-coated leather came free in her hands, as much because what was beneath was digging itself out of the sand as Mac's tugging. A faint muffled *coo,* then two limpid eyes stared up at her, blinking grains from their eyelashes.

A baby Myg? "Come here," Mac urged gently, carefully helping the tiny creature from its hiding place. "Shhhh. It's okay."

With a pounce that would have done a cat proud—or an aroused male Trisulian—the baby attached itself to the front of her jacket, doing its utmost to shiver its way through the warm skin of Mac's throat. She cradled it there with one hand as she got to her feet.

"I've a pretty good idea where Fourteen might be," Mac announced. "Let's go."

"We have to report this." At the shake of her head, he protested: "Mac!"

"Raising an alarm—likely too late, I might add—will only stop us from getting to the Origins Room. I have to get there, Sing-li. I have to work with my team." Mac looked at the too-familiar damage. "Ro don't tend to stick around."

He wasn't happy, but didn't argue.

They made their way to Unensela's quarters, Sing-li having contacted Mudge for the location within the building. He'd signed off the com link to frown worriedly at Mac. "Mr. Mudge says there was no answer from her room either. Do you think the Ro—?"

Mac, busy trying to convince a certain small and persistent Myg that a Human female was physically incapable of offering it a snack, merely grunted: "Doubt it." Unensela's quarters were on the uppermost residential floor. This time, they took the lift, Sing-li stepping out first to sweep the corridor with a glance. After a long second, he waved at her to follow. Mac didn't argue, too busy listening. She knew the sounds of the Ro, heard their *scurry . . . spit pop!* in her dreams.

"Clear," he said, then frowned. "What's that noise?"

"That noise" being a series of loud squeals that incited the Myg baby to squirm up to Mac's shoulder, chattering with excitement, Mac didn't feel particularly worried. "I think we've found out why Unensela isn't answering her com," she said.

A knock on the door did no better—the squealing having grown too loud anyway. The two Humans exchanged glances. "I don't know if we should just walk in, Mac."

"The Ro?" she reminded him.

"Good point." He pushed open the door . . .

. . . giving Mac perfect line of sight on a pair of madly vibrating paisley shorts, an unexpected alignment of body parts, and a wildly squealing female Myg who, upon spotting new arrivals, freed an arm to wave them inside with every appearance of sincerity.

Clandestine meetings indeed. At least his grandsires would be pleased.

As for that smell . . .

"Let's give them a moment," Mac suggested, stepping back into the corridor.

Sing-li didn't argue with that either.

Fourteen had exchanged his formal wig for his Little Misty Lake General Store hat, jauntily dipped over one ear. Mac was fascinated to see that his forked tongue, white until now, was engorged and distinctly pink. *No external genitalia indeed,* she speculated.

A happy Myg. Or he would have been, if it hadn't been for her news. "Whaddyou mean, dey've sdarted sending da signal?" The tongue was causing him problems.

"Idiot," this from Unensela, who seemed unaffected by anything other than containing the offspring who kept trying to jump to Mac. *She didn't blame it.* Neither adult Myg had evinced concern about the child having narrowly escaped the Ro; after his initial trauma at missing the successful signal, Fourteen had worried more about his clothes.

Probably why he'd so glibly offered her his firstborn, had he had one, Mac recalled, struggling with this variation on parental behavior. "I suppose now you'll want to celebrate," Unensela continued. She leaned confidingly toward Mac, necessitating another grab at the offspring. "I was consoling him on his failure," she explained. "Males. Any excuse."

Sing-li made a choked noise; Mac didn't bother turning around. "Could we focus on the problem at hand, please?" she asked both Mygs. "And walk a little faster?"

Fourteen put a protective arm around his partner, avoiding the offspring climbing on her shoulders. "Of course she can't," he claimed, both expression and tone highly smug. "Not yet."

Unensela squealed; Sing-li smothered another laugh.

Was she the only one intent on saving the planet? Mac began to wonder about their collective sanity.

When they reached the lifts, she drew Fourteen aside, scowling at his somewhat theatrical sigh at leaving Unensela's side. "I need you to do something for me, Fourteen," she told him, keeping her voice low. *Not that she knew the auditory acuity of a Myg,* she realized belatedly.

Abruptly serious, his tiny eyes riveted on her. "You haf my allegiance, Mac. You know dat."

And she was about to test it—severely. Mac bit her lower lip, then took him by the arm and walked him a few more steps away from where the others waited. Probably an unnecessary caution. The offspring, having discovered Sing-li's armor made interesting noises, were keeping both Human and their mother preoccupied. *But she'd rather not share this.*

"I want you in the signal room in the Atrium—yes, I know what's in the basement," she said at his attempt to look surprised. "Where do you think I've been?" Mac firmed her voice. "They're monitoring for a response from the Ro. I need to know when they get it, Fourteen. What it says. This isn't something the Sinzi-ra would approve," she warned.

"I will be your eyes and ears, Mac," he promised, puffing out his chest. "If anything happens, I'll send a message to your imp. I can do it so none are the wiser, even our omniscient host." The tongue only tripped him on "omniscient," the word coming out more like "omblifflivy," but Mac understood.

She gave a grateful nod, trusting he could read the gesture. "There's one other thing, Fourteen. This won't be as easy to hide. I want you to find a way to disrupt the outgoing signal—to do it if I say so, without question."

His chest collapsed in a quiet moan and the Myg put his hands over his eyes. She grabbed his wrists and pulled his arms down again, quickly but gently, hoping Unensela hadn't noticed the despairing gesture. *The smell she couldn't help.* "The Ro are to save us, Mac," he protested, unhappy but quiet in her hold. "This is not an act of *strobis*. I cannot."

"And if they are not saviors, Fourteen? What then? They've been spying inside the consulate. Who knows what they intended to do with you!"

"Idiot. I'm the only one genius enough to make progress with their code. They could have been trying to communicate with me."

Save her from wishful academics, regardless of species. "For that same reason, Fourteen, they could have wanted you dead." She held his eyes with hers. "Just go there, please. Keep an eye on things. Keep me informed. And, for all our sakes, have a plan in mind. I've a feeling whatever choice you have to make will be clear—I only hope you have time to make it."

Fourteen nodded, then reached out and tapped her nose. "And I hope to embarrass you about this for many years to come, Mac."

So did she, Mac thought, watching the lift doors close behind Fourteen.

So did she.

Night elsewhere, but on the main floor the illumination was daylight normal. Knowing the ways of researchers, Mac had assumed they wouldn't be the only ones awake in the dead of morning. She'd counted on it, in fact.

Sure enough, each of the six consular staff they encountered was towing a cart of coffee and pastries, including one outside the Origins Room. "Good evening, Dr. Connor," he said without a blink. "We noticed activity in your room and anticipated your group would also require refreshments. Was this correct?"

"Perfect," she said a little too warmly. *Should pacify the ones who don't wake well,* she thought, following the staff through the door. Sing-li, on her signal, came with her.

A series of high-pitched squeals announced them as they entered. Unensela's offspring left her, bounding across the floor to intercept the cart, only the staff's quick move to lift the tray beyond their reach saving the pastries. *Just as well,* Mac thought. The female Myg hadn't been pleased to see Fourteen sent on a mission of his own—although it seemed her pique was more because she didn't have a secret mission, than any worry about risk to him. *Implying,* decided Mac, *a certain lack of personal commitment in more Myg relationships than parenting.*

Mudge hurried up, relief on his face. "Everyone's here, Norcoast."

Except Nik, she thought, having swept the crowd with a look, but didn't say it aloud. "Good work."

"Where's Fourteen?"

"He's busy elsewhere—"

"What's going on?" Like most here, Lyle hadn't wasted time to do more than throw on clothes. His sparse hair stood on end and his eyes were bloodshot.

Mac pitched her voice to his ears only. "We're going to prove the value of your work once and for all. Or look like blithering idiots. Game?"

His lips stretched in a bitter grin. "Game."

"Give us a moment first. Sing-li?"

He followed Mac to a quiet part of the room, not that there were many options. When they stopped, he gave her a troubled look. "Mac, I have to raise the alarm."

"I know. One last thing before you do." She put her hand on his armor-coated chest, irrelevantly noticing tiny Myg prints marring its gleam. "I want the rest of you here."

He took a look around the room, then frowned at her. "This room isn't defensible, Mac, if that's what you're thinking. Those windows? The door's a joke. And who knows what the Sinzi buried in the walls? Specs have this place capable of morphing into a fortress—from the outside, at least."

She shook her head impatiently through all of it. "I want them here—you, too—in case Nik needs you."

"For what?" Low and worried. "Mac, what are you planning now?"

"See the signs, do you?" she said, trying to keep it light.

"Mac." A growl.

"Nik might have to retrieve our guest from the basement. Fast."

That earned a grim look. "You might be sent home if you're wrong, Mac. Nik—the rest of us—we won't be that lucky. Not if we disobey the Sinzi-ra and the Ministry. That's treason."

What had Nik said? "I'll spend us both—"

If I have to, Em, Mac told herself, cold and calm, *I'll spend them all.*

"Let's hope it doesn't come to that," Mac said aloud.

"Let's." Sing-li pressed his lips together for a moment, then gave a curt nod. "No offense, Mac, but we're not the kind of assets you're used to—can't risk being penned in here, for starters. Leave it with me."

Gladly, Mac thought, feeling one of the knots in her spine ease. "Whatever you think best, Sing-li."

"Trust me, you don't want to know what I think." But he smiled. "Anything else?"

"The door may be a joke, but can you make sure we aren't interrupted?" His anticipatory grin matched Lyle's. "Good."

Leaving Sing-li to contact the others—*and make whatever plans such people made for treasonous activities*—Mac headed into the middle of the room. She grabbed the nearest stool and climbed up on it, finding her balance.

"Good morning, everyone!" she called out.

The answering chorus was ragged, spiced with some complaints about her time sense, though less than she'd expected. The faces Mac could read looked understandably tired and puzzled. "In this room," she told them, her voice clear and calm, "are two very important things. You. Experts on understanding the past. And your data. Everything collected to date about life on the planet that spawned the Dhryn.

"We can't answer every question we have tonight. But we must answer one," she said. "One I believe you'll find worth losing a little sleep over."

"It better be!" someone called from a back row. Sing-li, a dark presence now blocking the only door, gave the speaker a menacing look. There was a ripple of uneasiness as the rest noticed.

"You tell me," Mac challenged. "Here's my question. Were the Dhryn—their biology, their technology—deliberately modified into a weapon by the Myrokynay, the Ro?"

Only the patter of baby Myg feet broke the ensuing silence. Even the consular staff, who'd been preoccupied dispensing coffee to those nearest, stopped to stare at her, his hands in midair.

Mac raised her eyebrows. "We don't have much time. Tonight, this Gathering began transmitting the Ro's contact signal. I, for one, would like to know who we're inviting to the party—before we throw open the door."

"You heard the lady," Lyle said into the stunned hush. "Let's get to it."

19

HYPOTHESES AND HORRORS

MAC COULD FEEL it along her nerves. She walked quietly from group to group, listening, absorbing, not saying a word. The focus was there; the drive had taken hold. *If she tried to stop them now,* she thought with satisfaction, *they'd ignore her.*

Even the meditation chamber was humming. *Literally.* Mac stopped beside the gray curtain, but could tell nothing about what was happening on the other side beyond some nice harmonics.

If her route tended to circle back most often to where Unensela and the climatologists pored over data, no one noticed that either.

Mac shifted two Myg offspring to her shoulders, balancing a third on one hip. *Almost no one,* she sighed, taking the trio with her. She went to stare out the window, seeing the patio where the Gathering met each morning. No sign of dawn, but there were glows out now, as yellow-clad staff moved over rain-wet tiles to set up tents between the trees. A little morning drizzle wasn't going to stop the Sinzi-ra's efforts to coax the Ro.

And beneath it all, the Atrium, where a signal was even now being sent.

Mac's shudder made the Mygs grab where they shouldn't and she snarled in protest. "I'm not a horse," she muttered, heading back to their mother.

Not that she knew for a fact Unensela was the biological mother of the pack. Caretaker, at least, although absentminded.

Before Mac reached the climatologists, Lyle intercepted her. "I think we have something," he said, jerking his head back to the circle of tables and consoles they'd dubbed "the view" for no reason anyone had explained to her.

Before joining him, Mac glanced at the door. Sing-li's shrug was the same as his last dozen. *No word from Nik.* He'd sent his report about the Ro; nothing, as far as Mac could tell, had resulted. No klaxons or alarms, no rush of searchers through the room. She supposed she should be grateful not to be disturbed.

It felt more like a serious threat was being ignored.

Carrying her passengers, Mac joined Lyle, nodding a greeting to Therin and his compatriots. "What is it? Sorry, one minute." She restrained the little Myg who'd spotted the Sthlynii's oral tentacles, giving the nearest Human, Kirby, a pleading look. Once he'd pried the annoyed offspring from her shoulder, Mac continued: "Lyle says you have something for me."

"You are standing on it."

Mac backed out of the empty circle of floor. Therin gestured to another Human, who lifted a pair of image extrapolation wands. Like Mudge, she knew the name of the devices, if not how they were used.

Seemed she was about to find out.

Without warning, the floor and the space above it filled with an image of dust and ruins, so perfect Mac felt as though she could put her hands into it. The archaeologist did just that, only reaching with the wands instead of hands as Therin spoke. Each time, it modified what was being displayed. "We've gone through our surveys and those from the IU team still on the planet. This is the largest Dhryn building either group has found." Dust disappeared and the building was restored before Mac's eyes. She walked around it. Perfect on all sides. The walls had that characteristic nonperpendicular slope so dear to the Dhryn. Its walls were coated with mosaics. "Note the size." A Human figure, a duplicate of Mac herself, walked into the image to stand beside the building.

Mac frowned at her doppelganger. "I'm too big."

"No, Mac," Lyle said, a note of excitement in his voice. "The building's too small."

Therin concurred. "We haven't found a single structure large

enough to contain one of the Progenitors. Including underground," he added, anticipating Mac's question.

"That's—" As Mac walked around the image, her little echo
doing the same until she glared at the operator. "Tents? Could they
have lived in the open?"

"I don't see how," said one of the others. "The climate was
harsh before the vegetation was stripped from it. And you said the
Dhryn offspring were born from a Progenitor's skin—that sounds
vulnerable. You'd want protection."

"He said there were ships waiting for them," Mac whispered.

"Pardon? What ships? Who said?"

She blinked up at Lyle. "The Haven Dhryn," she covered
quickly. "One talked about how the great ships were buried and
ready for them when they arrived. Could the Progenitors have lived
on similar ships, orbiting the planet?"

"They did not have these ships. They could not make them."
Da'a, the other Cey, heaved a deep breath, sending a quiver
through his hanging folds of skin. "I do not say the Dhryn are stupid. But we have no evidence from this world that they were space-
faring at all. There are none of the precursors of such technology."

"You could say the same for most of the technology in this
room," Mac pointed out. "Imports, with no history of development on Earth."

The archaeologists smiled and exchanged looks at this. Lyle gave
a grim laugh. "You can see the pattern of evolution in living things,
Mac. Trust us to know what to look for in what a culture can and
cannot do. The Dhryn might have wound up in space. Someone
else put them there."

"Before the Progenitors needed larger buildings." Mac frowned.
"How sure can we be that the Dhryn are from this world?"

A voice from behind. Unensela, without offspring. "Idiot. The
fossil record's solid. I've a progression of eight-limbed, primarily
colonial animal forms stretching back to preflowering plants. DNA
to match. The Dhryn started here, all right. Come and see what we
have."

"Weeee're nooooot done, botanist." The Sthlynii's diction
slipped momentarily.

Mac hid a smile and focused on Therin. "What else?"

The building image was replaced by a satellite view of the Dhryn home world. A few strokes of the wand pushed back time, until buildings sprang from ruins. Mac leaned closer and the image obligingly zoomed in. She fought vertigo as she inspected something that seemed unlikely. *Then again, she didn't want to be called a biologist,* Mac grinned to herself. "Did they have powered flight?"

"You noticed." From the triumphant look Lyle gave Therin and the others, Mac presumed there'd been a bet placed. She didn't bother reacting.

"No roads," she obliged.

"And no sign of flying machines either."

"The feeder form?"

"Irrelevant," Unensela snapped. "The prevailing winds would have blown them halfway around the continent. Only in there—" she stabbed her hand and arm into the image, distorting it and getting a protest from the operators, "—would they be able to float about without assistance."

"In there" was a series of deep rifts, running roughly north/south. They were immense and, in this presentation, filled with lush vegetation.

"Fantastic, aren't they?"

"They are more than that." Unensela made a rude noise. Mac prepared herself in case a smell was to follow. "The forest growth on this world was as cyclic as the climate. Seeds for the dominant species, large and filled with nutrients, were produced underground and stayed there, safe from extremes and foragers. The surface growth, even of trees, would die to the soil in each hemisphere in turn, starting at the pole, then germinate and regrow when conditions improved again. Food would have ebbed and flowed like a tide that took centuries to pass any one place." She disrupted the image again, jabbing at the rifts. "These—they would have been like roadways to anything following that tide. Your feeder Dhryn could use them."

Mac noticed a heated discussion underway to one side of the group. She caught the eye of one of the participants and gestured her closer. It was the gray-haired woman, Mirabelle Sangrea. "What is it, Mirabelle?" she asked.

"We've been mapping the Dhryn—well, you can't call them cities, Mac, not like you'd see on most IU worlds—we've started calling them havens." She smiled at Mac's raised eyebrow. "It seemed right. They built clusters of buildings, like beads, but, as you noted, unconnected. Therin? Could we display Sim 231 for Mac, please?"

The Sthlynii blew out his tentacles, but complied.

The view was again of the planetscape, but now dotted. Mac didn't need the Myg's triumphant "Hah!" to see how lines of dots, each representing a haven, paralleled a rift. Not every line of dots did so. Some were on their own. *But the overall pattern?* "Were these all inhabited at the same time?" she asked.

Mirabelle's smile widened. "There's evidence of sequential abandonment, then reuse."

"As if the Dhryn population moved down from one pole, going from haven to haven, then back again," Mac said.

"Yes. Well, until they stopped doing so—not long before the rest of the Chasm worlds were stripped bare of life. We're working on that interval. It definitely overlaps the time when the Dhryn abandoned ceramics."

Mac met Lyle's eyes, then looked around at the rest. They'd attracted another crowd, not everyone by any means, but a solid ring had formed, stood shoulder to shoulder in order to see. All appeared equally disturbed.

Da'a spoke first. "I see a piece missing, Mac."

"Only one?" Mac couldn't help but murmur. She nodded for him to continue.

"If the Ro took the Dhryn and modified them, produced these gigantic Progenitors as breeding machines, why doesn't Myriam— the Dhryn planet—show some early sign of it?"

"Because the entire planet was a trust," Mudge said loudly, pushing his way through to stand by Mac. "Protecting the diversity of the source material."

Mac grinned. "I knew I brought you for a reason, Oversight."

Her grin faded as she studied the strange world now slowly turning in front of them all, showing its seasons. "That had to be what the Ro did. Until they had new Dhryn, the species exactly as they wanted—modifications tested, sure to reproduce in kind—they'd want the real thing healthy and close at hand. But once they were satisfied—any living members of the original genetic stock would be a threat, a potential for reversion. They'd have to be destroyed."

"None of this absolves the Dhryn of guilt."

Lyle. Mac understood the pain in his face. *No time,* she told herself. "Right now the issue is the signal going out to those who may have modified the Dhryn into a menace. My next question, folks. Was it the Ro or not? You have," she made a point of looking at the windows, "until they answer."

With that, Mac turned and walked away. It was that, or scream at all of them to hurry, to forget another coffee, stop chatting with friends. *Not reassuring behavior in a team leader.*

Automatically, she glanced at Sing-li, only to see him heads together with Nik, here at last, both men deep in conversation. Mac changed direction to join them, but she wasn't as quick as Mudge, whose glad shout of "Stefan!" was enough to turn several heads.

There were times, Mac growled to herself.

Fortunately for Mudge's continued existence, Nik was more than capable of dealing with distraction. After a brief handshake and a quiet word—accompanied by the pair of them looking at *her*—Mudge nodded and walked away.

He did, however, pause beside Mac long enough to say: "At least Human authorities are taking us seriously, Norcoast. Stefan wants to talk to you."

She muttered something under her breath.

"Pardon?"

"Nothing, Oversight."

Nik smiled as she approached. A smile for others that did nothing to warm his eyes. "Is it my imagination, Dr. Connor," he said cheerfully, "or are these the same people we spent the last months keeping away from your doorstep?"

She collected herself, reading the message. *Keep it calm; keep it normal.* "Pretty much," she said as lightly. "But I don't think you needed to try very hard. They're better at hunting the past than the present."

"Let's hope so. You certainly have them working late—or is that early?"

Her ability to stay calm and act normal was, Mac realized, *severely limited at this hour.* "We need to talk," she said bluntly.

Nik said: "No argument there." Then he looked past her and that carefree smile reappeared. "Is that ? I don't believe it—that's Wilson Kudla, isn't it? Author of 'Chasm Ghouls—They Exist and Speak to Me.' I'm such a fan."

Mac and Sing-li were left standing dumbfounded as Mr. Spy, Nik Trojanowski, dashed to where the sweaty author and his trio of equally perspiring supplicants were emerging from their curtained-off alcove.

She didn't, Mac decided, *want to know what they'd been doing.*
Or, for that matter, what Nik was doing.

Sing-li coughed once. "You're supposed to go with him, Mac."
"I am?"
"Trust me."

Fuming at the waste of time, Mac stormed up beside Nik just as he was greeting the Great Man himself. *The slight stammer while asking for an autograph was,* Mac decided, *a particularly nice touch.* Kudla, despite being one of the most nondescript Humans she'd ever met, was virtually preening.

"And, may I, could I?" Nik touched the curtain with one visibly trembling hand. "I've never had success before—but where you've been meditating? It must work!"

"Of course," the Great Man intoned. "May the Ghouls speak to you as well." *His smug look in her direction,* Mac told herself, returning that look with a scowl, *said more than the specters ever would.*

"You'll want to see this," Nik promised Mac as the ghoul hunters walked off—hopefully to shower. Ignoring her protest, he took her real hand and pulled her with him through the curtain.

The alcove was little more than a tent, its fabric opaque and—Mac sneezed—a bit dusty. Small lights, designed to look like candles, ringed the junction between ceiling and walls. Mac did her best not to step on anything. It wasn't easy, given the number of small ornate gongs lined up in rows around what was, without doubt, a very well-used mattress.

Not a place she wanted to stay. Mac turned to protest "What's—" but Nik's mouth smothered the rest, the unexpected kiss making her completely forget whatever she'd planned to say anyway.

Before she could decide whether or not to lose herself in it, his finger replaced his lips against hers. "Shhh." His eyes were hidden behind the reflections on his lenses.

Satisfied she understood, Nik climbed on the mattress and, shaking out the small telescoping wand he drew from a pocket, used it to sweep the space around them, poking into every corner, even along the ceiling. "Clear," he pronounced an instant later.

Of Ro. Lo-tech. Effective.

She wanted to hug him. Instead: "Is anyone else checking?" Mac asked, her arms wrapped tightly around her middle.

"I'm told the consular staff is aware of the situation." Low, with some frustration. "What that means, I don't know. The Sinzi have defenses within the building but . . . no one was hurt and the Ro certainly aren't the first aliens to trash a room here." A shake of his head. "I came as soon as I could, Mac."

"I know."

He ran his fingers down her arm to the glove, giving the fingers a gentle tug. "You okay? You haven't had any sleep, have you?"

"Better than you," Mac asserted. "I grabbed a nap." *It wasn't a lie.*

"We can't stay in here long," he said, hand dropping to his side. His nose wrinkled. "Just as well. Sing-li brought me up to speed. Now, Dr. Connor." A note of familiar exasperation. "Why aren't you sleeping? Why aren't all these people sleeping? Why is that Myg in the signal room instead of sleeping? And—"

Mac raised one eyebrow. "And?"

"What the hell are you doing giving orders to my people?"

"Hopefully making a fool of myself."

"Well, you've got company," he said, shaking his head. "Remind me not to station anyone on Base again. The place corrupts."

She couldn't smile. "Nik, we've found evidence the Dhryn were taken into space, that their present state isn't their natural one—implying they were modified. My team's now hunting anything that ties in the Ro. When we find that—"

"If."

"When," she countered defiantly. "It's them, Nik."

He lowered his head a moment, then looked up at her over his glasses. His eyes might have been chipped from ice. "You can't be wrong on this, Mac."

"I'm not."

"You know what's at stake."

Mac looked at him, but saw a raindrop pausing on a leaf, the surge of salmon against a current, the curious tilt of a duck's head. Heard the cry of an eagle hidden in cloud. Felt the silky coolness of a slug resting in her hand. *And that was just Field Station Six.* A mere speck on this world. This world a mere speck among the uncounted number like it.

"Everything is at stake," she said, her voice hard and sure. "That's why I won't let the Ro get away with this. Please, Nik. Come and see the evidence we have. Decide for yourself."

"I did," Nik snorted. "Come now, Mac. Surely you didn't believe Sing-li could redeploy the Ministry's assets within the consulate on his own? You had to know it would be my name on those orders—my head on the block." His grin took on that dangerous edge, dimple showing. "Though you were late. I'd moved them into position around the Dhryn and launch pad an hour before."

"Then why—" Mac flung her hand at their surroundings.

"Call it one chance for you to pull the plug. To tell me it had been a mistake; the Ro were going to save us after all; that you and I should head back to your cabin. It needs some work, you know. The cabin."

The last almost made her smile.

Almost.

"Were you similarly ahead in dealing with the signal?"

His lower lip went between his teeth for a second. "That's trickier. Anchen, Hollans, the rest? They're hovering around the consoles, to be there when the Ro answer back. Hardly a group to take kindly to our request they turn it off. What's Fourteen up to?"

"He's to let me know if there is a response. I don't imagine I'll be informed otherwise. And—if I ask him, he'll try to stop the signal going out, somehow."

"Somehow." Nik filled the word with doubt.

Mac blushed. "Neither of us are spies. I know that. But it was the best I could do. I couldn't very well call and ask you. No one else would listen."

"Don't count on that. The Sinzi-ra, Hollans? They heard my concerns—our concerns. Emily Mamani's arrival, her appearance, shook them badly. They aren't sure about the Ro, not anymore."

"Not sure as in stopping the signal?"

"Not sure as in waiting to see what comes of it."

Mac shook her head. "Risky."

"Present situation to the contrary, they aren't fools, Mac."

"Comforting." She found a smile. "We'd better get out of here before anyone starts to notice. Especially—" she added with a wince, "Sing-li."

"One more thing, Mac." He hesitated.

No need to guess what drew down the sides of his mouth like that. "Emily."

"I wasn't able to talk to her. She's—it's as if she's detached from those around her, paying attention only to certain words, certain tasks. The Sinzi-ra has promised every assistance. But until we know more of Emily's state—"

"I'm aware of the priorities!" Mac interrupted, her voice sharper than she'd intended. She closed her eyes, sighed once, then opened them again. More gently. "Thank you, Nik. As you said. She's here. She's alive. That's infinitely better than yesterday."

He nodded, but Mac understood the pity in his eyes.

They left the tent, its closed-in warmth making Mac feel as sweaty as any ghoul seeker. The air of the open room felt like a reprieve. Nik, as usual, appeared able to wear a suit and remain immaculate under any circumstances.

From the activity everywhere, no one had paid attention to their sojourn communing with the departed. *Well, almost no one.* Sing-li, obviously waiting for them to emerge, gestured impatiently for Nik to join him. He looked upset.

That couldn't be good.

"I'll be right back," Nik told her, heading toward the door with long strides. "Check on your people."

Mac took only her first steps across the room before: "Mac? A moment?" She nodded automatically and turned toward the voice, only to have all six Myg offspring hurtle up her jacket, at least one finding its way inside the collar. "What the— Unensela!"

Then Mac paused, feeling how the tiny things were quivering. Putting a protective hand over as many as she could, she looked around for what had frightened them. Her heart hammered in her chest. Everything seemed as before, normal, busy. People moving in all directions or leaning over equipment. It wasn't enough to reassure her.

Not the Ro.

Please not the Ro.

It wasn't, Mac realized as Unensela came hurrying up to her, prying loose her now-hysterical little ones with a running commentary about the inconvenient unavailability of a certain male Myg and whose fault was that she'd like to point out.

It was Emily.

Where she stood opened like an eddy within a river: researchers gave her space, moving past with sidelong looks of dismay, none willing to risk curiosity.

"Hello, Em," Mac heard herself say, as if this was a normal day at the lab, and they were meeting over coffee.

The eyes. They were the worst. Flat, dull, the whites so bloodshot they made Mac's own eyes burn in sympathy.

Emily hadn't come alone. Two consular staff flanked her to either side, discreetly behind. They met Mac's inquiring look with that impassive, attentive expression. Watchers.

Not the only ones. They had Nik and Sing-li's attention as well— explaining Sing-li's urgent summons. Nik caught her eye.

Mac shook her head, very slightly.

"Need some help?" The words were Emily-normal; the voice anything but. It could have been a recording. *And what would Emily say to you, Mac? What sequence of syllables would make you believe she still existed within that frame?*

Play along, Mac thought, sick to her soul. "Always. You could help me with the—" *not near the Mygs,* "—cartographers. That group there."

The body turned in the direction Mac indicated, graceless yet with coordination and strength. *Not starved—emaciated from something else,* she judged, giving a frantic hand signal to Mirabelle as they headed her way. *How did you warn someone about your best friend?* Emily's bizarre appearance would likely do it for her.

Her being here, now, couldn't be coincidence, Mac decided.

It could be opportunity. *How much of you is left, Emily?*

"Welcome to the Origins Team, Em," Mac began. Her voice sounded strained even to her and she coughed to clear it. *She could do this. She* had *to do this.* "We're working on where the Dhryn came from—had some breakthroughs already this—morning." *The word was appropriate,* Mac told herself, even if dawn was still some hours away. "I think you'll be impressed by our findings."

Emily might have been a walking plague, the way silence spread ahead of their little procession and murmuring followed it. Mac scowled at everyone in general, to no avail, then her eyes found Mudge. She beckoned him with a curt nod.

He came, eyes filled with the horror Mac felt. "Dr. M-Mamani," he managed. "Good of you to join us."

"This is Oversight—Charles Mudge III—Emily. I'm sure you remember all my stories about him." Mac shot Mudge a warning look.

He gave a miserable excuse for an offended *harrumph,* but gamely offered his hand. *No lack of guts,* Mac thought gratefully.

Forced to stop walking or run over him, Emily looked down at his hand for a few seconds, then turned to stare at Mac.

She was frowning.

No, not frowning, Mac thought with sudden hope. She knew that thoughtful crease between Em's dark eyebrows, had seen it every time the other scientist focused on a problem. "What is it, Em?" she asked gently.

"Where is this place?"

Hadn't anyone told her? Mac felt a rush of sympathy. "On Earth," she offered. "You're home."

"Earth isn't safe." The crease eased away. "It will be, when the Myrokynay are made welcome."

Over my dead body, Mac said, but kept her expression as close to neutral as she could.

"Perhaps you could help us understand the Ro better, Em," she suggested, changing her mind about the cartography. "We've questions."

"Always glad to be of help, Mac." Cold. By rote.

Mac felt the sting of tears in her eyes and fought them back. "Great. Let's get a spot out of everyone's way, shall we? Oversight? Will you get Lyle and—Stefan—to join us please?"

She started walking, too abruptly, and bumped into one of Emily's shadows. The collision was startling enough, given how adept the consular staff were at avoiding contact, but even more was the feel of a small object being thrust into her hand. Mac didn't look down, she just pushed the thing into her pocket.

No telling what it was. From the feel, a cold metal cylinder of some kind. Perhaps the Sinzi-ra had sent her a message. Some kind of imp. *If it was a weapon*—Mac jerked her hand from her pocket. *New rule,* she told herself. *Don't fondle unknown alien objects.*

A moment later, the four of them sat at one end of the conference table, the staff standing their precise distance behind Emily. The rest of the room's inhabitants were too carefully uninterested. Unensela's offspring, now mute, had taken refuge under her lab coat. *Excellent survival response,* Mac thought. She avoided thinking against what.

Nik showed no expression beyond polite attention, although Mac had learned the signs. He wasn't pleased—whether because Emily was here at all, or because Mac was preparing to discuss their work with her, she couldn't tell.

So long as he was there. He'd warn her if the discussion went in dangerous directions. He'd act, along with Sing-li, and hopefully the two staff, if Emily herself became the threat.

Then why, Mac thought, dry-mouthed as she looked into her friend's eyes, *did she feel alone?*

"What are your questions about the Myrokynay?"

Lyle leaned forward eagerly. Mac presumed Mudge had given

him some idea who Emily was, though she'd no idea what. *An expert on the Ro? Their spy?* "Do they live on planets now?" he demanded.

"This is—" Mac began.

"Dr. Lyle Emerson Kanaci," Emily interrupted. "Administrator for Chasm Studies Site 157, financed by Sencor Research Group, a company owned by a consortium of Sthlynii, Cey, and Human corporate and governmental interests."

Nik raised a brow at Mac. Lyle flushed in blotches of pink, but didn't deny any of it. "What about his question, Emily?" Mac prompted. "Are there Ro worlds?"

Emily's immaculately manicured hands, even in the field, had been a source of bewilderment to Mac, who couldn't keep a nail intact in her office, let alone on a granite ledge. Now, the fingers crawling restlessly over the tabletop, back and forth, were dirty, with split, fractured nails at their ends. "The Myrokynay moved beyond the limitations of a planetary biosphere before the Sinzi knew what one was."

"Harding was convinced they hadn't originated in the Hift System. Too young for one thing," the archaeologist muttered, as if to himself. Louder, "If they have no planets to risk, why do they fear the Dhryn?"

"The Myrokynay fear nothing." The fingers were drumming now, distracting all of them. "They wish to help those of us at risk."

"Did they help the Trisulians?" Mac asked. Nik shot her a look of caution she ignored. "Emily?"

The fingers stopped. "Where is this place?" An air of confusion.

"Home," Mac told her, wishing her voice wouldn't shake. "You're home, with me, Emily. The Trisulians. They had your instructions on how to signal the Ro. Did they use them? Did the Ro—the Myrokynay—come?"

"You read my message, Mac." Emily's smile exposed yellowed teeth and swollen gums. "I told the Myrokynay you would. You're stubborn that way."

"The Trisulians. Did they send the signal?"

Emily's gaze wandered to the ceiling, to the far wall where Sing-li stood watch, brooding and focused on them, to the alcove, to the windows.

Mac half stood. "Emily?"

"Mac," Nik said quietly.

Okay, new subject. Sinking back into her chair, Mac made herself take a couple of breaths. "Emily." The dead eyes shifted back to her. "You told me the Myrokynay had been watching for the Dhryn to reappear since the destruction of the Chasm. Once the Ro found Haven, they took some of the immature Dhryn from their Progenitors—you said it was to test them. For what, Emily?"

"For signs the Dhryn were producing another migratory generation. Your own work uncovered this. I told them you were clever."

"The *oomlings* who were taken," Mac pressed. "What happened to them?"

The fingers started to crawl again. "Where is this place?"

Oh, Em. Mac hardened her heart, rejected pity. "They underwent metamorphosis into the feeder form, didn't they, Emily? Even though they weren't supposed to—like Brymn! The Ro can somehow induce that change, can't they?"

"Where—is this place?"

Mac couldn't stop. *She didn't dare.* "Then the Ro took them to different worlds and set them loose. That's how they aim the Dhryn, isn't it? By taking advantage of their instinct to seek more of the tastes returned by scouts. They returned those feeders to Haven, so they'd give those tastes to the Progenitors. Bait."

Emily's body rose from the table as if tugged by competing strings, arms and legs out of proper sequence. The rest stood as well, everyone but Nik focused on Emily. Mac met his eyes, seeing the warning there. *Careful,* he all but said aloud. *Don't lose her.*

The signal was being sent. *There wasn't time for care.*

She'd spend them all if she had to. "Emily," Mac urged, going around the table to where her friend stood, eyes wide and staring. "You used to think for yourself. Please. Listen to me."

Emily hesitated. Something almost sane looked out at Mac. "Mac?"

"Yes. It's me."

A shudder. Every rip in Emily's clothing glowed for an instant, as if the space held within her flesh had tried to accommodate a sun. "Mac," more sure. Her hand wrapped itself around Mac's wrist, fingers strong as they were cold.

"That's right, Emily," Mac whispered, her voice husky. "I'm Mac, your friend. We need your help. I need it. We have proof—"

"I found you," Emily said as if she hadn't spoken. Her grip tightened until Mac couldn't help but wince. "I'm to bring you. Now."

It seemed fitting that Nik's shouted "Mac!" coincided perfectly with the universe turning itself inside out.

- Encounter -

"WE HAVE INCOMING ships, sir," the transect technician reported, calmly, professionally. Only someone standing close by could have seen her hands tremble. "Sending to your station."

"Got it." One look at the display and her supervisor smacked his hand on the emergency com control.

"To all of Sol System. This is Venus Orbital," he announced. "We've incoming Dhryn. Two ships through—three— My God, how many are there?"

The technician assumed she should answer. "Fifteen Progenitor ships have now arrived through the Naralax, sir. There are more coming behind." She turned to look at him. "Should I keep count, sir?"

He shook his head, reaching for the control again. "This is Venus Orbital. If you're going to do something . . . do it now."

20

DANGER AND DISMAY

TIME SAT on a shelf.
Rolled off.

Dropped her on a hard surface, in the dark.

No, not dark. Light splintered over impossible shapes. She closed her eyes but couldn't escape it.

Not alone. Words. The sound was elongated, wrong. She tried to cover her ears, but couldn't find them.

"Here is Mac."

The disorientation, the pain, were all too familiar sensations. *No-space.*

Mac opened her eyes slowly. It didn't help. She turned her head and retched helplessly.

"The Myrokynay will be here soon, Mac."

Emily.

Explaining the how and the why, but not the where. Mac wiped her mouth and squinted at her surroundings.

A sand shark looked back at her, then curved its sinuous body in a disdainful arc to swim away.

Mac blinked and found herself staring at the scuffed toe of a boot, a once-expensive hand-tooled black leather boot. She rose on her elbow and looked up the leg. "This is the tank room," she said, unutterably relieved to be still within the consulate.

Where Nik could find her. Would *find her.*

"The Sinzi have been clever." Emily flattened her hand against the wall separating them from the night-lit water and its life. "It is disconcerting for the Myrokynay to perceive our world directly from theirs. They had to rely on allies such as myself to be observers. This novel interface?" She drew her fingers along the surface in a caress. "It permits the Myrokynay to witness our doings with new clarity, to be heard."

"So they're in the tank."

Emily started, as if she'd forgotten Mac was there. "In here? No more than they are in any one place," she said. "Only Tactiles ever limit themselves to our dimensions."

" 'Tactiles,' " Mac repeated, managing to sit. *Sitting was enough for now,* she assured her unhappy stomach. "Are Tactiles a kind of Ro?"

The illumination was dim, a mottled glow reflected by the coral within the tank itself. It played tricks with the dark floor and walls, hid the ceiling. Still, by it Mac thought she saw a flash of fear cross Emily's face. If so, it was the first true emotion she'd seen.

Which didn't bode well.

"They are tools," Emily said at last.

"Like the Dhryn?"

"The Dhryn are the enemy of all. They will destroy life until none is left. They must be stopped."

Mac ignored what sounded like a mantra, concentrating on getting to her feet. *There.* Wobbly, but better by the minute. "Short trip," she commented. "Does it get easier with practice?"

"What?"

"Moving through no-space."

Emily's hand fell from the tank. "I cannot move," she said. "I cannot feel. I cannot breathe. I cannot move. I cannot feel. I can—"

Shuddering, Mac broke in: "It's all right, Emily. You're going to be all right."

"Where is this place?" plaintive, in a small voice.

Mac eased back. The door was behind her. *With guards behind that.* She estimated her chances. Emily was taller, had always been faster. But her body had to be paying a price for the abuse it had suffered, the gaps in her flesh a terrible stress on her system.

As if guessing Mac's intention, Emily took three quick steps, but not to block Mac from the door. Instead, she went to a curl of pipe, hand reaching into the shadows. "You must not leave," she said calmly, pulling out the hidden weapon to aim it at Mac's stomach.

So much for physical advantage. Cinder's weapon. With their "new clarity," the Ro must have watched Mac hide it.

At the thought, Mac turned, careful to make it slow and easy, until she could see the tank.

"Why do they want me here?" she asked.

"You wish to stop the signal. You are an enemy of life."

Mac gave a harsh laugh. "Me? An enemy of life? You can't believe that, Emily Mamani. I don't care what they've stuffed into your head; you know that isn't true."

"You are Dhryn."

"Nonsense. Two arms," Mac held out her arms, dropping them again as the weapon rose in threat. "Two arms, five fingers, call an insect-eating primate ancestor. Human, Emily. Human like you." *Like you used to be,* she added to herself.

~~DHRYN ACCEPT YOU~~

~~DHYRN YOU ARE~~

Every word tore into Mac's skin, the sensation so real and agonizing she cried out even as she looked down at her body, expecting to see blood, even as she touched herself, unable to understand the pain.

Somehow, she raised her head, stared into the tank.

Illusion. It had to be.

The water, the coral, the fish—they couldn't have been replaced by this confusion of appendages and swollen dark mass, this shifting *emptiness* filled with disks that burned like stars, winking in and out of this reality with a distortion that threatened sanity.

Mac threw her arm in front of her face, looked frantically for Emily.

Emily had lowered the weapon, eyes on the tank, the lines of her face softened as if she gazed upon a lover.

~~YOU WILL NOT INTERFERE WITH US~~

Mac gasped and fought to stay on her feet. "Too late!" she shouted in fury. "We know about you! We'll stop you!"

~~YOU KNOW NOTHING~~

~~YOU ARE NOTHING~~

~~YOU WILL BE REMOVED~~

The words. *The pain was more than she could bear.* Mac felt herself drop to her knees, threw out her hands to save herself from falling flat.

"Why—why bring me here, then?" she forced herself to say. "What do you want from me?" When no answer dug its unseen claws into her flesh, Mac lifted her head to glare at the seething void that marked the Ro, her eyes weeping with the strain. "We can stop you. That's it, isn't it? I've learned about you. No one else has before. Well, get used to it," she shouted defiantly. "We'll find out the rest. You'll be nothing!"

~~YOU ARE HERE SO WE MAY WITNESS~~

Mac tried to cover her ears. It made no difference—the words came through her flesh, not the air.

~~YOUR ENDING~~

Agony!

~~WE SUMMON YOUR DOOM~~

Emily had fallen to the floor as well. Mac tried to crawl to her.

~~WE ARE WHAT WILL LIVE~~

"NO!" Mac surged up to her feet. Desperate for a weapon, a rock, anything, she snatched the Sinzi cylinder from her pocket. But as she raised it, it extended itself into a gleaming rod. A rod she'd seen used before.

A gift from Anchen, who'd believed her enough for this . . .

"No!" she screamed again, thrusting the rod at the tank. As before, it went through the wall as if nothing was in the way. Mac immediately threw herself back, holding on to the rod with all her strength. *Pulling something with it.*

She hadn't snared a shrimp; she'd hooked a whale.

A furious one.

Mac's hands couldn't hold it. She let go, fell in slow motion, saw the rod disappear into the tank.

Then, for an instant, everything *stopped*. Eternity ticktocked its way through her heart. She saw . . . she saw . . .

. . . reality snap back into focus. Mac had barely time before the wall gave way to grab Emily, hold her close as they were both swept by a torrent of now-dead fish and warm sea.

"Mac? Mac!"

"Mummph!" Mac spat out a mouthful of seawater. *Hopefully free of Ro bits,* she thought, spitting again in case. "Over here!"

The lights coming her way—their way, for she still held Emily—were flashing. Mac put up a hand to protect her sore eyes, then realized it wasn't just the hand lights. The door to the corridor was open, explaining why the floodwater had receded so quickly around her. But the light from that source was pulsating rhythmically. *An alarm?* About time. "What's going on?"

Nik, suit jacket replaced by an armored vest he hadn't bothered to fasten, splashed to her side. "I could ask you the same. Later. C'mon. We're under attack."

Mac flinched. "The Ro?"

"No." He helped her to her feet as someone else helped Emily. "The Dhryn. They're through the gate. They're coming here!"

"The Ro—"

"I told you—" Nik began, half carrying her toward the door.

"Listen to me!" she begged even as she found her feet and hurried with him. "The Ro are calling the Dhryn. That's what the damned signal's for, Nik! We have to shut it down. Now. It's calling them!"

He didn't hesitate. "Confine her," he snapped to the man carrying the unconscious Emily. "With the Dhryn—it's the only Ro-proof room I'm sure about. Let's go," to Mac.

They stepped over the flaccid body of a shark, wedged in the doorway, then Nik pulled her into a run, every urgent step splashing through the water puddled in the white corridor.

They ran through death as well as water. Large, small, brilliant, dull, it floated or lay abandoned, innocent eyes staring. It tripped her feet, made her even more clumsy. Mac tried to keep up, but at the second slip, she told him: "Go!"

Nik simply put one arm under hers and around her waist, taking most of her weight with ease. "You're the one who knows what's going on, Mac," he reminded her.

The floor shook under their feet. "Is that—are they here?"

"Not yet. The building's morphing. That's what took me so long to get here. Had to evacuate the outer rooms first."

He threw open the door to the other corridor, held it for her and the man carrying Emily like a sack over one armored shoulder. Fortunately—or more likely due to foresight by the Sinzi—the floor sloped up to this point, stopping the tank water and its cargo from spreading any farther.

Just as well, Mac told herself as they entered another kind of flood. Beings of every kind were moving in the corridor, the majority making their way through openings along the walls—doors, hidden until now. Like her closet, waiting for a purpose.

Emergency shelter. Did they know how it wouldn't be enough?

Some walked past the still-closed door to the Dhryn's cell, more were arriving down the corridor as far as Mac could see. A few had weapons out, but most were clutching other things. *Possessions,* Mac realized with a jolt. *Research.* Whatever could be snatched up; whatever couldn't be abandoned.

They'd evacuated the upper floors. To come here. She sought familiar faces. "Nik. My team. Oversight?"

"Safe as anyone else." Nik snapped orders over her head. Tall forms separated from the crowd, made a path for them. "Come on!"

No delay at the door to the Atrium. Those guarding it weren't Human, but they moved out of Nik's way. Given the look on his face at the moment, Mac thought that entirely wise.

Others pushed in behind them before the door closed again, so close Mac was shoved forward until a hand took her by an elbow. "Can't have you trampled, Mac," said a voice she knew very well.

Mac twisted her head around to make sure. " 'Sephe!" she said with relief. "I thought you were in Vancouver."

"Got a call."

Behind her were other familiar faces, all equally grim. Mac blinked to clear her eyes. The Atrium seemed deserted. They must have been evacuated as well. *No,* Mac realized, *not entirely.* The next step up to the left hosted a cluster of floating platforms. Telematics.

Another platform was waiting for them. "Let's go," Nik ordered. Somehow, they all fit—*likely overcrowding the thing*—but Mac didn't argue. She only hoped no one would fall off the edge.

But they made the short trip to the next step without incident, connecting their platform to another. Both shifted underfoot like docks on water as they hurried across.

A mass of beings had gathered around a series of screens toward the back. Nik led the way. "What's going on upstairs?" Mac asked 'Sephe quickly.

A gleam of teeth as her lips parted in a tight grin. "The Sinzi-ra sent as many of the attendees offworld as could be moved in the time we have. The rest are waiting it out down here." Her thumb jerked upward. "Every out-facing room and hall has been filled with impact-resistant foam. Every vent, door, window has been sealed. Quite the feat. Reminds me of your pods."

"That won't stop the Dhryn."

A shrug. "Then let's hope you can," the other woman said quietly, but with an earnestness that silenced Mac.

Those ahead moved aside to let Nik through. Mac, not particularly willingly, followed behind, walking between aliens who stared down—or up—at her with expressions she didn't try to guess.

She smelled anxious Myg before spotting Fourteen. He stood in the inner circle, nodded a greeting.

Three techs, all consular staff, sat in front of what appeared an ordinary communications system, manipulating their 'screens as matter-of-factly as if this was an ordinary day and those representing the power of the IU in this system weren't an audience. But their display was twinned so another, larger version hung in the air where everyone could see it.

Mac studied it. She didn't know the specifics, but she understood the management of incoming threads of data. This had to be a simplification—a focus on what the decision-makers needed to know. She approved, in principle.

But seeing the Dhryn ships speeding toward Earth—

"I've dreamed this." Mac didn't realized she'd spoken aloud until Nik turned and beckoned her forward.

"Tell them."

She didn't need urging.

"You have to stop!" Mac pointed at the display, the splatter of pulses down one edge that gave transmission status. "Don't send the Ro signal," she ordered. "It's calling the Dhryn! They told me!"

Reaction came from all sides. "Ridiculous!" "Who let this Human in here?" "Get her out."

Anchen stepped into the open. "We will hear her. Tell us your concerns, Mac. Give us your evidence."

"There's not time. Trust me, Sinzi-ra—please. Turn it off now!"

"She's right." When no one moved, Nik did, heading for the console.

A figure blocked him just as quickly. Cinder. "What do you think you're doing, Nik?"

"Out of my way," clear threat, partner or no partner.

"This isn't necessary." Hollans came up beside the Sinzi, eyes going from Mac to Nik. Whatever he read there—*besides desperation,* Mac thought wildly—made him turn to the alien. "Shut it down. This is our world, Sinzi-ra."

More harsh words filled the room. "This is IU territory." "You have no authority here, Human!" "The Ro will save us!"

Hollans raised his voice: "I've a right to be heard. So do these two. Until we're sure about the Ro, I say shut it down!"

The display was growing complex. Mac assumed some of the moving specks were Human ships, on their way to intercept the invaders. Others had to be evacuating—trying to save what they could.

Grabbing what couldn't be lost, like the beings stuffed into the shelters behind her, waiting for . . . what?

Time's up, Mac told herself with despair.

"Fourteen!" she shouted. "Now!"

Her shout might have been a signal of its own. Nik used the distraction to launch himself at Cinder, the rest of the Ministry agents thundering past Mac to support him, an even greater number dressed in IU yellow leaping out to stop them. No weapons were fired, likely because of the proximity of so many prominent scientists and diplomats, but there were as many cries from those scampering out of the way of the conflict as there were from those now struggling hand to hand. Or hand to whatever.

Only two hadn't moved. Mac and Fourteen. He looked at her, then put his hands over his face, shaking his head. "Oh, no," she whispered.

Then Mac realized someone else hadn't moved either. Great complex eyes met hers as she stared up at the Sinzi-ra. *Not one individual,* Mac thought suddenly. *Six.* A species reliant on innate diversity; a culture that sought the same across space itself. "You gave me the means to save myself from the Ro," Mac told Anchen, her voice as calm and certain as if giving her own name. "You suspected them yourself."

"Noad convinced Hone and Econa there was risk. He is prone to intuition." Anchen made this sound a failing. "Still, all of us, I, are grateful you weren't harmed. We had no idea the Myrokynay could use our tank this way. Their attack against you was more than a serious breach of protocol. We are troubled."

If any single mind in that body would be—*not in charge, but feeling the greatest pressure of events*—Mac decided, it would be that of Atcho, the consulate administrator. Despite the battle raging around them, she took a step closer. "The Ro make no connections, Anchen. They intend to be the only life, to end ours. We mustn't help them. Please. Stop the signal. Now."

"I concur." Two long fingers lifted into the air. Their tips snapped by one another. A too-quiet sound, considering the grunts and scuffles on every side, but the techs must have been waiting for it. Hands stroked the display.

The transmission stopped. Mac staggered with relief.

"Hold!" Hollans bellowed, the word repeated by others.

Like that, it was over. Mac could hardly believe such intense fighting could end as suddenly as it began. She also found it incredible that the combatants of an instant before were helping each other stand, as if this had all been some kind of practice scrum.

Not all. There was something unfinished and deadly in the way Nik and Cinder remained facing one another. Mac saw it. So did Sing-li, who came up to both. She heard him say in an urgent voice: "Save it for the Dhryn."

"Look, Sinzi-ra!" cried one of the techs. "The ships!"

"What is it?"

"They've stopped forward motion. The Dhryn—they're just sitting there."

Mac thought this a very good time to sit herself and, spotting an unoccupied bench, headed for it with a single-minded concentration that would have suited one of her salmon.

- Encounter -

"**R**EPEAT THAT!"

"All enemy vessels have ceased movement toward Earth, sir. They're maintaining a fixed position relative to the gate."

Captain Anya Lemnitov chewed her lower lip. An old habit. "Nav. Time to intercept."

"Thirty minutes at our present speed, sir. If they keep sitting there like ducks."

"Bloody big ducks."

Lemnitov grinned without humor at her Weapons officer. "Then I hope you've an appropriate solution planned, Mr. Morris."

"Of course, sir." But she wasn't surprised when her old friend came to stand beside her, dropping his voice for her ears only. "It'd be easier if they were our usual troublemakers. Smugglers. Insurance defrauders. Lost tourists."

"Sol's been lucky," she countered. "Boring. Peaceful. Maybe we were due for a shake-up. We'll do okay. *Tripoli* hasn't let us down before."

"What worries me are the claims that each of those ships can split into hundreds, maybe thousands more. If they do, well, we can't stop more than a fraction of them, Captain. And the Dhryn don't care about casualties—only their target."

Target? Home to most of those here. She was Mars-born, but had an apartment in Prague that two cats and a lover kept warm. "We do our part; others do theirs," she reminded him. "Confirm ready status to fleet command."

"Captain?" Uncertain, from the com tech.

Morris and the captain exchanged looks. "What is it?" she asked.

"Incoming message from command, sir. Orders—sir, we're ordered to hold position as well. No hostile moves."

Lemnitov stood up. "Do they say why? Belay that," she grunted. "They never say why."

"That's crazy! We can't just leave them there, Captain."

"Calm down."

"What if they split—getting moving before we can? Do you realize how many would slip past us? Reach Earth?"

The entire bridge hushed, everyone listening, every eye on the captain. Lemnitov deliberately took her seat. "Settle back, folks," she ordered, crossing her legs and getting comfortable. "We're parking."

She didn't dare show her fear.

But whoever had ordered Sol's defenses to stand down before the nightmare that was the Dhryn had better be right.

If not, none of them would live to complain.

21

STRAINS AND STRESS

"**I** WILL HAVE ORDER and attention."

How did she do it? Mac wasn't bad at harnessing a room, although it usually involved shouting or leaping on a tabletop. *Brandishing something unlikely helped.* The Sinzi-ra simply spoke those words, in her quiet voice, and everyone presently bickering, stopped.

It didn't mean they suddenly agreed with one another, Mac realized, surveying the room from her seat, this time to the left of Anchen herself. Promotion or protection? *Both likely applied.* From what she'd heard so far, more than a few of those here felt the Dhryn had stopped by coincidence and that they should continue all efforts to contact the Ro.

Others, now believing the Ro were as much a menace as the Dhryn, and one capable of breaching the walls at that, wanted the Sinzi-ra to abandon the consulate and run for safety.

That left, Mac counted in her head: herself, Nik, Hollans—who'd proved himself, as far as she was concerned—and the Sinzi-ra herself. Hollans, meanwhile, had upset the majority here by ordering Earth's defenses not to engage the Progenitors' ships, the situation, he'd insisted, being too volatile.

So the only thing they'd agreed on to this point was that the Dhryn wouldn't stay cooperatively still much longer.

Mac yawned, covering her mouth with her gloved hand. *Which,* she sniffed, *smelled like dead fish.* The staff had done wonders cleaning the corridor; they could give lessons to those students prone to fish tank disasters. *Always a few.*

She should have asked them to clean her as well.

"We are in crisis," Anchen continued. "The IU has sent urgent messages to all members warning them not to activate any signal or device provided by the Myrokynay. We have not—yet—extended this warning to avoiding the Myrokynay themselves," this with an elegant wave of her fingers that managed to convey informed caution.

Mac shifted unhappily in her seat, but didn't say anything. *One problem at a time,* Nik had told her on the way to this meeting. *One enemy.*

As far as she was concerned, there was only one. *But,* Mac thought thankfully, stifling another yawn, *she didn't have to make such decisions.*

"We have also made it clear that the transects must remain open, regardless of the risk of attack. Our connections to one another are not only defense, but lines of safety. We will resolve this problem as a group, for the good of all."

"What about the Dhryn?"

"Ah. For this we must turn to Mac."

Mac, well into a very pleasant "not asleep, really, resting my eyes" daze, snapped back to attention at her name. "We do?" she said blankly.

"While not all here agree, you have proved to me that your doubts about the Ro were well-founded. Their motives remain unclear and potentially antagonistic; their methods are not those of civil discourse." *Now there was an understatement.* "However, now I must call upon your other area of expertise, Mac."

Salmon?

"It is time to share with all of you that we have, in this building, a representative sent by the Dhryn." Even the Sinzi-ra had to wait out the round of outcries this created, finally holding up one finger for order. "He was unwell. There were doubts he would live. Thanks to Mac, who knew this individual and is fluent in his language, he is recovering. More to the point, he presents us with an opportunity to negotiate with the Dhryn Progenitors threatening this world."

That silenced everyone—who then turned to direct their appropriate visual sensory organ or organs at a certain weary salmon researcher.

Might as well paint a target on her forehead, Mac decided. Given the worried look Nik sent her, the same thought had occurred to him.

Everyone, including the Sinzi-ra, waited for her to speak. *She'd much rather join Emily in a drugged stupor—sleep for a day would be nice.*

Mac swallowed and said the only thing she could: "I'm not a negotiator, Sinzi-ra, but I'm willing to try."

Nik stopped her in front of the Dhryn's door, where they were shielded from sight by a rather reassuringly protective clump of Ministry agents. *Most of whom she knew by name.* "Here." He held out a loaded syringe.

"Why did I know you'd have that handy?" Mac asked, but took it. A field kit dose of Fastfix, a cocktail designed to let the Human body continue past its natural collapse point. She'd used one before and knew to quickly drive the tip into her real arm, ready for the sharp pinch. In minutes, her electrolyte balance would head for normal, and stimulants would convince her she'd slept like a baby. *If ever there was a time,* Mac thought, and returned the now-empty syringe with a faint smile.

"You do realize this negotiation idea is a long shot. At best."

He arched his eyebrows as if shocked. "This from the person who single-handedly destroyed the Sinzi's no-space tank system?"

"You don't know I destroyed it. The Ro probably did the damage. I—" Mac flushed, "—okay, maybe I poked it."

"Proving my point. Put some of that 'shove the universe' attitude of yours to work for us. You can do this, Mac, if anyone can," he said, low and sure.

"That's just it, Nik. It doesn't have to be me—" The rest of Mac's explanation was cut off by the opening of the door.

"Greetings, Mackenzie Winifred Elizabeth Wright Connor Sol!"

The booming greeting was the most cheerful thing she'd heard
in a while. Mac walked up to the cell bars. "You look—you look
great," she said with wonder.

While she'd been awake, at work, worried, jumped on by baby
Mygs, transported through no-space, and tortured by an impossible-
to-bear alien's voice—not to mention the flood of dying fish and a
brawl in the signal room. *And,* Mac summed up dourly, *another
meeting with a long table,* the Dhryn had been resting.

The result? One about-to-stagger Human and a robust, hearty
alien. With, she noticed, every one of the little rings she'd brought
adorning his ear ridges, and a bold, yet pleasing accent of burgundy
at eyebrows, cheek ridges, and lips. Mac doubted she could have
done as good a job with a mirror.

The golden irises of his eyes almost glowed. "While you,
Lamisah, have neither rested nor bathed. What's wrong? And why
does that one sleep without waking?" A gesture to the left.

Where Mac saw the new addition to the room. A smaller version
of the jelly-bed, with Emily lying on it, unmoving. She resisted the
impulse to run to her side. Two was already there, standing atten-
tively.

"She's—" Dhryn had no words for illness or its treatment. *'A
Dhryn is robust or a Dhryn is not.'* Mac sighed. "That's my friend
Emily."

The Vessel, who'd been sitting, abruptly stood. "Emily Mamani
Sarmiento?" he exclaimed. "*Lamisah* to my beloved Brymn Las?
She is found?" He hurried to that side of his cell. "This is wonderful news, Mackenzie Winifred Elizabeth Wright Connor Sol!" But
once there, he stopped and stared at the unconscious woman. "She
is damaged."

Two, who'd stood impassively as the larger blue alien rushed
toward her, gave Mac a look of inquiry. Mac walked along the cell
bars to stand beside the Dhryn, careful not to look at Emily.
"Brymn Las told you—the Progenitor—about Emily?"

"Of course. And that she was taken from your side by the monstrous Ro." Empty food containers in the cell shook as the Dhryn
said something too low for Mac to hear. *Likely something she'd agree
with,* she thought bitterly.

Unfortunately—or otherwise—Brymn's last chance to communicate with his Progenitor had been before they'd learned of Emily's betrayal. *Not the time to share,* Mac decided. Instead, she said quietly: "The Ro damaged her. We hope for the best. Vessel, we have to talk about something else—" Mac started walking toward the door to the cell.

But the Dhryn stayed where he was, leaning as close to the cell bars as he could without touching them, implying they were in some way dangerous to touch. *Not an experiment she'd been interested in trying.* "*Lamisah,* wait. Did they place their channels within her flesh?"

Mac nodded, startled by the question. "Yes. Links to no-space. But how—"

"Aieee! Then the Ro have not yet released their grip. If they do not steal her from you again, they will take what is theirs. You must be ready! Bring those among the not-Dhryn who understand the workings of a Human body, who can deal with extreme damage." The Dhryn gazed at Mac with distress. "You doubt me, *Lamisah?*"

"I have seen no awareness of—" Mac was forced to use the Instella words "medicine or biology" before continuing: "—among Dhryn. Brymn Las told me these subjects were forbidden. 'We do not think on it.' "

"Ah." The hint of a smile on those burgundy-tinged lips. "And why should Dhryn waste a moment's breath puzzling at that which is incarnate in every Progenitor? We are the study of life, *Lamisah.* The workings of living things, Dhryn or not, are our passion. Like yours! This is why I know," the smile disappeared, " that Emily Mamani Sarmiento must be in the care of those with such knowledge or she will end."

Mac didn't argue further. She turned to Nik, who'd stayed close behind her. "The Ro can still harm Emily," she told him. "The Vessel—I don't know how he knows, but he says she could need medical assistance at any minute. Please, Nik."

He gave her a dismayed look but nodded. "We can't risk moving her until we have another shielded location. I'll get someone on it, Mac, but you need to work on the problem at hand. The ships."

"I know." Mac took a deep breath, feeling a rush of energy that had more to do with the Fastfix taking hold than any remaining adrenaline in her system. As she did, she checked who else had come into the room with her.

Nik, of course. 'Sephe and Sing-li, now standing to either side of the door. The rest must have stayed outside to loom appropriately.

Under the circumstances, Mac highly approved.

One and Cinder stood on the other side of the cell, as if awaiting instructions. The Trisulian seemed calm enough, although one eyestalk was definitely bent in Nik's direction. *Still angry or wanting to apologize?* For all Mac knew of the species, it could have been neither.

Last and not least at all, the four who had come in that first time: Anchen, Brend Hollans, Genny P'tool, and the still-silent Imrya with her recording pad.

"What ships?" the Vessel echoed, in Dhryn.

They could yell at her later, Mac decided. She knew her strengths. Negotiation and diplomacy weren't among them.

She opened the door and walked into the cell. The Dhryn met her in the middle. "What ships?" he said again, almost impatiently. "What's happening, Mac?"

"How do you feel about crowds?" she asked, then patted the Dhryn's shoulder. "Dumb question."

"Indeed," the Vessel replied. "Even the presence of not-Dhryn is better than being alone."

"That's good. Because you're going to be meeting quite a few shortly. And you must speak to them so they can understand you. Their language. Please."

Real alarm tightened the muscle beneath Mac's fingers. "You said they would take you away from me, *Lamisah*!"

She nodded, swallowing hard. "That may happen. If it does, I want you to trust those you see here, in this room. And anyone Nik—Nikolai Piotr Trojanowski—brings to you. Will you do this for me? It is," she added sincerely, "what you need to do for all that which is Dhryn."

An arm draped itself heavily and awkwardly over her shoulders.

"You are also that which is Dhryn. I will not permit you to come to harm, *Lamisah*."

Despite their audience, in this room, beyond it, despite the contradiction between fear of this species and memories of friendship, Mac let her forehead rest against the Dhryn's cheekbone, managed to stretch her arms as far around his body as she could. The alien stood perfectly still. Brymn had done the same for her. Their species might not share the use of physical contact for comfort; both shared the need.

Mac stepped free, giving the Vessel a final pat, and swallowed to moisten her throat. "Nik?" she called.

He joined her in the cell. Hollans looked as though he wanted to say something. Mac shook her head once, receiving a tight-lipped nod in return.

Nothing like a demonstration, she decided. "Nik, the Vessel would like to know what ships you were talking about. Tell him."

The understandable outbursts from those outside the cell didn't matter. *Nothing mattered,* thought Mac, except the instant comprehension in his eyes, the determination that replaced it. "Twenty-three Dhryn ships—Progenitor Ships—have entered this solar system," Nik said, moving to stand where he could look straight into the Vessel's golden eyes.

A long silence, then: "Why have they come?" Instella, clear and unaccented, yet with an undertone that rattled the furnishings.

"A signal—a call—has drawn them from the Great Journey," said Mac, careful not to mention the Ro. "We've stopped it and they've stopped. But they haven't left."

Nik continued at her look. "We've tried to communicate with the ships, but there's been no response."

"Because you are not-Dhryn," the Vessel explained, as if this should be obvious.

The Ministry's top alien liaison merely nodded. "That's why we need your help—to open negotiations with them."

"Negotiate what?" It seemed honest puzzlement. "The Great Journey has begun. That which is Dhryn will not be distracted by other concerns."

Hollans had come close to the bars. "You're waging war for the Ro, aren't you?"

Mac winced. *That wasn't going to go over well.*

Sure enough, the Vessel immediately wrapped his arms around himself in that complex, defensive positioning. "Who is that being?" in Dhryn, flat and angry.

"*Erumisah* for Humans," Mac said in the same tongue, giving Hollans a warning glare. In Instella, *hopefully,* she continued: "Vessel, that which is Dhryn shouldn't be here. We," she put her hand on her chest, "—I—don't want to be food for Dhryn."

A shocked "o" of his mouth, but he replied in the same language. "Is that why you think they have come? To consume your world as others were consumed? Impossible!"

"The dead planets of the Chasm. You—your Progenitor—spoke to me of remembrance. Of regret. Do you want that legacy again?"

"I do not speak of it."

"You must!" A touch on her sleeve stopped her from more.

Nik's eyes were gleaming behind his glasses. "Vessel. What could turn that which is Dhryn from one path to another?"

She knew she'd been right to have him do this, Mac thought, relieved.

The Dhryn's torso tilted up slightly. *Threat,* she judged it, *but not at them.*

Yet, anyway.

"A risk to the Progenitor."

Mac looked at Nik in dismay. *If Earth's defenders, nose-to-nose with the Dhryn ships, weren't considered such a risk, what would be?*

He didn't seem flustered. *Or didn't show it,* she thought enviously. "How would such a risk be discovered by the Dhryn?"

"The Progenitor would reveal it."

Around again, she thought, frustrated, but kept silent.

"You are a Vessel," Nik said calmly. "You can speak to other Progenitors—tell them this world is dangerous, that they should avoid it."

A rapid series of blinks, like blue shutters covering those huge eyes. Then: "This world is not dangerous to a Progenitor," the Dhryn said in a reasoning tone. "You two are my *lamisah*. The rest," a gesture to the silent group outside the cell, "I am to trust."

What had she thought about rocks and hard places? Without thinking, Mac breathed: "Let me try again."

Nik studied her face, then nodded. "Go."

Mac sat cross-legged on the floor. To keep his eyes on her, the Vessel had to relax and lower his head. "Things are not as they should be, Vessel," she said carefully. "That which is Dhryn has been shown a wrong path. A path that risks all Progenitors. I believe this."

"I do not wish to speak of—"

"Stop!" Mac said sharply, looking up at the larger being. "You were sent to talk to me."

Miserable, with yellow liquid oozing from one nostril. Tears. "Yes, *Lamisah.*"

"Explain to me. How does a Progenitor reveal a risk to her Dhryn?"

His mouth closed tight. Mac was about to ask again when she felt the floor beneath her start to vibrate. The reverberations traveled up her spine, jarring her teeth. "Like that," she said with satisfaction. *Though at a much greater intensity, given the size of a real Progenitor.* It would be like an earthquake.

She'd felt it on Haven, before the planet split to release the ships, the Progenitors using their own bodies to warn their people. A warning that traveled through the ground and air, over vast distance, unstoppable.

A warning that this time might save more than Dhryn.

There was something about watching capable people getting things done, Mac decided happily, *that satisfied the soul.*

Either that, or she was experiencing Fastfix euphoria.

The distinction wasn't important. She stayed where Nik had essentially parked her, near Emily's bed, while he and others swarmed about to make and send a recording of what had been dubbed the Progenitor's alarm cry. *Which was more an alarm* throb, Mac corrected, not that the name mattered.

They'd circumvented the need to bring in additional equipment—or move the Dhryn—by simply sliding aside a good portion of the ceiling. It also removed a good portion of the Dhryn shielding, exposing them all to the Ro, but Mac doubted the secretive beings would bother entering a room packed to the rafters.

Not to mention the presence of armored beings of every sort, intent on anything that wasn't part of capable persons getting things done.

"You look pleased, *Lamisah.*"

Mac glanced through the bars at the Dhryn. "I do?" She considered the idea. "Relief," she said finally.

After all. Others knew. Others were taking action. She wasn't waiting to hear what was happening—she was in the midst of it all.

Okay, maybe that last wasn't such a great thing. Mac looked down at Emily. Even drugged unconscious, a state Anchen recommended for now, her face wasn't relaxed. Muscles spasmed in seemingly random order. Her arms shifted as much as the cover allowed. Mac hadn't guessed the bed could be adjusted into a restraint. It put a new light on climbing into her own later.

If there was a later.

She watched the lift they'd slung from the other side bring down its next load. The Vessel watched as well. He'd stayed as close to her as possible but didn't seem upset.

Which made sense. They were proposing to warn the Dhryn, not harm them.

A tactic that didn't satisfy everyone. Mac narrowed her eyes. The Imrya had spent most of her time with Cinder in the last half an hour, a conversation whose topic she could guess well enough.

"Let it go, Mac," easy and quiet.

She glowered at Nik. "Have you talked to her yet?"

His laugh wasn't amused. "In all this? We'll sit down over some beers when things calm down. Cinder and I—we've enough history to get past a difference of opinion."

"So you don't think the Dhryn should be exterminated as soon as possible?"

The Vessel's only protest was a faint distressed sound.

"Gods, Mac," Nik shook his head at her. "Do you know any direction besides straight ahead?"

She was unrepentant. "Not when I know where I'm going. Nik—we need to—"

One came up to them. "We're ready to test the simulation, Mr. Trojanowski, Dr. Connor." A polite pause as he sorted out protocol. "Honorable Vessel."

"Go ahead."

The lights dimmed to request silence. The techs inhabiting the jumble of equipment now along the far wall gave a signal. Instantly, the walls and floor began to shake. Objects not secured fell and rolled.

While the Dhryn stood and ran as hard as he could in the opposite direction.

As that was the direction of the descending lift, the massive alien managed to knock most of the gear from it to the floor, sending himself rebounding to lie on his back.

Someone thought of shutting off the simulation.

"Well," said Mac brightly as the Dhryn picked himself up, apparently no worse for wear, "that worked."

Anchen touched fingertip to fingertip. "I had hoped we would be negotiating with the Dhryn, not shouting at them to run. You remain sure this is the only option?"

Nik shrugged. "Right now? Yes, Sinzi-ra. Given the time and situation, there's no choice."

Genny P'tool spoke up: "It will be a test. If it works, if the Dhryn are repelled, then we can provide this to other members of the IU."

"Even if it works," Mac cautioned, "it may only work once. The Dhryn are obeying instinct, but they obviously haven't lost their ability to function as intelligent beings. They can operate ships—navigate transects to find a specific target. They are making decisions. They'll soon realize they should ignore alarms that come from outside their ships."

"They don't learn to ignore the Ro's call."

"We can't know that," Mac insisted. "Some might be trying to.

This Progenitor did—" a gesture to the Vessel. "And there's another difference. Organisms will seek food even if sometimes the clues are wrong. It's too essential a need. But they can't keep reacting to false alarms. It's better to risk ignoring a valid alarm, than to starve hiding from false ones."

"That which is Dhryn mustn't starve." The Vessel's comment, low and implacable, sent a shiver down Mac's spine.

Hollans turned pale as well. To his credit, his voice stayed calm. "Understood, Dr. Connor. But if it might save even one more world, it's worth a try, don't you think?"

Anchen's fingertips snapped past one another. "We will not test the patience of the Dhryn. Send the alarm."

- Encounter -

THE PROGENITOR'S warning is felt by all that is Dhryn.
  The Great Ships turn to flee.
The Progenitors must endure.
Conflict . . . confusion . . .
The Progenitors on each ship call for Vessels.
No time for consultation. In this, the will of all comes first.
The Call has been silenced.
The cry is paramount.
All that is Dhryn must *move*.

"Say again."

"The Dhryn ships have come about, sir. Projected course—the gate to the Naralax Transect! They're running!"

In the midst of cheers and whistles from her bridge crew, Lemnitov heard an astonished: "From us?"

She gave her Weapons officer a sideways grin. "Don't think we're scary?"

"Do you?"

"There have been days . . ." Seeing the scan tech trying to get her attention, the captain raised her voice. "Quiet down, people. We can celebrate at the next way station. What is it?"

"You need to see this, sir."

"Main display."

The center space of the bridge filled with the images of ships.
Dying.

That which was Dhryn had lost the call.

That which was Dhryn has turned to flee.

~~FAILURE~~

It is not the Way to risk the Progenitors.

~~WITHDRAW~~

Holes appear down every seam of the Great Ships; their silver sides, like so many petals, fall open to vacuum. Gouts of air vent and freeze, icy splinters coat the figures that tumble into space.

Within, the Progenitors die even as they try to shield their newborn with their vast hands, *oomlings* floating free in every direction as gravity fails with all else.

As the last heartbeat sounds in silence, that which was Dhryn tumbles toward the Naralax Transect.

Nothing more than debris.

- 22 -

AGONY AND AFTERMATH

EMILY SCREAMED, a drawn-out shriek that choked on moisture. Mac hurled herself to her side, hearing other cries but understanding only this one.

"Emily!" Mac tried to free her from the blanketlike restraint, but the jelly-bed held firm. Emily's body spasmed in another scream, muted to a gurgle by the blood still pouring from her mouth.

"I need help here!" Mac shouted.

She was pulled aside, others pushed past. She didn't resist, trying only to see what was happening.

But when she could see, Mac screamed herself and turned away. Someone held her.

No one could erase what burned behind her closed eyes, the bloody ruin of arms and legs, the wet gaping abdomen.

The Ro had taken back what they'd put in place of Emily's flesh. *Returning nothing.*

"Dead." "It's confirmed. Dead." "Dead." Like a contagion, the word sped through the room. Mac choked back her tears, pushed away to free herself, heard clearly what at first made no sense: "All of them, you're sure?" "Yes, all dead."

All of them? *All of* who?

"AIEEEEEEEEEEEE! LAMISAH!"

Half blind, Mac fought to reach the new scream, struggling to get past what seemed an army intended to hold her in place as gently as possible. She flailed out, got ready to kick.

"Mac. Mac. They're helping Emily. Hang on. This way."

Nik. With the voice, movement in the right direction. No more screaming, although disquieting mutters of "dead" kept circulating around her, part of confused fragments of conversation.

Others were caring for Emily. Only she could help the Dhryn.

Emily.

Inside the Dhryn cell was peace of a sort. The area outside was crammed with people, the outer door opening and closing with a steady growl of permissions asked and given. Overhead, more noise, a heady buzz from the other side. *Cheering?*

Mac focused on the Vessel, a huddle of patent misery in the middle of the floor. Had he even stood again after running into the lift? She couldn't remember. Nik, faster than she, was already at his side. "We didn't do it," he was saying, confusingly if urgently. To her: "The Dhryn ships. They self-destructed. All of them. After they'd powered up on a heading to leave the system."

"Why would they do that?" she asked numbly.

"They didn't," Nik said between his teeth. "Their ships must have been rigged. Some kind of triggering pulse was sent from inside the consulate. We'd never have caught it, but we were set up to listen for a reply to the Ro signal. We're tracking the source." She'd never seen such naked rage on a face before. "It—Emily was affected at the same time."

The Ro.

Too cold for anger, Mac bent over the Dhryn, touched him gently. "Vessel. *Lamisah.* Do you understand now? The Ro are the enemy. They tried to use these Dhryn against us; when that failed, they destroyed them. We have to work together; find a way to stop the Ro before more die."

Low, in Dhryn, muffled by an arm. "I must go back."

Mac kept talking in Instella for Nik's sake. "What do you mean, 'you must go back'? Back where? Why?"

The arm shifted to reveal one golden eye. The Dhryn made the effort to reply in kind. "I was sent here to talk to you, Mackenzie Winifred Elizabeth Wright Connor Sol. To learn the truth. I have, to my unending sorrow, done so. Now, I must return to my Progenitor and tell her."

Mac sat back, giving Nik a startled look. "We can't—" she began cautiously. He put a finger to his lips, then leaned close to the Dhryn's ear.

"I'll make sure you get there, *Lamisah*," she heard him whisper. "But please, don't speak of this to others until we've made the necessary arrangements."

As he spoke, Nik looked straight at her.

Oh, she knew that expression.

Full-scale plotting.

And no one had better get in his way.

"She's alive. I admit to being surprised. I had thought her body would give up the first night."

Mac pressed her lips together and stared out at the ocean. The Sinzi-ra had come in person to report on Emily's condition. She was grateful for that.

Once the Dhryn were gone, the consulate had morphed back to its normal state, giving them all back their beds and belongings, restoring access to the research rooms. She was grateful for that, too.

She wasn't grateful to have been sent to her bed the moment it was available. *Not,* Mac admitted, *that she'd been good for much by that time.* Fastfix made you pay. She had vague memories of a quiet, comfortable corner, some floor of her own, annoying people who claimed she was in the way and made her get up.

Mac shook herself. "Emily's always been strong," she said. "Thank you for your care of her. Strong or not, I'm not sure she would have survived what the—what the Ro did to her without Noad."

An elegant sweep of fingers to head, the meaning unmistakable. "It remains to be seen how much of her has survived, Mac. You should be prepared."

How could she do that? Mac asked herself. Aloud: "What else do I get to know, Anchen?"

"Whatever you wish. You have more than earned my confidence, Mac."

"Is the IU going to release the Vessel? Let him return to his Progenitor?"

They were sitting on the terrace. The storm front had passed, leaving a clear sky. The breeze lifting from the ocean played with Mac's hair and set the beads by the door in motion. It wasn't enough to move the Sinzi's fingers, yet she pretended it did, waving their tips before her great eyes like silver-coated reeds swaying in the wind.

Delay, Mac judged it. *Why?* She decided on patience, and was rewarded a moment later.

Anchen put down her fingers with what seemed reluctance. "Mac. The destruction of the Dhryn ships. How do you judge this act?"

"Murder. The slaughter of innocents."

"Innocents who may have been responsible for the deaths of billions. For the eradication of entire biospheres."

"I've seen eagles gather by the hundreds to feast on salmon as they spawn. If I could ask the salmon's opinion on that slaughter, I'm sure it would differ from the eagles'. I have none."

"So you see the Dhryn as part of nature."

Mac's lips twisted. "I see them as a perversion of nature. A perversion created and manipulated by the Ro. Who are, in my opinion, guilty of murder on all counts."

"To those who do not think as you—or I, Mac—the Ro's destruction of the Dhryn ships was an act of salvation."

Mac frowned. "How can that be? The evidence—"

"Is not definitive. Not yet. Not to all. Human ships are collecting debris, hunting clues. Meanwhile, you must continue your work, Mac." A lift of those tall shoulders. "But, as you do, be aware of this ambivalence among us. There will remain division, factions to be pacified and contained."

Too much to hope it would be simple, Mac told herself. *That all would see the same threat, interpret the same actions as she did.* She thought of how hard it was for her and Mudge to agree—and they started from the same information and had similar goals.

"For how long?"

"Until we know the Myrokynay's intentions beyond doubt."

"If they win," Mac grumbled, "we'll know, won't we?"

Anchen formed her triangular mouth into a smile. "Let us hope to gain this knowledge first. We must establish communications with both the Dhryn and the Ro, Mac. Since the Ro have proved—uninterested—in civil discourse, I will send our Dhryn back to his Progenitor, trusting to form a useful connection."

Mac's eyes sought the horizon again. Late afternoon. Some scudding cloud. That ridiculous blue sky hanging over a sea sparked with light. A sea with life spared for another day.

Good-bye.

"I'll go with him," she said.

A cool sharpness, light as the tip of a feather, stroked the back of her hand. For an instant, Mac couldn't remember if it was her real one or not. She looked at the Sinzi-ra. "I mean it."

"And I am grateful for your courage. But you cannot, Mac." Anchen stroked her hand once more. "We need you here, to continue leading your team. Even if they could manage without you," she said, anticipating Mac's protest before she did more than draw breath to make it, "Emily cannot. What hope she has to recover may depend in part on the presence of a—good—friend. I have a third reason—do you wish to hear it?"

Mac scowled but nodded.

"The Ro followed you once before, using the tracer signature within your body. It's true they had Emily's help and her device—also that they knew your destination and could stay close. But do you wish to take the chance that they could repeat this feat and, through you, find the Vessel?"

"The Ministry might have a way of masking it—changing it."

"Which brings me to my last reason, Mac. Although you accepted temporary citizenship within the IU in order to be part of the Gathering, your kind has claimed you back from us. The Ministry of Extra-Sol Human Affairs is unwilling to risk both of its experts on the Dhryn in such a venture. I find I concur."

"Both?" Mac nodded slowly. *Of course.* She'd heard Nik say it. *It just hadn't registered.* "Nik's going."

"Yes."

"When?"

Anchen gestured westward, sunlight glinting from her silver rings. "Today. I am sorry you did not have a chance to say good-bye in person, Mac, but the launch must be secret. We sought no agreement for this mission. We fear an act against the Vessel—followers on their trail. You can send a note to me. I will make sure Nik receives it."

A note, Mac repeated to herself, feeling as though the terrace had tilted toward the sharp rocks below.

And she'd wasted the last twenty-four hours asleep.

The knock at her door shortly after Anchen departed didn't surprise Mac. Who was knocking did.

"Come in, Mr. Hollans," she said, quite sure she was doing a lousy job of hiding her disappointment.

"Dr. Connor. If I might speak with you?"

If he made it quick. "Sure." He walked through the arch to the sitting room.

So much for quick.

They took seats in opposing jelly-chairs. The fish tank table—every one, Mac had been told—had been replaced by a solid slab of local stone, polished and gray. She tucked her feet under the Sinzi gown. He was, predictably, in the brown suit. There were dark circles under his eyes, lines of strain around his mouth.

"Dr. Connor—"

"Mac."

He almost smiled. "Mac. I came to apologize."

"I've a temper," she admitted with a shrug. "Besides, you were right. Dhryn were killing Humans. I needed to know." Mac paused uncertainly. "Did you have family—at the refinery?"

He shook his head, then gave a strange laugh. "Yes. In a way."

"In a way?"

"My job—when I'm not working with Anchen—is to watch out for the ones who leave home. I don't know many of them as individuals; I don't need to. Those who go to space are different. They're travelers, restless, eager for something new and bigger. The seeds of our kind, in a way. Fragile, sometimes foolish. Sometimes with evil intent, often brave. They deserve to do better than survive out there. I want more for them than that. Sorry. I'm probably not making much sense." He rubbed his face with his hand. "Been a long few days."

Mac eyed him cautiously, then made up her mind. "I knew someone like that," she offered. "Just had to go to space. I didn't understand why he couldn't be satisfied with Earth. I argued with him, tried to keep him here." *With her*.

"Let me guess. He left anyway."

She nodded. "And didn't come back. It's taken me this long to understand, a little anyway. It wasn't that Earth was too small for Sam. He saw what I didn't, back then. Earth isn't isolated, complete in itself. This world is part of something else, larger, waiting to be known. He wanted that something, be it space or other worlds. Guess I'm not making sense either," she finished, frustrated.

A true smile this time, frayed with exhaustion, but offered as one friend to another. "Sounded all right to me," Hollans said, then stood. "Mac, I also came to make sure you understood why I asked the IU not to send you with the Dhryn. Nothing to do with your abilities." His smile turned rueful. "Believe me, Mac, I've become convinced. But—" he paused.

Mac stood, too. "Anchen told me. Nik Trojanowski is going and you can't risk us both." She was surprised when the words came out sounding normal.

"So you think he can do it?" A little too casual, given the anxiety she read in his eyes.

Mac didn't hesitate. "Nik doesn't speak the language," she admitted. "That's a disadvantage among Haven-raised Dhryn. But— he understands the Dhryn. And, to be honest, he understands this—" Her wave was meant to encompass not only Earth and the consulate, but all the IU. "—unlike me. You're better off with someone out there who won't shove the universe at the wrong time." She paused, then said: "And the Vessel does know where he's going, in case you were wondering."

"But I thought you said—"

Mac blushed, just a bit. "The Dhryn don't lie, Mr. Hollans. But I'm not a Dhryn."

A curt—and very relieved—nod. "Thank you, Mac. That helps."

She walked him to her door, scuffing her bare toes in the sand. About to leave, he stopped and turned to look at her. "We'll do our best for Dr. Mamani. Under the circumstances, I've arranged for the charges against her to be dropped."

"Charges?" Mac repeated, then stopped her automatic protest. *What hadn't Emily done?* "Thank you."

She closed the door.

As for the circumstances?

"He believes you're going to die, Emily," Mac said, her forehead against the doorframe. "Don't start being convenient now."

No messages. No more visitors. Mac's nerves stood the peace and quiet as long as they could, which was not at all, then she dressed and went out.

"Hi, Mac."

The voice from nowhere made her jump half out of her skin. "Don't do that!" Mac hissed.

'Sephe's lips stretched in that magical smile of hers. "Your feet left the floor."

Mac snorted, then shook her head. "I've things on my mind. Why exactly are you standing outside my door?"

"Even I pull guard detail." Not that 'Sephe was in full armor, although she wore one of the vests and had a weapon hanging at her hip. Underneath, she wore a bright red dress, complete with matching sandals.

"I thought the Sinzi had put up Ro detectors of some kind." Mac had heard the explanation given to another and tuned out all but the key, to her, part. *Safe, for now.* "Disrupts their ability to exit from no-space within the building."

"Untested technology to stop an unseen foe?" 'Sephe arched one eyebrow.

"And not everyone in this place is a friend of mine," Mac suggested.

A sober look. "Let's say we're going to stick a little close for a while. If you don't mind."

"Do I have a choice?" but Mac softened it with a smile of her own. "I don't mind the company, 'Sephe." In fact, she'd hoped for it.

"Where to?"

By way of answer, Mac held up a palm-sized salmon. It had been the smallest one hanging from her ceiling, and one of the nicest. A traditional Haida rendering, pale wood with dramatic lines in red and black, shaping eye and sweep of tail, offering meanings as well. *The cycle of life. The whole as a sum of its parts.* The dangling thread still attached caught on her finger and she wrapped the excess around the tail. "A token for a traveler," she said somewhat breathlessly.

"Mac, you know there's a security blackout. Clock's started—"

"Then why did you let me sleep so long?" she snapped, then, desperately: " 'Sephe. Please."

Muttering something that wasn't Instella or English—or polite—under her breath, the Ministry agent turned and led the way down the corridor to the far lift. Mac stayed close behind, not daring to say another word.

Theirs didn't seem a particularly clandestine route—down a regular lift—main hall—outside along the patio, walking on top of the Atrium—but Mac knew better. They passed one too many faces she knew, faces that gave 'Sephe a look of disbelief and Mac one of pity.

This route was guarded.

She had to trust they were guarding against her as well, that 'Sephe wouldn't have given in this easily had Mac's impulse posed a risk.

That wasn't to say others might not. "There you are, Norcoast!"

'Sephe gave her a warning look. Mac just shrugged. *There were some people you couldn't lose.* "About time you woke up," Mudge went on as he caught up. "They wouldn't let me see you. Are you all right? I've had a briefing from the Sinzi-ra herself. Fine job you did. Risky, but—"

"Oversight," Mac interrupted, "we're in a bit of a hurry here. Do you mind if we talk about all this later?"

He harrumphed, his cheerful expression changing to suspicion as if she'd thrown a switch. "What's wrong? I thought we won. What's going on. Where are you going?"

Mac rolled her eyes, then grabbed Mudge by the front of his jacket, pulling him along in the direction 'Sephe had indicated until he scampered to keep up. 'Sephe, with a heavy, completely clear sigh, took a few longer strides to get ahead and lead. "We didn't win," Mac told him as they passed under the trees. "Not yet. And, thanks. I'm all right."

"This is the way to the landing pads." Mudge grabbed her arm, tried to slow her down. "What's going on? Are you leaving, Norcoast?"

Mac rested her fingers over his for an instant, smiling what she hoped was a reassuring smile. "No. But a friend is. I want to say good-bye, that's all. You can wait back at the consulate."

"And miss a chance to see the latest Sinzi machines?" he said. "Nonsense, Norcoast."

She'd tried. "Fine. But don't slow us down."

Much to Mudge's chagrin, the last part of their journey angled away from the landing field. Instead, 'Sephe paused on the path beside a bench like all the others, checked all around, then led them off the path into the forest. Behind a dense planting of shrubs with thorns Mac decided would make quite reasonable knives, they came to an access port built into the volcanic rock. "Through here," 'Sephe said quietly. "Watch your step."

The warning came suspiciously late, Mudge having gone first and a faint cry of pain coming from the open doorway.

'Sephe grinned at Mac. "I told him."

Mac followed 'Sephe, who, after closing the door, took her down three uneven steps, then up a fourth where a low rail required those passing it to duck underneath. Mudge was there, rubbing his head. "This doesn't seem very efficient," he complained.

"If you have to run through here," 'Sephe assured him, "you've other things to worry about."

The corridor wasn't Sinzi white, but crudely carved into rock, in some places so irregular that the ceiling protruded downward. 'Sephe activated the lights in each twisting segment as they approached, checking the way ahead but stopping short of making them wait while she did so.

Just when Mac felt they were probably under the ocean, the corridor widened into a disarmingly normal cargo loading space, complete with busy servos and workers moving crates to and from a series of rakish-looking surface-to-orbit craft lined up before immense closed doors.

Mudge made a happy sound.

'Sephe jerked her head toward what appeared to be a temporary shelter within the cargo bay. "In there, Mac. Don't be long."

Now that she was here, Mac's feet felt glued to the floor. She held out the salmon. "Take this for me—"

"Mac."

"Please." She shoved it into 'Sephe's hand and ran back into the tunnellike corridor.

She'd said good-bye to Sam.

She couldn't say good-bye to Nik.

"Stupid rail." Mac sat on the bench and rubbed her hip. She'd forgotten the trap and almost flipped right over the bar, saving herself in time.

Bruising her hip nicely.

She leaned back, grateful the bench had a back, although it wasn't quite meant for her particular body plan. *And those odd holes in the middle . . .* Mac bent over to look, trying to match their shape to the posteriors of the aliens she'd met here.

Rustle . . . rustle.

She froze in place. The sound was surely innocent in a tamed wood like this. Mac listened, but heard nothing further.

Suddenly, a wooden salmon appeared under her nose, peering up at her through one of the holes.

"Funny," she managed to say, sitting up with a jerk.

The salmon withdrew and Nik came around the bench to sit beside her. He didn't say a word, just held the carving on his lap, in both hands, apparently studying it for all he was worth.

Shy?

Mac looked at him. Gone were the glasses, the suit, the cravat. Now he wore a spacer's jumpsuit, faded enough to likely be his own, pockets everywhere. It might have been dark blue once. Maybe purple. The boots were newer.

"You didn't dream last night." Quietly, as if to the wooden fish.

She gave an exasperated snort. "If you were there, why didn't you wake me up?"

"I hadn't seen you sleep like that before." Mac watched the dimple suddenly deepen in his cheek. "You snore."

"I do not," she protested and was fascinated by the upcurve of the corner of his mouth.

"It's a cute snore."

"Oh, that helps."

They fell silent again, Nik watching the salmon, Mac watching him.

"I made some notes for you," she said abruptly. "I gave them to Anchen."

"Got them. Thanks. And this." He put the salmon in one hand, and drew out the amulet from around his neck, the one the Progenitor had sent with Parymn. Still not looking at her, Nik brought it to his lips, then put it back inside his coveralls. The salmon went in a pocket. He leaned back, his head tilted to stare up into the trees. "I left you some notes, too. Gave them to your friend, Oversight."

Mac memorized the strong lines of his throat, pleasantly tormented by the pulse along the side, the soft shadow below his jaw. "Aren't you supposed to be leaving? Soon."

"Now. They're holding the launch for me."

Time's up. Mac's hands felt strangely heavy. "Nik. Why didn't you wake me? We could—" She couldn't help the huskiness of her voice. "A night. At least that."

She watched his throat work as he swallowed. "I considered it." The voice was light. Then Nik lifted his head and her heart pounded at the heat in his eyes. "Then I realized I'd want tomorrow and the next night. That I couldn't imagine any amount of time with you being enough. That I had to leave then or I wouldn't leave at all."

"Oh."

He didn't smile at the single syllable she managed, gazing into her eyes as if he couldn't do anything else, motionless.

Sometimes, Mac told herself as she reached for him, *you had to give the universe a shove.*

The universe didn't seem to mind at all.

READING AND REUNION

MAC NUDGED the glasses on the table in a half circle, careful not to touch the lenses. They'd been with the notes Nik had left her. Mudge had thought them an odd sort of gift. Then again, he still thought Nik was Stefan.

They were an odd gift, she smiled to herself, *but useful.* Through Nik's lenses, the white walls and furnishings of the consulate showed their true Sinzi glory. Not a bad perk for being the Sinzira's favorite Human.

There'd been no news. Not yet. The Ro were silent. The Dhryn might have all been killed—not that anyone believed it. Researchers were poring over every scrap of wreckage and space-chilled flesh. Nik hadn't reported in—that they'd told her. The two, Human and Dhryn, weren't traveling alone, although Mac hadn't been pleased to learn Cinder had been one of those selected. But Nik could handle it. She had her part of the puzzle. The Origins Team was busy and productive.

Although there had been, Mac scowled, *far too many meetings.*

"Where did I leave off?" she mumbled to herself, picking up the clumsy thing. The book wasn't a real antique, but a copy. A stack of others lay in the sand—gifts from her Dad. *The format was,* Anchen had assured her, *a welcome change for her eyes,* easily tired these days from practicing her reading skills.

"Ah. Here."

Mac had wrestled one of the jelly-chairs to where the afternoon sun would fall over her shoulder. Winter had already given them a frost or two, but also clearer skies. She curled herself up and looked over at Emily with a wistful smile.

Against the white pillow, her face was composed, at peace. As it had been for the last twenty-seven days. The skin had recovered some of its luster, though not all. The cheeks were still sunken, the arms above their prostheses too thin. Her bones, graceful yet ominous, pressed outward as if anxious to leave. The hair alone seemed right, shining black and thick.

Every third breath was that soft little snore Em had denied utterly when awake. Mac listened for it in the night, obscurely comforted.

"Any change?"

Two put a glass of water on Mac's desk, in reach of her hand. "No, Mac. Do you wish me to stay?"

"It's okay. Unless you want to hear the rest of this story?"

The staff came as close as ever to smiling, a crinkle at the corner of her eyes, a tilt to her head. "No, Mac. I heard sufficient of the last seven to know how it will end."

When Two had left, Mac took a drink, then found her page. True, the selection tended to a certain similarity in plot, but there were exciting bits. This part, for example. She cleared her voice and started to read aloud. " 'The trail through the bog had grown cold since midnight—' "

"There's no sex in that one either."

"There doesn't have to be sex in everything you read," Mac said automatically, turning the page.

Then, realizing what had just happened, she stopped. The book fell from her hands as she looked toward Emily.

Dark eyes, tired *sane* eyes, met hers. "I should have remembered," Emily said, voice weak but feathered at the edges with that familiar, amused warmth. "You never let go of anyone, do you, Mac?"

Grin or cry?

Instead, Mac took Emily's outstretched hand gently in hers. It didn't matter that neither were real.

"Welcome back, Em."